W9-CHB-318

Praise for

CHASING THE SUN

"A satisfying conclusion with this sweet nineteenth-century western . . . Fans of the series will enjoy another visit to the Wilkins clan, while new readers are sure to admire Warner's vivid descriptions of love and life in the land of enchantment." —*Publishers Weekly*

"Coming to the end of an enjoyable saga is like bidding far-flung relatives and friends good-bye after a holiday or vacation. If the reader is immersed in the tale, tears and a feeling of sorrow follow the turning of the last page. And that's exactly how I felt reading the last paragraph of the Wilkins brothers' story . . . Without a doubt, Kaki Warner is a writer to watch, an author with a promising future. She's definitely an addition to my must-buy authors list." —*All About Romance*

"What an excellent series she has written . . . Kaki Warner really hits all the angles and makes this series such a warm, romantic read." —*Smexy Books*

"Warner does a superb job . . . [She] swept me into the lives and hearts of the rugged men and strong women of the Wilkins family . . . Through her exquisite writing, I've come to know and love these people." —*The Romance Dish*

"A true page-turner, *Chasing the Sun* is full of action and adventure described with Warner's trademark detail. Once again, her characters' relationships provide a story filled with emotional, humorous, and gut-wrenching moments." —*Romantic Times*

OPEN COUNTRY

"Warner earned readers' respect as a strong western writer with her debut, the first book in the Blood Rose Trilogy. With the second, she cements that reputation. Her powerful prose, realistic details, and memorable characters all add up to a compelling, emotionally intense read." —*Romantic Times*

"A thoroughly enjoyable historical romance." —*Night Owl Reviews*

continued . . .

"Vivid imagery . . . [A] beautifully spun tale that will leave readers satisfied, yet yearning for Jack's story."   —*The Season*

"A wonderful historical tale starring a strong ensemble cast . . . [A] superb Reconstruction era romance."   —*Genre Go Round Reviews*

PIECES OF SKY

"A wonderful read I couldn't put down . . . Reminds us why New Mexico is called the land of enchantment. A truly original new voice in historical fiction."   —Jodi Thomas, *New York Times* bestselling author

"Romance, passion, and thrilling adventure fill the pages of this unforgettable saga that sweeps the reader from England to the Old West. Jessy and Brady are truly lovers for the ages!"   —Rosemary Rogers

"Readers may need a big box of Kleenex while reading this emotionally compelling, subtly nuanced tale of revenge, redemption, and romance, but this flawlessly written book is worth every tear."   —*Chicago Tribune*

"In her auspicious debut, Warner kicks off the Blood Rose Trilogy . . . Warner develops [the] romance with well-paced finesse and great character work . . . Warner makes great use of the vivid Old West setting."
                    —*Publishers Weekly*

"Generates enough heat to light the old New Mexico sky. A sharp, sweet love story of two opposites, a beautifully observed setting, and voilà—a romance you won't soon forget."   —Sara Donati, author of *The Endless Forest*

Colorado Dawn

KAKI WARNER

BERKLEY SENSATION, NEW YORK

THE BERKLEY PUBLISHING GROUP
Published by the Penguin Group
Penguin Group (USA) Inc.
375 Hudson Street, New York, New York 10014, USA
Penguin Group (Canada), 90 Eglinton Avenue East, Suite 700, Toronto, Ontario M4P 2Y3, Canada
(a division of Pearson Penguin Canada Inc.)
Penguin Books Ltd., 80 Strand, London WC2R 0RL, England
Penguin Group Ireland, 25 St. Stephen's Green, Dublin 2, Ireland (a division of Penguin Books Ltd.)
Penguin Group (Australia), 250 Camberwell Road, Camberwell, Victoria 3124, Australia
(a division of Pearson Australia Group Pty. Ltd.)
Penguin Books India Pvt. Ltd., 11 Community Centre, Panchsheel Park, New Delhi—110 017, India
Penguin Group (NZ), 67 Apollo Drive, Rosedale, Auckland 0632, New Zealand
(a division of Pearson New Zealand Ltd.)
Penguin Books (South Africa) (Pty.) Ltd., 24 Sturdee Avenue, Rosebank, Johannesburg 2196,
South Africa

Penguin Books Ltd., Registered Offices: 80 Strand, London WC2R 0RL, England

This book is an original publication of The Berkley Publishing Group.

This is a work of fiction. Names, characters, places, and incidents either are the product of the author's imagination or are used fictitiously, and any resemblance to actual persons, living or dead, business establishments, events, or locales is entirely coincidental. The publisher does not have any control over and does not assume any responsibility for author or third-party websites or their content.

Copyright © 2012 by Kathleen Warner.
Excerpt from *Bride of the High Country* by Kaki Warner copyright © by Kathleen Warner.
Cover illustration by Alan Ayers.
Cover design by Lesley Worrell.
Interior text design by Tiffany Estreicher.

All rights reserved.
No part of this book may be reproduced, scanned, or distributed in any printed or electronic form without permission. Please do not participate in or encourage piracy of copyrighted materials in violation of the author's rights. Purchase only authorized editions.
BERKLEY SENSATION® is a registered trademark of Penguin Group (USA) Inc.
The "B" design is a trademark of Penguin Group (USA) Inc.

ISBN 978-1-61793-481-0

PRINTED IN THE UNITED STATES OF AMERICA

For Heather, Adeline, Kenzie, and Jackson
With all my love

Prologue

Maddie turned the key in the lock at her parents' small stone cottage, paused for a moment to gather her courage, then opened the door and stepped inside.

Silence greeted her. That oppressive kind of silence that came when a house has been left empty too long and the life and energy once trapped within its walls was slowly draining away. A fanciful notion. But funerals always made her melancholy.

Still wearing her coat and clutching her reticule in cold, numb fingers, she walked slowly through the rooms.

Everything looked the same, like a tintype frozen in time—her mother's bonnet draped over the arm of the settee, the same array of photographs lining the walls, a book left open on the table beside her father's chair. Even the air smelled familiar—a subtle blend of old smoke with a hint of her father's pipe tobacco and her mother's sachet. But beneath it, barely detectable, hung the damp mustiness of an empty house and the beginnings of decay.

And they had only been dead a week.

In the kitchen, she dropped her reticule on the table and stripped off her coat and gloves. Moving by rote, she set a fire in the cook-stove and lit the lamp sitting on the table, then went through the rituals of preparing tea. Once she had the kettle heating and the tea caddy and sugar bowl on the table, she set out her mother's favorite cup, a napkin, and a spoon.

Then she sat down in her father's chair, dropped her head onto her folded arms, and wept.

An hour later, she was still sitting there, her tears long spent, nursing her third cup of tea and trying to decide what to do with the rest of her life.

Her parents were dead. Her marriage was a failure. She would probably never have children or a home of her own. Even this house would have to be sold to cover the cost of her parents' funerals. With no other family and no resources, her future stretched bleak and empty ahead of her.

So what was she to do? Go back to Scotland? To a father-in-law who couldn't abide the English, and a mother-in-law who rarely left her room? Angus's sister, Glynnis, was so busy running the Kirkwell lands she had little time for a husband, much less a friend, and his two older brothers were so involved with their own pursuits they were rarely at home, and when they were, they called her the English girl because they couldn't remember her name. With her husband gone years on end, what reason had she to go back?

She looked down at the heavy signet ring Angus had given her before he rode off to rejoin his cavalry regiment over a year and a half ago. She hadn't seen him since. In over four years of marriage, he had written her two letters and visited her once. Four years, languishing at the family's remote Highland estate, the unwanted English bride of a Scottish earl's son, while he played soldier in Ireland.

She had given up her dreams for that?

She almost yanked the ring off her finger and threw it across the room. But she hadn't the energy for even that. After her hurried dash across half of England to get to the funeral on time, then standing in the icy drizzle as Vicar Collins presided over the small graveside service for her parents this afternoon, she was so emotionally drained just lifting her teacup took an effort of will.

It was all rather meaningless, anyway, if the target of her ire wasn't even there to make note of it.

Beyond the window, the wind huffed and moaned. Tiny pellets of sleet rattled against the windowpanes. Gusts sent drafts back down the stovepipe to burp puffs of smoke into the still air.

Perhaps he had died. That's what soldiers did, especially rash, high-spirited cavalrymen who took needless risks. But she had always thought Angus Wallace was too big, too headstrong, too fearless to die. Besides, if something had happened to him, his family would have been notified—if not his wife, then surely his father, the Earl of Kirkwell.

If not dead, then what?

Utterly indifferent.

The realization left her breathless with despair.

Fearing another onslaught of tears, she looked around the room, seeking distraction. Her gaze fell on the framed photograph hanging beside the door that led into the parlor. A calmness came over her as she studied the smiling faces of her parents, remembering that last holiday at Brighton, and how Papa had cajoled her mother into donning one of those scandalous bathing costumes and testing the waters. Maddie had tried to make them sit still all afternoon. Finally, when they stopped to rest on the wall overlooking the beach, she saw her chance.

It was one of her first attempts at portraiture, and a poor one at that. Blurred lines, misplaced shadows, shoddy composition— all marks of a novice photographer. But it was her favorite, because there was more to it than just an image on paper. For the first time she had captured not just form, but emotion. There was a story behind those smiling faces. She had seen it, and coaxed it out of the shadows, and trapped it in tintype for all the years to come.

Perhaps she could do that again.

That notion burst into her head, half formed and elusive. But it grew with every heartbeat until it filled her mind. Dare she?

For the next two days, as she set her parents' house to rights and packed away their things, that thought dogged her footsteps like a lost cat.

It was absurd. So far beyond reason and practicality it wasn't worth pursuing. Yet, after her third restless night, she surrendered to the lure of possibility and resolutely climbed the stairs to the attic where her photographs and equipment were stored, determined to at least give it a try.

The Scottish had a saying: "Be happy while you're living, for you'll be a long time dead." And Maddie intended to be happy. She deserved it, Angus Wallace be damned.

The next afternoon, she was sitting before Mr. Reginald Farnsworth Chesterfield's desk at *The Illustrated London News* nervously clasping her gloved hands in her lap and growing more convinced by the moment that grief had robbed her of her senses.

Daughters of baronets and wives of third sons to earls did not seek employment. They did not set up shop, or peddle their wares, or go into business, especially such a male-dominated business as photography. They stayed at home and tatted and traded vague reminiscences about their absent husbands and childless, empty lives until God finally took pity and allowed them to die.

"Hmm," the gray-haired publisher said as he pulled another photograph from the portfolio she had brought for his perusal.

Hmm? What did that mean?

She tried not to fidget. A chance. That's all she wanted. She would work for a pittance—or at least enough to keep her parents' house so she would have someplace to live. She would even take an assignment on speculation, just to prove she could do it.

Minutes ticked by. Maddie's confidence dwindled to quivery jelly. After almost a half hour of silence, she was on the verge of snatching up her portfolio and fleeing the building.

This was all a horrid mistake. It was time to accept her fate and go back to Northbridge, and learn to speak Gaelic and eat haggis without gagging.

"I had to look at them one more time," Mr. Chesterfield finally said as he slid the photographs and *cartes de visite* back into the heavy canvas folder. "Just to be sure."

Maddie tried to keep her breathing even.

After tying the closure tabs, he tipped back his swivel chair and studied the ceiling, his brow furrowed in thought, the forefinger and thumb of his right hand idly plucking at the gray hairs sprouting from his top lip. "It's a rather forward-thinking notion," he mused, more to himself than to her. "Revolutionary. Still . . . It just might work."

Abruptly he swiveled around and stared at her across his desk. "Have you seen the photographs of Matthew Brady?" he demanded. "Those he took in America during their recent rebellion?"

"Y-yes." Her voice sounded like a mouse squeak, so she cleared her throat and tried again. "They are most evocative." Astounding. Haunting. Compelling. Everything she wished her photographs could be.

"And those of William Jackson," he pressed. "And Tim O'Sullivan?"

"The ones of the American West? They're fascinating. Each image seems to tell a tale all its own."

"Yes!" The elderly man beamed, showing small, crooked teeth beneath his gray muttonchops. "But they only present one side of the story, don't you see."

Maddie didn't but nodded politely, her fixed smile starting to wobble. "One side."

"The male side, as it were."

"Ah. The male side." She wondered if he was insane. And what he would do if she cast up her accounts on his desk. Perhaps she should leave before she did.

"But to see it from a whole new perspective, that's the challenge. That would certainly catch your eye, would it not?"

"Indeed." Clearly insane.

"Of course it would! So what do you think, madam?"

Maddie felt that thickness in her throat again. "About what, sir?"

"The female perspective!"

"Well . . . insomuch as it's the only one I have, I rather like it."

He gave a sudden bark of laughter that made her jump. "You misunderstand. I'm asking if you would like to travel to America, Mrs. Wallace, and photograph the West from the female perspective."

Maddie was too astounded to respond. *America?*

"I have been wanting to send an expeditionary photographer over there for some time." His voice grew more enthusiastic with every word. "But a woman! Now that would be unheard of. Revolutionary!" He startled her anew by slapping the flat of his hand down on her closed portfolio. "You have the talent for it, madam. But have you the will? What say you?"

She couldn't say anything. Her tongue wouldn't work.

"I would advance you travel expenses," he added before she could form a response. "And those of your husband, of course, as I assume he will be accompanying you."

"I . . . ah . . ."

"Unless you think he might object? Shall I contact him directly? I realize this is highly unusual, but if he—"

"There is no *he*," Maddie blurted out, astounded by her own audacity and the lie she was about to tell. But how could she *not* do it? A new start. A new life. A whole new *country*, even. "That is to say, I'm"—*forgive me, Angus*—"a widow."

"A widow?" The idea seemed to delight him. "Well, then, there's nothing to hold you back, is there?"

"Not a thing." And for all intents and purposes, she truly was a widow. Angus had left her in spirit almost two years ago. This physical parting was simply the final step in accepting the death of her marriage so she could begin a new life without him.

"Excellent. I'll book passage for . . . shall we say, two weeks? That should give you time to gather what equipment and supplies you'll need. Have the bills sent to my office." He smiled, all but rubbing his hands together in glee. "Any questions?"

Dozens of them. Thousands. "No."

"Excellent! Then we're agreed." Hopping up, he held out his hand.

Maddie rose on shaky legs and placed her fingers in his, hoping he didn't feel the tremors in her hand. "Agreed."

And as simply as that, it was done.

Two weeks to pack, put the house up for sale, restock her supplies, and send a note to Northbridge to inform them of her plans in case Angus ever inquired about her absence.

America. Just the thought of it made her giddy.

One

The Fifth Viscount of Ashby—or Ash, as his new London friends called him—rode slowly down the muddy street, Tricks padding wearily at his side, his rough coat dripping rain and mud.

A sad place, Heartbreak Creek. Judging by the faded store shingles hanging over the warped boardwalk, and the hulking structure perched on the bluffs above the canyon that sheltered the town, it had once been a prosperous mining community. But now the machinery sat silent, the mine dark, and few people walked past the unpainted wooden buildings with their sagging roofs and boarded storefronts. It looked no different from a dozen other wee villages he'd ridden through in the last months.

He had seen worse in Ireland—which would probably never recover from the devastation of the potato famine—and in Scotland, where the Clearances had left a trail of empty huts and overflowing graveyards across his beloved Highlands. But it was always disturbing to see a town die.

Yet, despite the obvious decline, there were still signs of life in Heartbreak Creek. Two wagons stood in front of the Mercantile, Feed, and Mining Supplies store, and the hotel looked freshly painted and bore a fine new sign over the front doors. But without steady commerce from mining, timber, or the railroads, the town would soon die.

So why had she come to such a bleak place? To hide from him? He had once been a forward rider with the Rifles of the Light Division, and a man never forgot training like that. Dinna she realize that no matter where she went or how far she ran, he could still find her? She had led him a merry chase, so she had. The lass was as elusive as peat smoke, but he sensed that finally after twenty months of searching, he was getting close.

Reining in at the rail in front of the hotel, he stiffly dismounted, twisting as little as possible as he swung down. For the last hour, pain had been gnawing at his left side like the starving hounds of hell, and he knew he would pay a high price for riding so long in the rain. Cold dampness always made his slow-healing wound ache—the crossing had been a bluidy nightmare, made worse by the constant pitch and roll of the ship. But the dizziness had eased once he'd stepped onto solid ground in Boston Harbor, and he hadna suffered a single headache in well over a month.

"Stay," he ordered Tricks as he looped Lurch's reins over the rail.

The dog grinned up at him, tongue lolling, his bushy brows spiky with rain and clumps of mud.

"I mean it. You're bluidy filthy, so you are. And since you willna allow a bath, you'll stay out here. That's an order."

Ignoring the animal's pitiful whines, Ash stepped through the double front doors and was pleased to see that Heartbreak Creek Hotel was as dapper inside as it was out. Dark paneling gleamed. Lush green plants rose out of tall clay urns. There were no patches or stains on the upholstered chairs gathered around a tufted hassock, and no dusty cobwebs dangling from the sparkling chandelier. Even the bald spot atop the head of the old man at the front desk looked polished, and the brass clasps on the braces worn by the freckled bellboy posted inside the doors would have satisfied the most demanding sergeant.

A well-run establishment. Ash nodded in approval.

"Hidy," the clerk said as Ash crossed to the front desk. "Help you?"

"Aye. I need a room. One with a big bed."

The old man's grin showed a lack of teeth, and those that remained were marred by rusty stains. "Planning a party, are you?"

Ash looked at him.

The grin faded. "All our beds are the same size."

"Then one without a foot rail."

The clerk gazed past Ash's shoulder. His faded blue eyes widened. "Great Godamighty! What is that thing?"

Ash dinna have to guess what had caught the old man's attention. "A wolfhound. The room?"

Still staring toward the door, the elderly fellow said, "Dogs—assuming that hulking beast is a dog and not a starving, long-tailed bear—ain't allowed inside."

"I told him that but he dinna listen. You're welcome to give it a go."

Whirling, the old man fled through the open doors into what appeared to be the dining area. "Miss Hathaway! You better come quick!"

Bollocks. Ash felt a gob of mud hit his ear and turned to glare at Tricks, who was slinging water and mud in a ten-foot arc as he wagged his long, thin tail. "Now look what you've done," he accused. "I should sell you to the Chinamen, so I should."

"Sir!" A woman marched out of the dining area, the clerk hot on her heels. A blond woman, with eyes as green as Ireland and a look on her pretty face that would send the devil into retreat.

"Animals are not allowed in this establishment." She waved a hand at the double doors. "Take him outside immediately!"

"He willna stay there without me."

"Then I'll bid you good day, as well."

The old man snickered.

Ash sighed. "I've come a long way, so I have, and I'm in desperate need of a warm, dry room. One with a long bed, so my feet willna hang off the end. Can you make an exception this one time?"

Her pretty eyes narrowed in suspicion. "A long way from where?"

"Scotland."

"I told you he wasn't from around here," the clerk muttered.

"Yancey, I'll handle this!"

But Ash could see his answer had startled her, and he wondered why.

"What is your name, sir?" she asked.

"Ashby."

"That's it? No first name?"

Ash shrugged. "Some call me lord."

Understanding came quickly—the woman was blade sharp. "Lord Ashby? Is that a joke?"

"Regretfully, no. I'll pay double," he added to distract her.

"Why are you here? In Heartbreak Creek?"

"I'm seeking a woman."

The clerk snorted. "Aren't we all."

With a hiss of exasperation, she whirled on the old man. "Yancey, please assist Miriam upstairs. Billy"—she waved to the freckled boy watching with wide-eyed interest from his post by the front door—"fetch Sheriff Brodie, if you will. Now."

After the boy dashed out the front door and Yancey stomped up the staircase that rose along the wall separating the lobby from the dining room, she returned her attention to Ash. "What woman?"

Ash frowned, put off by the challenge in her tone. Not many would dare. Especially a female. But he had no wish to sleep on the ground again tonight, so he kept his tone pleasant. "Madeline Wallace."

"Why?"

"I have news of her family."

"What news?"

Bugger this. He started toward the door.

"Ah . . . double, you say?"

He stopped, debated, then thinking of the cold dampness that awaited him if he left, turned back. "Aye. But the bed canna have a foot rail."

"You'll bathe your dog?"

Ash thought of the last attempt. "Aye. If you have four stout men to aid me."

"You can bathe him in the trough around back. I'll send out Yancey and Billy with drying rags." Her green eyes flicked over him. "You may use the tub in the washroom off the kitchen. But not the dog. And we don't have stables here, so you'll have to take your horse to the livery on the edge of town."

It took Yancey, Billy, and two lengths of rope to get Tricks into the trough, but the deed was done without loss of limb. When Ash left the washroom an hour later, clean and freshly dressed with his pouting and mostly clean wolfhound at his heels, he found a man leaning against the wall beside the door, working at his nails with a penknife. By his expression when he saw Ash, it was apparent he had been waiting for him.

"Heard you were looking for Maddie Wallace," the man said, studying Ash through dark eyes from beneath the brim of his black flat-crowned hat. He was even taller than Ash and solidly built, and he would have carried an air of authority even without the sheriff's badge pinned to his vest.

Ash nodded. "I am."

"Mind if I ask why?"

Ash did, so he dinna respond. Tricks plopped onto his belly by Ash's boot, his rangy body taking up most of the hallway, and began licking the dampness from his front legs.

"Impressive dog," the man said as he folded the penknife. "Is he as dangerous as he looks?"

"Not to me."

The sheriff nodded and slipped the penknife into his pocket. Bending down, he let Tricks sniff his open hand, then gently stroked the knobby head.

Ash was surprised. Like most of his breed, Tricks was standoffish with strangers. By accepting the sheriff so readily, it only confirmed Ash's assessment of the man. A reasonable fellow who wore his position well.

The sheriff straightened. "See that table in the back corner?" He pointed across the hall to the open door that led into the dining room. "The one with the ladies?"

Ash followed his direction and saw the blond woman seated with a dark-skinned woman and a pregnant sandy-haired woman. All three were staring their way. And frowning. "Aye, I see them."

"The blond is Lucinda Hathaway," the sheriff explained in a friendly tone. "Owns the hotel. Yankee. Smart. Carries a pepperbox pistol. Far as I know, she hasn't killed anyone with it. The dark-skinned woman is Prudence Lincoln. She lives at the school the ladies set up for ex-slaves and anyone else who wants to come learn. Whether she likes it or not, she's under the protection of a Cheyenne Dog Soldier. Ever heard of them?"

Ash had. He'd never seen one, but he'd heard of their legendary fierceness in battle and admired them for it. He was Scottish, after all. But right now he was less curious about Indians than why the sheriff was telling him all this.

"Now that blue-eyed beauty," the man went on, his voice softening as he looked at the sandy-haired woman. "She's Edwina Brodie. She might fool some with her southern charm, but she's pretty handy with a shovel and once even faced down a mountain lion with a bucket of salad greens. And if that's not enough to give a man pause . . ." Swinging his gaze back to Ash, he gave him a hard look. "There's me."

Ash heard the challenge but gave no reaction. "And who are you?"

The sheriff touched the tips of two fingers to the brim of his hat. "Declan Brodie. I'm temporary sheriff here at Heartbreak Creek. And her husband."

The warning was clear, although Ash had no idea why Sheriff Brodie had issued it. Maddie Wallace was the woman he had come to see, not these females. "Why temporary?" he asked.

"Because I'm a rancher," Brodie explained, which explained nothing. "As you can see," he went on, glancing back toward the women, "the ladies are upset. It's not good when they get upset."

"Which of us is in trouble?" Ash asked, although he had a fair idea.

Brodie flashed white teeth in a crooked grin that changed his austere face to one that women might find handsome. "Hell, I've got four kids and a pregnant wife. I'm always in trouble. But this time, it's you."

"What have I done?"

"That depends." No longer smiling, the sheriff stepped toward Ash.

Immediately Tricks rose.

The sheriff paused, looked from the dog to Ash, but came no closer. He showed no menace, yet Ash sensed an unbendable resolve within the man. He respected that, since it was a trait they had in common.

"Why are you looking for Maddie?" Brodie asked again.

That was the second time the sheriff had casually used the shortened version of Madeline's name. Ash dinna like the sound of it on another man's tongue. "As I told the Hathaway woman, I have news of her family," he said stiffly. "Is she here?"

Brodie remained silent. Ash suspected he was being assessed by the lawman, and although he dinna like it, he withstood it without showing his growing irritation.

The women continued to watch them and whisper quietly amongst themselves. Ash could feel the censure in their eyes and wondered what he'd done to cause it.

"She's off making pictures," the sheriff finally said. "Should be back in a week or so, then she'll be leaving again for the big meeting up in Denver."

"Meeting about what?"

"Political thing. Statehood. Delegates are coming from all over the territory. Promises to be quite a gathering."

"She's a delegate?" That surprised him. Despite her father's leanings, she had showed no interest in politics before. But then, that she was here instead of Scotland where she belonged showed how little he knew her.

"No, I am. Part of the job. Or so I've been told."

Ash heard the disgust in the man's voice and guessed the sheriff wasna excited about the trip. But he'd heard enough to know this was the woman he sought, and his natural impatience caused him to speak more sharply than he intended. "I canna wait another week. Where is she now?"

The sheriff reared his head back and subjected Ash to another lengthy assessment.

Ash was weary of it. "It's important that I speak to her."

"You'll not hurt her?"

"I dinna hurt women."

After more scrutiny, the sheriff sighed, as if he'd come to a decision he might later regret. "She headed up to the Alamosa a month ago."

"The Alamosa?"

"Alamosa River. Things are hopping up there since the strikes."

Brodie must have seen Ash's confusion. "Gold strikes," he clarified. "Miners are pouring in from all over. She wanted to document it. Photograph it. She's a photographer. Didn't you know that?"

Of course Ash knew. It was through her photographs that he had tracked her this far. But he thought the woman had more sense than to go haring off to a place as dangerous as a wide-open mining town. "She dinna go alone, did she?"

"She's got Wall-eyed Willy with her, not that he'd be much protection."

Bluidy hell.

"You going after her?"

"Aye. I'm going after her." After tracking the lass from Scotland to England to Boston, then halfway across America, Ash wasna about to lose her in some western mining town. *Daft woman.* But first, he had to send word to his banker in Boston, telling him to let his family know where he was and that he'd found her. "Is there a telegraph office in town?"

NEAR BRECKENRIDGE, COLORADO TERRITORY

Sixty miles away, in an abandoned mining shack not far from the Blue River, loud voices cut through the night.

"You moron!" Cletus Cochran caught his brother, Silas, on the side of his head with a backhand that sent the younger, smaller man flying. "You idiot! I told you to watch him, not kill him!"

"I didn't mean to, Clete, I swear." Si cowered, one hand pressed to his cheek, the other raised to ward off another blow. "But he got loose and was about to get away, and when I tried to stop him, he started hollering and hitting me and I was afraid—"

"So you cut his damn throat?" Clete's kick sent Si hard against the wall. Dust and dirt rained down from the sod roof, momentarily dimming the pale lantern light and making him cough.

Si cried out, sliding down the rough planks and rolling into a ball. "It was an accident, Clete! I didn't mean to. The knife just slipped. I swear."

Clete kicked him one more time because he could, then turned and studied the dead body sprawled on the dirt floor. There was blood everywhere, on the log walls, on his brother, even on the pale, thin roots hanging down through the beams overhead. Si must have cut an artery. The place smelled like a goddamn slaughterhouse. "Did he tell you anything?"

Eyeing his older brother, Si pushed himself into a sitting position. "No, Clete. Mostly he just yelled."

"You freak. I should have killed you the day you were born."

"Ma wouldn't let you. That's what you said."

"I should have killed her, too, just for birthing you."

Suddenly remembering, Si reached into his pocket. Pulling out a small leather pouch, he offered it to his brother. "Look, Clete. I found it in his pack. I think it's gold."

Clete snatched the pouch from Si's hand and opened it. Nuggets. All sizes. Sharp edged, not rounded and smooth like the placer gold men were digging out of the Blue River north of town. There was even a strip of rope gold. He held it toward the lamp. "This here's from a vein, Si. Proof the bastard struck big. I knew it."

Si grinned and nodded vigorously. "You were right, Clete. You were always the smart one. Everybody says."

"Shut up." Clete dropped the gold back into the pouch and shoved it into his pocket. His brief triumph gave way to unreasoning fury when he realized that with the man dead they would never know the location of the strike. He wanted to hit something, kick his brother until bones snapped. Kill him. "Now we'll never find the claim, you moron, because you killed him. I ought to kill you, too, and get it over with. Where's that knife?"

"No, Clete, wait! There's something else." Si scrabbled over to the dead man's pack. He dug for a moment, then pulled out the cards and papers and offered them to his brother. "Look, Clete. Pictures. Pretty pictures. And papers with writing on them."

"Idiot!" Clete kicked Si's hand and sent the cards and papers flying. "I don't care about damn pictures. I want to know where the strike is."

"He didn't say, Clete, I swear it."

"Quit blubbering, you whiny bastard. I can't take it anymore." He made a show of looking around. "Where's the knife?"

"No, Clete! I'll stop!"

"Stupid, crying moron." Clete paced, his hands opening and closing at his sides, his mind still fogged with rage. Why didn't anything ever go right? All they needed was for the man to tell them where he'd found the gold, but his idiot brother couldn't even do that right.

"Just watch him," Clete had instructed his brother. Then he comes back to find the man dead and Si blubbering about pictures. *Son of a bitch!* Now how would they find the claim? *Damn him.*

He paced a few more loops, then stopped before Si. "Give me the pack. Maybe there's something in there that'll at least tell us who he is."

All he found of interest were some letters from an Aaron Zucker in Pennsylvania addressed to Ephraim Zucker of Breckenridge. Brothers? Clete studied the dead man's battered face. He looked like an Ephraim. Small and skinny like Si, but twenty years older. Late thirties.

A plan formed. Clete played with it, studying it from all angles.

Assuming the dead guy was Ephraim Zucker, and if Clete posed as his brother Aaron, from Pennsylvania, he could ask around and maybe retrace Ephraim's trail back to where he'd found the gold.

Might work. Might not.

Hell, it was their only shot.

He tossed the pack to his brother. "Bury this. And him. Deep. And don't you botch this up, Si, or by God, I'll gut you. You understand?"

"Yes, Clete. I'll do it. You can count on me."

"Yeah, right. Moron." He started for the door.

"Where you going, Clete? You're not leaving me, are you?" .

Clete heard the fear in the whiny voice and knew his brother was about to start wailing again. He gritted his teeth. If he hadn't promised Ma he'd look after the pathetic little freak, he would have shoved him in a river when he was born seventeen years ago. He might anyway, once this was over. A man can't spend his whole life wiping up his idiot brother's snot.

"I'm going back to the saloon where we first saw him. See if anybody knows him. You bury him and the pack, then wash off all that blood and wait here. I'll be back."

"You promise, Clete?"

"Shut up."

As soon as the door slammed and Si knew he was alone, he swung his fists in the air and kicked his feet in a furious pantomime of what he wanted to do to his brother. "I hate you, Clete," he cried, tears running down his cheeks. "You bastard, moron, freak, shut up, I hate you."

After a while, the tears stopped. Wiping a sleeve over his runny nose, Si crawled over to where the pretty pictures had fallen. He picked them up and studied each one, feeling sad about the man on the floor.

He looked over at him. "I'm sorry," he said. "But you shouldn't have run at me. It scares me when people run at me."

He hadn't intended to hurt him, but when the man saw the knife in Si's hand, he had rushed at him and then things happened all at once, and the next thing Si knew, the man was on the floor and blood was running everywhere. "It was an accident. I swear."

The man didn't say anything because he was dead.

"I'll keep your pictures safe. I will. I promise." And Si carefully slipped them into the secret place beneath the torn lining of his jacket where Clete would never find them. He added one of the letters and the folded papers to his stash, too. Someday he would learn to read and the papers would be good to practice on. He'd show that whiny moron bastard brother of his that he could be smart, too.

He stood slowly, his back stiff from his brother's kicks. Seeing a rusty shovel leaning against the wall by the door, he picked it up, then inched open the door.

It was really dark outside. Sound whispered around him—leaves rustling, something moving through the brush, a mouse gnawing on the wood under the stoop.

He began to tremble.

Si hated the dark. Bad things lived in the dark. Things even worse than Clete with his spooky mismatched eyes and mean hands. Si looked fearfully around but saw nothing move. Sliding a trembling hand into his pocket, he wrapped his fingers around the cross pendant Ma said would keep the demons away, then stepped out into the yard.

Walking as fast as he could, he crossed to a grassy spot well away from the shadows of the woods. Humming softly and with his eyes fixed to the ground so he wouldn't see the bad things and they wouldn't see him, he began to dig.

Two

Cursing softly, Ash braced his elbows on top of the boulder he was leaning against and adjusted the focus on his new binoculars.

Damn newfangled contraption. He liked his old field glasses better. The offset lenses might have been bulkier, but the image was brighter. This roof-prism design darkened everything too much.

He twisted the adjustment again. The figure beside the creek blurred, then came into focus. A woman. Auburn hair. Undressing. *Undressing?*

He pulled the glasses down, then quickly raised them again and scanned until he found her. Definitely undressing. In the open. Like a wee highland fairy. This couldna be the woman he'd been tracking across two continents for over a year and a half. The woman he sought was a gently bred Englishwoman. Much too proper to do such a thing.

But just to be sure, he continued to watch.

Nice form. Long legs. Skin as pale as pink marble even with these darker lenses. And that hair had the look of the Highlands in it, catching the sun like burnished copper as she lifted her arms—*Bluidy hell.*

Leaning forward as if that might bring the image closer, he peered in disbelief at the silver dollar–sized birthmark below her right breast.

God bless Scotland. He'd found her. *Damn her hide.*

Lowering the glasses, he pushed away from the boulder, then flinched when something jabbed into the middle of his back. Something hard and round and cold. Like a gun barrel.

"Hands in the air," a gravelly male voice ordered. "And don't move, you damn lecher."

Unclear how he was expected to do both, Ash hesitated, then raised his hands. "I'm not a lecher."

Another jab in his back almost knocked him off balance. "You were spying on a lady."

"I wasna spying. And any woman who parades herself about half naked like a Newmarket tart on race day is no—"

"Show some respect!" A sharp crack on the side of his head sent him staggering.

Pressing a palm to his temple as if that might slow the familiar dizziness, he let loose several Gaelic curses, adding more from India, and a few from Ireland.

"What's that? Foreign talk?"

"Bugger off, ye manky bastard."

"Damn foreigners. You're everywhere. Keep your hands up and turn around."

Hands raised, he turned slowly to keep his balance, and found a rifle—a Winchester Model 1866, by the look of it—an inch from his nose. Behind it, a grizzled old man peered up at him out of a face full of whiskers. At least, one eye peered up at him. The other was pointed off to the right somewhere, which told Ash this was probably the walleyed man Sheriff Brodie had mentioned. Concentrating on the one aimed in his direction, Ash debated putting down the old man now, or waiting to see what he wanted. He'd truly like to have that Winchester. His breech-loading Snider-Enfield cavalry carbine was no match for these newer American lever-action repeating rifles.

The gun barrel banged against his nose to get his attention.

"Manky. That's good, right?" When Ash gave no answer, the barrel banged again.

"Dinna do that," he ground out, his temper fraying.

The eye glanced up at his raised hand. "What's that you're holding?"

"Field glasses."

"Hand them over."

"No."

"No?" The old fellow was clearly taken aback by the refusal. Then he grinned, showing more gum than teeth. "You're a big one, ain't you? But I doubt you're big enough to win out over a bullet. Care to try?"

Ash glanced around, wondering if the old man had come alone. "What are you doing out here?"

"Huntin'. And looky what I found." He poked at Ash with the rifle.

"Do that again, old man, and I'll hurt you, so I will."

A gummy grin. "Which of my eyes looks most concerned?" But wisely, the fellow took a step back. "I'd like to plug you here and now, foreigner, but she'd hear and get upset, and then I'd have to sit through another lecture. No thank you. So we'll let her decide what to do with you. Open your coat." When Ash did, the old man frowned at his sword belt. "No gun?"

Ash shook his head, glad that he'd left his pistol in his saddle-bag.

"You army?"

"Cavalry. British. Retired."

"Don't sound British."

"That's because I'm Scottish."

"Then why'd you call yourself British?"

Ash sighed. "Can I put away my field glasses?" He dinna want them damaged when he disarmed the old fellow.

"Where's your sword?" the man asked after Ash stowed the glasses in the *sabretache* case on his sword belt. "And get your hands back up."

Ash raised his hands again. "Ireland." What was left of it, anyway.

"I thought you were Scottish."

"I am."

"Then what were you doing in Ireland?"

"Fighting for the British."

"You foreigners confuse the hell out of me. I'll let her sort it out." The rifle waved in front of Ash's face. "But make no mistake. You'll show the lady respect or I'll drop you where you stand. Understand?"

"Aye."

"I what?"

"Aye—*yes*—I understand. What about my horse?" He rotated an upraised hand to point toward the brush where he'd left Lurch tied. He dinna mention Tricks, not wanting to involve him unless necessary.

"I'll get him later. After she decides if I get to kill you or not. March."

They marched, although it was a far cry from any of the marches that had been drilled into Ash during seventeen years of military service. Following a faint trail, they cut through a forest of scorched stumps and blackened tree trunks, evidence of a fire that had swept through years ago. After several minutes, he called over his shoulder, "Can I put my arms down now? My hands are going to sleep."

"Shut your piehole."

Taking that as a yes, Ash lowered his hands. He knew he could take the old man at any time—just slow down until the rifle was within reach, then do what he had been trained to do. Whirl, grab and twist, then kick. But his left side remained weak from his old injury, and after that crack on his temple, quick movements made his head spin, so he marched stoically on. Besides, he was anxious to see the woman up close, still not convinced he'd finally found her.

Blasted, headstrong woman. She'd eluded him for months, but he had her now. The idea of that made him smile.

"What's the woman to you?" he asked, skirting a huge rock. "You seem protective of her. Bodyguard?"

"Maybe we're courting."

Ash stumbled, coming down so hard on his left leg it sent a shock of pain up through his still-sore ribs. "Courting?" he choked out once he caught his breath. "Is that a jest, man?"

"Why would it be a jest? You think I'm too old for her?"

"Well, because . . ." He sputtered for a moment, his steps slowing, his mind reeling. "Because the lass is already married."

"Was, maybe. But her husband died. Keep moving."

"Died how?"

"Soldiering. Veer right."

Musing over that bit of information, he followed the trail down a steep, sandy slope riddled with round river rocks that made footing treacherous. From below came the sound of rushing water. As they descended, firs and juniper and spruce gave way to aspens, the faint yellow of their rustling leaves hinting at the winter to come. He looked around, wondering if the woman was bathing nearby, then realized the old man had taken them in a wide flanking maneuver that put a dense copse of trees between them and where she had been.

"What was he like? Her husband?"

"Foreigner, like you. Deserted her, the bastard."

"I thought you said he died."

"Same thing, as far as she's concerned."

Rocks shifted beneath Ash's leather-soled cavalry boots, and he had to grab onto a sapling to keep from sliding down the slope toward a fast-moving creek. "She speak of him much?"

"Not as much as you do. We'll cross there."

The air cooled as they climbed down into the shallow water tumbling over the rocky creek bed. He felt the cold against the leather of his oiled boots and wondered how the woman could bathe in such frigid water.

On the other bank, they picked up the trail again. He smelled woodsmoke and heard a dog barking, and guessed there was a cabin nearby. Seemed odd, living up here. He'd heard the winters in the Colorado Rockies were brutal. Not what he would expect from a woman like her.

Madeline. Even now, he couldna say her name without unleashing a storm of memories—confusing, painful memories that disrupted the control he fought so hard to maintain. A soldier thrived on order and structure. It protected his body as well as his mind. But this woman brought only chaos.

In truth, he had worked hard *not* to remember her or think about her. And for five years he had almost succeeded, keeping her so far in the back of his mind he could barely recall the sound of her voice, or her laughter, or his own desperation to feel her skin against his own. Because of her, he had gone against his family's wishes. Because of her, he had jeopardized his military career. Because of her, he was here now, called to another kind of duty, and finding the prospect of seeing her again just as disturbing as it had been on his last visit home three and a half years ago.

Why had she left him? What had he done?

"You, Angus! Shut your yap!"

Startled, he looked around, then realized the old man was talking to a dog that was tearing out of the brush, barking and snarling.

Ash glowered down at the wee beastie menacing the toes of his boots. It was a pathetic excuse for a dog. More like a ball of hair sprouting improbably large, pointed ears, a stub of a tail, and four tiny feet. And she'd named it Angus? *Bugger that.*

"Best hope she's in a forgiving mood," the old man warned as they stepped out of the trees into a clearing.

Instead of a cabin, he saw an odd-looking wagon parked beside a smoldering fire. Not a canvas-covered buckboard, but more like a peddler's wagon, with hard sides and small glass windows and crates strapped on top. There was even a smokestack rising out of the bowed wooden roof and a wee proper back door opening onto fold-down steps. Rigged out like a shepherd or gypsy wagon, by the look of it, but with a black tentlike structure attached to one side and bold lettering above the windows in such a filigreed script he couldna make out the words. Two mules stopped grazing to watch their approach, and the woman from the creek stood by the rear step—fully dressed, more's the pity.

The sight of her sent a shock of recognition through him, followed by a flash of emotion so intense he had no name for it.

Finally.

The dog ran toward her, the stub of a tail wagging furiously. He debated whistling for Tricks, just to show her what a real dog looked like, but decided not to further complicate what already promised to be a difficult situation. But with each step, his apprehension grew. He'd faced artillery barrages with more confidence.

"Who do you have there, Mr. Satterwhite?" she called, lifting a hand to shade her eyes from the glaring noon sun.

"A letch I caught spying in—"

"Who do you think, you daft woman?" he cut in, taking the offensive to hide his confusion. "Is this any way to greet—"

"I warned you," the old man muttered behind him just before the gun barrel cracked against his head.

"Mercy sakes, Mr. Satterwhite!" Maddie Wallace cried, running to where the stranger laid facedown in the grass. "What have you done?"

"He was ogling you. Want me to shoot him?"

"Gracious, no! Oh, dear, he's bleeding."

"Barely."

Maddie bit back a retort. She really must do something about Mr. Satterwhite. This was the third time he had accosted a complete stranger, and had almost caused a riot in the mining camp by the Alamosa River. Didn't he understand that she was here to make photographs, not enemies?

Shooing the dog aside, she bent over the still form. "Help me roll him over, Mr. Satterwhite, so I can see if he's still alive."

The injured man was quite tall and so sturdily built it took all their strength to get him onto his back. As soon as Maddie saw his face, she jumped back, almost tripping over Angus.

Good heavens! What was *he* doing here?

Her heart started beating so hard she felt suddenly light-headed and half nauseated. Then seeing the blood from the cut on the man's temple, she got herself in hand and inched forward again. "Oh dear, Mr. Satterwhite. Have you killed him?"

The old man nudged the prone figure with the toe of his crusty boot. "Probably not."

"Probably?"

"I think his chest is moving."

"You *think?*"

Satterwhite reared back, his crooked eyes round beneath his white brows. "Don't go hysterical on me, missy. The dirty letch was spying on you. He deserved what he got." The bushy brows lowered. A speculative look came into his bristly face. "Why do you care? You know him? Is this another of your *suitors?*" He said that last word with noticeable disgust.

Maddie studied the familiar face that she had never expected to see again. She had a hard time catching her breath. Nothing seemed to be working right. Her head felt like it was spinning off her neck. "I th-think he's my h-husband."

"Your husband? The dead one?"

Maddie nodded, unable to take her eyes off the man lying so still at her feet. He looked like her husband. The same strong nose and uncompromising chin. Deep-set eyes. She resisted the impulse to pry up a lid to check the color. No one had eyes the same bright mossy green as Angus Wallace. But that scar cutting through one dark brow and giving it an upward, almost quizzical slant, was new. And this man was turning gray, although his brows and lashes and the stubble of beard shadowing his sun-browned face remained dark brown. And yet, that widow's peak was the same . . . and those strong hands, and the long line of his neck . . .

Dizziness assailed her. Why was he here? What had possessed him to come looking for her after all this time? Her chest tightened. She opened her mouth and gulped in air but still couldn't seem to fill her lungs.

"Best sit down, missy. You're looking right pale."

Moving on wobbly knees, she allowed Mr. Satterwhite to lead her around the back of the wagon to the single ladder-back chair that stood beside the coals of that morning's fire. As she sagged onto the cushioned seat, she grabbed at the gnarly hand on her arm. "Do please check, Mr. Satterwhite. I m-must know if you've killed him."

"By the bones of Saint Andrew! Of course he dinna kill me!"

Maddie gaped at the figure staggering around the back of the wagon, one hand braced against the ladder support, the other pressing a red-stained handkerchief to his brow. Lifting a foot, he shook it furiously, trying to dislodge her snarling dog from his boot. "And call off your rat before I snap his bluidy neck!"

"Angus, hush!"

"The hell I will, madam!"

"No, the other one."

"The other one?" Mr. Satterwhite looked around. "How many husbands you got?"

"Oh, dear. I-I think I'm going to faint."

"Not until I get some answers, madam!"

But everything was already swirling away.

Bollocks.

Ash lunged, catching her just before she toppled into the fire. Fending off the yapping rat, he lowered her to the ground. "Tie up that bluidy dog," he ordered the old man. "And get some water!"

"Is she dead?"

"No, she's not dead! She fainted." Or so he hoped. Uneasy with the old man hovering somewhere behind him with a loaded gun in his hands, Ash glanced over his shoulder. "Scatterwell, is it?"

"Wilfred Satterwhite. Some call me Wall-eyed Willy, but if you do, I'll shoot you. Maybe fifteen times, since this here's a repeater."

"What's her name?"

Satterwhite blinked in surprise. "You don't know?"

"Her name!" Ash had to be certain. With her eyes closed, it was hard to tell. Yet every part of his being had recognized her instantly.

"Missus Wallace. Who are you? You really her husband?"

Ash wasna sure. The woman had apparently touted it about that he was dead. Maybe she'd contracted herself to someone else. The thought made his hands shake. "I'm Angus Wallace. No, Ashby."

"Which?"

"Both."

"Named her dog after you. Makes sense to me."

"Get the water. And either lock up that yapping dog or shoot it."

The old man snatched up the wad of fur and stomped off, muttering under his breath.

Ash blotted at the cut on his head, checked the handkerchief, and was relieved to see the bleeding had stopped. But the pain was just beginning. He felt it closing in, pressing against the edges of his vision, building with every pulse beat. He calculated he had about an hour before it drove him to his knees.

He studied the figure on the ground. His wife. The woman he had tried so hard to forget yet had crossed an ocean to find. He recognized her . . . but she seemed different from the woman he'd married. Older. Prettier. More . . . rounded. He sank back on his heels, distancing himself from both the woman and the disconcerting realization that even as angry as he was with her, he could still feel an attraction. But she'd always had that effect on him. Just being in the same room with her had robbed him of reason.

He remembered her as being sweet and pretty. Tractable. Always smiling, with round pink cheeks, and good teeth, and a cheerful aspect even when his father had given her his best scowl.

And passionate. So passionate it had been like a drug to him.

Shoving that thought aside, he continued his assessment. He could see time had aged her, replacing those round girlish cheeks with clearly defined cheekbones and sculpting a stronger line to her jaw. Stubborn, almost. The wide mouth was the same—he remembered that well enough—and that arch in her brows that always gave her the look of a wide-eyed innocent.

Innocent? Ash snorted, then winced when pain exploded behind his eyes as if a battery of twelve pounders had gone off inside his head. How innocent could a woman be if she would willingly desert her husband, toss her marriage aside, and run off to some foreign country just to make tintype pictures?

Well . . . That might not be fair of him. He had seen her work. It was more art than photograph. The woman had an eye, so she did. And a way of looking at the world that transformed the mundane into the beautiful.

But that was no excuse for deserting her husband.

"Here's the water, Your Majesty." The old man stomped toward him, dribbling a trail of liquid from the long-handled ladle he held in his outstretched hand. "But I'd advise you not to throw it on her."

Ash took the ladle, realized he couldn't force an unconscious person to drink, debated disregarding Satterwhite's advice and throwing it in her face, then drank it himself. It was cold going down, but seemed to ease the pounding in his head. He handed back the ladle. "Get my horse."

"Get him yourself."

"And you'll tend her while I'm gone?"

Satterwhite went to get his horse.

"Mind the dog," Ash called after him, then turned back to the woman, uncertain what to do. He wanted her to wake up so he could yell at her. He wanted her to stop lying there so pale and still. He wanted to stop wanting her.

Reaching out, he tapped her cheek with his index finger. "Wake up."

She ignored him. Typical female tactic.

He tried to see in her features the young woman who had caught his eye six years ago when the Tenth Hussars had bivouacked in her village en route to their new deployment in Ireland. She'd become a beautiful woman since then. Older, but better. Unlike him, she showed no gray in her dark auburn hair, and her face wasna marked by seventeen years of hard soldiering. Granted, he was thirty-four now, and quite a bit older than she was. Nine or ten years, if he remembered right, which would make her somewhere in her mid twenties. Still young enough to produce heirs, which, after all, was why he was here.

Duty. Would he ever be free of it?

"Is—is it truly you, Angus?"

Looking down, he saw that his wife had awakened and was gawking up at him. "Aye. But 'tis Ashby now." He was still having trouble getting accustomed to that change.

"Where's your mustache?"

On reflex, he fingered his bare upper lip, which had once sported the flaring mustache that was the mark of the Tenth Hussars. "I shaved it off."

She slapped him hard across the cheek.

Rearing back onto his heels, he blinked at her in shock. "What was that for?"

"For deserting me, among other things." Laboriously, she pushed herself into a half-reclining posture, her elbows braced behind her.

He tried not to notice how that pulled the fabric of her dress tight across her breasts, which seemed fuller than—*Wait. He* deserted *her?*

"I see you're still the vexing, high-handed man you were when you ran off like the dog you are. Oh, do move away, Angus, or Ashby, or whatever you call yourself now. You're crowding me."

"*I* ran off?" He stood too quickly and almost lost his balance before the spinning stopped. "If you'll recall, madam, I returned to my regiment. As ordered. And because of you, late. What might your excuse be?"

"You left me. I had no choice. Where's Mr. Satterwhite?"

"Choking the dog, I hope."

"Then you'll have to do." She extended a hand in his direction.

He could see it was shaking, and was gratified that she seemed as unsettled by this meeting as he was. He also noticed she wore the signet ring he had given her to mark her as his. It looked incongruous on her delicate hand and had a thick cord wrapped around the back to keep it from slipping off her slender finger. But even after all this time, she still wore it, and he took that as a good sign.

"Well? Are you going to help me up? Or have you forgotten how to be a gentleman?"

He refrained from flinging her into the trees. "I dinna desert you," he said with rigid calmness once she was settled in her chair and had finished fussing with her skirts. "I left you in the care of my family at our ancestral home."

She shot him a look. "Ancestral home? That pile of rubbish?"

"Rubbish? Northbridge has been the seat of the Earls of Kirkwell for nigh onto five generations. It is not a pile of rubbish."

"They've repaired the skirt wall, then?"

He was momentarily struck dumb by how much he wanted to shake her, throttle her, wipe that smirk off her face. Get his hands on her any way he could.

She dismissed his silence with a wave of her hand. "As I said. A pile of rubbish. Have you come for a divorce?"

Caught off guard by the abrupt change in subject, it took him a moment to find an appropriate answer. She had always had a talent for making him lose track of his thoughts. To cover his lapse, he returned to the rigid role of military officer. "As appealing as that notion might be, madam," he snapped, "I have come to take you back."

"Back? In a casket, I assume?" She smiled sweetly. "For I assure you that is the only way I will return to the loving bosom of your family."

Ash clasped his hands behind his back before he used them on her. "My family is greatly reduced, madam. You will find them scant bother."

She blinked up at him, her deep, brown eyes no longer flashing anger. "Reduced?"

He cleared his throat of a sudden tightness. "My father died of a seizure a while back, and my mother, as well as Neil and his wife, were taken in the fevers of sixty-nine."

"Taken?"

"Died." What was she—a bluidy parrot?

"Oh, dear." She reached up.

He tensed, wondering where the blow would land.

But this time she only rested her fingertips on the sleeve of his coat above his bent elbow. "I'm so sorry, Angus. Truly."

And suddenly there she was, the woman he remembered, her expressive eyes filled with tears, her face softened by emotion. She had looked at him that same way the last time he'd seen her, when he had ridden off to rejoin his regiment after a night he would never forget.

He looked down at the fingers so pale against the dark fabric of his coat. It was just a hand. Slim and fine and small next to the thickness of his arm. But he remembered it well, and how soft it had felt sliding up his bare back, and he fought a troubling urge to cover it now with his own hand—to anchor her to him, to reassure her, or maybe to keep her from hitting him again—he wasna sure which. "They dinna suffer long."

"Your older brother and your sister? How did they fare?"

He cleared his throat and looked away. "Donnan and Glynnis survived, although when I left, Donnan had yet to regain his full strength." Deciding to press on while she seemed in a receptive mood, he stiffened his spine and braced his legs. "Which is why I have come."

Her hand dropped away. "Oh?"

"Neil had no sons. Nor does Donnan, you see."

She waited.

"And considering his age and the poor state of his health, it's unlikely that he will."

"Which leaves you."

"Aye."

For a moment, silence. Then she burst into laughter. "And you think—you and I—we—should continue the prestigious family line?"

He felt his face grow warm. "Aye. 'Tis our duty."

"Duty!" Laughter faded. "Back up before I strike you again."

He inched back—as a courtesy, of course, not in retreat.

"Do you honestly think that after completely ignoring me for almost six years—*six years*, Angus—all you have to do is show up and issue your orders and I will happily jump to do your bidding?"

He had hoped so. It worked that way with the men under his command. And besides, he hadna completely ignored her. He'd come home that one time . . . and risked much to do so. Most officers went much longer between visits with their wives.

Luckily, Satterwhite's arrival prevented him from mentioning that before he had time to think it through.

"Here's your horse," the old man called as he led Lurch toward the wagon. "Spookiest animal I ever saw. Jumps at everything he sees."

"He's deaf. Give him water and unsaddle him, then tie him where he can see me."

"Mr. Satterwhite is not your flunky."

"What about the dog?" Ash asked, ignoring the muttered comment.

"I didn't see any dog."

"Isn't that Lurch?" his wife asked, studying the horse as the old man tied him to the side of the wagon. "You brought him from Scotland?"

Surprised that she would remember after so long a time, Ash nodded.

"He wasn't always deaf, was he?"

"No." Sensing questions coming that he dinna want to answer, he tried to divert her. "There are things we need to discuss—"

"What happened to him?"

Bollocks. "He was injured in an explosion."

"When?"

"Two years ago."

"Were you with him?"

"Aye."

"Were you injured?"

"Aye."

Her cheeks seemed to lose color. "Badly?"

Realizing that he had pressed the heel of his palm against his throbbing temple, he lowered his arm and once more clasped his hands behind his back. "Badly enough to end my military career," he said curtly, needing no reminders of that senseless, blood-soaked afternoon. "As I was saying, madam, there are things we need to—"

"Ah. Now I understand." She leveled her gaze at him.

It was disconcertingly direct. That artist's eye again. Intrusive. As if she saw past all his carefully erected barriers to the doubt and confusion he always felt when she was near. Charging at a full gallop toward a line of armed infantry soldiers made him less nervous than did his own wife.

"Now that you can no longer follow the drum, you have come to me to amuse you. Is that the right of it, Angus?"

"I assure you, madam, at this moment I am anything but amused." He glowered at her to prove it.

She laughed, apparently unfazed by a look that had caused more than one raw recruit to soil himself. "I wonder, Angus—or Ashby, as you now fashion yourself—why you persist in calling me 'madam.' Have you forgotten my name, perchance?"

Another wave of heat rushed up his neck. Of course he remembered her name. But it helped him keep his distance if he dinna speak it aloud.

"You have, haven't you? How utterly like you."

Yet he had glimpsed tears in her eyes before she'd looked away, and sensed the hurt behind her brittle smile. *Bluidy hell.* He hadn't intended to make her cry. He hadn't intended for this meeting to go so badly. But she addled him, being so different from the woman he had expected to find—all prickly, and outspoken, and . . . independent. The change unsettled him.

And repelled him.

And in some odd way he dinna understand, it also pulled him closer.

"Of course, I remember your—"

"It's Madeline," she cut in, still not looking at him. "Maddie, to my friends. Alexandra Madeline Gresham Wallace."

"Not anymore. Madam. Madeline."

She blinked at him, that shadow of hurt still reflected in her eyes. "So you've divorced me, after all?"

"Not yet." He softened that with a smile, not sure if he was joking. "But since the passing of my father and Neil, our status has changed. Donnan is now Earl of Kirkwell, and as his heir, I am now Viscount Ashby." He punctuated that with a curt bow. "My fellow officers have—had, that is—shortened it to Ash, happy to remind me of the gray in my hair. And you are now Lady Madeline, my viscountess."

"Your vi-viscountess?"

"My viscountess."

"But I do not want to be a viscountess, yours or anyone else's. I am perfectly happy being a tintypist."

"I'm afraid you have no choice, madam. Madeline."

"Oh, dear. I never—" Abruptly the air went out of her. Her eyes rounded. A look of terror came over her face as she stared past his shoulder. "Duck!" she screamed just as something slammed into his back and drove him to the ground.

Three

"Get off me!" Ash yelled over his wife's shrieks. "Down!" From the corner of his eye, he saw Satterwhite running from the wagon, the rifle at his shoulder. "No! Don't shoot! It's my dog! Don't shoot!"

Finally getting a grip on the wriggling body straddling his chest, he shoved Tricks out of licking range and rolled to his feet. "You boggin' noob!" he railed, wiping his dusty sleeve over his damp face. "I told you to stay."

Madeline let the stick of firewood she gripped in both hands drop to the dirt. "Th-that's a dog?"

"Aye." He glowered at the animal grinning up at him. "An Irish wolfhound, and he's but a wee pup, so he has much to learn. You won't be needing that." He motioned to the rifle in the old man's hands.

Satterwhite slowly lowered the rifle. "I've ridden smaller burros. The thing must be eight or nine hands high."

"Aye," Ash said proudly. "The lad's big for his age, so he is."

"B-But he attacked you." His wife edged back from the panting dog, her brown eyes as round as buttons in her pale face.

"Not my Tricks." Bending, he brushed dust from his trousers

and inspected his boots for new scratches. "He's just glad to see me. Fair exuberant about it, so he is, but he means no harm." He straightened to find both his wife and Satterwhite gaping at him. "What?"

"Does he bite?" the old man asked.

"Not unless I tell him to." *And Tricks decides to obey.*

Tentatively, his wife reached out a hand.

Ash started to warn her, but the hound was already giving her fingers a thorough sniff, then anointing them with a slobbery kiss.

"Good boy," she crooned, smoothing back the wiry eyebrows that were almost as high as her waist.

Ash watched, as perplexed by the hound's affectionate behavior as his wife's reaction. Few of the gently bred women of his acquaintance would extend a hand to such a ferocious-looking beast, much less smile at his damp show of acceptance. But then, his wife had never been orthodox—not in her emotions, or her photography, or her passions. At one time he had wondered if married women were allowed to be so open in their affections toward their husbands—he had never seen such between his parents, or his brothers and their wives—not that he had complained. In fact, the memory of that ardor had warmed him during many a lonely night.

"Why Tricks?" she asked.

"Because he does tricks."

"Indeed?"

Trying not to sound boastful, Ash said, "He can bring down a wolf or a boar, or even a stag or horse. And he can rip out a man's throat on command." That was conjecture, of course, since it had never happened. But Ash suspected Tricks would do it if the occasion warranted. He ruffled a rough-coated ear. "He's a braw lad, so he is. Protective and intensely loyal. It's in their natures."

"That's not *tricks*. That's savagery."

Ash shrugged. "He's a war dog. That's what they do." Seeing she needed further reassurance, he added, "He can also sit and heel. He's verra smart." He lifted a hand. "Tricks, sit!"

The dog flopped on his back and displayed his privates.

"Oh, aye," she mimicked with a smirk. "The braw lad is verra smart, so he is." With a dismissive wave of her hand, she turned toward the wagon. "Come, Mr. Satterwhite. Let's collect what you will need for your rabbit stew this evening."

Bemused, Ash watched her walk away, squinting through the dwindling haze of his headache at the way the breeze molded her skirt to her rounded arse. "See what I mean, lad?" he said, idly rubbing his temple. "She's not like other women, who will do anything for a title. She's unpredictable, so she is, and independent to a fault. A woman with ideas and the backbone to see them through. A potent combination."

When Tricks dinna respond, he looked down to find the dog staring after his wife, his jaws open in a toothy grin. "Shut your geggie, lad. You look like a drooling gawk. But I agree. We'll not be giving up on her yet."

Maddie managed to make it up the steps and into her wagon before her wobbly knees betrayed her.

Angus-the-dog rushed her, yipping and trying to climb her skirts. Dropping down onto her narrow bed, Maddie gathered her pet in her arms and pressed her heated cheek against the fluffy fur.

"He's here, pup. He's actually here."

The dog licked her face, then wiggled out of her arms and went to scratch at the door.

"I can't let you out, Angus. His great beast will eat you." She pressed a trembling hand to her brow. "Oh, dear. I'll have to change your name, won't I?" Then she remembered that Angus-the-man was now Ash-the-viscount, so what did it matter? She stifled a laugh even as tears burned in her eyes. She didn't know why she was laughing and crying but couldn't seem to stop either. She felt giddy. And panicky. And terrified.

My husband is here. Now. Just outside the door.

Or had she dreamed it?

Leaning over, she inched back the curtain over the small window.

Definitely no dream. More like a nightmare. He stood where she had left him, talking to his overgrown dog. From the safety of the shadows, she studied him as she hadn't dared do when they were face-to-face.

He still cut a fine figure. Tall and lean. His long legs as muscular as she remembered, his shoulders as wide, and his back still ramrod straight.

Insufferable, pompous ass.

She had hoped he'd grown fat and bald and toothless. But other than deeper grooves around his mouth, fine lines fanning out from his remarkable green eyes, that scar across his eyebrow, and the gray in his hair, he was the same man who had haunted her dreams for the last six years. Except that now he was a peer of the realm. Lord Ashby.

The bounder.

Angus-the-dog whined and sniffed at the narrow gap under the door.

Dropping the curtain, Maddie sat back, wondering what she should do. She had no interest in being a viscountess. Or in returning to Scotland and being dumped in that drafty castle so he could go galloping off to Edinburgh or London on some pursuit that didn't include her. Over the last two years, she had carved out a life without him—a fulfilling life—a fine, happy life, thank you very much—and she had no intention of giving it up.

She sighed. "He can do it," she told the dog still whining at the door. "Legally, he can force me to go back with him." He could even beat her, or lock her in a mental hospital, or take control of her parents' home and any money she made from her photographs. "So what am I to do?"

The dog stretched up to bat at the door latch.

"I know. I'm his chattel as surely as those two mules out there are mine. And he can make me do anything or live anywhere he wants."

Unless, of course, she did something to convince him that that would be a poor idea and she was not a suitable wife for a peer.

Hmmm. Now there's a thought.

Leaning over, she lifted the edge of the curtain again. Now he was talking to Mr. Satterwhite, no doubt ordering the poor old man around like one of his troopers. With a sniff, she let the curtain fall.

"It would have to be something that wouldn't land me in jail," she mused aloud. "Something that would bring harm to no one, especially myself, but would be so reprehensible he would gladly put me aside. Any ideas, pup?"

Angus-the-dog squatted and puddled by the door.

"Oh, I couldn't do that," she said, rising to clean the mess. "I'm not that desperate." Not yet, anyway. But there must be something just as odious she could do to scare him off.

Shadows lengthened as Maddie paced the tiny wagon, chewing her thumbnail, thoughts racing through her head. By the time Mr. Satterwhite knocked on the door to tell her dinner was ready, she had discarded a dozen ideas and had finally decided the whole notion was silly.

But one thing was certain. She couldn't—wouldn't—go back to the sterile life she had worked so hard to leave behind.

At a yapping sound, Ash looked up from Satterwhite's recitation of the merits of the Winchester repeater over his British Snider-Enfield to see his wife peering out of the open door of her wagon with a wiggling ball of fur in her arms.

"Will you please tie up your dog?" she called.

"There's no need," he called back.

"You're certain?"

"Aye."

Ash studied her as she came down the steps. His headache was almost completely gone now, allowing him to better see and admire the changes in his lady wife. She had lost none of her grace, he noted. She still moved with the regal glide that marked her a lady of quality—back straight, head high, each step measured. She looked every bit the viscountess he needed her to be—except for the squirming, yapping rat she clutched in her arms.

He stood as she approached.

"You're sure it will be safe?" She eyed Tricks warily. "I can't keep my dog locked in the wagon forever. We've already suffered one indiscretion."

"You or the dog?"

He thought he saw a smile before she pinched it off. He had missed that smile and the way it involved her whole face, and how it had made him feel when she'd directed it at him.

After positioning her chair away from the smoke, he held it while she settled, then returned to his seat on the log beside Satterwhite, who was stirring a bubbling pot suspended over the coals. "If I tell Tricks to leave your wee dog alone," he said, raising his voice over the constant yapping of the rat, "he will obey. As long as I'm not threatened."

"Like he obeyed your command to sit?"

Satterwhite snickered. Ignoring him, Ash reached down to pat the wolfhound reclining beside his leg, his dark eyes fixed on the rat. "Tricks isna vicious. He will do as ordered." *Unlike you*, he almost added.

"In case he doesn't," Satterwhite offered, one eye looking hopefully toward the wagon, the other aimed at Ash, "want me to get my pistol?"

"Not unless you want me to have it. Come, lass. Put your dog down. I'll watch Tricks until they're acquainted."

Hesitantly, she lifted the dog from her lap.

Ash felt the wolfhound tense under his hand and murmured softly in Gaelic until the dog relaxed.

As soon as the rat touched dirt, it charged.

Madeline leaped from her chair.

"Wooee!" Satterwhite hollered, lifting his scuffed boots out of the raging mite's path.

"Hold fast!" Ash ordered.

His wife obeyed. The rat dinna.

Without rising to his feet, Tricks lifted his head out of the frenzied creature's reach as the dog yipped and jumped in his face.

"Easy, lad. The thing is mostly hair and gristle and wouldna go down easy anyway."

Eventually the wee beastie wore itself out. Panting, its pink tongue drooping from its open mouth, the rat settled on its haunches and attempted to stare down the bigger dog.

Tricks responded by lifting a hind foot and scratching his ear.

"See, lass? All is well."

"I thought for sure the big one would eat the little one." Satterwhite sounded disappointed.

Ash studied the rat, trying to determine its ancestry. "One of those Mexican dogs, is it?"

"Half." Still watchful, Madeline sank back into the chair. "The mother was a Corgi of low virtue who was also a sound sleeper. An unfortunate combination," she added with a pointed look in his direction.

He ignored it. "I find it odd," he said pleasantly, "that you named your wee dog after me. I might even have been flattered, had the animal been male."

"Angus is a girl?" Satterwhite bent to study the dog's furry underparts. "I never knew that. 'Course I never looked that hard, either."

"She is." His wife focused her attention on smoothing the skirt draped over her knees. "And her name is Agnes."

"Agnes? You said it was Angus, missy."

"I fear you misheard, Mr. Satterwhite."

Ash watched her lips twitch. A smile, perchance? It gave him hope that the fine sense of humor he remembered might still lurk beneath that starchy reserve. "A common mistake, so it is."

"Indeed."

Turning to the old man, Ash said in a friendly tone, "In the future, Satterwhite, you willna call my wife 'missy.' She is a viscount-ess and should be addressed as my lady or Lady Madeline or Viscountess Ashby."

"Oh, rubbish," his wife interjected. "And I suppose next you'll insist I call you Lord Ashby. Don't be such a stick. Missy is fine, Mr. Satterwhite. We are friends, after all." Turning back to Ash, she added as if he were a blithering numptie, "Americans do not recognize titles, *Angus*. And as I have not yet accepted yours, I choose not to use it."

He managed to keep his voice calm. "It's not a matter of choice, *Maddie*. I am Viscount Ashby. You are wedded to me. Thus, you are Viscountess Ashby. And even though it's customary for peers to be addressed by their titles rather than their given names, if Ashby is too lofty for you, I'll answer to Ash." He punctuated that with a wide grin.

She looked away, her lips pressed in a thin, flat line.

Again, Ash wondered why she was fighting him on this. Most women he knew would jump at a title. Yet, she wanted none of it. Why?

Or was it him she wanted naught to do with?

"Stew's done, Your Majesties," Satterwhite announced. "Grab your plates."

They ate the burned food beside the fire. Although it was still early evening, the sun had dropped behind the trees and long shafts of dappled light slanted across the wispy grass. Already the air was cooling, and Maddie was grateful when Angus—Ash—added an-other log to the coals.

Ash. It suited him. As did the gray hair. With his imposing fig-ure and handsome face, and now a lofty title, he would have no trouble finding another woman to be his viscountess. Then she would be free to take her pictures and travel when and where she wanted, and answer to no one.

She frowned. Put that way, it sounded rather lonely. Was that truly what she wanted? To dwell on the fringes of her friends' lives? To rock their children to sleep without ever holding her own? Could she be content to never again feel a man's arms around her?

If it meant having control of her own life . . . absolutely.

Ash had been a skilled lover, and she had missed that intimacy these last six years. She liked men. She liked the way they moved and laughed and smelled—the texture of their skin, the strength in their bodies, the power they took and gave in the marriage bed.

They? *He.*

Memories eddied through her mind as she looked across the fire at the only man who had ever made love to her. Would it be the same with other men? Would she ever find that wonder and bliss again?

Perhaps she should find out. There were several men in Heartbreak Creek who had shown interest—admittedly, most had been patrons of the Red Eye Saloon next to the hotel, and their attentions had been more like harassment than true interest. Even Mr. Satterwhite had made an offer, although Maddie knew the only reason he had done so was out of his determination to see her protected. Mercy sakes, the dear man was old enough to be her father. Her grandfather, even.

Still, the idea bore consideration. Perhaps if she encouraged advances from other gentlemen—not Mr. Satterwhite, of course—Ash would become so disgusted with her he would go on his way and leave her to her tintypes. She could continue to reside in Heartbreak Creek near her dear friends Lucinda and Prudence and Edwina, and all would be as it was.

With a sigh, she pulled her shawl tighter around her shoulders and stared with disinterest into her plate of stew.

Unless Angus—Ash—was so intent on getting his heir, he dragged her back to Scotland to suffer the arduous task of petitioning Parliament for a divorce so he could marry someone who could give him a son.

It was all so wretchedly unfair. She fingered the heavy signet ring on her finger and wondered why she still wore it. The man who had given it to her was long gone. A figment of a lonely young woman's imagination.

Suddenly aware that her husband was watching her, she forced herself to take a nibble of the dry-as-dust hardtack that Mr. Satterwhite insisted on serving with every meal.

Not that she could do any better. She was an artist—not a cook. When she had interviewed Mr. Satterwhite for the position of driver and cook and he had proclaimed himself excellent at both, she probably shouldn't have taken him at his word. But after spending several months in his company, she was glad she had. He was a dear old thing, even if he was a ghastly cook. And she had greatly enjoyed his companionship on her treks through mining camps, Indian reservations, army posts, and lonely homesteads. With his help, she had captured the spirit of the West so vividly that after Mr. Chesterfield at *The Illustrated London News* had received her first shipment of whole plate negatives, and *carte* portraits, and stereoscopic panoramic slides, he had written immediately back, demanding more and hinting at a leather-bound compilation of her work.

She was making a name for herself—by herself. Mr. Satterwhite was part of that success, and she couldn't give up on him, no matter how poor a cook he was, any more than she could give up on her work, no matter what Angus—or Ash—said. Somehow, she would make her husband understand that having known the joy of independence these last two years, she would never willingly give it up. Not even for a husband, or a title.

She watched Ash sneak pieces of stringy meat to his dog when Mr. Satterwhite wasn't looking, and tried to stay mad at him for his cavalier treatment of her. But gentler memories kept intruding.

Her husband wasn't a bad man. As a young cavalry officer, he had been brash and energetic and perhaps too ready to rush to the next adventure. Not that she blamed him. She had lived with his family. She knew how suffocating and judgmental they could be. But in the years since she had last seen him, he seemed to have settled somewhat. This older man she now had to think of as Lord

Ashby was more subdued, perhaps a bit jaded, and there was a weariness behind his green eyes that hinted at painful experiences. The rough edges were gone, leaving behind a seasoned, hard-faced ex-soldier who was accustomed to getting his way.

She would have to tread carefully with this new Angus. This man looked to have a clear idea of what he wanted and the confidence to do what he must to get it. He wouldn't take kindly to insubordination. Especially from a wife.

Tossing the last of the scraps into the fire, he rose from the log bench. "If you'll excuse us, lass, Satterwhite and I must tend the animals."

Earlier he had introduced his big gelding to her mules, Maisy and Buttercup. After a few snorts and sniffs, they had accepted each other and had been allowed to wander loose as they'd grazed the clearing throughout the afternoon. Now he went to collect Lurch, careful to approach from the front so the deaf animal would see him and not be startled by his sudden appearance. Then following Satterwhite and the mules, he led him to the creek for a last drink before staking him close to the wagon for the night.

Maddie watched him, seeing in his distant form the young man she had once found so captivating.

With his long-legged lankiness and his gentle touch with horses, he was well suited to be a cavalryman, despite the fact that his initial enlistment had been with the Riflemen of the Ninety-Fifth. She hadn't known him then, as he had already transferred to the Hussars when she'd met him, "hoping to be sent to China for the Second Opium War."

Instead, the Tenth Hussars had been sent to Ireland, where, as he'd written in his last letter several years ago, he had been promoted to the rank of colonel "for no good reason other than I complement the flashy uniform and sit a horse well." An odd thing for a man to say about himself and his own success.

Yet despite his obvious disenchantment with the military, he hadn't sold his commission, or come home to see his wife, or written to her again. And now, after years of silence, he was back in her life—with a new title and a new name and all the power he needed to bend her to his will.

Disheartened, she rose and began gathering the empty plates and dirty utensils. She wondered how he would react if she told him she wanted a divorce. If they were no longer married, she could continue her work, and he could find some fertile young thing to bear his heirs in exchange for the title of viscountess and a short letter every year or so. Divorce was the only sensible solution.

And yet . . .

It was almost dark when Ash returned from the creek with Lurch and Tricks. The breeze had died, and stars were winking to life in the cloudless dome overhead. It would turn cold in the night. He could feel it in his side.

His wife sat huddled by the fire, lost in thought. After staking Lurch near the wagon, he untied the bedroll from his saddle and crossed toward her, Tricks at his heels.

"Sit," he told the dog. This time Tricks obeyed. Dropping the bedroll, Ash stepped over the log then sat, his hands extended to the warmth rising from the coals. "It's a braw night, is it not? Reminds me of the Highlands."

"Except for the lack of fog and drizzle and stink of wet sheep."

So much for friendly conversation. Too weary to wrest pleasantness from an angry woman, he let it go. "Where do you want me, lass?"

She looked at him, then at the bedroll, then back at him. He admired the way her brown eyes caught the flames and her fine cheekbones were tinted goldish pink by the glow of the coals. "Want you?"

"To sleep. In the wagon or out—"

"Not in the wagon!"

He studied her for a moment, then gave what he hoped was a reassuring smile. "You're not afraid of me, are you, wife?"

"Why would you think that?"

Ash had seen fear in many forms over the years, from white-faced recruits in India to shrieking men being carried into the surgeon's tent in the Crimea during the siege of Sevastopol to the blank terror on a man's face just before Ash fired the bullet that would kill him. But he'd never expected to see it on his wife's face. He was unsure how to respond, or what to do to allay her fears.

"I bear no grudge because of your desertion," he assured her. "You've naught to fear on that score."

"*My* desertion? What about yours?"

Ash sighed. Well, he'd tried. "Where does Satterwhite sleep?"

"I don't know. Somewhere out here. Perhaps by the fire." Leaning forward, she dropped her voice to add, "He's afraid of bears."

"Bears? Are they a problem?"

She sat back. "They have been. But not lately. They're drawn to the smell of food, which is why we hang our supplies." She pointed to where the old man had thrown a rope over a high limb and was now hoisting up a canvas bag of foodstuffs until it hung at least a dozen feet off the ground.

"Tricks will alert us if they come near." Reaching down, he patted the wolfhound's knobby head. "He's verra canny, so he is."

They lapsed into silence. She poked at the coals with a stick, sending up a swirling plume of sparks. Somewhere in the shadowed forest an owl hooted, which brought the wolfhound's head around, his eyes scanning the trees. From farther away came the bugle of a bull elk, another sign of winter closing in.

He wished she would retire to her wagon so he could sleep. Even though his headache was gone, a lingering weariness remained. And her nearness further weakened him, teased him with memories best forgotten—the softness of her skin, the way she moved when he touched her, the sounds she made when he did.

Bollocks. It promised to be a long night.

After tying off the rope suspending the bag from the tree limb, Satterwhite stepped into the brush at the edge of the clearing. A few minutes later, he walked back out with an armload of firewood and carried it into the wagon. It wasn't long before a puff of smoke coiled above the stovepipe sticking out of the roof.

Ash studied his wife, wondering why she was wary of him and why he'd come this far seeking a woman who dinna even want him. Had he been that bad a husband? Or was it as she had said, because he had ignored her? A poor excuse. A soldier couldn't rush home whenever the mood struck him.

But maybe he could fix that now, show her some attention, perhaps even coax out a smile. "What will you do when it's too cold to travel these mountains?" he asked pleasantly.

"I'll go home. That's where we're headed now. My shipment of albuminized paper and silver nitrate has probably arrived from E. and H.T. Anthony's of New York, and I need to send my latest negative plates to London for engraving."

"Home, you say. And where would that be, lass?"

She pulled the shawl tighter and anchored it beneath her crossed arms. "Heartbreak Creek. It's a little mining town about fifty miles from here."

"Aye. I was through there recently." He gave a wry smile. "You're a difficult woman to track down, so you are."

"I wasn't in hiding, Angus—Ash. In truth, I didn't think you would care enough to come after me."

Not care enough to track down his own wife and the woman who would bear his heirs? He almost laughed. Yet, in view of her resistance to him, he wondered if he should have bothered to come after her. But he had come this far, and if he was ever to fulfill his duty, he would have to resolve this marriage, one way or the other. A sad state of affairs, so it was.

With a sigh, he leaned forward and rested his crossed arms on his bent knees. Since his wife seemed so set against him, perhaps a divorce would be best.

And yet . . .

A moth circled above the fire until the heat and smoke sent it plummeting into the flames. He felt like his own life had been in a similar downward spiral since leaving the Hussars. He'd been on the move and under orders for over seventeen years. But now that his military life was over, he no longer knew where he belonged, or what his duty was. His title was only a courtesy rank given him as the heir to an earldom; no lands or responsibilities came with it. So other than securing the line by producing heirs—which he couldn't accomplish without a wife—what was he to do with himself? Gamble his nights away? Learn to tie a neckcloth properly? Wait for Donnan to die? Such a useless life was repugnant to him. He almost envied his runaway bride for finding a purpose she could believe in.

"Heartbreak Creek," he said after a while. "An odd place for a gently bred Englishwoman to call home."

"I have dear friends there. A family almost."

"Aye. I met some of them." He stared into the flames and thought of the loyal blond hotel owner and the tall, overprotective sheriff. "But you have family in Scotland, too."

"No. *You* have family there. Mine are all gone."

"Gone?" He turned his head and looked at her.

"If you'll recall, my parents died in a carriage mishap."

"Did they?" Why hadna he been told? Then he remembered what an uproar the house had been in when he'd returned—the fevers still running their courses, the funerals coming one upon the other, his own disoriented state. Still, he should have known. "When?"

"Three years after we married. In September of sixty-eight."

A month after the explosion. "I'm sorry, lass. I dinna know."

"Yes, Ash, you did. Or would have, if you'd actually read any of the letters I sent you." With a look of disgust aimed in his direction, she rose from the chair. "I have an assignment in Denver coming up and must return to Heartbreak Creek to gather supplies. Mr. Satterwhite and I will be leaving at first light. We'll try not to wake you. If I don't get a chance to speak to you again, I'll bid you good-bye now and wish you safe journey back to Scotland."

Ash watched her walk toward the wagon. Not walk—more like parade march, with that stiff-backed stride. The woman had spirit. And a lot of anger. He wondered if it would be possible to rid her of one without breaking the other.

Satterwhite came down the steps to meet her, the rat right behind him. They spoke for a moment while the rat did her business, then his wife and the dog went inside and Satterwhite walked to the front of the wagon. After pulling a bundle from beneath the driver's bench, he crossed toward Ash. "It'll get cold tonight," he said, dumping his bundle of bedding on the ground beside the fire. "Hope you got something warm to wrap up in."

Ash looked at the wagon and thought of his wife in there all snug and cozy. With a sigh, he picked up his bedroll. At least he had Tricks to warm his back. "I'm a Highlander," he said as he spread his blanket on the dirt. "We invented cold."

"Doesn't say much for your intellect," the old man muttered.

Ash laughed. "Oh, it's not so bad. On cold, clear nights like this you can see every star in the heavens. I've spent worse nights in worse places, so I have." He stretched out, hands clasped behind his head, his dog snug on one side, the smoldering fire on the other, and an endless array of stars winking down at him from overhead.

Silence settled around him, so sharp and clear he could hear Tricks breathing beside him, the hiss and pop of the fire, aspens rustling in a breeze that felt as soft as a woman's breath on his cheek.

It was odd sleeping in the open without the sound of soldiers moving around him, voices calling out on the picket lines, or the distant boom of cannon and crack of rifle fire. Usually he liked the solitude of it. But tonight he felt a little lost in all the dark stillness. Like one of those lonely stars hanging overhead.

"So," he said to the old man, suddenly needing to fill that empty silence. "Tell me about Heartbreak Creek and these friends she has there."

Four

The first thing Maddie saw when she opened the door of her wagon the next morning was Ash coming up the trail that led to the creek, his hair wet, his braces off and dangling by his thighs, and his shirt hanging open.

The second thing she noticed was the puckered web of ropey, purplish scars that covered the left side of his rib cage. She gaped in shock. When had he suffered such a massive injury?

Then she remembered the explosion he'd said had left his horse deaf and himself so badly injured it had ended his military career. But that had happened two years ago, yet the wound was still red in spots, as if it had only recently begun to heal. Had he been recovering all that time? And why hadn't she been told about it? Hadn't she the right to know if her husband had been so gravely injured?

But then, how would anyone have known where to reach her? Other than her publisher, and now her husband, no one had ever tried.

Agnes darted past her through the open door and down the steps, then came to a full stop when her toes touched the cold, dew-frosted grass. Balancing on her front legs, she lifted her rear high off the ground and glanced back at Maddie for help.

"Go on, you silly thing. Do your business."

Her voice drew Ash's head up. When he saw her in the doorway of the wagon, he pulled his shirt closed and angled toward her, side-stepping Agnes as she ran to greet Tricks. "So you're finally up, lass. Will you be wanting breakfast, before we go? I believe there's some of Satterwhite's hardtack left." He stopped at the foot of the steps, which put their eyes at the same level. "I saw how much you enjoyed it last evening."

He had the finest eyes. Green and lively and full of laughter. They were the first thing that had drawn her to him. Even now, she felt their power and had to force herself to look away. "No. But thank you."

"Then stow your belongings," he called back as he walked on toward the cold fire where his jacket and bedroll lay draped over the log. "We're hitched and ready to leave whenever you are."

We? "You intend to travel with us?"

"Aye."

"Even though we're headed in the opposite direction?"

"Opposite from what?" he asked over his shoulder as he tucked his shirt into his fitted cavalry-style trousers.

The fabric of his shirt clung to his damp skin, giving her an inspiring view of his sturdy body in motion. As she let her gaze drift over him, a sudden image flashed in her mind—that long back, the gentle dip of his spine, those broad shoulders and narrow hips tinted pink by the setting sun as he had dressed by the window before he had left to rejoin his regiment. She remembered lying in bed, watching him, a feeling of possession taking hold as she realized that for the rest of her life that fine strong body was hers to touch, to claim, to enjoy.

If she'd only known then the pain that awaited her.

"Opposite from the direction you're headed," she finally answered, coming the rest of the way down the steps.

Dipping his shoulders, he shrugged on his braces, then turned to face her. "And what direction is that, lass?" he asked, reaching for his jacket.

Away from me. "East. Toward Scotland." She waved at the trees.

"That's south." With a broad hand, he smoothed back his damp hair. It needed a trim, and where it had started to dry, the gray hairs glistened in the sun like spun silver. "And will you be coming back to Scotland with me?"

"No."

"Well then." Bending, he picked up his bedroll. "I'll not be going to Scotland, either. Not yet, anyway. Come, Tricks."

Maddie frowned after him as he and his dog crossed to where Lurch stood saddled. *Blast.* The last thing she wanted was for her husband to insinuate himself further into her life. He'd happily ignored her for the last six years—why couldn't he leave her alone now?

With a huff of irritation, she looked around for Mr. Satterwhite and spotted him at the front of the wagon, harnessing Buttercup and Maisy. Careful of her footing on the slick, frosty grass, she marched toward him. "He's coming with us," she muttered when she reached the old man.

"If you mean the foreigner," he said as he tested the curb on Maisy's bridle, "I know."

"But why? He has no reason to hound me all the way to Heartbreak Creek. I'm not going back to Scotland with him. Ever."

"So you said." Satisfied with the rigging, the old man walked back toward the front of the wagon.

Maddie followed. "Besides, the man eats like a horse and we're already running low on supplies. You said so, yourself."

He climbed up into the driver's box and unwound the reins from the brake handle. "I know."

"You *know*?" Maddie gripped the wheel, the metal rim cold and gritty against her palm. "That's all you have to say?"

"What do you want me to say?"

"That you'll help me."

The old man sighed heavily. He muttered something under his breath, then turned to her, an impatient look in the faded blue eye pointed her way. "Help you do what, missy? Shoot him?"

"Heavens, no!" She drew back, her whole being recoiling from the suggestion. "How could you even think such a thing, Mr. Satterwhite?"

"I wonder." Another sigh. "He's your husband, missy. And he seems a good man. I'd give him a chance. You riding up here, or in back?"

"What? I—in back, I guess." Why was he acting this way?

"Then get your dog and let's be off. It'll take us three days to reach Heartbreak Creek as it is."

Hurt, Maddie whirled and marched to the rear, her eyes stinging. She desperately needed her friends. Lucinda and Pru and Edwina would help her figure out what to do. *They* wouldn't let her down.

She came to an abrupt stop when she found Ash waiting by the step, Agnes tucked under his arm. The wretched beast was licking his stubbled chin like it was coated with honey.

God. Was everyone turning against her?

She glared at him.

He smiled back, and the wicked twinkle in his eyes told her he must have overheard every word of her conversation with Mr. Satterwhite.

"Up you go, love, so I can secure the stair."

"'Love'?" she mimicked. "What happened to 'lass'? Or have you suddenly become English now that you're a member of the peerage?"

He grinned and sketched a bow. "I'm a bit of both, *leannan*, with a wee drop of the Irish thrown in."

She snatched her traitor dog from his arms and stomped up the steps.

"And don't fret about going hungry," he added as she opened the door. "If it's fresh meat you're needing, I'll be sure you get as much as you want. As you'll remember, wife, I'm verra good with my gun."

She slammed the door so hard the window rattled.

.   .   .

It was midafternoon, and the ache in Ash's side was so constant he could hardly sit the saddle when Satterwhite finally reined in the team.

"How's this?" the old man asked Maddie, who had long since released herself from her self-imposed isolation in the back of the wagon and moved up front to the driver's box.

"It's lovely, Mr. Satterwhite." She turned to Ash with a tight smile. "But does it meet your approval, Lord Ashby?"

Still miffed, he saw. He had already rejected a similar meadow that would have been impossible to defend. Old habits in old soldiers die hard, he'd found. Assessing this one with a military eye, he saw a grassy clearing with a wee creek on one side and a rocky bluff on the other. "This will do, Satterwhite. If you'll set camp, Tricks and I will forage for supper."

He let Lurch and Tricks drink in the creek, crossed, then rode a short way past it before reining in behind a jumble of boulders. "Shite," he hissed, using his arms to hold most of his weight as he swung his leg over the saddle. Gripping Lurch's mane, he leaned against the stirrup leathers, teeth gritted, his eyes closed, and waited for the pain to dim to a dull throb.

Earlier, he had been about to trade his saddle for a seat beside Satterwhite when his wife had decided to move up front. He could have taken her place in back, he supposed, but his pride wouldna allow it. Now he was paying the price. "Buggering, bluidy, humpin'—"

"What's wrong?" his wife asked, startling him so badly that when he whirled to face her he almost lost his footing.

"Hell and damnation, woman! Are you daft, sneaking up on a man that way?" He saw her frowning at the hand he held clasped to his side, and jerked it away. "What are you doing out here? It's not safe for you to be wandering about alone."

"Are you hurt?"

"Of course I'm not—"

"It's your injury from the explosion, isn't it? I saw the scars this morning when you came up from the creek."

"So you've come for a second look, have you?"

Instead of being put off by his insulting tone, she came closer. "The wound looked relatively fresh."

"I was about to relieve myself, madam. If you plan on watching, I'd advise you to step back."

"Don't be crass. When did it happen?"

The woman was bluidy relentless. "In spring. Leave."

"Just a few months ago? No wonder it still pains you."

"Two years ago." Deciding to get it done so she would leave him to get on with his business, he added impatiently, "Bits of metal and wood lodged inside and prevented healing. A surgeon in London removed the last piece just before I sailed. And I truly do need to relieve myself, lass, so I'm asking you to leave. Now."

She left, calling back over her shoulder as she disappeared around the boulder, "Don't worry about hunting something for our meal tonight. We'll make do with leftover hardtack."

When he led Lurch out of the woods an hour later with four grouse dangling from his hand, he was greeted by the smell of woodsmoke and the sight of his lady wife cutting the old man's hair while she lectured him about threatening strangers. "We've come to take photographs, not shoot people, Mr. Satterwhite. And no more brawling. Or drunkenness. Do please remember that. There. All done." With a final pat on his head, she stepped back and assessed her work. "You look quite lovely."

Lovely? Satterwhite?

At Ash's approach, she looked up and smiled. "Excellent. You're just in time. Mr. Satterwhite, if you'll tend to the animals and those fine grouse, I'll get started on Lord Ashby."

Started on what? And when had he been elevated in rank from Ashby to *Lord* Ashby?

Satterwhite rose. Scratching at the back of his now-bare neck, he walked over to take Lurch's reins and the bird carcasses. "Watch yourself," he whispered. "She's in a mothering mood." The old man nodded his shorn head toward the fire. "She's cooking that for you."

Ash looked at the pot of something chunky and whitish yellow sitting over the low fire. A rancid odor rose with the curling steam. "I'm not eating that," he muttered.

Satterwhite grinned up at him. His crooked eyes darted back and forth, the right eye meeting Ash's gaze for a second, then the left. It was unsettling. Ash wasn't sure which one to look at.

"It's not for eating. It's a poultice." The old man cackled nastily. "Good luck, Your Majesty."

"Sit, please," his wife called, patting the chair.

Ash glanced at the mound of white hair that had once warmed Satterwhite's pate, and shook his head. "I don't think so."

"No?" Wearing a sweet smile that was at odds with the resolve in her brown eyes, she pulled a folded straight razor from her apron pocket. "You would rather start with a shave?"

"No. No shave. I'll do that myself." And what was she doing with a straight razor?

She dropped the razor back into her pocket. "A trim it is, then. Sit."

It was odd. Through all the years, in different times and other circumstances, Ash had had his hair hacked off by a sergeant's bayonet, delicately trimmed by a dandified barber in a London gentlemen's club, and cut in various camp followers' huts on foreign fields of battle. But none of those experiences made him quite as nervous as seeing his wife come at him with a pair of pointed scissors. The woman had stored up a wealth of anger in his absence, and it seemed, unaccountably, to be aimed at him. But he had faced rioting sepoys in India, Russian artillery in the Crimea, Irish insurgents, and more than a few Scottish brawlers. And Angus Frederick Wallace, Fifth Viscount of Ashby and retired colonel of the Prince of Wales's Own Tenth Royal Hussars was definitely not a coward.

So he sat.

Maddie studied the silver streaks in the glossy waves that hung over the banded collar of her husband's shirt. For most women, turning gray was a disaster. But in men, it could be an enhancement, lending a bit of dignity, an assurance of maturity, stability, and even a hint of wisdom gained through hard experience. In Ash's case, the gray threaded through the deep sable was such a striking contrast to the dark brows and lashes it made him appear even more virile than when he'd left her six years ago.

Deserted her. She needed to remember that.

The soft, silky waves were especially eye-catching against such a strong neck. Incongruous. Sensual. Like satin sliding through a man's fingers, or lace draped over a muscled arm, or a broad callused palm stroking a woman's pale hip.

Her satin. Her gown. Her hip. Images that were burned so indelibly into her memory that even after all these years they still whispered through her mind like a lover's sigh.

Nitwit.

Furious with where her thoughts had strayed, Maddie snipped off a great chunk of hair at the back of Ash's neck, then stared at what she had uncovered. A long ridge of scar tissue wound above his ear and up to his temple—from the same explosion that had scarred his side? But even more curious were the markings on the back of his neck. A square cross surrounded by four smaller crosses, and beneath it in block letters, *ICH DIEN.* "What's this?" she asked, running her fingers over the markings.

"A tattoo." He shrank away from her touch. "Don't do that."

"Does it hurt?"

"No. It . . . ah . . . tickles."

"What does *Ich dien* mean?"

" 'I serve.' 'Tis the motto of the Tenth Hussars."

She traced the center cross with her fingertip. "And the design?"

He shifted in the chair. "A Jerusalem cross. The Prince of Wales got one during pilgrimage several years ago, and eventually most of the officers in his regiment followed suit. Are you finished with my hair yet?"

Strangely, the longer she touched his neck, the redder his ears became. "Are you blushing?"

He turned his head and looked up at her, and when she saw the look in his mossy green eyes, she snatched her hand away. "Do turn around so I can finish."

"Finish?" His slow smile revealed his lovely white teeth. He had lost none of those, she saw. But the tiny chip in the corner of the third on the left was new. It gave his smile an almost boyish appeal, which was totally at odds with the unboyish heat in his remarkable eyes. "Finish what, lass?"

She cleared her throat. "Your hair. Turn, please."

Laughing softly, he did.

She continued to comb and trim and cut while he sat stiffly, his shoulders wider than the slatted back of the chair, his bent knees splayed, his big hands resting on his thighs. He wasn't a patient man, she remembered, and he seemed no better now, as evidenced by the drumming of his fingers on the top of his thighs, and how every now and then, his chest would rise and fall on a deep sigh.

"Be still," she admonished him.

"I'm trying."

"Are you still in pain?"

"No." The answer was as curt as a slammed door.

"You shouldn't sleep in the open on the cold ground."

"A soldier's plight. Are we done yet?"

"When the weather is inclement," she went on, ignoring the question, "Mr. Satterwhite sleeps beneath an oiled canvas, which he attaches to the front roof of the wagon and drapes over the driver's bench. He says it works beautifully and keeps him warm and dry."

"The bench is too narrow. And my feet would stick out."

She smiled, seeing the image in her mind.

On the other side of the clearing, Mr. Satterwhite finished staking the mules and Lurch. Then he picked up the grouse carcasses and, trailed by both dogs, took them down to the creek and away from camp to clean them.

She snipped and cut.

Ash fidgeted.

On the fire, the cornmeal poultice began to bubble.

Using the end of her apron to protect her fingers from the hot metal, she set the pot on a rock to cool. "Or . . ." She hesitated, undecided. Then discarding her reservations and all rational thought, said, "Or . . . I suppose you could sleep in the back of the wagon."

His hands stilled. Beautiful, strong hands. Looking at them sent quivers of awareness dancing along the nerves beneath her skin. She remembered them well. Her husband might have wielded a sword, but he also knew how to touch a woman.

"Do you think your bed would be big enough, lass?"

She frowned at the back of his head. Then realizing where his thoughts were headed, she let out a breath. "No. But the floor would."

He turned to look up at her again.

She thumped his shoulder. "I invited you into my wagon, Ashby," she said, fighting back a smile. "Not my bed. Now take off your shirt."

That was a mistake, she realized as soon as the unveiling began. Not only because seeing the puckered ridges of scar tissue brought tears of sympathy to her eyes, but because even with the scarring, Ash's body was a thing to behold. Unlike many men of his age and station, he was still lean and firmly muscled from his years of military service, and the sight of it—the memories of it—awakened yearnings and feelings Maddie hadn't felt in years. She found it odd, though, that the graying on his head didn't extend to the dark hair on his chest or the long thin arrow of it disappearing past the waistband of his trousers.

Wadding up the shirt, he tossed it aside, jarring her back to attention. "Get on with it, love, before I die of the cold."

Instructing him to stand, she handed him the piece of muslin she had earlier coated with lard. "Wipe this over your side. It will keep the poultice from sticking."

Wrinkling his nose at the smell, he did as instructed while she smeared the hot cornmeal and flour paste onto a folded strip of linen. "It might seem very warm at first," she said, seeing his flinch as she laid the linen over his scars. "But as it cools it will draw out the pain."

While he held the poultice against his side, she quickly wrapped strips of muslin around his rib cage to anchor it in place, following that with wide strips of cotton batting to hold in as much heat as possible.

"There," she said, after tying off the ends of the wrappings. "Hopefully the heat will last three or four hours. Try to move as little as possible so the wrappings don't come loose." She straightened to find him studying her with a bemused, thoughtful expression.

"That's a fine field dressing, lass. Where did you learn such a skill?"

"I wasn't always a viscountess." Waving a cornmeal-caked hand toward the trees and the rocky peaks rising behind them, she added with a wry smile, "One can't live in this raw place without learning a thing or two about survival."

"Verra wise." He picked up his wrinkled shirt and pulled it over his head. "Can you shoot, as well?"

Her smile faded as less pleasant memories tugged at her. "A dear friend was abducted by Indians several months ago. She survived, thank the Lord, even though she is still struggling to come to terms with her ordeal. But now I carry a double derringer in my reticule, and I have a scattergun under my bed. And, yes. I can shoot."

"That's wise. This stinking poultice could draw unwanted company." His gaze drifted past her to where Mr. Satterwhite and the dogs were walking out of the trees, then made a slow sweep of the brush surrounding the clearing. "And bears might not be the only predators roaming these woods."

Five

"Mr. Satterwhite," Maddie said later as they were finishing their evening meal beside the fire, "I've decided to alter the sleeping arrangements."

The elderly man looked up from his seat on an overturned water bucket. Ash was leaning against a boulder nearby, the dogs waiting patiently at his feet as he stripped the meat from a drumstick with his teeth.

An innocuous scene . . . had her husband not been eyeing her like a starving dog in a butcher shop throughout the entire meal.

"Alter how, missy?"

"The ground is too cold for Lord Ashby, so I'd like for you to set up the photography dark tent for his use."

"Too cold? Even for a Highlander?" The old man smirked over at Ash, who had stopped chewing and was watching her through narrowed eyes. "Then by all means, let's set up a nice comfy tent for the wee lad."

Taking advantage of Mr. Satterwhite's distraction, Maddie slipped the last bits of charred grouse off her plate and into the fire. "I think that would be best, in view of his condition."

"Condition?"

Ash tossed the bone into the brush. "I have no condition."

"And predators," Maddie added, wiping her fingers on her apron.

Mr. Satterwhite's skewed eyes widened. "Predators? You mean like bears?"

"Those, too." She sent Ash a questioning look, a bit confused by his stiff, angry posture. "A reasonable concern, considering all the bones he's been tossing into the brush. But he may have a point. So in the event unwanted guests do come calling, Mr. Satterwhite, I think it prudent if you were to stay in the tent, as well."

Mr. Satterwhite blinked from Maddie to the glaring Scotsman. "Both of us in there? Together?"

"Why not? It's warm and safe and dry. That way we will all be out of the weather, off the cold ground, and safe from any wandering bears." She beamed brightly at the two men staring at her.

Neither smiled back.

"Excellent. Then if you will set up the tent, please, Mr. Satterwhite?"

"It smells in there," Satterwhite complained.

"That's the eggs." Resting her palms against her bent knees, she explained to her husband, "I have to coat the print paper with egg whites, you see, although it's the sulfur in the egg *yolks* that makes them smell, and not . . . well, never mind. It won't harm you, Mr. Satterwhite."

"What about all those other chemicals you use? I could blow up in my sleep and never know it. And that tent won't stop a bear."

"Oh, I doubt—"

"Go!" Ash waved an arm toward Satterwhite. "Set up the tent. But be assured I willna be staying in it with you."

Muttering, Satterwhite tromped toward the wagon.

"My Lord, there's no need to badger—"

Ash whirled, his expression thunderous, his brogue even stronger in his anger. "You insult me, madam, to treat me like an old man with aching bones, or a cripple who must be coddled."

"I didn't mean—"

"I may no' be the soldier I once was, but I can still do my duty without hiding in a tent!" Spinning on his heel, he stalked away.

Maddie blinked after him, her face hot with embarrassment. She had only meant to make him more comfortable. And also, after thinking through her earlier offer for him to sleep on the floor of her wagon, she had realized that would never do. Neither of them was stupid. They both knew if she allowed Ash into her wagon, it would only be a matter of time before he charmed his way into her bed, as well. And what if she became pregnant? She would have to return to Scotland then. And that would ruin everything.

Sighing, Maddie dropped her head into her hands. The man was her weakness. He had been so from the moment she had seen him riding past in his bright blue uniform six years ago. Even after their long separation, being near him again had aroused all those needs and wants and urges that had sent her flying into his arms in the first place.

Lifting her head, Maddie wiped her palms down her apron and reminded herself this was not some grand, romantic reunion. Her husband hadn't come all this way seeking *her*, but rather the woman he expected to bear his heirs. And when she had fulfilled that duty—*if* she could even do so, after last time—he would abandon her like a bad habit, just as he had before.

She pressed a hand to her stomach, as if somehow she could reach through the layers of cloth and flesh and bone to the empty womb resting within and soothe that dull ache of loss that never seemed to go away.

It was after midnight when Ash sensed movement, and he looked up from the fire to see his wife standing in the shadows at the edge of the light, holding something bulky in her arms.

Frowning, he rose from her chair. The moon had already moved a quarter of the way across the night sky, and the air had a frosty bite to it. Satterwhite had been snoring in his tent for two hours. What was she doing wandering about in the middle of the night?

He had gotten over his initial fury but was still angry that she thought him less capable because of his injury. He'd withstood that same pitying condescension from his commanding officer, his doctors, and his family. But he wouldn't tolerate it from his wife.

"I brought extra quilts," she said as her little dog rushed past to greet Tricks, who lounged by the warm rocks circling the fire. "Where shall I put them?" She stepped closer and into the light.

He could see she had been fretting. In their short days together just after their marriage, they might not have had time to learn much about each other, but his wife had seldom been able to mask her thoughts from him. She was too open. Too unguarded. Too ready to accept what was put before her. That artist thing again, he supposed. But whatever it was, that trusting, hopeful smile had captivated him from the first.

Captivated him now. He was that weak.

"What do you have there?" she asked, nodding to the tin he'd forgotten he still held in his hand.

Heat rushed up his neck and he was grateful for the concealing darkness. "Dirt." Then hearing how daft that sounded, he added, "Many a soldier carries a wee something in his pack to remind him of the place he left behind." And dirt from home to sprinkle over his grave if he dinna make it back.

"That's from Northbridge?"

"Aye."

"Did you miss it terribly?"

He had to think for a moment. In truth, he'd spent most of his life away from his family's lands, and when he thought about them at all, it was with a confused mix of memories of his siblings and fights with his father, and an almost overwhelming need to escape. "At first I did," he admitted. "I missed the idea of it. Of belonging someplace."

"And later?"

He shrugged. "The military became my home. My fellow soldiers were my family."

"And yet you still have the tin."

"Habit." Embarrassed to have revealed so much, he slipped it into his pocket and reached for the quilts. But once he had them, he wasn't sure where to put them and so dumped them on the chair. "Thank you," he said, facing her again.

They stood in silence for a moment. Then two. Then longer. He was about to say something to smooth the awkwardness when words tumbled out of her in a rush.

"I've also come to apologize. For our misunderstanding earlier. I meant no insult, Ashby. And I certainly don't see you as a cripple. But seeing how much pain you were in—"

"I'm fine."

She looked away, her hands twisting like she was working dough, the signet ring he had given her flashing in the firelight. In view of her feelings, he wondered why she still wore it.

"I only meant to help, but I seem to have made a tangle of it. I'm sorry."

Some of the stiffness eased in his back. "I'm fine, lass," he said in a gentler tone. "It's been a long and difficult healing, so it has. But I should not have taken my frustration out on you. We'll not speak of it again."

She let out a deep breath. Her hands seemed more relaxed now.

He studied her face in the firelight, then came to a decision he knew he would probably regret. "And I offer apologies, as well. I can see it was a shock, me showing up after all this time. It's obvious you have reservations about going back to Scotland with me, so if it will ease your worries, I give you my word I won't force my attentions on you. Even if I've every right to do so as your lawful husband."

Judging by her expression, he probably shouldn't have said that last part, so he hastily added, "In truth, it will try me sorely to be in the presence of such a beauty as yourself and keep my hands to myself, so it will."

She blinked at him. Then laughed. "You've been in Ireland too long, milord, to be spouting such blarney with a straight face."

He spread his hands in innocence. "You're a beautiful woman, lass. Even more so than I recall."

"You didn't even recall my name," she reminded him.

"I was too busy recalling the rest of you."

Another bit of silence, but uncomfortable for a different reason.

A log settled in the fire, sending up a burst of tiny orange sparks that faded into the stars overhead. The crescent moon skimmed the treetops, and for an instant, silhouetted against its glowing face, a bat swooped on a circling moth. Ash shifted his weight from one foot to the other and tried to think of something to say.

"Did the poultice help?" she asked after a time.

"Aye."

"You removed it?"

"And burned it."

She arched a brow. "You were truly afraid it would attract bears?"

"I was afraid you would make me wear it again. It itches."

She laughed. He liked the sound of it. He liked standing here in the near darkness, with her scent drifting in the woodsmoke and her voice gentle in his ear.

"You never told me how you were injured."

And he dinna want to now, preferring to keep that sad memory buried in the back of his mind. But she had seen his scars and probably thought she had a right to know how they had gotten there. And since he wasn't yet ready for her to leave, he told her.

"We were escorting a munitions detail," he began. "Transferring a shipment of explosives from the dock to the armory. It was fairly routine. I was laughing with Major Ridgeway about something inane—I canna even remember what—when the caisson beside him blew up. The next thing I recall is waking in a hospital bed a fortnight later."

"Oh, dear." Her hand touched his arm. "I'm amazed you survived."

"Only because Ridgeway and his mount took the brunt of the explosion. Three other good men were not so lucky."

"How sad." Her hand fell back to her side. He missed the heat and weight of it. "It must have been painful. How long were you in the hospital?"

"Over two months. It was a confusing time." Realizing he was running his fingertips over the scar hidden beneath his hair, he clasped his hands behind his back so they wouldn't betray him again. "I was given laudanum for the pain, so I dinna remember much. If your letter came then, I have no memory of it. I'm sorry about that."

"My letter?"

"The one telling me of your parents' deaths. Had I known and been able to travel, I would have come to you."

She stood unmoving, her eyes glittering in the firelight. Something shifted in her expression, but in the dim light, he couldn't be certain what it was. "Perhaps if I had known of your injury," she said with a sad smile, "I would have come to you. It might have changed everything. Now we'll never know."

He dinna know how to respond to that, so he said nothing.

"Well . . ."

Seeing that she was about to leave, he threw out a hand. "Stay." Then hearing how brusque that sounded, he softened his tone. "It's a braw night. Perhaps you'll sit awhile?" He motioned to the chair, saw the quilts piled on the seat and hurriedly shoved them to the dirt.

She eyed the rumpled bedding.

"Here." Snatching a blanket from the ground, he held it out. "You'll need this. To ward off the chill."

Gingerly accepting the proffered blanket, she shook off pine needles and dirt, then tossed it around her shoulders like a shawl. "Thank you," she murmured, and stepping over the rest of the quilts, sank into the chair.

He added more wood to the already blazing fire, then stood guard over it, hands clasped once more behind his back.

Silence again. It stretched to an agonizing length before she finally broke it. "I so enjoy the nights here in the West." He looked over to see her smiling up into the night sky. "In England, and in Scotland, too, it is often so overcast all one sees are clouds and more clouds. Until I came here, I never knew there were so many stars in the heavens."

His gaze drifted down the curve of her neck, and a memory flashed of another moonlit night when he had kissed that small hollow at the base of her throat and felt the rapid beat of her pulse against his tongue. "Aye. It's beautiful, so it is," he murmured, looking away.

Despite the awkwardness and the heavy silences and troubling memories, he was glad of the company. Too much silence and solitude opened his mind to dark memories and questions he couldn't answer.

And the woman beside him posed the biggest question of all.

He dinna want to return to Scotland without her. He dinna want to go back to the stilted, purposeless world of Viscount Ashby, heir to an earldom. He dinna want to go back, at all.

At his feet, Agnes circled three times, then settled against the sleeping wolfhound's warm side, curled into a tight ball, her nose tucked under her front legs. How simple life was for dogs. A friendly pat, a full belly, and a warm place to wait out the night. That was all they needed.

When had his own life become so complicated that he no longer took time to enjoy such simple contentments? And what had he to show for it?

Idly, he watched sparks rise with the curling smoke. As he listened to the music of the flames, he thought of the thousands of other campfires he had stared into through the years, and of the soldiers who had stood beside him, sharing its warmth on a lonely night.

He missed that bond. That camaraderie. The ribald jokes and deep laughter. The trust and discipline that gave meaning to the days and hope through the long nights. He understood the soldier's life. It had defined him for over seventeen years, and now that it was lost to him forever, he felt adrift. Irrelevant. Such a lack of clear direction was intolerable to a man more suited to action, a man trained to fight and protect. It created within him a driving need to find something else to give him purpose. Ash looked at the woman beside him and wondered if she would ever be part of that.

"Is it me, lass? Something I've done that prevents you from returning home?" With her beside him, he might find his balance again.

She looked up at him, one side of her face cloaked in shadow, the other tinted pink by the fire. He felt her mind probing his and remembered how intelligent she was, and how clearly she saw the world with her sharply assessing artist's eye. "Why did you marry me?" she asked.

Ah, he thought, both dismayed and challenged by the counterattack. He thought for a moment, debating whether he should tell her he'd been taken with her beauty and her fine form and that touch of the Highlands in her coppery hair—all true, of course, but not the sole reason he had asked her to marry him. Then realizing he had naught to lose since the lass was already set against him, he decided to give honesty a go.

"The earl dinna want me to." Damning, but true.

Her mouth opened, closed, opened. "That's the reason you married me? To defy your father? Are you jesting?" Her voice had risen with every word, a clear indication that he had erred.

On reflection, Ash decided that perhaps the unvarnished truth might not always be the best approach where a woman was concerned. Throwing out a smile to cover his retreat, he said, "Well, that and because I thought you were the loveliest lass I'd ever seen in my life and I was determined to have you as my own."

"You're pathetic."

"You don't believe me?" Ash was hard-pressed to keep his face straight at such a blatant attempt at cajolery. When she smiled back at him, he felt like he'd won a great prize.

"In truth," he added in a more serious tone, "he grew weary of waiting for Glynnis to accept Fain McKenzie. And the only other way to expand our hold was to make an alliance with the McRaes who bordered us on the east. It was ever about the lands with the earl. Naught else."

"That sounds like a practical match. Why were you opposed?"

"I wasn't until I met you." She gave an unladylike snort that made him laugh again. "But I also have to admit that as far as Mary McRae goes, I've seen prettier faces hanging over a paddock fence."

"That's cruel."

He shrugged. "Everyone has a right to be ugly, but that poor lass abuses the privilege." He rocked on his heels, hands still behind his back. "Now I would like for you to be honest with me and answer the question I posed. Why will you not go to Scotland with me?"

She dinna answer straightaway, and he hoped she wasn't picking her words and would answer him true. He needed to know now if he could fix this or if he should cast aside all hope and petition for a divorce.

In his tent, Satterwhite snorted and snored. Beside the fire, Tricks twitched in his dreams, rousing his wee friend to a sigh and a tighter curl against his side.

"You hurt me." Her accusation carried a quiet dignity that cut deeper than a blade. "And I don't want to be hurt again." She shrugged. "But your indifference was not the only reason I left."

Indifference? Never that. In fact, so much the opposite, it had scared him. "I sent you letters," he reminded her. "And I came to visit."

"Yes, you did. You wrote exactly two times and dropped by once on your way back from Newmarket after purchasing remounts."

Actually, he had defied orders to come see her as soon as the sale was completed. And after he'd forced himself to leave her the next afternoon, he'd had to ride through the night to get back to the ship before it sailed. Again, he'd risked everything—and again, all she saw was that it wasn't enough. "I'm sorry, lass. I would have come more often had I been able."

She made a dismissive motion, then let her hand fall back to her lap. "That aside, I have made a new life here. A fulfilling, happy life—peopled with dear friends and challenged by interesting, meaningful work to which I am totally committed."

Looking down into her upturned face, he saw the fire and passion that at one time had been directed at him, and he realized with sudden clarity that by armoring himself against this woman, he had lost something valuable and irreplaceable. Something he never even knew was within his grasp until it had already slipped through his grip. "Your tintypes."

"Precisely. There is a man in London who, even now, is clamoring for more of them."

Ash nodded. "Chesterfield, at *The Illustrated London News*. I spoke with him. In fact, it was through him that I tracked you here."

"I'll have to remember to thank him," she muttered.

"I would have found you without his help. Remember, I was a forward rider with the Riflemen in my early career." He smiled down at her. "Chesterfield showed me some of your photographs. You're verra good, lass. Your spirit shines through in every picture."

She looked away. "Mr. Chesterfield has been most encouraging."

"As well he should. He sells a lot of newspapers because of you."

He watched her stroke imaginary dust from her skirt—a gesture he was beginning to recognize as one she used when she was nervous or feeling shy—and sensed his words had pleased her. Which pleased him.

So he expounded. "In fact, all London is talking about the talented A. M. Wallace."

"All?" A smile teased her lips. "Even the children and illiterate? How remarkable."

Tipping his head, he studied her face in the fire glow, willing her to look up at him. When she did, he asked, "Why don't you put your full name on your work, Maddie, instead of just your initials? Are you ashamed of your talent?"

She shrugged. "If subscribers thought I was a man, I would have a greater chance of success. There are less than a handful of female photographers, and their work is rarely taken seriously because of their gender. Also"—she sent him a pointed look—"I thought it would make me more difficult to track."

He grinned. "And so it did. I had to use all my persuasive powers to convince Chesterfield to tell me where you were." Along with the threat of Newgate Prison for abetting the desertion of the lawful wife of a peer.

"Ah. I thought so. 'Tall, overbearing, and unpleasant.' That's how he described the man seeking information about me. Who else could it have been but you?" Her teasing smile took some of the sting out of the words. "I just don't know why you went to the bother of finding me."

He looked at the ring he'd given her that she still wore, and wondered again if she might still harbor feelings for him. "You're my wife."

"So it's all about possession, then?"

He grinned. "Not *all*."

She opened her mouth—to berate him, no doubt—when a rustling sound in the brush drew her attention.

Ash turned and studied the trees. Beside him, Tricks lifted his head and stared fixedly toward the creek, his nose quivering as he drew in scent.

Moving without haste, Ash picked up his Snider-Enfield, which he'd loaded and left propped against the stack of firewood. Holding it by his side, he scanned the trees that ringed the meadow.

He saw nothing. Heard nothing. Glancing over at the mules and Lurch, barely visible at the edge of the firelight, he noted they stood quietly, ears relaxed, heads drooping as they dozed. After a moment, the wolfhound lost interest, and with a wide, tongue-curling yawn, dropped his head back onto his paws.

Reassured, Ash rested the rifle back against the wood and straightened to find his wife watching him. "It's naught, lass. You're safe. Tricks and I will watch over you."

"I can see that. And I thank you for it." Tossing off the blanket so that it draped over the slatted back of the chair, she rose and snapped her fingers. "Come, Agnes. Let us leave our guardians to their duty."

The little dog bounded up, stretched, gave Ash's boots a sniff, then trotted ahead of her master toward the wagon. Tricks continued to sleep.

Seeing her turn away, and wanting to keep her there for just a wee bit longer, he blurted out the first words that came into his mind. "I canna read."

Bluidy hell. Why had he admitted that?

She stopped, slowly turned. He couldn't see her face clearly in the dim light, but the sudden stiffness of her body told him he'd blundered badly. *Bleeding, bluidy, humping—*

"You can't read?"

Heat rushed into his face. That old panic gripped his throat so tight for a moment he couldn't respond. "What I mean is," he finally managed, "I can read, but it's . . . difficult. That's why I dinna write more often."

She watched him, waiting.

"The letters jumble up and make no sense." He looked away, shame burning through his chest. "I canna explain it."

He heard her come closer and braced himself. If she showed him pity, he wasn't sure what he would do.

With a sigh, Agnes returned to the wolfhound's side.

"Is it your vision? Because of your injury?"

He dared a glance but saw only concern in her eyes. Letting out a deep breath, he felt some of the tension go with it. "I wish it were that simple, lass. My eyes are fine. In fact, during my time with the Green Jackets I won most of the regimental rifle competitions. This"—he gestured vaguely toward his eyes—"is an affliction I've suffered all my life." He thought of the beatings, the ridicule, all the long hours sweating over pages and columns that were indecipherable in his head. "But I'm verra good at other things," he said emphatically. "I'm not simple."

"How could you be? You attended University, did you not?"

"Aye."

"And fooled them all, it seems."

He allowed a tight smile. "So I did."

Lifting the blanket from the back of her chair, she draped it once more over her shoulders, then sat. Pulling the rough wool tight against the chill, she crossed one leg over the other and looked up at him. "How?"

He gave a scornful laugh. "The son of a lord—even a third son—is given some latitude. And I have a sure memory, so I learned to do numbers and verses in my head."

"And if something needed to be read or written?"

"Harry Ridgeway would help me."

She thought for a moment. "The same Major Ridgeway who died in the explosion?"

"Aye."

He could almost hear her mind fitting pieces together. "And your letters to me? They were also written by Major Ridgeway?"

Another wave of heat up his neck. "At my dictation," he defended.

A pause, then in a dry tone, "That accounts for the lack of ardor, I suppose. Did he also read my letters to you?"

"No. I pieced those together as best I could." He frowned down at her. "You should attend your penmanship, lass. Your ps and qs and ds and fs and ts all look the same, so they do."

She met his scolding look with a smile. "I'll work on it."

"So you should." Rocking back on his heels, he looked up into the night sky, feeling suddenly as if a heavy weight had been lifted from his shoulders. She hadn't laughed or mocked him, so maybe she could accept his affliction and think no less of him. If she stayed with him at all.

"Thank you for telling me." Rising from the chair, she carefully folded the blanket and set it on the seat, then bent and scooped up Agnes.

"I never meant to hurt you, lass."

She looked up at him, the flames reflected in her eyes.

She looked so beautiful standing there in soft golden firelight that he wanted to reach out and feel the warmth in her skin to assure himself she was real. "And I was never indifferent to you. Ever."

That shift in her expression again, but she looked away before he could define it. "It occurs to me," she said as she idly scratched Agnes's ear, "that I don't have to be in Denver until the end of the month. Perhaps it would be best for your injury if we delayed our return to Heartbreak Creek for a day. The mules can use the rest, too."

"I'm fine, lass."

"And I noticed earlier," she went on as if he hadn't spoken, "that with the sun riding low as autumn wanes, it creates the most extraordinary contrasts of shadow and light. I should like to photograph that."

Ash smiled. "And I should like to watch you do so."

"Excellent." A quick smile, then she turned away. "Until tomorrow, then."

"Tomorrow, lass." Ash watched her all the way inside her wagon, then lifted his head and smiled into the starlit sky.

Six

Ash lay propped against his saddle, one hand tucked behind his head, the other balancing a steaming mug of tea on his chest. Across the clearing, Satterwhite carried yet another box of photography equipment from the wagon to where a folding wooden table had been set up in the grass.

He supposed he should go help. Or at least call Agnes so she wouldn't keep getting underfoot. But he wasn't yet fully awake after spending a restless night plotting strategy, and besides, if the snoring that had come from the photography tent all night was an indication, the old man was well rested. As was his wife, it seemed, judging by the briskness of her step as she moved back and forth from the tent to the clearing.

He admired the way the rising sun haloed the wispy copper curls that had escaped her topknot and bounced about her face with every step. No measured, ladylike glide today, he noted in amusement. But the march of a woman on a mission. His wee wife had always been especially energetic in the mornings, he remembered. God bless her.

A shadow drew his gaze, and he looked up to see a wide-winged hawk drift by on currents rising off the warming earth. He watched it, feeling a spark of kinship with the solitary bird, as if his unfettered spirit soared beside it.

He had told her of his affliction, and she hadn't seemed to mind. A wondrous, liberating thing, so it was.

At his side, Tricks yawned, which made Ash yawn.

He really should get up.

Instead, he lifted his head off the saddle, took a sip of tea, and sank back with a contented sigh. What a braw morning it was.

Across the clearing, Satterwhite cursed as he tried to wrestle the wooden leg of a gangly tripod from Agnes's snarling jaws. Nearby a brownish bird perched on Lurch's withers, checking his mane for lice, while at the edge of the wood, wee yellow birds with black crowns and black-and-white wings darted in and out of the high branches, scolding a striped ground squirrel. Nary a cloud marred the icy blue of the sky.

He wouldna mind waking up to this every morning of his life.

Glancing over at the pot of water steaming on the coals, Ash debated whether to use it for another cup of tea or for shaving. He hated shaving in cold water. Or maybe he should ask his lady wife to shave him with that straight razor she kept in her apron. *There's a right fine idea.*

Closing his eyes, he pictured it in his mind—sweet Maddie leaning close, her curls tickling his nose, her lips pursed in concentration just inches from his own, as if begging him to—

"Are you going to be a slugabed all day?"

He opened his eyes to find his wife frowning down at him, elbows akimbo, hands on hips . . . which presented an inspiring view of the underside of her full breasts as they pressed against the taunt cloth. "Hmm?"

"It's well past dawn. Aren't you ever going to get up?"

Oh, he was definitely up. Bending a leg to hide evidence of that, he smiled and lifted the mug. "Will you join me in a cup of tea, lass?"

"I've had my tea. Hours ago."

"Then perhaps you'll renew your offer to shave me?" He rubbed a palm over his stubbled cheek.

Muttering, she whirled and marched toward Satterwhite.

"Or if you'd like," he called after her, "you can watch while I do it."

"Exposing a negative plate is a delicate process," Maddie explained to Ash a half hour later as she bent to check the thumbscrews attaching the bulky box camera to the tripod. "And to prevent light from ruining the image before the plate is to be exposed, I use this." She held up the corner of a black cloth draped over the back of the camera. "The entire process must be completed in the dark and before the collodion emulsion on the glass has dried. Usually about five minutes."

"Sounds complicated." Leaning a hip against her folding table, Ash crossed his arms and suppressed a yawn. Although he appreciated the final product, he wasn't that interested in the process of photography. He was more a man of action. But as part of his campaign to win over his reluctant wife, he was willing to suffer through a lecture or two. Besides, he enjoyed spending time with her.

"The tedious part is the preparation."

"Is it?" She had such pretty eyes. A rich, deep brown with yellow flakes in the irises, and lashes that were so long the sun shining through them cast spiky shadows across her cheeks. "Show me."

He liked watching her work, her hands deft and sure, her attention so focused on what she was doing he had plenty of time to focus on her, which he happily did. She was an intriguing woman, this stranger who was his wife—smart and independent and saucy. He wanted to learn as much as he could about how her mind worked before he began his full frontal assault.

Success is as much in the planning as the execution, his old commander often said.

And Ash was planning on success. He wouldn't let this woman drift away from him a second time.

Satisfied that the camera was secure, she returned to the table to sort through one of the crates. Finding what she sought—a thick piece of cotton paper—she placed it on the table. "First I coated this with a mixture of egg whites and salt. Then once it dried, I dipped it into a solution of silver nitrate and water." She paused to send him a bright smile. "That's what makes the paper sensitive to light exposure, of course."

He smiled back. "Of course."

Her gaze dropped to his mouth, then quickly away. "Then I dry the treated paper in darkness until I'm ready to place it in a frame with a glass plate that has been treated with the collodion emulsion mixture."

"Collodion?" He especially liked that arch in her brows that gave her face a perpetual expression of wonder. It always drew him closer, as if being near her might cause some of that joy in life to rub off on him.

"It's a liquid emulsion made of cellulose nitrate and ether and a few other ingredients. It creates fumes that are quite noxious, and if allowed to accumulate, can become highly flammable. That's why I mix it outdoors."

Ash blinked. "Flammable?"

She gave his crossed arm a reassuring pat. "Oh, I'm most careful. I store all my chemicals in airtight tins. And I hear they're on the brink of developing a new dry process, which would eliminate—"

"Ether?" Ash straightened, his arms falling to his sides. He looked down at the boxes stacked at their feet, then at the wagon. "You store ether in there? With a woodstove?"

He must have shouted it because she stepped back, her eyes round with surprise. "Of course not. I'm not demented. Only the negative plates are stored inside. I keep all the dangerous substances in crates on top of the wagon. That way if something does go wrong, the explosion will go upward rather than down, and the plates won't be damaged."

"Plates? You're worrying over *plates*? What about you?"

Another step back. "Don't be silly. I take all necessary precautions. It's not as if I'm dabbling in that experimental magnesium powder that can set your hair on fire or blow off your fingers."

"Holy mother of mercy." But before he could voice further objections, she slid her arm through his, and as soon as he felt the soft press of her breast against his arm, he completely lost his train of thought.

"I'll show you." She led him toward the camera, and still bemused, he followed docilely along like a spring lamb.

"We'll start with a photograph of Buttercup and Maisy." Releasing his arm, she moved the camera and tripod into position so that it faced the grazing mules. "First we focus." She slid back the rear section of the camera and pointed to a glass pane in a wooden frame. "This is the focusing screen. We look through it at what we want to photograph." Holding up the dark cloth, she motioned him forward. "Step under. Look through the glass and tell me what you see."

Bending, he draped the cloth over his head and peered through the glass. "Nothing. It's blurry."

"Exactly!"

Moving out from beneath the cloth, he found her grinning up at him like he'd earned a great prize. One couldn't fault the woman's enthusiasm. Or his reaction to it.

"So how do we make the image sharper? By sliding this rear section in and out of the camera box." She demonstrated.

In and out. One of his favorites. In fact, he'd been told he was quite good at it. Once even by her. "Fast or slow?"

"Pardon?"

He motioned with his finger. "That in-and-out part. Should that be done fast or slow, do you suppose?"

She stared at his finger. A slight flush eased up her throat. "Slow, I should think. To maintain focus, as it were."

"Focus. Of course. One wouldn't want to lose focus at such a delicate time." Clasping his hands behind his back, he gave her his best smile. "Pray continue."

"Ah . . . yes, of course."

After aligning the image, she put a cap over the lens protruding from the other side of the camera box and removed the glass focusing screen from the rear. "Now comes the tricky part." She held up a plain glass plate. "I must coat this with the collodion emulsion to sensitize it, then insert it into this holder."

Insert. Another favorite. "Then what?"

She pointed to a wooden frame with a dark plate on one side. "That plate will protect the glass from extraneous light until I'm ready to expose it. But first"—she carefully slid the glass pane into a flat pan—"I coat it with the chemical solution—collodion emulsion—to sensitize the glass. Then I put the wet glass in the holder and slide it into the camera. All that must be done out of the presence of light. And finally, we're ready to take a photograph. Isn't that exciting?" She beamed up at him.

He beamed back, and hoped he wasn't required to remember all that.

"This will only take a moment, but I'd advise you to step back while I mix the emulsion. Just in case."

"In case of what?" he asked, distraction forgotten.

But she was already under her dark cloth, with only her rounded arse poking out as she bent over the table, mixing her witch's brew. He cocked his head to study the shapely contours, then stepped back to get the full effect. The woman had a lovely arse. He was looking forward to reacquainting himself with it.

At a sound, he straightened to find Satterwhite glaring at him from over by the wagon. "What?" he mouthed, feigning innocence.

Shaking his head, the old man snatched up two water buckets and stomped toward the creek, Agnes and Tricks in tow.

Still under the drape, Maddie reached out to locate the camera, then working blind, slid the frame into the rear of the camera. "Ready?" she called out in a muffled voice.

"Ready," he answered, having no idea what she was talking about but enjoying the show just the same. *Trim ankles. Narrow feet.* He recalled how soft the soles had felt sliding up the back of his calves.

"I've removed the dark protective plate," she called from under the drape. "Now I'll remove the cap from the lens in front"—which she did—"and the exposure will begin. Count to nine."

Ash did, wondering if he might finagle a kiss if he did it right. When he reached nine, she replaced the lens cap and protective slide, then removed the holder from the camera. Wrapping it in the dark drape, she gave Ash a triumphant grin. "Now to process the plate in the dark tent. Come along."

Ash put on an expression of regret. "As much as I would like to," he hedged, "I feel I should help Satterwhite. I hate to see a man his age carrying those heavy water buckets by himself. Do you mind?"

She did, he was gratified to notice. But politely masking her disappointment, she waved him on. "Not at all. Go do what you need to do. I'll be a while."

Several hours later, Maddie slammed the door on the wagon and plopped down on her bed with a snort of disgust.

She was in desperate need of her friends. Ever since that conversation with Ash beside the fire the previous night and his attentiveness throughout the morning, she had begun to question her decision to send him on his way. Was she so weak-willed where the man was concerned that she could so easily overlook years of neglect just for a smile and an hour of polite conversation?

Conversation? She wanted a great deal more than that.

She was absurd. A ninny of the first order. One of those simpering, clingy, dependent women she so despised. But the ladies of Heartbreak Creek would quickly set her back on track.

With a sigh, she flopped back, arms thrown wide, hands dangling over the edges of the narrow bed. She stared up at the low ceiling, which she had papered with newspaper clippings of her favorite photographs, many taken by Matthew Brady during the War of the Rebellion, and others by Tim O'Sullivan, who so beautifully chronicled the expansion of the West. There were even a few of her own up there.

And the newest—a lovely albumen print she had taken in secret just this morning—was of Ash, with Tricks at his knee, talking to

Lurch. His head was slightly downcast, a fall of gray brown hair on his forehead, his eyes fixed on the horse's face. His hand looked large and pale where it cupped Lurch's dark jaw, and the horse seemed to lean toward him, his head slightly tucked on his glossy neck. Trust. Somehow she had captured that bond between the man and his horse. And along with it, the power and grace and magnetism of the man, himself.

And now that magnetism was working on her.

It was vexing in the extreme. She was being an utter fool . . . as her friends would no doubt be delighted to point out.

Lucinda would find her infatuation with her own husband immensely amusing. She would laugh and make some astute and clever observation that would cut straight to the heart of the matter. Edwina would immediately take her side, of course. But against what? Ash? Her own weakness? It didn't matter with the fiercely loyal Southerner. She was the champion of them all, no matter what. And Pru, the beauty and possessor of the highest intellect in the group, would calmly explain that giving up a budding career as an expeditionary photographer and returning to the life—and the man—she had fled, would be illogical, at best.

She would listen, shed a few tears, and they would comfort her. Then hopefully she would be able to put aside this growing attraction to Ash and send him on his way so she could get back to her exciting and fulfilling life. Just two more days, and those would be spent traveling. Surely, she could manage that.

With determined steps, she left the wagon. As she came down the stair, she saw Ash and Mr. Satterwhite standing by the table in the clearing, arguing over some inconsequential thing, as they were wont to do.

"Gentlemen," she called, crossing toward them. "If you would please help me pack up these boxes and load them onto the top of the wagon, I'm hoping we can depart for Heartbreak Creek first thing in the morning."

·   ·   ·

They awoke to a heavy dew that clung to the grass and dripped from sagging spruce limbs. By the time they were ready to go, the mist had thickened to a cold drizzle that slowly sucked the yellow leaves from the aspens and turned the trunks of the firs and alders dark brown.

Maddie rode beside Mr. Satterwhite, Agnes in her lap. Even though the overhanging roof extending above the driver's bench protected them somewhat from the rain, the cold dampness soon made her bones ache. She could see it was having a similar effect on Ash's healing injury.

She felt bad for him. Earlier, she had offered to let him take her place up front, but he had refused—stubborn, prideful man that he was—and now rode alongside, a dripping flat-crowned coachman's hat covering his head, and an oiled duster draped over his legs. Tricks trotted at his side, his rough coat matted with rain and mud.

Before long, the drizzle gave over to a steady rain that didn't let up throughout the morning. Soon the wagon track became a slippery morass, and Buttercup and Maisy were struggling for footing on the inclines, and sliding hock deep in mud on the downward slopes. As the hours passed and the rain continued, runoff cut deep grooves into the sodden earth.

By early afternoon, when the rain showed no sign of slacking and their progress had slowed to a crawl, Maddie turned to Mr. Satterwhite. "Perhaps we should stop for the day," she shouted over the drumming of rain on the top of the wagon. She was chilled to the bone, Agnes was shivering, and it was apparent from the paleness of his face and the tight line of his mouth that Ash was suffering, as well. Even Mr. Satterwhite was showing the strain, sitting hunched over the reins, his head drooping.

"We've got one more crossing," he shouted back. "It's the deepest, so we'd best cross now before the water rises too high."

"How far?" Ash called, angling Lurch close to the wagon.

"Mile. Maybe two."

"I'll scout it." Kicking Lurch into a trot, he went ahead of the wagon, Tricks loping alongside.

As they disappeared down the road, Maddie turned again to Mr. Satterwhite. "He's in pain. We should stop as soon as we can."

"He's in pain? What about me?" Mumbling under his breath, he snapped the reins and pushed the mules to a faster pace.

When they rounded the bend a few minutes later, Ash was sitting on Lurch beside the rushing creek, a worried look on his face. "Over two feet deep and moving fast. I'll lead the team across."

Mr. Satterwhite nodded and urged the mules forward.

Maddie clung to the arm rail as the wagon bounced over the rocky streambed. Ahead, reining Lurch with one hand and gripping a rope hooked to Maisy's driving bridle with the other, Ash called encouragement to the frightened mules. Soon water churned around their knees and the animals were lifting their hooves high and setting them down cautiously. Buttercup, the more timid of the two, began to tremble.

Looking down, Maddie saw that the wheel on her side was half-submerged, and clutched Agnes tighter.

"Get on! Get on!" Mr. Satterwhite shouted as the mules scrabbled on the uneven streambed, struggling to drag the wagon over a large rock. With a bounce that almost tipped the wagon over, they cleared the obstacle. But when the heel chains slapped against Buttercup's rear legs, the startled mule leaped forward, knocking Lurch off balance. The horse went down, throwing Ash out of the saddle, and suddenly both mules were lunging toward the opposite bank.

Lurch regained his feet and splashed after them. No sign of Ash.

Shouting "Whoa" in a panicky voice, Mr. Satterwhite reared back and wrestled with the reins. From inside the wagon came the crash of tumbling boxes and shifting furniture as they careened over the streambed.

Maddie looked back, saw Ash rise, dripping and cursing, out of the water, and went almost giddy with relief. Bracing her legs, she fought to stay seated, one hand gripping the roof support, the other clutching Agnes to her chest. With a jarring bounce, the wagon cleared the stream and started up the muddy incline, Lurch racing wild-eyed alongside. A loud grating sound came from the axle beneath the bench, then just as the wagon reached flat ground, the wheel under Maddie gave with an explosive crack.

The wagon tipped to one side, flinging Agnes from her arms and Satterwhite against her shoulder. Maddie flailed for a handhold. The wagon teetered, then rocked back, finally slamming to earth at a precarious angle over the broken wheel.

Hands grabbed her, yanked her to safety.

"Are you all right?" Ash demanded, running his hands up her arms to grip her head. "Are ye hurt, Maddie? Speak to me!"

"Yes. N-No. I'm all right."

"Sweet Mary." He pulled her hard against his body, one big hand pinning her head so tightly to his chest she could feel the vibration of his thundering heartbeat against her cheek. "Ye scared the bluidy hell out of me, ye daft woman. You'll no' do that again."

He was muddy and wet, but she sank into the cold, solid strength of him. One—or both—of them was shaking. She didn't know which.

After a moment, he pulled back. Hands gripping her shoulders, he bent and peered into her face. "You're sure you're not hurt?"

"I'm all right, but Mr. Satterwhite and Agnes—"

"They're fine. Everyone is safe."

She looked around, spotted Lurch and the dogs waiting in the shelter of the trees, and Mr. Satterwhite trying to calm the mules, who stood trembling, their mud-coated sides pumping as they dragged in air. "Thank God," she said on a shaky breath. "We all made it."

"All but the wagon." Releasing her arms, Ash turned to study the damaged wheel. "That hub is shattered, I'm afraid."

"C-Can we fix it?" Now that the danger was past, the fear and cold were setting in, and her teeth began to chatter.

"You're chilled. Satterwhite!" Ash had to yell over the sound of the rushing stream. "Set up the photography tent for my wife while I see what can be done about this wheel."

"Don't b-bother with t-the tent. Look." Maddie pointed a

shaking finger at the patches of blue sky that showed through the thinning clouds. "It's s-stopped raining."

Ash was as miserable as he had been at the siege of Sevastopol during that terrible winter fifteen years ago, and every wound he had suffered in the years since was aching like a buggering son of a bitch. *Bluidy wheel. Bluidy hub. Bluidy, humpin' mud.*
Biting back a groan, he straightened, one hand pressed against his cramping back, and flung the mallet to the ground in disgust. "There's no help for it. The hub canna be repaired. It will have to be replaced."

Satterwhite kicked the hub. "Hell."

"I'm not supposing you carry an extra wheel?"

"Nope."

"Bollocks." They stood staring down at the remains of the right front wheel, then Ash sighed and asked, "How far is it to the nearest blacksmith or wheelwright?"

Idly rubbing his left arm, Satterwhite thought it over. "That'd be Becker's Fort at Hellbent Falls. It's not really a fort. More like a trading post. And Becker died in an Indian raid about four or five years ago, so I'm not sure why the place still carries his name. The falls are gone, too, sent underground by a rock slide a decade ago. But last time I came through there, they had a smithy, and he had wagon parts."

"How far," Ash asked again, striving for patience.

"Twelve, maybe fifteen miles." Satterwhite pointed up the road in the direction they had been headed. "About ten miles up is a big burned-out cedar stump. Beside it is a trail that branches left."

Ash nodded and started to turn away, when Satterwhite added, "But that's not it, so don't take it."

Wearily, Ash turned back.

"But if you was to backtrack about half a mile from that stump," Satterwhite expounded, "you'd find a cutoff to the east. That's the one that'll take you into Becker's Fort."

"You're sure?" Ash asked, fearing he was being sent on a fool's errand by a bigger fool.

"Well . . ." Satterwhite stopped rubbing his arm and scrunched one wandering eye closed in deep consideration. After a moment, he opened the eye and nodded. "Yep. That's it. Pretty sure. Your Majesty."

Ash considered choking him, but his hands were so cold and sore from wrestling with the wheel he wasna sure he had the strength to do it properly. "You'll watch out for her while I'm gone?"

The old man drew back. "I watched out for her well enough before you showed up, didn't I?"

Shaking his head in exasperation, Ash started away again.

This time Satterwhite stopped him with a hand on his arm. "You are coming back, aren't you?"

Ash glared down at the gnarly fingers, then jerked his arm free. "What do you think?"

"I think I'm getting too old to haul her around. And I think she's not safe out here on her own and needs someone to watch out for her. And much as it pains me to say it, I think that someone should be you." Satterwhite stepped closer, his white-whiskered jaw jutting. "So I'll ask you again, soldier boy. Are you coming back, or not?"

Soldier boy? Ash was so angry he almost reached for the saber he no longer wore. "I have journeyed over a year and more than five thousand miles to find her," he said through clenched teeth. "Do you truly think I would return to Scotland without her?"

Satterwhite's face went slack. "Scotland? You're going back to Scotland?"

"Of course, I am, ye bluidy noob! I'm heir to an earldom, so I am. I dinna seek it, nor do I want it, but that's the task I've been given. So, aye, I'll go back. I have duties there."

"You have duties *here!*" Clapping both hands to his head, Satterwhite stomped a tight circle. "You mule-headed, yammering, fancy-pants foreigner, you're blinder than I am!"

Ash had opened his mouth to toss out a few insults of his own, when Satterwhite whirled and jabbed a finger into his chest. "And what about missy? You planning to drag her back with you?"

Dumbfounded, Ash looked down at the finger planted on his chest. How many men would have dared do such a thing? Sane men. Dinna Satterwhite realize what a soldier in training for seventeen years was capable of? What *he* was capable of?

Blitherin' numptie. Striving for the cool calmness that had earned him a reputation for levelheadedness under fire, Ash stiffened his spine and clasped his hands behind his back. "It is my hope that Viscountess Ashby will return with me to assume the duties of her station."

"Which probably doesn't include going into places no proper lady would dare venture just to take her pictures. Right?" Another jab.

"Remove your hand. Now."

Satterwhite did, then heaved a great sigh of disgust. "You'll kill her."

Ash blinked. "I'll what?"

"Missy has a kind and gentle heart. You can see it in every picture she makes. It's in the way she looks at the world. Hell, in the way she looks at me—a broken-down old man with eyes that make children duck behind their mother's skirts. She sees the beauty in us all. And you would take that away from her."

"*Haud yer wheesht!*" Ash shouted, his accent getting away from him. "I wouldna dae any sech thing!"

"You take away her photography, you take away her joy. Is that what you want?"

Ash blinked at the old man, deafened by the ring of truth in his words. That joy in life was what had attracted him to Maddie in the first place. Attracted him, still. But a member of the peerage couldn't go haring about in disreputable places just to pursue a hobby. It wasna safe. Or proper. Or acceptable. Such behavior would make her the laughingstock of society, and he dinna want that for the lass.

"Of course it's not what I want." But if Satterwhite was right, and Maddie insisted on continuing her photography, he might allow her to open a wee studio in a fashionable part of town. He wasn't a harsh man.

And at that moment, and with that thought, Ash realized he had already made his decision about his marriage.

He wouldn't petition for a divorce, and he wouldn't go back to Scotland without his wife. Somehow, he would convince Maddie to accept him and the life he could give her. He was offering a title and a life of ease, for God's sake. "Dinna fret about milady," he said with cool stiffness, having regained his temper. "I will take proper care of my wife and keep her safe, so I will. And as for Scotland, when I come back from Becker's Fort, I'll talk to her about it and show her that I'm a—"

"Damned fool."

"—reasonable man," Ash ground out over the interruption. "But while I'm gone, you'd best watch out for her—"

"Like I've been doing all these months?"

"—because if anything happens to the lass, I'll—"

"Everything is fine in here," Maddie called, coming around the back of the wagon. "A broken lantern and the stovepipe knocked askew, but that's the extent of it. None of my negative plates were broken, thank goodness. And do stop threatening Mr. Satterwhite, Ashby. He is an excellent guardian."

"Thank you, missy."

Ash sent the old man a warning glare. "Just in case, I'll leave you Tricks."

Muttering under his breath, Satterwhite stalked off.

"And anyway," Maddie continued, stopping beside Ash and the ruined wheel, "I'm more concerned about how stable the wagon is." She frowned at the huge rock propped beneath the end of the axle where the wheel had been attached. "It looks rather precarious."

Ash refrained from giving the wagon a hard shove just to prove her wrong. But it had taken all his strength and a stout log to lever the wagon out of the mud so Satterwhite could roll the rock under it, and he was in no mood to go through that a second time. Besides, his side hurt like hell. "It will be fine for one night, lass. If I leave this afternoon, I should be back by tomorrow night. It should take no more than a day to repair the hub."

Or perhaps, two, if he had to wait for a new one to be made. Which might not be that bad a thing. For surely, even in a remote trading post, there would be a warm bath, a warm meal, and a warm room to let. Anxious to reach it and get out of his mud-caked clothes, he turned to his wife with a smile. "So give us a kiss, love, and off I go."

She reared back, her eyes wide. "W-What?"

"A kiss and a hug. Just in case."

"So now it's a hug, too? And in case of what?"

"One never knows." When she still dinna move, he opened his arms wide. "For auld lang syne, then. Luck. Good-bye. Come, lass." He wiggled his fingers and smiled encouragingly. "One wee kiss."

"Well . . ."

Actually, it wasna wee, at all. And not only because he wrapped his arms so tight around her she couldn't move. But because his sweet, loving wife kissed him back, and took such time and care in the doing of it, he still couldn't sit his saddle comfortably for an hour after he left . . . which was about the same time Tricks caught up to him and it started to rain again.

Seven

"That monster dog of his has run off." Mr. Satterwhite dumped an armload of wood beside the fire, then brushed his hands down the front of his wet duster. "Hope we'll survive with only me to look out for us."

Maddie tilted her parasol toward the back so the rain dripped on her oiled canvas jacket rather than puddling in her lap. "I'm sure he meant no insult."

"Oh, I'm sure he did. It's no wonder you ran off and left him. Damned foreigner—oops, excuse me, missy."

Maddie wasn't certain if the apology was for the coarse language or because he had directed it at foreigners—of which she was one. "I didn't run off and leave him. He left me."

"To return to his regiment, you said. Did he have a choice, then?"

Maddie felt her conscience nipping at her but willed it away. "Perhaps not. But he could have written." Or had Ridgeway write.

With a deep groan, the old man settled on a rock beside the sputtering flames. Leaning forward, he stirred a pot bubbling on the coals—some sort of stew, seasoned with jerky, potatoes, carrots, and their last onion. It almost smelled good enough to eat.

"But not everybody can read and write, missy. With these crooked eyes of mine, I sure never learned the knack."

"I'm sorry for that, Mr. Satterwhite. But I assure you Lord Ashby could have sent more than two letters in all those years. He was educated in Edinburgh, after all."

Oddly, she took pride in that accomplishment, knowing now how difficult it must have been in light of his affliction. "The University of Edinburgh has been called the seat of Scottish Enlightenment, you know."

"The seat. Well, that explains a lot."

Maddie chose not to respond to that. Instead, she watched rain sizzle in the coals and tried not to listen to that voice in her head. The one preaching sin. Telling her that the wonderful kiss she had shared earlier with Ash didn't have to be the end of it.

But it could be the *beginning* of the end. Perhaps if she gave in to these wild urges she could put the man out of her mind and her heart forever.

She almost laughed aloud at the absurdity of that. She had scarcely been able to do that when he was six years and half a world away. How was she to put him out of her thoughts when he was within arm's reach?

Thankful for the concealing rain, she brushed a hand over her stinging eyes. As soon as she was back among her friends in Heartbreak Creek, she would feel better. They would give her the strength to resist this foolish infatuation. And yet, weak creature that she was, on the next breath she was wondering if he had made it to the outpost before the rain started—if his side was hurting him—if he was thinking about that kiss, too.

She was beyond hopeless.

With a weary sigh, she pulled the canvas jacket tighter and wondered if this rain would ever cease. It had begun again not long after Ash had left, but had soon slowed to a relentless, misty drizzle. Clouds hung so low they draped the treetops, and even the mules that stood shivering under the wide boughs of a tall spruce seemed disheartened. It was a wretched evening to be sitting outside beside a steaming fire. She would have much preferred to be in her snug wagon with Agnes. But Mr. Satterwhite, out of some misguided concern for her reputation, had refused to come inside with her and out of the rain. And since she didn't want to leave him out here cooking supper all alone, here she sat.

"Did you ever write to him, missy?"

So they were back to that again. "Several times. But when he didn't respond, I stopped." She tried to remember what she had written, and how many *p*s, and *q*s, and *d*s, and *t*s, and *f*s she had used.

"So you gave up." He said it as if she'd done something wrong.

Sweeping a clump of wet hair out of her eyes, she turned to look at him. "You think I should have continued to write to a man who couldn't be bothered to write back?" Or have someone else do it for him?

"He might have been a tad busy, being a soldier and all."

"I cannot believe you're defending a man you called a *damned foreigner* only five minutes ago."

"Well, he is a damned foreigner—pardon my language. But he's still—overall—a good man."

First Agnes and now Mr. Satterwhite. She felt utterly abandoned.

"Can't believe you'd leave the man just because he wouldn't write you letters," he muttered, idly massaging the muscles of his left arm.

"It was more complicated than that."

He watched her, waiting.

"I was"—she paused, trying to find the kindest words, then decided on honesty—"a disappointment to his family. I'm English. One of the oppressors." She said it in a derisive tone, although in truth, after the Clearances, the Scots might have had ample reason for their animosity toward the English. "In addition, my father was possessed of no great fortune. They wanted a Scottish woman from a more lofty family, preferably one who could bring either land or wealth to the family. Add to that my 'ill-bred and unladylike' passion for photography, along with my father's democratic ideas, and ours was not the hoped-for alliance."

"Yet His Majesty chose you. In spite of what his family wanted."

"Well . . . yes."

That admission clung to the back of Maddie's throat like the taint of sour milk. She had made so many misjudgments, it seems.

"What about your own family?"

Realizing she had worried a thread loose on the lapel of her jacket, Maddie pulled her hand away. "I am an only child. My parents died in a carriage mishap two years ago. After I went to London to settle their affairs, I simply never returned to Scotland.

"Just like that? You just walked away?"

She could feel his censure. It made her defensive. "And what should I have done? A family who barely acknowledged my presence and a husband who hadn't come home or written in over two years—what reason had I to stay?" Hearing the self-pity behind her words, she tried to deflect it with a laugh to show that their indifference had had little impact on her. But it sounded brittle and false even in her own ear.

"My defection, if you will, was unplanned," she went on. "While I was in London, a friend suggested I take my photographs to her uncle, who was publisher of a London periodical. He liked them and asked if I would be interested in spending a year or two photographing the West from a woman's perspective. He even said he would pay me."

"When was that?"

"September of sixty-eight."

"Two years ago."

The unspoken message was clear. It was time to go back.

"Did you tell His Majesty of your plans?"

"I wrote to his family, told them I was leaving for a while, and instructed them to pass the message along if Lord Ashby should ask." But how could he? she realized, that twinge of conscience now gnawing in earnest. Lying injured in his hospital bed, Major Ridgeway no longer there to write for him, and unwilling to risk ridicule to ask help from someone else? Still, he could have sent word . . . somehow. "It was a wonderful opportunity, Mr. Satterwhite. The dream of a lifetime."

"Then why are you crying, missy?"

Surprised, Maddie lifted a hand and felt wetness on her cheek. She quickly blotted it away. "It's raining, if you haven't noticed."

"Oh, I've noticed," he muttered, rubbing his arm again. "But here's the thing. You can't spend the rest of your life hiding behind your camera. You've got to start living life. Go home with His Majesty—or make him stay here—just do something. I can't be carting you around forever. It's hard work and I'm getting too old for it."

"Don't be silly." Maddie gave a scoffing laugh to cover how deeply his words had hurt her. *Hiding?* Was that all her work amounted to? "You're not old, Mr. Satterwhite. Seasoned, perhaps. A man of great vigor—"

"I'm seventy-three. That's way past vigor."

Something in his voice caught her attention. Pushing her hurt aside, she studied him from beneath the brim of her parasol. He did look tired. The day had been a difficult one. And seeing the way he winced as he rubbed his left hand made her wonder if he had injured himself while helping Ash with the wheel. "Are you well, Mr. Satterwhite?" she asked, growing concerned. "Is your hand hurting you?"

"No. In fact, it's a bit numb. Probably the cold. And don't try to change the subject and think I won't notice."

"What subject?" Even though she tried to make a jest of it, she was becoming more worried by the minute. She shouldn't have insisted Mr. Satterwhite come on this trip. She should have hired someone else. But she had always felt so safe with her old friend— heavens, hadn't she just blurted out the whole sorry tale of her disastrous marriage, something she had only recently shared with the ladies in Heartbreak Creek? The fact was, Mr. Satterwhite had become more than a friend and confidant. Over the months, she had come to think of him as a substitute father.

But looking at him now, she could see she had been selfish in the extreme to have pushed him so hard. "Have I done you a disservice, Mr. Satterwhite? Should I have let you rest this one out?"

He gave a bark of laughter that ended in a cough. "And leave me sitting outside the assay office playing checkers with that old cheat, Chalmers? Not on your life. These last few months . . ." His voice faltered.

He looked into the fire, blinking hard, the quiver in his whiskered chin betraying his emotion. "I wouldn't have missed them for the world, missy."

Maddie heard the good-bye in his voice and wanted to weep. How would she manage without his steady presence, his kindness, his wry humor . . . even his wretched cooking? Reaching out, she put her hand on his shoulder. "Nor I, Wilfred. You've been a god-send."

He turned his head away, but not before she saw the glitter of tears in his faded, crooked eyes. "What I'm trying to say, missy," he went on in a gruff voice, "is that I'm getting too old to be spending my days on that hard driver's bench and my nights on the cold ground. You need a younger, stronger man to look out for you and keep you safe."

"I need you."

"You need your husband. And a life that'll amount to more than a collection of tintypes in some dusty book on a stranger's shelf. And that's all I'll say about that." Leaning forward, he wrapped his kerchief around the handle and lifted the stew pot from the fire. "Supper's ready, Your Majesty. Grab a plate."

With a sigh of contentment, Ash tipped his head back against the high rim of the oversized wooden tub and closed his eyes. Steam curled about his head, dampening his eyelashes and beading on his freshly shaven face. On the other side of the drape, the voices of other patrons of Mrs. Renfroe's Chinese Laundry and Bathhouse faded to a distant, low rumble, punctuated now and then by a woman's soft laughter. He could almost feel the hot water loosening the knotted muscles in his back and legs, and soaking away the ache in his side from his long, wet ride.

He must have dozed off, because the next thing he heard was a dog's low growl. Opening his eyes, he saw a scantily clad woman standing just inside the drape, holding a bottle of amber liquid in one hand, two shot glasses in the other, and staring in horrified disbelief at the wolfhound stretched on the floor beside the tub.

"What's that?" she asked.

"A dog." He pointed at the bottle in her grip. "What's that?"

"Whiskey. Does he bite?"

"If he must. Scotch whiskey?"

"Rye."

Ash sighed and pushed himself upright, sending a splash of water over the edge of the tub. "Beggars canna be choosers, I suppose. Pour a wee dram for us both, lass, and we'll send up a toast to our fallen brothers."

"I don't got no brothers." Still eyeing Tricks, she edged into the room, her bare feet slapping on the wet floor. "I'm Betty. Some call me Betty Will, but it's really Williams. What kind of dog?"

"Wolfhound."

She was young. Too young to have such weary eyes. Ash had seen a thousand such faces—in every port, every camp, behind every supply train that followed the troops. As common in a soldier's life as flies.

Stopping beside the tub, she filled a glass and bent to pass it over, giving him a fine view down the front of her corset. "You talk funny," she said, moving back to perch on the edge of the tub. "Not from around here, I'm guessing."

Ash tossed back the whiskey, shuddered, then held up the glass for more. "Scottish by birth, British by law, Highlander by the grace of God."

"That up by Denver?"

"Just east of it." He downed his second drink, licked lips that were already going pleasantly numb, and handed back the glass.

"My thanks, lass." He settled back, sending another wave over the rim.

"You want company?" Smiling coyly, she drew a tattered corset string through grimy fingers with nails chewed to the quick. "I'll show you a real good time."

Ash tried to imagine it but could only picture Maddie's flushed face, her lips pink and swollen from his kiss, her eyes slightly out of focus, and her fine, clean body pressed against his. Would he truly quash that passionate nature if he took her back to Scotland? Was there not some way they could reach a compromise?

"It's fifty-cent night," Betty said, cutting into his thoughts. "A dollar would get you the bottle, too. How 'bout it?"

He put on a regretful smile. Despite her youth, the poor lass had probably been cocked more times than his carbine. He wanted no part of that, especially with a woman like Maddie waiting. "Tempting, love, but not today."

"Tomorrow, then?"

"I'll be gone tomorrow." At least he hoped he would.

When he had explained his specifications for a replacement wheel, the blacksmith had allowed that he had a forty-two by two-inch steam-bent hickory wheel out back somewhere, but it needed repairs on the hub. To Ash's inquiry about how long that would take, the dour man had replied he would get it done when he got it done. Maybe tomorrow. Maybe not.

Ash was not surprised to learn the man was Scottish.

After leaving the smithy, he had gone to the only hotel in town, secured a room, then had come here to Mrs. Renfroe's for a shave, a bath, and a change of clothes—and apparently a rogering, if one's standards were sufficiently low—which his were not.

Tossing Betty a coin for the whiskey, he sent her on her way.

An hour later, after dousing a vigorously protesting Tricks in his bathwater, he and the wolfhound left the bathhouse, clean, refreshed, and mostly dry. Standing on the boardwalk, he looked around.

The rain had dwindled to a fine mist, and other than the lights shining through the windows of the vice palace at one end of the street and the hotel at the other, the town looked deserted.

Hoping the kitchen was still open, he crossed to the hotel, which also housed the only eating establishment in Becker's Fort.

Naturally, Tricks caused a stir when they entered the dining room. But after Ash explained that the dog might get upset if they were separated, and promising that they would both behave, they were allowed inside. The meal was surprisingly good, even if the meat was suspect. After enjoying two plates each, he and Tricks went upstairs, where he watched spiderwebs flutter from the ceiling over his bed and tried to figure out how he could convince his wife to trade in her camera for a life with him in Scotland.

Maddie stood in the dark beside the remaining front wheel, hands on hips, and struggled to keep her voice from betraying her exasperation. "Mr. Satterwhite," she called up to the old man teetering on tiptoe as he struggled to attach a length of canvas to the overhanging roof above the driver's box. "I must insist you stay inside tonight. It is far too cold and damp out here and I know you're not feeling well."

He muttered something she didn't catch.

"Or we can set up the tent."

"And have the wagon fall over on me in the night? No thanks."

"Then as I've said innumerable times," she went on at increased volume, "if you won't set up the tent, and you're not comfortable staying with me in the back of the wagon, I will be happy to take the driver's bench for the night."

"Will you?" He peered over the side of the wagon. "And will your oversized husband be happy when he returns to find you sleeping out here in the cold and me cozying up in your bed?" He squinted an eye at her. "The bed he's not even allowed in, I might add."

"Oh, bother." She waved the notion aside. "That doesn't signify in the least since he's not truly my husband."

"No?"

Taking a moment to pluck a wet curl from her cheek, Maddie struggled to maintain composure. "What I mean to say, Mr. Satterwhite," she continued in a less strident tone, "is that Lord Ashby and I are estranged. And he will certainly understand the necessity of your moving into the wagon. I'm sure he wouldn't want you to become ill, either."

"You're right about that," he agreed, turning back to his task. "He'll want me hale and hearty when he snaps my neck."

"He would do no such thing! Lord Ashby is a gentleman."

"So now you're defending him?"

Maddie threw up her hands. "Fine! Sleep out here, if that is your wish! But don't come coughing to me when you wake up with a chill."

"That's a promise."

Contentious curmudgeon.

Somewhere in the distance a wolf or coyote or some such howled, which brought an answering yip from Agnes in the back of the wagon. At least the rain had stopped for a while. Maisy and Buttercup had moved from beneath their sheltering spruce canopy to graze in the meadow, and stars were peeking through the tattered clouds. If it continued to clear, the temperature would probably drop below freezing.

Too weary to continue a losing argument, Maddie sighed in defeat. "How many more blankets would you like?"

"Three if you got 'em."

As the weather promised, it was a long, cold night. Maddie spent most of it huddled under the covers, either worrying about Ash or worrying about Mr. Satterwhite. At least she knew Mr. Satterwhite was all right, since his whiffling snore could be heard quite clearly through the wood partition that separated the driver's box from the back of the wagon. But Ash could have gotten lost or been accosted by a wild animal, or upon reaching his destination, found that Becker's Fort was little more than a ghost town. He could even be ill from riding so far in the cold rain.

You twit. He had survived six years without her worrying about him. He could certainly make it through one more night. Not that she was worrying, of course.

Flopping over onto her back, she pulled the pillow over her head to muffle sound, and prayed that morning would come soon, lest she stuff a pillow over Mr. Satterwhite's snoring head, too.

She awoke to frosted windowpanes and someone calling her name. She rolled over, blinking in confusion, wondering if she had actually heard a voice, or if it was another of those unidentifiable sounds Mr. Satterwhite made in his sleep.

Agnes crawled out from under the covers and yawned, her ears pricked toward the door. Still only half awake, Maddie leaned up on her elbows and listened.

There it was again. Muffled. Weak. "Missy."

Alarmed, she flipped back the covers and stepped to the window. Wiping the frost away, she peered out.

At first she saw little but the fog of her own breath. Then she noticed movement on the other side of the smoking fire. Mr. Satterwhite, his hands clutching his chest. As she watched, he sagged to the ground.

Whipping a blanket off the bed, she threw it around her shoulders, yanked on her walking boots, and raced from the wagon.

"Mr. Satterwhite," she shouted, almost slipping on the icy grass as she ran to kneel at his side. "Wilfred, can you hear me?"

His face contorted in pain. His fingers grabbed at his chest. "Missy."

She fluttered around him, wanting to help, but not knowing what to do. "What's wrong? Talk to me."

He gasped for air, his crooked eyes wild and unfocused, his back arching off the ground. "Jesus." It was a long, hissing exhalation that ended abruptly. He sank back. His fingers relaxed. Slowly, his hand slid off his chest to flop, palm up, on the frosted ground.

Silence.

Oh God.

Maddie knew. But it was too sudden. Too shocking. She didn't want to believe it. "Mr. Satterwhite!" She gave his shoulder a hard shove. "Wilfred!"

He didn't respond. Didn't blink. What color was left in his whiskered face began to fade away.

"Wilfred! Say something!"

He didn't. And that loosened a wave of terror that burst from her mouth in a torrent of angry words. "Come back! Don't you dare leave me!" Grabbing his shoulders, she shook him so hard the back of his head made a soft thump when it struck the earth. "Wake up! Wake up now!" She shoved hard against his chest.

A sound burst out of his slack mouth. Startled, she lurched back, almost tumbling onto the frozen ground. Hardly daring to breathe, she watched him, waiting for him to rise up.

He didn't. And she knew then that the sound he had made was just air escaping his lungs when she had pushed on his chest. He was gone. Pressing both hands to her mouth, she rocked back and forth, her mind numb with despair. *Please, Wilfred. Come back. Don't leave me.*

But she knew.

And this time she couldn't deny it.

Lifting her face to the clear, sunlit sky, she cried out in anguish, startling the mules and sending a squirrel chattering through the branches. Then strength left her and she dropped her face into her hands and wept. For him. For her. For all the unspoken words she had meant to say.

After a while, the chill reached through the blanket and her thin nightdress, and she began to shiver. She tried to rise, but she had knelt for so long her legs had gone numb. When she finally managed to stand, Agnes got tangled in her feet, almost making her fall on Mr. Satterwhite.

For a moment, she stood blinking down at him through her tears, not sure what she should do. Try to drag him into the wagon? She would never get him up the steps. Bury him? In the frozen ground? No, she would wait for Ash. He would know what to do.

Her stomach churning, she bent down and closed his lids and

jaw. He felt so cold. Even knowing nothing would warm him now, she pulled the blanket from her shoulders and laid it over his body.

The draped mound looked smaller than she would have expected. Not quite real. Not really true. But when she saw the pale tips of his fingers showing at the edge of the blanket, she knew it was true and her friend was gone, and she had never had a chance to tell him good-bye. The reality of that was like a fist against her chest.

Blinded by tears, she stumbled to the wagon and collapsed on her bed, her mind whirling with useless regrets. After she had cried herself out, she rose and dressed in her warmest flannel underskirts, her work dress, and wool stockings. Then she sat at her tiny vanity and pinned up her hair.

She wanted it to look nice. She wasn't sure why. Perhaps to honor her friend. Perhaps because she dreaded going back out there and doing what she knew needed to be done. But her hands were shaking so badly it wasn't as neat as she would have liked. Finally unable to delay longer, she donned her heavy coat and kid gloves, called Agnes, and left the wagon.

She had a time of it removing the canvas drape from over the driver's bench, and ended up losing her temper and yanking on it so hard the cloth ripped on one corner. The violence of it released some of the pain and gave her a false strength that kept her moving.

She spread the canvas beside Mr. Satterwhite then removed the blanket she had draped over him. She was glad she wore gloves now because he looked pale and waxy, except where his skin was beginning to mottle, and she feared she might cast up her accounts if she had to touch his dead flesh. Yet as ghastly as it was, the sight of his deterioration helped, because he no longer looked like her friend. Mr. Satterwhite was gone now; she was simply cleaning up behind him.

Once she had rolled him up in the canvas, she folded the loose ends over his head and feet so that every part of him was covered, then cut lengths of rope and tied them around him to hold the canvas in place. As she straightened, she saw that the sun was high overhead. Half the day had passed and she hadn't untethered the mules, or put wood on the fire, or fed Agnes. The thought of eating anything, herself, was so repugnant it made her stomach roll.

Glad to stay busy, she tended those duties, and soon had a fire crackling and a stack of wood ready beside it. The normalcy of such mundane tasks soothed her, insulated her from the chilling reality of the dead body lying on the other side of the fire. But as that first wave of shock and grief began to recede, the enormity of her predicament began to penetrate her numb mind.

She was utterly and completely alone in an isolated spot away from the road, with few supplies left, a broken wagon, and only a tiny dog, a scattergun, and a near-useless palm pistol for protection. If Ash didn't come before dark, the animals would.

They would come for Mr. Satterwhite.

A new kind of terror engulfed her, filling her mind with such horrific images her mind started to spin. It took all her strength to bring the fear back down so she could think again.

Ash would come. He would return soon and take care of everything.

Clinging desperately to that thought, she went back for her weapons, just in case a creature came nosing about. She debated staying inside where she would be safe and warm until Ash came. But how could she leave Mr. Satterwhite out there alone?

Shaking but resolved, she gathered up her weapons and a blanket, and went back to the fire. After positioning her chair upwind of the smoke, she set the loaded guns within reach, stoked the flames, then sat with a blanket over her shoulders and Agnes on her lap to await Ash's return.

It shouldn't be long. He said he would only be gone a night and a day, and there weren't many hours in the day left. He was probably already on his way and would come riding through those trees any moment now. He would come back to her like he said. He wouldn't let her down this time.

· · ·

"Tomorrow!" Ash gave the smithy his most intimidating scowl. "I need it sooner!"

The beefy man retreated a step, hands upraised. "Takes that long for the hub to set up. Then I have to seat the spokes and tack on the metal rim. Otherwise, wouldn't last ten miles."

Ash bit back a string of curses. He'd told Maddie he'd be back by dark. Now it would be another day. *Bluidy hell.* He dinna like leaving her with just an old man to look out for her. This colder weather would bring all sorts of predators down from the high country. Bears, mountain lions, wolves. He'd seen in the Crimea the damage wolves could do, and how when they hunted in a pack they could take down anything on two legs or four. "If it's ready by daybreak," he told the blacksmith, "I'll pay you double."

At least Maddie could shoot, he consoled himself as he headed back to the hotel. And with Satterwhite and his repeater, she would be well protected. Still, it worried him.

He glared down at Tricks, trotting happily at his side. "You should have stayed with her, you mangy cur. If anything happens to her, I'll sell you to the Chinamen, so I will." Leaning down, he added sternly, "And they eat dogs."

As he straightened, he realized what he'd done. Threatened his loyal companion over a woman who, up until a few days ago, he hadn't even been sure was still alive. The same woman who had deserted him and led him on a merry chase across an ocean and half a continent. A woman who dinna even want him.

"She's doing it to me, again," he muttered to Tricks. "Just like six years ago, when she made me cast aside good sense and my family's blessing, and enticed me to stay with her longer than I should. Which almost cost me a promotion, so it did. And all because of one wee kiss and a smile. But not this time, Tricks. This time I willna let her weave her spells about me. I promise you that."

Tricks looked up at him, his dark eyes round and sad.

Ash sighed and ruffled the dog's wiry brows. "You're right, lad. But I can at least try."

Eight

When the last of the sun finally slipped behind the trees and plunged the small clearing into twilight gloom, Maddie's spirits sank with it.

Ash wasn't coming back.

She should have known. The man's promises were as substantial as the smoke rising from the fire. She had to accept that. Still, it hurt—hurt almost as much as Mr. Satterwhite's passing, for in a way it, too, was a death—of hope, of faith. She had actually begun to believe that despite their rough beginning, Ash was coming to care for her. How foolish was that?

Furiously, she swiped a hand over her burning eyes. *Well, no more.* She had shed her last tear over that man.

An animal cried out, startling her. The sound was barely heard over the babble of the creek nearby, so she wasn't sure what it was—a squirrel, maybe even a bird. But it served to remind her that she couldn't dwell on Ash's desertion now. She had a night to get through and a plan to devise that would allow her to salvage what she could from the wagon and get back to Heartbreak Creek. But first . . .

She glanced over at the canvas-wrapped body on the other side of the fire. First, she had to figure out what to do with Mr. Satterwhite, because she certainly wasn't going to leave him to the animals. She owed him more care than that.

She supposed she could suspend him from a tree like they did their supplies. Loop a rope around him, throw the other end over a sturdy branch, then use Maisy to hoist him up. An excellent plan if she hadn't cut up the rope to bind the canvas around Mr. Satterwhite's body. And besides, she thought, looking around, she wasn't sure where the mules were. She had been too distraught earlier to restake their pickets, thinking they wouldn't wander far. They probably hadn't, but she didn't have time to go chasing after them. The sun was sinking fast and she needed to tend to Mr. Satterwhite while there was still sufficient light.

That left burying him. With sunshine throughout the day, the ground had probably thawed enough to make digging possible. He was too heavy to move far, so she would have to dig right where he was now—close to the fire and the light, and where the ground would be warmest.

"Off you go," she said, shooing Agnes from her lap. Rising on cold-stiffened legs, she went to the storage box on the underside of the wagon to get the shovel.

The light lasted about as long as her gloves did. This close to the creek, the dirt was littered with river rocks, from round, fist-sized stones to others almost too heavy to lift. After an hour of hacking at the earth, she had dug a hole barely big enough to hold her valise, much less a human being. Her back was a mass of cramping muscles, blisters were already forming beneath her shredded gloves, and she was almost out of firewood.

Throwing down the shovel in disgust, she grabbed her scatter-gun, dumped a handful of cartridges into her jacket pocket, and tromped into the trees, hoping Mr. Satterwhite hadn't already scavenged all the available wood. Agnes trotted ahead of her, sniffing here, piddling there, and almost tripping Maddie in the growing gloom. No sign of the mules. Luckily she found ample wood, although most of it was damp from the rain. After several trips back and forth, she had a substantial pile drying beside the fire.

As darkness descended, the temperature dropped. Knowing she would stay warmer if she were active, she picked up the shovel and resumed digging. Slowly, the hole grew—as did her blisters—until finally it was too dark to see and her hands could take no more.

So discouraged and weary she wanted to weep, Maddie forced herself to stay calm so she could think clearly. She considered her options. There were only two: Give up, retreat to the wagon, and let the animals have Mr. Satterwhite. Or stay out here by the fire, standing guard over him with her scattergun until daylight, then come up with another plan.

With a sigh, she draped a blanket around her head and shoulders and set her guns within reach. Then pulling her chair as close to the fire as she dared, she cuddled Agnes in her lap and settled in to await the morning.

It was a beautiful, moonless night, so crisp and clear the stars seemed to hang just above the treetops. Occasionally, odd streaks of light would shoot up in wavy spikes behind the trees to the north, then fade, then rise again, sometimes with a greenish hue, or even a blue. At first, she thought it might be someone coming—perhaps a wagon with a night lantern swinging from a hook. But though she listened hard, she heard no sound other than the rushing creek, and after a while, the streaks faded.

Later—she didn't know how long—Agnes awoke her when she jumped off her lap and ran, barking, toward the brush by the creek. Drowsy and disoriented, Maddie lurched to her feet, almost tripping over the blanket. "Agnes," she called, grabbing the scattergun. "Agnes, come away from there!"

Agnes continued on, her yips growing more distant as she moved along the creek. With shaking hands, Maddie made sure both barrels of the scattergun were loaded, and worked the lever. Then remembering the repeating rifle Mr. Satterwhite had kept beneath the driver's box, she raced toward the wagon. After retrieving the gun and a box of bullets, she climbed back down just as Agnes came squealing out of the brush.

And she wasn't alone. Behind her raced a lean, snarling form.

A wolf.

With a cry, Maddie dropped the rifle and lifted the loaded scattergun to her shoulder. "Agnes!"

The little dog veered, changing direction faster than her larger pursuer could. Yelping in terror, she tore toward Maddie, nails clawing up wet earth, her tail tucked tight against her belly.

At the sound of Maddie's voice, the wolf stopped. Then head low, it began to circle, its nostrils flaring as it assessed this new threat.

Maddie tracked it with the gun, her hands gripping the stock so tightly her arms shook. She could hear it panting. Could see the glitter of firelight reflected red in its eyes.

"Go away!" she shouted, her voice shrill with terror, the scattergun wobbling against her cheek.

The wolf dropped to a crouch. Those unblinking eyes studied her for a moment, then shifted to Agnes, cowering by Maddie's skirts.

A low snarl. Lips pulling back from long, yellow teeth.

Then it lunged.

Maddie squeezed both triggers. The impact threw her back against the side of the wagon. Acrid smoke stung her nose and eyes. Ears ringing, she frantically dug in her pocket for more cartridges, then saw the wolf was down, biting at a dark, wet crater in its chest, its legs thrashing in the dirt.

The twitching slowed, then stopped.

She slumped against the wagon, trembling and lightheaded, a whimper rising in her throat. She had never before shot at anything but targets, and seeing the dead creature sprawled at her feet gave her a feeling of both triumph and revulsion.

Agnes's whine brought her out of her frozen state. She whipped around, looking for other figures lurking in the shadows, but saw none. Yet wolves rarely traveled alone. More could be coming and she had to be ready. In sudden and unreasoning flight, she tossed the guns back into the driver's box, grabbed Agnes, and tossed her up, too. "You silly fool," she scolded, climbing up beside her. "Next time you run off, I'll let them have you. See if I don't."

With shaking hands, she reloaded the scattergun, muttering

against the darkness and her blistered hands. "We can't sit up here all night," she told the dog shivering at her side. "It's cold and I left the blankets by the fire."

Besides, she needed the light to figure out how the rifle worked. She knew the bullets—didn't Mr. Satterwhite say it held fifteen rounds?—went into a tube beneath the barrel, but she couldn't see well enough to open it. She assumed the lever was like the one on the scattergun, and when worked out and back, would send a bullet into firing position. If she could get it loaded, the repeater would be much better protection than a two-shot scattergun. As would the fire.

She listened and looked around but heard only the sound of the rushing water in the creek. Nothing moved in the shadows. Knowing Agnes would be safer and less troublesome in the wagon, Maddie scooped her up, collected the guns, and hopped to the ground. Half expecting to be leaped on from behind, she ran to the back of the wagon. When she made it safely, she seriously considered staying inside.

But Mr. Satterwhite was out there. Alone.

"You can do this," she chanted as she gathered her guns and more blankets. Then locking Agnes inside, she went back to her chair by the fire.

"I hope you see what I'm doing for you, Mr. Satterwhite," she muttered, once she was settled and both guns were loaded and ready at her side. "I might not have told you as often as I should how much I appreciated you, but surely sitting out here in the cold all night while keeping the wolves at bay will partially make up for that lack."

He didn't respond, but an owl somewhere in the trees did. Maddie studied the bushes where the wolf had chased out Agnes, but saw nothing.

The darkness pressed closer, stripping the night of all but cold, still air and the sound of the creek. She looked up, seeking reassurance from the stars overhead, and almost wept with gratitude when she realized a late-rising quarter moon had arrived to push back the dark.

The heavens rotated and the temperature dropped. She tossed more wood onto the fire and pulled the blanket tighter around her head.

Weariness tugged at her, and more than once she found herself jerking awake in the chair to find the fire low and her body shivering with cold. As the hours passed, her thoughts grew sluggish, her will weaker. Then she would remind herself how well Mr. Satterwhite had looked after her, and resolved she would do no less for him.

"Don't worry, Mr. Satterwhite," she said, trying to rub warmth back into her chilled arms. "I shan't leave you." She knew it was insane to be talking to someone hours gone. But she had never felt so alone or lonely, sitting here in the cold, in the middle of the night, with a dead companion for company and only a dim circle of firelight to hold the terrors at bay. It was unreal. Otherworldly. And hearing the sound of her own voice helped dispel the shadows crowding all around and reminded her that despite the presence of death, she was still among the living.

A wiser woman would have retreated into the safety of the wagon. After all, Mr. Satterwhite was dead. But he was her friend, too. And while she hadn't the chance to sit with her parents after they had died, she could at least do so for the man who had watched over her like a father.

"You were wrong about Ash," she said after a while. "He's not a dependable man—his absence tonight is proof of that. He could charm a bird out of the sky, yet was never there when I needed him. But you always were, weren't you, Mr. Satterwhite? I thank you for that."

The fire hissed and snapped and whistled like a living thing. Far away, coyotes howled, calling the pack to hunt. Picking up the rifle, she rested it across her lap and stared into the darkness.

"We were so taken with each other at first. I was only eighteen, you see. Defenseless against such a fine-looking officer in his dashing blue uniform. And that smile . . ." She shook her head, remembering. "How could a gullible country maid not fall in love with a face like that?"

She sighed and plucked at her tattered glove where the leather had stuck to a ruptured blister. "Why are men so inconstant, Mr. Satterwhite? Oh, not you, of course. You have been as steadfast as any friend could be. But other men. Handsome men like Ash. Is it due to some innate fickleness of heart, do you suppose? Or is the fault with we women who expect too much and are thus so easily disappointed?"

Feeling a warm trickle on her cheek, she reached up to brush a tear away. "How tiresome you must think me, Mr. Satterwhite, to weep over a man who scarcely remembered my name. But he was dear to me once. In truth, I fancied myself in love with the man, naïve creature that I was."

More tears, hot on her cold cheeks. They infuriated her, evidence of a weakness she couldn't put aside, and with a slash of her hand, she wiped them away. Steadying the rifle in her lap, she hiked her chin. "But you mustn't worry about me, Mr. Satterwhite. I shall be fine. I have my friends, and my work, and my pride—tattered though it is— and they will see me through. So rest easy, dear friend. I survived the rogue once, did I not? I shall certainly do so this time."

A noise caught her attention, and she looked over to see the low branches of a spruce flutter violently. Quickly shifting the rifle to ready position, she watched down the long barrel, breath caught in her throat.

A limb cracked as something ran through the brush. Something big, moving fast. Then suddenly, the branches parted, and a huge form burst into the clearing. Maddie almost fired, then recognized Buttercup, with Maisy crowded behind her. They ran past Maddie, then whirled and stared back the way they had come, heads high, nostrils flaring.

Maddie scanned the brush but saw nothing amiss. Releasing an explosive breath, she lowered the rifle from her shoulder but kept it ready in her lap. "You silly chits! Where have you been?"

They continued to stare at the shadows, ears pricked. But after a moment, even though Buttercup remained alert, Maisy lowered her head and began grazing on the frosted grass.

"I should shoot you both for frightening me that way!" Pressing a shaking hand over her thudding heart, Maddie slumped back in the chair. As she did, she saw that the trees were more distinct now, rising in sharp silhouettes against the eastern sky. She laughed out loud, the sound hoarse and wobbly and carrying a hint of hysteria.

More tears threatened, but this time they were tears of relief. "Look, Mr. Satterwhite," she said, pointing toward the heavens. "We made it. The new day has come."

A sudden prickling sensation alerted her. A sense of being watched. She froze, eyes straining against the dim light. Movement. A low growl. Shadows shifting, drawing closer.

The wolves had come, too.

Ash was on his way just after daybreak, the wheel strapped across his back. It was slow going at first, since the rim stuck out past his shoulders and above his head and kept getting hung up on low-hanging branches. But once the narrow track joined the wider road that led past the creek and meadow where he'd left the wagon, he was able to put Lurch into a ground-eating lope.

An hour later, as they started across the creek, the smell hit him. Not the putrid stench of a battlefield after the smoke has cleared and the burial parties are loading their carts. But the faint, yet unmistakable, reek of blood and the beginnings of decay. It was an odor familiar to every soldier, and smelling it now sent a jolt of panic through Ash.

He reined in on the other bank, struggled out of the rope harness, and heaved the wheel into the brush, startling Lurch into a hopping sidestep.

"Find!" he ordered Tricks as he leaped to the ground. But the wolfhound was already disappearing into the brush, hackles up, head low.

With shaking hands, Ash retrieved his pistol from his saddlebag and checked the load. Not wanting to take time to load the Enfield, he pulled the short double-edged bayonet from its sheath inside his boot, and armed with both blade and gun, ran after Tricks. Dreading what he might find, he stopped just inside the trees and quickly scanned the clearing.

Other than a pile of rocks and canvas beside the fire ring, the camp looked no different from when he'd left. No sign of the mules or Satterwhite. Maddie sat slumped in her chair beside the cold fire,

Satterwhite's repeater in her slack hands. No blood. Asleep? He saw no movement except for Tricks and Agnes at the edge of the brush on the other side of the clearing.

He returned the blade to his boot and ran toward his wife.

At the sound of his approach, she jerked awake, the rifle coming up.

Ash grabbed the barrel as it swung toward him, but when he tried to pull it from her grip, she fought him, a whimper rising in her throat.

"Maddie, 'tis me. 'Tis Ash. Let go of the gun."

"Have they come back?" She looked frantically around, her eyes wild. "Are they here?"

He shifted to follow her gaze, and saw Tricks nosing a crumpled form by the edge of the woods. Not human. Dark, smaller than a bear. A wolf? Another lay near the wagon. Definitely a wolf. *Bluidy hell.* And where was Satterwhite?

As he swung back to Maddie, his gaze fell on the pile of rocks and canvas on the other side of the fire pit. Not a pile. A canvas-wrapped form and a half-dug grave. He realized then what had happened—Satterwhite had died—the wolves had been drawn to the scent of death—Maddie had held them off to protect her dead friend. Had he not done the same thing during that grisly winter at Sevastopol when the wolves had poured nightly out of the hills to feast on the day's dead?

Setting the pistol nearby on a rock, he went down on one knee beside the chair, his hand still on the barrel of the rifle. "It's over, love. You and Satterwhite are safe now. I'm here."

"Ash?"

"Aye. 'Tis me." This time she dinna resist when he took the gun from her hands and set it aside. "Are you hurt, lass?"

"You didn't come back."

"I did. I'm right beside you, so I am. Are you hurt?"

"My h-hands." That wild look was starting to fade from her eyes, but he could tell she was still confused by the way she looked at her shaking hands as if seeing them for the first time. She was wearing gloves, torn in places and showing dark stains on the worn leather. "I have bl-blisters."

"Let me see, love." He tried to be gentle, but the leather had dried to her crusted skin, so he had to pull to loosen it. When he finally got the gloves off and saw the ruin of her hands, he had to work hard to keep his voice calm. "Tell me what happened, Maddie."

"Mr. Satterwhite died." Her voice wobbled on the words. "His heart, I think. It happened so fast. He just fell. I tried to bury him, bu-but I couldn't. I didn't even have a chance to say good-bye."

As she spoke, he pulled out his handkerchief, ripped it in two and carefully wrapped the pieces around her hands to keep out dirt until he could clean them properly. "You got these blisters from digging?"

"There were so many rocks. I tried. I did. But I-I couldn't. So I waited for you." She looked up at him, her brown eyes glittering and wet. "But you never came. Why?"

Not trusting his voice, he said nothing and continued binding her hands. He felt a tremor move through her. Then another. Her breathing changed, and after he tied off the wrapping, he looked up to see the bleakness in her eyes had been replaced by such fury it was like a slap in the face.

"What took you so long?" she accused. "You said it would only be a day and a night. Why didn't you come back?" With each word, her voice had risen and the shaking had grown worse.

Sitting back on his heels, he watched her and waited. He'd often seen such violent reactions in young soldiers once the rush and horror of battle was past, and he knew it would eventually play itself out.

Still, he was surprised when she hit him.

"Why aren't you ever here when I need you?" She hit him again, apparently oblivious to the pain it must have brought to her injured hands. Tears were running down her face now, and her words were so garbled it was difficult for him to make them out. But the rage was unmistakable.

"You weren't here when Mr. Satterwhite died—or when my parents died—or when I lost the baby. You're never around when I need you!"

Baby? What baby?

Afraid she might further hurt herself, Ash leaned up and put his arms around her, trapping her against his chest. "Ssh, lass," he whispered against her ear. "You're safe. I'm here now."

She began to sob, great, wrenching cries that made her whole body shudder. "No! You aren't! You never have been!"

She fought him for a moment more, then as abruptly as the rage had come, it just as quickly burned itself out. Weeping, she slumped against him—not so much in surrender, as in defeat, which Ash knew were two verra different things.

He rose, lifted her from the chair, and carried her to the wagon. After stripping off her jacket and boots, he loosened the collar of her dress, then helped her into the bed, covering her shivering body with the quilt.

She dinna fight him, dinna speak. But her drooping eyes never left him, and the defiance he saw in them was clear: their first skirmish might have ended, but a war still raged in her head.

By the time he'd gotten the wee stove going, she was asleep.

Straightening as best he could in the cramped, low-ceilinged quarters, he studied her. Her eyes looked bruised. Dirt streaked her cheeks, following the path of long-dried tears. Her hair was a knot of auburn tangles around her ashen face. Poor lass. She looked like a discarded doll, roughly used and cast aside by a careless hand.

Something unfamiliar clenched in his chest. Regret, remorse, maybe even pity. He should have taken better care of her. She was his wife and he had failed her too many times.

Disgusted with himself, he turned and left the wagon.

Moving through habits so engrained he dinna give them a thought, he retrieved Lurch and the wheel from where he'd left them in the brush, unsaddled the horse and watered him. At the big gelding's whinny, the mules came running back. After staking all three away from the wagon so they wouldn't disturb Maddie, he turned his attention to the dead wolves.

They weren't as big as the grays in the Crimea, but they were prime animals, and it sickened him to think of the damage they could have done if Maddie hadn't been armed. Trailed by Tricks and Agnes, he dragged the carcasses deep into the woods and heaved them into a ravine, then headed back to camp, gathering wood along the way.

The wagon door was still closed.

Once he had the fire going, he picked up the shovel and set to work on the grave his wife had started.

What baby?

Noon came and went. After patting down the dirt over Satterwhite's grave, he checked on Maddie and found her still asleep.

Unable to stay idle, he busied himself with other chores through the early afternoon—gathering more wood, taking Lurch and the mules for an afternoon drink, feeding the fire, cleaning his weapons. Routine tasks that wore out his body and dulled his mind. But not his appetite. Realizing he hadn't eaten since before dawn, he grabbed Satterwhite's repeater, tied Tricks and Agnes to the back steps, and went to hunt up something for supper.

This time he got a turkey. After dressing it back at camp, he tossed the offal to the dogs and skewered the split carcass on a spit over the coals.

He went to check on Maddie again. Still asleep.

Since he couldn't reset the wheel with her inside the wagon and he'd run out of things to do, he sat in her chair, arms crossed over his chest, boots braced on a rock beside the fire.

What baby? And why hadn't he been told about it?

He could understand her anger over the rest of it. He had neglected her sorely, so he had. But he'd told her of his affliction and explained why he hadn't written, and she'd seemed to accept that. As for his other lapses, he'd been in the hospital and hadn't known of her parents' deaths until she'd told him a few days ago. And he'd been gone when Satterwhite had died.

But the baby? Why had she not told him of that?

Unless it wasna his baby.

No. He couldna—dinna want—to believe that.

Nine

Maddie awoke to late afternoon sunlight and the sound of the door opening. Sweating and disoriented, she tried to roll over but was so tangled in skirts and blankets she could scarcely move. Wondering why she would be abed at this hour, and fully clothed, at that, she leaned up on one elbow and looked over her shoulder to see Ash peering through the doorway.

"So you're awake then, lass?" Without waiting for a response, he came all the way in, turning to wrestle their biggest bucket through the narrow opening. Setting it down not far from the woodstove, he straightened, wincing when his head bumped against the low ceiling. "I thought you might want to wash."

Maddie blinked at him, trying to clear the fuzziness from her mind.

"Do you . . ." He motioned vaguely in her direction. "Need help?"

She looked down, saw her wrapped hands, and it all came rushing back—Mr. Satterwhite, the wolves, Ash returning. "No." Kicking her feet free, she sat up and swung her legs over the side of the bed. The sudden movement made her head spin. She started to slide.

His arm caught her. "Steady, love."

Sagging weakly against his grip, she waited for the dizziness to pass. When it did, she straightened, breathing deeply to clear her head.

He continued to hover over her, his big form taking up all the space in the cramped quarters.

"I'm fine," she said, pressing a trembling hand to her forehead.

He took a step back but was still a looming figure that dominated the small room.

She felt him. Felt the weight of his gaze. She didn't need to look up to be keenly aware of each breath he took, of the scent of him, of the danger he posed to her in this weakened state.

"You needn't stay."

He didn't respond. She was afraid he might question her about things she barely remembered saying to him earlier just after he had returned. She had been angry and exhausted. In her distraught state, she might have said more than she should have, revealed more than was wise.

"I'll get water, then," he finally said.

Before he could close the door behind him, Agnes rushed in and leaped onto the bed, wiggling and hopping in her face for kisses. By the time Maddie got the exuberant dog under control, Ash was back with two buckets of steaming water. He poured them into the bigger bucket, then straightened, bumping his head again. "There's food," he said, rubbing the top of his head. "Will you be coming out, or eat in here?"

Fearing he might want to join her in the wagon, she shook her head. "I'll come out."

He started for the door.

"Mr. Satterwhite? Is he . . . ?"

He paused in the open doorway, his shoulders as wide as the opening. "I buried him." He looked back at her. "You did a fine job protecting him, lass. It's sorry I am that I wasna here to help you." Then before she could think of a response, he left, quietly closing the door behind him.

A half hour later, she left the wagon, clean, refreshed, and a trifle nervous, although she wasn't sure why. Perhaps because Mr. Satterwhite was no longer there to act as a buffer. Or because being out here alone with Ash created a feeling of intimacy that made her uneasy.

She remembered how furious she had been with him earlier—the harsh words she had said. Even now, remnants of that anger and sense of betrayal still smoldered inside her.

But she also remembered his gentle care of her. And that confused her. The man, himself, confused her. It seemed for every step they took forward, something happened to pull them back. She could make no sense of it, and even though she had slept the afternoon away, she was still too weary to puzzle it through now.

As she came down the steps, Maddie glanced over, saw the mounded grave, and felt sadness mingled with relief. At least Mr. Satterwhite was finally at rest.

Ash rose from her chair as she approached. "Feeling better?"

"Yes, thank you." And suddenly quite hungry. The smell of roasting meat reached all the way to her empty stomach, reminding her that she hadn't eaten in over a day. "What have you there? Turkey?"

"Aye. Along with two shriveled potatoes, four carrots, and a can of peaches. A feast."

He held the chair as she took her seat, then bent and picked up a small round tin that was resting on a rock beside the fire. "But first, we must tend those hands."

When he took the lid off the tin, a foul odor escaped. "What is that?" she asked, wrinkling her nose.

"Wound salve." As he dropped to one knee beside her chair, he tipped the can to study the label. "Good for saddle sores, galls, wounds, and hoof rot. At least, I think that's what it says. Hold out your hands."

She balled them into fists. "No. Truly. They're fine." *Hoof rot?*

"It's not just for horses, love. Tricks has benefited from it, too."

She looked at the tin, then up at him. "You're jesting."

He smiled. It didn't reassure her. "It won't hurt. I promise."

He had to coax her fists open. But he was right—it didn't hurt, although it smelled ghastly and had the feel and consistency of axle putty. "What's in it?" she asked as he rewrapped her slimy hands with another torn handkerchief.

"A soldier's hope. There. All finished." He rose, slipped the tin into the pocket of his jacket, and wiped his greasy fingers on his knee-high cavalry boots. "Good for leather, too, so it is." Grabbing a knife stuck point-first into the log beside her, he began carving on the turkey still spitted over the coals. "Grab a plate, Your Majesty. Supper's ready."

She faltered, then did as he asked. "Mr. Satterwhite often said that."

"Aye. A remarkable man, your Mr. Satterwhite."

Blinking hard, she watched him pile succulent pieces of breast on the plate she held out. "Yes, he was. I shall miss him."

"I'm sure even now he's frowning down at my poor attempt at cooking, but I couldna just let it burn." After filling his own plate, he settled back on the log beside her chair. "I hope you dinna mind."

She gave a shaky smile. "I shall press bravely on."

"He would expect no less."

They ate in silence under the hopeful eyes of Tricks and Agnes. Watching the amount of food Ash consumed, she doubted there would be many tidbits left.

"He had to make a new hub," Ash said after a while. "The wheelwright. That's what took me so long."

She didn't respond.

"I would have come sooner, lass, had I been able."

A tired refrain. She was weary of it. But when she turned to tell him that, she saw the worry in his eyes and her anger faded away. What did it matter if Ash had come yesterday or today? Mr. Satterwhite's heart would have stopped whether he had been here or not.

"I'll put on the new wheel first thing in the morning." Leaning forward, he cut a drumstick from the rapidly dwindling carcass, then sat back. Tearing off a bite of meat with his fine, white teeth, he stared into the fire, his jaw working as he chewed.

It was a nice jaw, despite the stubble. Strong and square, with a slight dip in the middle of his chin. Not quite a cleft. *More like a wee fairy's thumbprint,* he had told her once when she had explored it with her fingertip. Then her lips. Then her tongue. And with that wayward thought, the memory of him burst into her mind— the salty taste of his skin, the warm, male scent of him, the dark promise in those moss green eyes when she had raised her body over his.

"What baby?"

Startled, Maddie choked on a bit of potato, then coughed to clear it. "Pardon me?" she asked in a strained voice.

He took another bite, watched her while he chewed, then swallowed. "You said you lost a baby. What baby? And why dinna I know about it?"

Irritated by the challenge in his tone, she answered more sharply than she intended. "Because your father asked me not to tell you."

Suspicion gave way to surprise. "Why?"

Appetite gone, she set her plate on the ground. Immediately Agnes pounced. Tricks would have, too, but halted at a word from Ash. "He felt you shouldn't be bothered. 'The lad has more important things to attend,'" she mimicked in his father's gruff voice. "'He canna help what he canna change.' He was right, of course."

Ash muttered something in Celtic under his breath.

Maddie didn't need to understand the words to catch the meaning. "I'll not argue with you on that score. But on this occasion, I agree with him."

Ash turned his head and looked at her. She saw the anger and pain in his eyes and wondered if it was for her, or the babe who would never be, or his father's high-handedness. It was a sad thing on all accounts. But remembering her own grief, she softened to his. "What could you have done had you known, Ash? You had only been back with your regiment for three months, and were newly promoted, at that. They wouldn't have allowed you to leave again so soon. And even if they had, by the time you reached home, the crisis would have been long past. These things happen."

He frowned, that one scarred brow arcing up, instead of down. "You sound as if it dinna matter to you. Did you no' want the babe?"

To cover a sudden, sharp swell of emotion, Maddie bent to pick up her plate. "Of course I did." Hearing the wobble in her voice, she cleared her throat and tried again. "Of course I did. More than anything in the world. Especially since it will probably be my one and only chance to ever bear a child." Setting the plate on the log beside her, she pressed her hands on her thighs to still the trembling.

"It doesn't have to be, lass. Come back to Scotland with me and I'll give you all the bairns you want."

She tipped her head back to watch a flock of tiny yellow and gray birds flit by, hoping the breeze would dry her tears. "And leave me in the back of beyond to raise them on my own while you go haring off to who knows where? No thank you."

Muttering something under his breath, Ash abruptly stood. He paced all the way around the fire and stopped at her other side to loom over her, hands clasped behind his back.

"Then what do you want from me, Madeline? I'm offering you position and luxury as a peeress of the realm. What more do you want?"

"My work. My friends. Children. A real marriage. Not a life defined by duty." Realizing they would never come to agreement on this subject, Maddie rose and brushed the crumbs from her skirt. "I would like to leave as early as possible tomorrow. I need to get back. I have another journey ahead of me and I must prepare."

"Denver."

She nodded.

"You'll not be going alone." It was a statement, not a question, and the presumption of it irritated her.

"I won't be alone. Our sheriff is one of the delegates. His wife and the woman who owns the hotel will be accompanying me, as well."

He looked at her as if awaiting further explanation.

"It's some statehood thing." She made an offhand gesture, battling a sinking weariness that went deeper than flesh and bone. Even her spirit felt bruised. "It's been an ongoing struggle. But this time, the railroads are involved. I want to photograph it."

"It doesn't sound safe."

Bending, she scooped up Agnes. "If things get out of hand, Sheriff Brodie is most capable. I'll be quite safe."

"Aye, you will. Because I'll be going with you as well."

Surprised at the edge in his voice, she studied him but saw nothing in his expression to explain it. "Why?"

"You're my wife. If you need protecting, I'll do it."

"That's not necessary."

"It is to me."

NEAR BRECKENRIDGE, COLORADO TERRITORY

"What you doing?"

Silas Cochran whirled in the chair to see his brother standing in the doorway of the rustic cabin. "N-Nothing, Clete. I ain't doing nothing."

"Yeah, you are, moron. You're always doing something." Cletus Cochran slammed the door closed behind him, and without taking his gaze from Si, took off his dripping hat and hung it on a peg beside the door. "What's that you got there?"

"Nothing." Si tried to stuff the photographs back into his pocket with the other papers he'd taken from the dead man's pack, but a blow to his shoulder knocked him sideways in the chair and sent the pictures flying across the rough tabletop.

"Don't lie to me, Si."

"I'm not, Clete, I swear." Hunching his shoulders in case Clete hit him again, Si struggled to gather up the pictures, but his hands were shaking so bad they kept slipping from his grip.

"Tell me, Si."

"Just some pictures. That's all."

"Pictures? Where'd you get pictures?"

Si felt his older brother looming at his shoulder. The shaking spread from his hands throughout his whole body. "F-Found them."

"Where?"

"I d-don't remember."

"Yeah, you do." Batting Si's hands aside, Clete reached down and spread the pictures across the table.

When Si saw the smudges his brother's dirty fingers left on the shiny paper, he started to cry. Afraid Clete would see, he slumped deeper into the chair and kept his head down as tears rolled down his cheeks to drip from his wobbling chin. *I hate you,* he chanted silently, gripping his thighs so hard he could feel blood bump against his thumbs. *I hate you, I hate you, bastard moron, shut up, I hate you.*

Clete separated one of the photographs from the pile and held it up to the faint light coming through the fly-specked window. He frowned at it, his pale brows low over his mismatched eyes. "This is that guy. Ephraim Zucker. The one you killed before we could find out where his claim is."

Si swiped a sleeve over his runny nose. "It was an accident, Clete. I told you."

Clete punched him between the shoulder blades, driving Si hard against the edge of the table. "Did I say you could talk?"

Clutching his chest, Si fought to draw in air.

"Did I?"

Si shook his head, gasping, still not able to speak.

"Then don't, moron."

For a long time, Clete looked through the pictures one by one.

Si watched him, knowing each picture by heart—the dead guy smiling and sitting on a stump, or standing by his mule, or leaning on a pickax handle outside his little sod cabin. But it wasn't the man that Si liked best. It was the pretty country where the man was. The little creek, the grassy meadow, white-trunked aspens, and mountains so high they wore clouds for hats. He especially liked the peak behind the cabin that looked like a face turned sideways. That was Si's favorite. Whenever he felt sad about killing the smiling man, he would look at that picture and imagine being inside it, standing next to the smiling man in that pretty place far, far away from Clete. And that always made him happy.

"This may not be a bad thing," Clete said after a while.

Si watched him pick up his favorite picture of the peak with the sideways face, and he had to ball his hands into fists to keep from snatching it from his brother's grip.

"This could be the key." Staring off out the window, Clete tapped the picture against his dirty thumbnail. "The way we find that claim." He stopped tapping and squinted at the tiny white letters in the corner of the picture. "A. M. Wallace. You know who A. M. Wallace is, Si?"

"No, Clete."

"'Course you don't. You're a moron. A freak of nature. I swear, if you had dung for brains, you'd be twice as smart as you are right now."

Si watched him, rage bubbling like puke in his throat.

"Lucky you got me to watch out for you, ain't that so, Si? Ain't it?"

"Yes, Clete."

"Damn right." Suddenly Clete laughed and clapped Si so hard on his back it made him cough. He tossed the pictures onto the tabletop. "Pack up, moron. We're leaving."

Relieved to get his pictures back, Si quickly gathered them up and stuffed them into his pocket. "Where we going, Clete?"

"Where do you think, moron? To find us a photographer."

HEARTBREAK CREEK, COLORADO TERRITORY

By the time Ash and Maddie neared Heartbreak Creek late the next day, dusk had sucked the sun's warmth from the air and a chill breeze out of the north had already left a dusting of white across the high peaks.

"Turn here." Maddie pointed to a rough track that cut behind the hotel and ran parallel to the main street. "The livery is just past the blacksmith's shop. I usually leave the wagon there. Fred Driscoll will take care of the team."

Ash remembered him from when he'd been through before—a short, bowlegged man with a quiet demeanor that had easily won Lurch's trust.

He reined the team onto the track, then glanced over at his wife.

She had hardly spoken ten words all afternoon and now sat on the edge of the bench seat, staring intently ahead, her fingers worrying the empty fingertip of her glove.

His glove, actually, which he had insisted she wear to keep dirt out of the wrappings over her blisters. They dwarfed her trim hands and made her appear more vulnerable than he knew her to be. But he sensed it wasn't only the poor fit of the gloves that had deepened that furrow in her brow the closer they had come to Heartbreak Creek. Regrets, perhaps?

He had a few of his own.

He should have settled the question of their marriage before they'd left neutral ground. Heartbreak Creek was her territory. He was the intruder here and that put him at a distinct disadvantage. Now, in addition to having to allay Maddie's misgivings about returning to Scotland, he would have to contend with her friends and convince them it was the right decision. Something he wasna even sure of himself.

And in addition to that, he had overexerted when putting on the repaired wheel that morning, and now his side had stiffened from sitting so long, and his head felt like someone was pounding nails into it from inside.

"Out front is fine," his wife said as they pulled up to the livery. Ash reined in and was wrapping the reins around the brake when Driscoll came out of the open double doors into the barn.

"Evening, ma'am. Ashby." He tipped his battered hat, then looked around. "Where's Wilfred?"

"Gone. It was so sad, Mr. Driscoll." As she handed Agnes down to the liveryman, Maddie told him of Satterwhite's death, omitting the part about Ash being gone and her ordeal with the wolves. "I shall miss him terribly. He was such a dear. But"—she swiped a hand over her cheek—"it was my good fortune that this gentleman"—she shot Ash a smile that carried a hint of warning when he came to lift her down—"kindly helped me get the wagon back home."

"Evening, Driscoll," Ash said over Maddie's head as he lowered her to the ground. "Get that mule back on its feet?"

"Yes, sir, I did. And thanks for your advice." He showed tobacco-stained teeth in an evil grin. "I had words with the smithy. Promised to use the right size horseshoes next time."

At Maddie's look of curiosity, Driscoll explained that the farrier had used shoes that were too narrow, which put undue pressure on the hoof and decreased circulation to the frog on the underside. "Didn't see it myself," he added with a shake of his head. "But as soon as Ashby popped off those shoes, Muriel perked up fine. Saved me a good mule, he did."

"Indeed." Maddie pulled off Ash's oversized gloves, unwound the wrappings, and stuffed them into her coat pocket. "If you would be so kind to tend the animals, Mr. Driscoll, I shall be back in a day or so to ready the wagon for my next trip." She handed Ash his gloves and started walking back the way they had come. "Come along, Agnes."

Ash took a moment to remind the livery owner about Lurch's deafness and hand over enough coin to cover the cost of extra grain for all the mounts. Then slinging his saddlebags over his shoulder, he went after his wife.

With his much longer stride, he and Tricks were on her heels before she'd crossed the rutted road. "Why are we in such a hurry, lass?" he said to her stiff back.

She stopped and turned so abruptly he almost plowed into her. Pulling back, he pressed the fingertips of his left hand against his pounding temple to slow the spinning.

"When you came through Heartbreak Creek earlier looking for me, who did you talk to?"

Letting his hand drop, he squinted at her through his narrowing vision. "The woman who owns the hotel and the sheriff. Why?"

Leaning closer, she dropped her voice. "What did you say to them?"

Amused despite the grinding pain in his head, he bent and whispered, "About what?"

"Us. Why you were looking for me."

"I told them I had news of your family in Scotland."

She gripped his arm. "You didn't tell them your name? Or that you were my husband?"

He caught a whiff of old smoke and the flowery soap he remembered from their brief time together. And Agnes. "It wasn't their business."

"Thank God." Releasing his arm, she turned and continued walking.

Thank God? No longer amused, he put out a hand to stop her. "You don't want your friends to know we're wed? You're ashamed of me, lass?"

"Oh, no," she said hastily. "It's not that at all. But they—well—I may have said things."

"Things?"

"About you. Our marriage. Your . . . em, desertion."

He opened his mouth to correct her on who had deserted whom, but she shushed him with a finger pressed to his lips, which made him forget what he'd been about to say. Uncanny, that.

"Let's not get into that now," she warned in a low voice, taking her hand away. "And don't call me lass. Or love. Just Maddie. Or better yet, Madeline. It wouldn't do to arouse vulgar speculation until we settle the marriage thing, don't you agree?"

No, he dinna. But rather than get tangled in an argument in the middle of the street, he said no more.

When they reached the back stoop of the hotel, the Hathaway woman swung open the door. "We were starting to worry. We expected you back two days ago." Her welcoming smile faltered when she saw Ash and Tricks. "I see he found you."

Ash nodded in greeting, but before he could speak, his wife planted herself solidly in front of him.

"I have the most dreadful news, Luce. Mr. Satterwhite died. His heart, I think. It was so unexpected."

"Oh, no. I'm sorry to hear that. I know how fond you were of him." Stepping aside, the blonde motioned them into the back hallway, giving Tricks a thorough inspection as he went by. "But I don't see how it could have been unexpected. The man was at least ninety."

"Seventy-three. He was only seventy-three, and quite vigorous for his age. Is that Edwina and Pru?" Maddie asked as Agnes charged down the hall toward two women coming through the lobby doors.

Ash recognized the rounded, fair-haired woman as Sheriff Brodie's wife and the dark-skinned woman as the one under the Cheyenne Dog Soldier's protection. Reinforcements. The pounding in his head rose to a deafening thud.

"When I saw your wagon go by," Miss Hathaway said, nodding to the two women staring curiously at them from the lobby, "I sent word to Declan at the sheriff's office. I thought we could dine together and hear all about your trip. And poor Mr. Satterwhite, of course."

"I should like that." Calling to her friends, Maddie went to greet them, leaving Ash standing in the hall with the blond Yankee.

She slanted a glance up at him. "Of course, you're welcome too, Mr. . . . Ashby, was it?"

"*Lord* Ashby." That cool smile dinna fool Ash—he knew an adversary when he saw one. But despite her prickly ways, he liked the wee Yankee, recognizing in her a backbone as unbendable as his own. It was clear, too, that she was verra protective of Maddie, and like most soldiers, Ash valued loyalty above all else . . . even if it got in his way. But what he needed most right now was a wash, a bottle, then blessed quiet while he waited for the liquor to take effect and the pounding to stop. "Perhaps another time."

Mistakenly reading his refusal as a reluctance to intrude on a female gathering, she said, "I've asked Sheriff Brodie and Thomas Redstone to join us as well, so you needn't fear being overrun by ladies."

"As fearful—and intriguing—as such a fate might be, I must decline." Shifting the heavy saddlebags slung over his shoulder, he glanced at the closed door into the washroom. "However, if I might trouble you for a bottle of your finest and use of your washroom . . ." He let the sentence hang on a hopeful note.

Her gaze flicked over his rumpled clothing, still stained with mud from his battle with the wheel that morning. "Of course. You'll find hot water on the stove and drying cloths in the cabinet. Please don't use them on your dog. If you need your clothing laundered, put them in the burlap bag on the hook behind the door and Billy will take it down to the Chinese laundry later. I'll send Yancey with the bottle." She started away, then turned back. "Will you be needing a room, as well?"

"Best check with my—with Madeline."

It was obvious the response confused her, but rather than get into it in the hallway, Ash reached past her to open the washroom door. "Come, Tricks."

Yancey brought the bottle, collected his money, then left. Ash had just settled into the tub when the door latch rattled. He watched the door slowly creak open an inch. Then two.

He was about to reach for the pistol he had set on the stool by the tub—another old soldier's habit—but then saw that Tricks, lapping up water that had sloshed out of the wooden tub when he'd sat down, showed no alarm. So Ash left the gun where it was and waited.

A freckled face peered around the edge of the partially open door.

Ash was a bit disappointed. He'd hoped it might be Maddie.

"Hidy, sir," Billy said, goggling at the wolfhound that probably outweighed him by a stone.

"Afternoon, Billy."

"Got any laundry you want me to take?"

"So I do. There on the hook."

"Oh. Okay." Opening the door just wide enough to reach around, the boy yanked the burlap bag off the hook, then jerked back as if expecting Tricks to lunge.

Tricks continued to lick the floor.

"If you want, sir, I'll watch your dog while you're in the dining room."

Ash bit back a smile at the reluctant offer. "Would that be your idea or Miss Hathaway's, I'm wondering?"

"Miss Hathaway's. But Mrs. Wallace said it would be all right and your dog wouldn't hurt me."

"She's right. Tricks wouldna hurt you. Especially if you took him out back and gave him a plate of scraps."

"Oh. Okay. Out back?"

Reaching over to the pile of coins he'd left on the stool beside the pistol, Ash retrieved one and tossed it to the boy, who snatched it from the air with practiced efficiency. "He's partial to beef."

"Oh. Okay." The door creaked open a little wider. "Come, Tricks."

The wolfhound yawned and sat on Ash's boot.

"Perhaps it would be best, lad, if you brought the scraps in here."

A look of relief came over the freckled face. "Yes, sir. Do you want some, too? Food, I mean?"

Ash picked up the bottle he'd set on the floor beside the tub. "I have all I need right here, lad."

When Ash left the washroom nearly an hour later, his tongue was pleasantly numb, his side no longer hurt, and the ache in his temples had settled to a dull pounding like the crashing of waves against a distant shore. The rhythmic churn of it reminded him of the shipboard crossing and made him slightly nauseated.

Or maybe that was the spinning in his head.

Or the alcohol.

He probably should have eaten.

But he was clean, Tricks was fed and no longer gave him hungry looks, and if he could just find a warm, dry place to stretch out, he would probably make it through the night.

He put a hand against the wall to steady it and looked around, trying to remember where he was.

The hotel. Heartbreak Creek.

Voices and the smell of food drifted down the hall from the dining room, adding to the disquiet of his stomach. He wondered if the Hathaway woman had assigned him a room. He dinna want to go into the dining room where all her friends were gathered and ask. He dinna want to answer questions or be gawped at or watch his wife turn away and pretend she wasna wed to him. *Bugger that.* He just wanted to find a quiet, dark place to wait out the pain.

Executing a slow, careful about-face, he paused to wait for the spinning to stop, then carefully opened the back door.

Cold air slapped him in the face. He blinked, wondering if his eyesight had failed him completely, then realized it was night. Tiny pellets of icy snow peppered his face as he titled back his head. Bracing a hand against the door frame, he drew in great draughts of air.

The pounding eased. His vision cleared somewhat and his stomach settled. Shoving wet hair out of his eyes, he pulled the door closed, righted his balance, then stepped off the rocking stoop and headed down the street, Tricks at his side.

Faithful, loyal Tricks.

He wouldna turn away from him. Not ever.

Ten

From the window of the dining room, Maddie watched Ash step out onto the back stoop. For a moment he paused in the light from the hallway behind him, his face raised up to the sky, his head and shoulders haloed by tiny sparkling snowflakes. He looked big and ominous in the slanting light . . . and slightly off balance as he shut the door and stepped into the street. Then she lost him in the swirl of snow.

Where was he going? Why hadn't he joined them?

She sat back, staring into the darkness beyond the window as sound rose and fell around her, blending into a meaningless drone of voices and laughter, the clatter of tableware on china, the clink of glasses. Sounds that bespoke merriment, the enjoyment of a meal shared with dear friends.

Then why did she feel so disconnected from it? It was as if she had stepped into another room and was watching from afar.

"Was the news he brought so bad?" Edwina asked at Maddie's side.

Pulling her gaze from the window, Maddie realized conversation at their table had stopped and all faces were turned her way.

Dear, beloved faces.

Edwina and Declan, their improbable mail-order marriage turning into something more than either expected. Patient Prudence, still struggling to come to terms with her abduction by Lone Tree, yet taking time to share her learning with displaced ex-slaves and itinerant railroad workers. Thomas Redstone, the Cheyenne Dog Soldier who stayed staunchly by Pru's side, waiting for her to realize she loved him as much as he loved her. And dear, cynical Lucinda, with her valise of purloined railroad shares, and her confused feelings about the man she had left at the altar.

This was her family now.

This was where her future lay.

How did Ash fit into that?

"What's wrong?" Edwina's hand fell over Maddie's where it rested on the table beside her plate. "I declare you look like a two-headed turkey at a turkey shoot. Has that elusive Scotsman upset you?"

Ash wasn't elusive. Far from it. It seemed every time Maddie turned around, he was there—in her sight, in her mind—intrusive, intriguing, inescapable.

But was he not part of her family, too?

Maddie glanced around the dining room and saw that most of the tables had emptied. Only a handful of diners remained at the two tables along the far wall, and they seemed too engrossed in their own conversations to take note of theirs.

Dreading the storm she was about to unleash, she turned back to the expectant faces watching her. "That elusive Scotsman is my husband."

For a moment, silence. Then Lucinda threw her napkin onto the table. "That wretch lied to me! He said his name was Ashby. *Lord* Ashby."

"It is."

"I thought Angus Wallace was your husband?"

"He is." Seeing the questions coming, Maddie raised a staying hand. "But he recently came into the title of Viscount Ashby, and it's customary to address peers by their titles rather than their given names."

"Oh, my goodness gracious." Pru's smile lit up her strikingly beautiful face. "I suppose that makes you a viscountess, does it not?"

"A viscountess?" Edwina clapped her hands and laughed. "Well, if that isn't the most exciting thing. Our Maddie a real English lady. Should we curtsy, do you think?"

Lucinda's smile was more sardonic than gleeful. "Are we now to call you *Lady* Ashby?"

Edwina started to add another quip when Declan reached over and gently rested his hand on the back of her neck. Immediately her entire attention turned to him. If she'd been a cat, she would have arched her back. Maddie found it endearing the power the sheriff held over his feisty, southern wife—or rather, the power the feisty southern wife granted to him.

"Why is he here, Maddie?" Declan asked.

"To take me back to Scotland."

This time the sheriff couldn't hold back his wife's outburst. Other raised voices joined Edwina's, drawing glances from the other diners. But the protests soon played out, and when they did, Declan continued in his calm, reasonable way. "Do you want to go back?"

"No. Perhaps. I don't know." She gave a helpless shrug. "It's complicated."

"But I don't want you to leave," Edwina protested.

"She will not go." Pushing his empty plate aside, Thomas Redstone folded his forearms on the table.

Usually when he was in town and acting as Declan's temporary deputy, he dressed in his "whitewashed" attire—meaning trousers rather than leggings, a collarless work shirt and blue army jacket in place of breechcloth and war shirt, and instead of a topknot with an eagle feather, his long black hair and narrow temple braids pulled back and tied with a strip of leather. But Edwina had mentioned earlier that Thomas had just returned from another of his mysterious forays into the mountains and had not taken time to stop by his room in the Brodies' carriage house to change out of his Indian garb. He looked quite fearsome. Ash would have loved it.

Regarding Maddie through eyes as black as chips of basalt, Thomas said in his flat, solemn voice, "Unless it is what Madeline Wallace wants, he will not take her away."

Maddie translated that to mean Ash wouldn't be *permitted* to take her if she didn't want to go. Thomas would make certain of it.

She smiled her gratitude to the Indian warrior.

He didn't smile back but gravely nodded his dark head, which brought a sway to the eagle feather in his topknot.

A strange man, Thomas Redstone. One quarter white, three quarters Cheyenne, he straddled two cultures but seemed to belong to neither. He had gained the respect of his people by suffering the ordeal of the Cheyenne sun dance ceremony, then had gone on to earn a place with the Dog Soldiers because of his courage as a warrior. But through adversity and tragedy, he had forged a stronger bond with Declan, and when the tribes had been slowly driven from Colorado Territory, Thomas had stayed behind. Now he watched over his new tribe in Heartbreak Creek.

And Maddie loved him for it.

She loved them all. The thought of leaving these people and this place forever brought such a constriction to her throat she could scarcely breathe. And if she had to give up her photography, too . . . she simply wouldn't survive it. "Ash would never force me to go back," she said and hoped it was true. "But it's either go to Scotland or petition for a divorce. Because Ash is now a peer, that would require an act of Parliament, which could take years."

"Then why doesn't he stay here?" Edwina asked.

"He can't. As heir, he has duties to the earldom and the lands that go with it." She looked down at the signet ring that had caused the worst of her blisters. Yet she still wore it. In fact, through all the years, she had never taken it off, thinking in some silly superstitious way that if she did, harm might befall the man who had given it to her. "Ash has ever been a creature bound by duty."

Edwina slapped a hand so hard on the table her glass wobbled. "Well, I don't give a fig. He treated you shabbily by not writing or coming to see you, and for that, he certainly doesn't deserve a second chance."

"He had reason."

"Such as?"

Unwilling to belittle her husband by revealing his affliction and the reason he didn't write, Maddie said instead, "He was injured, for one thing. And still suffers because of it."

Shame heated her cheeks when she realized she hadn't even asked him how he fared after his battle to mount the wagon wheel earlier that morning. Perhaps he had hurt his side and that's why he hadn't joined them.

Or perhaps he hadn't felt welcome.

Blast. Now she would have to hunt him down and see what was wrong. She'd get no sleep otherwise.

"I had set aside a room for his use," Lucinda said, her green eyes cutting sharply into Maddie. "As well as your usual one. But the big suite is available, if you'd prefer that."

Maddie shifted in the chair as all eyes fastened on her. She knew her answer would determine how they would treat her husband . . . as an accepted part of the Heartbreak Creek family, or as an interloper to be shunned.

She sighed. Well, the big suite did have two bedrooms separated by a small sitting area, and she and her husband had just spent a day and a night in closer proximity than that. Masking her unease behind a smile, she nodded. "The big suite will do nicely."

"I'll have Yancey freshen the rooms and get your keys when we finish here."

The gathering broke up soon after. Before dispersing, Edwina invited them to a late Sunday dinner at the Brodie house the next day. "We saw Pastor Rickman outside the mercantile. Apparently Fred Driscoll told him about Mr. Satterwhite, and he wants to hold a short memorial service for him after services. I thought we would eat at two. And be sure to bring along Lord Ashby or Angus Wallace or whatever he's called," she told Maddie. "I have some questions for the fellow."

"Oh, dear," Prudence murmured.

"Now, Ed," Declan seconded as he helped his pregnant wife from her chair. "Don't you start anything."

"Oh, hush. As if I would." Edwina narrowed her blue eyes at her overgrown husband. "But aren't you just the littlest, teensiest, weensiest bit curious why he did what he did? It near broke her heart."

"I can hear you," Maddie chided. "I'm standing right here."

"I don't know what he did, or care why he did it," Declan said flatly. "Now come along."

Edwina rolled her eyes. "Men."

As the other four filed out, Maddie turned to Lucinda. "She's gotten so big. Will she be up to the trip to Denver, do you think?"

"Edwina will do what Edwina will do. The only one who could stop her is Declan. And he wants her to come along, since he worries like a mother hen whenever she's out of his sight."

An incongruous image, Maddie thought, considering Declan's size and unflappable nature.

"I doubt I'll be able to attend dinner tomorrow." Lucinda motioned for a kitchen worker to come clear the table. "And don't give me that look, Maddie. It's not because I think your husband is a cad for treating you the way he did—injured or not. But I have to ready my presentation for Denver. Now that the Denver Pacific has completed the main line from Cheyenne, they might be seeking a southern route across the Rockies, rather than relying solely on the Transcontinental. This will be our best chance to convince them to come through Heartbreak Creek Canyon."

Maddie knew Lucinda had high hopes of using the railroads to further rejuvenate the town she was working so hard to revive. The issue of the town's foul water still had to be resolved, but with the mine out of production and the water cannon no longer pouring dissolved chemicals into the water table, Lucinda was convinced it would only be a matter of time until the water became less harmful to the railroad tenders and locomotives.

Maddie wasn't so sure. Judging by the brown teeth of some of the longtime local inhabitants, the water might have been unsuitable even before silver was discovered on the hillside above the town.

But she couldn't worry about that right now. She had a husband to track down, a marriage to settle, and her own preparations to make before the trip to Denver. With so many people converging from so many walks of life, it would be a photographer's mother lode.

"Ash intends to accompany us," she told Lucinda as they walked toward the lobby. "He thinks I need protection."

"Perhaps he's right." Lucinda paused at the front desk to get a key for Maddie and to tell Yancey to move Maddie's things to the big suite. "Hopefully with Grant in office," she continued, "there will be no more vetoes. But Teller and Evans are still feuding about who should be the second US Senator, and tempers are running high. If this attempt to gain statehood fails, there could be violence. We might need every protector we can get."

"Oh, I hope not." Moving around the front desk, Maddie stepped into the office to retrieve her coat and Agnes, who was curled into a ball on Yancey's cot. "But my father would have loved the uproar. He had very strong political opinions. Democratic ones, at that."

In fact, Baronet Gresham had been so devoted to those ideals he had drained his small inheritance in futile attempts to organize collective cooperatives for coal workers, or draymen, or anyone else who would listen. A bit of a dreamer, her father was.

"Perhaps that's why you aren't jumping at the chance at a title."

"Perhaps." After donning her coat and scooping up Agnes before she could bolt into the dining room, Maddie said her good nights and went down the hall to the back door.

Agnes, having spent the evening inside the office, was enthusiastic for an outing. Wiggling out of Maddie's arms as soon as they stepped onto the back stoop, she trotted happily down the lane, weaving in and out of puddles and adding a few of her own.

The snow had stopped, yet seemed suspended in the thick fog, as if gathering momentum for another try. Most of what had already fallen had melted on contact, so there wasn't enough accumulation to make footing hazardous.

Deciding Ash might be checking on Lurch or chatting with Driscoll, Maddie pulled her coat tight against the chill and headed in the direction of the livery.

The barn was dark except for a pale wash of light shining out the back and a lit window in the front office where Mr. Driscoll slept. As she drew nearer, she noted a faint glow in the shadows and saw the liveryman sitting on an overturned bucket by the open double doors, smoking a pipe.

"Evening, ma'am. Come to check on the girls?"

"I'm sure the mules are fine, Mr. Driscoll. It's Ashby I'm looking for. Have you seen him?"

The hostler gestured with the pipe toward the back of the barn. "Yonder in your wagon. Saw him go in. Heard some cussing and banging around earlier, but nothing since. Dog's still here, though, sharing a stall with his horse. Need a lantern?"

"I see you left one lit in the back of the barn. It should be sufficient, thank you." Leaving Agnes digging for mice in the manure pile, Maddie went through the barn and out the rear double doors.

No light showed in the wagon.

Moving carefully on the damp steps, she quietly opened the door.

The small stove was unlit and the room was as cold inside as it was out. It had a deserted feel to it. Maddie was about to close the door and look elsewhere for Ash when she heard soft exhalations from the bed. Opening the door wider so the dim lantern light from the barn could shine in, she saw Ash's long form sprawled on his back on her bed, his booted feet protruding well past the end. "Ash?" she called.

He lurched upright, a pistol in his grip. "Halt!"

Maddie almost fell back down the steps. "Don't! It's me! Maddie."

"Holy Christ." The pistol clattered to the floor. He flopped onto his back, both hands clasped to his head. "Bluidy hell! I almost shot you!"

"I-I'm sorry." Maddie pressed a hand over her thudding heart and struggled to catch her breath. Was the man expecting an Indian attack? "I didn't mean to startle you."

"Dinna do that ever again."

"I assure you, I won't." It was obvious from the scent of spirits hanging in the still air that he had been drinking. That surprised her—Ash had never been much of a drinker before. But then, during the short time they had spent together, they had been too intoxicated with each other to need additional stimulants.

He pulled his hands away from his head. With a groan, he pushed himself upright and swung his feet to the floor, then sat there, hands gripping the mattress by his hips, his head hanging.

Maddie waited, wondering at his stillness, his silence, the weary slump of his shoulders. After a moment, when he still hadn't moved or spoken, she stepped forward. "Ash? Is everything all right?"

He looked up, his expression shadowed by a fall of gray brown hair over his eyes. "What are you doing here?" he asked gruffly.

"I was about to ask you the same thing." She took another step then stopped, her skirts almost brushing his boots. "Are you hurt?"

"I'm fine. Go back to your . . ." He started to wave a hand in the direction of the hotel, then groaned and clapped it to his temple instead. She heard him mutter something in Gaelic.

"Is it your side?"

His hand fell back to the mattress. "A bit of a headache, is all."

"From drinking."

"That, too."

Not sure what to make of that, Maddie remained silent, debating whether to apologize for asking him to keep their marriage a secret, or to berate him for taking too much drink.

"I told them about you," she finally said.

His head came slowly up. "Told them what?"

"That you're my husband."

"Oh, brave lass. And what else did you tell them?" He gave a harsh laugh that carried no mirth. "That I canna read? That I'm half crippled? That you're ashamed to own me as your husband?"

His vehemence stunned her. She would never have guessed her big, capable husband hid such doubts beneath his stiff-backed posture. She didn't know how to respond, what to say. But sensing she would only anger him more if she acknowledged those doubts by offering reassuring platitudes, she decided to treat it like the foolishness it was. "No, I didn't tell them any of that. Nor did I tell them that you talk to yourself when you think you're alone, or that you couldn't carry a tune in a five-gallon bucket, or that your knees are ticklish, or that you have a mole on your—"

"Bluidy woman." Before she knew what he was about, he grabbed her arms, jerked her forward between his splayed knees, and kissed her.

It wasn't a tender kiss like the one he'd given her before he'd left to have the wheel repaired. This one was raw and savage and filled with need.

And Maddie responded to it like a woman starved. When he finally pulled back, she was shaking, her breath trapped in her throat.

Setting her away from him but still gripping her arms, he stared into her eyes, his expression so bleak she almost turned away from it. "And did you tell them that, Maddie Wallace?"

Her thoughts in chaos and her body singing as it hadn't in long, empty years, Maddie leaned toward him. "Ask me again."

"Oh, lass . . ." It was a gentler kiss this time, as if to soothe his earlier assault. She stood over him, pressing against him, her fingers in his hair, the heat of him burning through her dress, her body shivering as his big hand slid up her back, then around to her waist and up . . .

. . . to push her away.

"I canna do it."

She froze, staring down at his bent head, the words careening around in her head. What was this? The ultimate rejection after she had finally allowed herself to weaken?

"You can't do what?"

"This. Us. Here." He lifted a hand to his left temple. "In this wee room and ridiculous bed, with the children watching and my head—"

"Children?" Hearing breathing behind her, Maddie whirled to see Tricks and Agnes regarding them quizzically from the open doorway. When had they arrived?

Then Ash's other words brought her around again. "Your head? What's wrong with your head? I thought it was just a headache." But even as she spoke, images filled her mind—the scar above his temple, the way his hand kept returning to it, the drinking and his self-imposed exile out here in this cold wagon. He was in pain, and too stubborn and prideful to mention it.

So it wasn't her, after all. She didn't know whether to dance a jig or slap him hard.

"It's your injury, isn't it? And don't say you're fine when it's obvious you're not, Angus Wallace. Why didn't you say something?"

He shrugged, then winced and rubbed his temple again. "It only comes now and then. Less often as the months pass, unless I do something to aggravate it."

"Like wrestle with a broken wheel," she snapped, astounded at the man's hardheadedness, "then ride in a bouncing wagon all day."

"Well . . . aye . . ."

"What do you do for it?"

He choked off a bitter laugh. "Drink. Sleep. Avoid light. Dinna fuss, lass. It will be gone by morning."

"You are such a nincompoop. Get up."

He lifted his head and squinted at her, his eyes reflecting back the pale light coming through the open door. "Nincompoop?"

"There's no need for you to stay out here," she went on, motioning impatiently for him to rise, which he did, but rather gingerly. "Lucinda has set aside the big suite for us."

"Us?"

"I cannot believe how utterly ridiculous you are. Be careful not to bump your head on the ceiling." Shooing the dogs back out, she steered him toward the door. "It's big and roomy and overlooks the back, so it'll be nice and quiet. Let me go down the steps first in case you fall."

He paused on the threshold, his hands braced on either side of the door frame. "And you'll catch me if I do, lass?"

Recognizing the absurdity of that, she backed away from the bottom of the stair and called the dogs out of the way. "Just be wary. It's slick."

"This is exactly why I dinna say anything," he muttered, carefully negotiating the narrow treads. "You're treating me like a bluidy cripple."

"Nincompoop," she corrected. "Which you are."

Once he reached the ground, she slipped her arm through his and guided him toward the barn. Seeing no light in the office, she surmised Mr. Driscoll had retired for the night, and paused to turn down the lamp bolted inside the door. The sudden darkness awakened her other senses, and as they walked down the center aisle, Maddie heard horses moving in their stalls—the stomp of hooves, chewing, the rustle of straw. The air was redolent with the earthy, musty scents of manure and grain and hay. And the man beside her.

Why hadn't he told her? Did he think she wouldn't care that he was in pain?

"I can walk on my own, ye ken," he muttered as they left the barn and turned toward the hotel.

In his weakened state, his Scottish accent was stronger. Hearing it reminded her of other times when his brogue had slipped past his reserve—whispering commands and soft encouragements in the dark cocoon of their draped bed. The memory of it brought heat low in her belly.

"I know. But you're big and warm, and I'm cold."

He didn't respond. But he didn't pull his arm away, either.

The earlier fog had thickened to a heavy mist that dripped from sagging spruce boughs and muffled the sound of the creek running fast and high a few yards from the road. There was an oppressive stillness to it that reminded Maddie of foggy nights in the poor, working areas of London where her father held his union meetings, and where angry words often erupted in violence. Instinctively, she pressed closer to the man beside her.

Seeking protection from a man who could scarcely walk on his own.

Yet it felt right. And good. She needed this man. And in allowing his stiff-backed pride to bend enough to reveal to her this new weakness, he was showing that he needed her, too.

But that didn't change anything. He was still bound by the duties of his position, and she was just as determined to maintain her independence.

"I can carry a tune."

She looked up at him.

"You said I couldna, but I can. I'm a piper. Do you no' remember that morning I played 'Scotland the Brave' at your window?"

Of course she remembered. Even now, the memory of awakening from a dead sleep to that caterwauling raised the hairs on her arms. But she had never thought the sounds a bagpipe made even remotely resembled a tune. "Yes, I remember it well."

"Aye. There's naught like the call of the pipes on a misty morn."

"I so agree."

The dogs trotted zigzag patterns down the rutted track, drawn to every scent. Ahead at the hotel, lamplight from the upstairs rooms lit the darkness like square beacons of light leading them safely through the damp, gray mist. It was beautiful and eerie and Maddie wondered if there might ever come a day when photography equipment would be able to capture that simple contrast of light and dark.

"You'll be giving me another chance," Ash said, breaking into her thoughts as they neared the hotel. Not so much a suggestion, as an order. Ever the soldier, Angus Wallace was.

"Will I?"

"Ye will." He looked down at her, that fall of hair now clinging damply to his brow. "I crossed an ocean and half this country to find you, lass. Do ye ken how hard that was for a man who can hardly read a map and mixes up his rights and lefts?"

"And yet, here you are."

"Aye. Because of you. So you'll be giving me a second chance, so you will."

Definitely an order. She said nothing, and kept her head down so he wouldn't see her smile.

By the time they made it up the stairs to their suite, Ash was starting to sag again. His face had lost color, and a deep furrow drew his dark brows together over his narrowed eyes. Each of his steps was careful and measured and came down softly so as not to jar.

She unlocked the door and ushered him inside. While the dogs explored every nook and cranny of the sitting area, Maddie walked on to the bedroom on the left. "This should be the quietest, I think." After snapping the drapes closed, she pulled back the counterpane on the bed. "And this bed has no foot rail, which should suit you better."

Ash stood in the doorway, watching her.

"I remember how you hated banging your toes and not being able to stretch out." The words awakened images that brought heat to her cheeks. She motioned to the bed. "Sit, please. I'll help you with your boots." When he didn't move, she added, "Unless you'd prefer to sleep the rest of the night in them?"

He sat on the bed. Kneeling beside his knee, she began unlacing the closure that went up the outside of his right boot beside a sewn-in sheath for his long knife. She was so intent on her task she didn't realize he had reached out until she felt something touching her hair. Surprised, she looked up.

"You have beautiful hair, lass." Instead of meeting her gaze, he watched his fingers smooth back a lock that had slipped loose from the pins.

His hand felt big and heavy and warm against her scalp. She refrained from leaning into it like a purring cat.

"I wondered if it was as soft as I remembered." When he let his hand fall back to the bed, it was trembling. "I'm sorry to be so weak." He had such a sad, weary look on his face it brought a catch to her throat.

Unable to bear it, she looked down and began loosening the laces on his left boot. "You're not weak. And you needn't apologize to me."

"Guid." She heard the smile beneath the brogue. "But I was apologizing to myself for allowing my mind to make plans my puir body canna fulfill. An unusual happenstance, so it is. Especially for a Scotsman."

"Indeed? I've never heard that." Biting back a smile, she finished unlacing and motioned for him to lift his foot. After pulling off his boots, she set them at the foot of the bed, then stood. "Shall I help with the rest of your clothing?" She tried to sound matter of fact, but her voice came out higher and thinner than usual.

"I'll manage, love. A man can suffer only so much coddling."

"Indeed? Then I'll not badger you about food. Good night." She started for the door.

"Food?"

She stopped and turned back. "I was thinking a bit of cheese or a slice of ham might settle all that alcohol I heard sloshing around, but I wouldn't want to coddle you beyond forbearance."

His smile made her smile. "I'll endure it. For you, love."

"You're too kind."

When she returned with a plate a few minutes later, he was sprawled on top of the bedding, one arm over his eyes, the other dangling off the mattress so that his hand rested on Tricks, who was stretched out beside the bed. He still wore his trousers and shirt, although he'd slipped off his braces and loosened the buttons at his collar. He was snoring.

Her poor wounded warrior.

Setting the plate on the bureau out of the wolfhound's reach, she tiptoed from the room.

Eleven

He watched her slowly awaken, her breath catching on a deep inhale as she stretched like a cat in the sun. Leaning on one elbow beside her, he gently coaxed her onto her back and was rewarded when she arched against his stroking hand, a small sigh escaping her throat. "Morning, love."

"Ash . . . ?"

"No, 'tis the archbishop of Canterbury."

Her eyes blinked open, slowly focused on his. He felt her body go still. He watched her, waiting, his palm resting over the small birthmark just below her breast. If she rejected him now, he would go into his bedroom, load his pistol, and put it to his head.

Or maybe not.

As long as there was Maddie, there was hope.

With her fingertip, she traced an old saber scar by his neck. "If you're the archbishop, then where is your shepherd's crook?"

" 'Tis right here, lass." He leaned down and kissed one corner of her mouth, then the other. Lifting his head, he grinned down at her as he trailed his fingers over her breast. "Would you like to touch it?"

Maddie laughed softly, her gaze drifting from his beautiful eyes with that scar through one dark brow, across the bristled curve of his jaw, down his strong neck to the rounded slope of his shoulder. Tendon and muscle and bone. But put together in a way that made her heart sing. "Apparently, the pain in your head is gone."

"Aye. 'Tis moved elsewhere."

She tried to ignore what his hand was doing. But every caress, every stroke left shimmering heat in its wake and a trembling anticipation of where he would touch next. She moved restlessly, needing . . . wishing . . .

"Open to me, love."

She did and then he was there, right where she wanted him to be, touching her as only he had ever done. "Ash . . ."

"Are your blisters healed?" he asked, kissing her brow.

"W-What?" Awash in sensation, she could hardly form a thought. "Blisters? Yes. Mostly." *There. Yes . . . there . . .*

"Then touch me, lass," he whispered against her lips. "Now."

It was madness.

Not at all what she wanted.

The absolutely wrong thing to do.

But almost of its own accord, one hand slid up to pull him closer while the other reached down.

Yet even as his touch set her skin on fire, and his scent filled her senses, and her body sank into shivering sensation, some small fragment of her mind still clung to reason. "If we do this," she murmured against his throat where the pulse beat fast and hard, "it won't change anything."

"But 'tis a grand way to open discussion to the possibility, is it no'?" His big body jerked when she found him. "Och . . . sweet Mary . . ."

"Mary has naught to do with this, lad." She squeezed.

He groaned.

Then there were no more words, only the rush of their bodies coming together—as if the years apart had never been and the pain they had dealt each other had never happened. It was a frantic, breathless, dizzying dance of hands and mouths and straining bodies that gave and took until finally they were spiraling into bliss.

Over. Too soon. Too fast.

He rolled away, panting. "Jesus . . . lass . . ."

She lay as he had left her, gasping up at the ceiling, her heart beating so hard and fast she felt battered by the force of it. "Well." She blew hair out of her eyes. *Well, indeed.*

When he didn't respond, she looked over to where he lay sprawled beside her amid the tangled bedding, the sound of his breathing filling the room. She tingled all over, her nerves still quivering beneath her skin. Watching the muscles of his broad chest flex and contract with every breath made her tingle anew.

"That was . . ." She paused, searching her befuddled mind for the right word.

"Magnificent?" he supplied. "Astounding?"

"Short and sweet, I was going to say. But definitely—"

"Short?" He lifted his tousled head off the pillow to stare at her. "Too short?"

She heard the worry in his voice and tried not to laugh. "But definitely," she continued, "well worth the wait."

"Bawdy lass."

She smiled over at him.

The first glow of dawn highlighted the window on the other side of the bed and bathed his strong body in soft morning light, sculpting tendon and rounded muscle and tipping his dark chest hair with gold. He was so beautiful, so perfect—the warrior replete. She framed it in her mind, each shadow and hollow and sweat-slicked curve sharply defined in the lens of her artist's eye—frozen in this moment for all time—hers forever.

I love you.

Rolling onto her side, she rested her hand over his thundering heart, wishing she could hold him there beside her forever.

"Mole where?"

She frowned, caught off guard by the change in subject, then smiled, remembering. "On your—what do you call it? Arse."

"I dinna ken that."

"I should hope not."

Laughter showed in his eyes. "I've missed you, Maddie, so I have." His smile faded into something raw and unfamiliar to her. "Dinna run from me again, lass. I couldna bear it."

Tears pressed behind her eyes. Biding time until they passed, she traced a fingertip over his lips. "I didn't run. I drifted away. And you let me."

"I ken I was wrong. But I'll not be doing that again. I swear it."

In that unguarded moment, she glimpsed the brash, handsome, young man who had captured her heart six years ago. Who held it captive still.

Yet, nothing had changed.

No matter the fine words, he would leave her again. He couldn't help it. Duty would call, and honor would not allow him to disobey, and she would be left bleeding in his wake, just as had happened before. The thought of it was an unseen weight that pressed against her heart until the pain of it stole her breath away.

Oh, Maddie. You foolish, foolish woman.

She pulled her hand away.

Oblivious, he sighed and closed his eyes. "You make me daft, lass, so you do. But I'm no' complaining."

Tears burned in her throat, behind her eyes. Why had she opened herself up to the same heartache that had nearly destroyed her once already? Had she learned nothing?

"Ash, what have we done?" *To ourselves. To each other.*

He opened his eyes and looked at her. They were the cool green of tarnished copper, or the earliest spring grass, or a high mountain lake fed by icy peaks. Changeable. Mysterious. Compelling.

"Forgotten already, love? Must I show you again?" He said it lightly, but she heard the tension in his voice, felt it in his arms when he pulled her on top of him. Skin to skin, heart over heart, they stared into each other's eyes—separated by only that unbridgeable gap between duty and desire.

"Puir lass." Reaching up, he cupped her head in his big hands, his fingers so long his thumbs reached to her temples. "I ken ye're confused, love. As am I. But this I know, Maddie Wallace. We belong together. Apart, we're less than we were meant to be. But together, we can be more than either of us dreamed."

"In Scotland?" She tried to keep her voice from wobbling but failed. "I don't need a title, Ash. I need my work."

"You need *me*." He said it with fierce certainty, his eyes hiding nothing from her. "You need me." He kissed her lips, then her closed lids, blotting away the tears she could no longer hold back. "And I need you." Brushing his lips across her cheekbone, he whispered into her ear. "Ride me and I'll prove it."

He took her to the heights again, his hands hot on her body, his mouth marking her like a brand. Where the first time had been a tumultuous rush of need, this was a slow, sweet reacquainting that spoke of deeper emotion. She abandoned herself to it, trembling with the joy of it, and resolving for this moment, at least, to forget the past and the pain awaiting her.

Instead, she looked down as she moved above him—watched his lips pull tight against his clenched teeth, felt the tremble in the powerful muscles beneath her thighs, and knew somewhere within his armored warrior's heart he loved her still.

As she loved him.

But when it was over, and she lay in his arms, her body trembling and her heart drumming against his, the unspoken words hung in the air around then.

And still, nothing had changed.

The sun was barely above the jagged peaks when Maddie pushed back the covers and rose. Moving quietly so she didn't wake Ash, she dressed and pinned up her hair, then wrote a short note and left it on the bureau by his shaving mug where she knew he would find it. Then calling the dogs waiting restlessly in the sitting room, she left her husband sprawled asleep on the rumpled bed and left the suite.

Luckily at this early hour only Yancey was in the lobby, so Maddie didn't have to suffer any of Lucinda's probing looks. They would come, she knew, but at this moment what she wanted—what she desperately needed—was to focus all the turmoil in her mind through the lens of her camera.

Blocking from her mind the memory of Ash as she had last seen him, she walked briskly under the dawning sky, following the dogs down the muddy track toward the livery, her imagination churning as she mentally framed images, calculated angles and perspectives.

Unlike her life now that Ash was back in it, a photograph was sharp and clearly defined. Precise. Predictable. A one-dimensional view with no surprises. If it didn't turn out, she could throw it away and try again. There was comfort in that. A sense of control.

Life was so much messier.

She stopped, captivated by a puddle in the road where the first streaks of sunlight shining through the treetops cast bright reflections in the water and highlighted every rut in the road.

Tucking her skirts around her legs so they wouldn't drag in the mud, she squatted to view the ruts from a ground-level viewpoint as they stretched away from her. Motion. Energy. The track leading the viewer's eye toward the bigger, more distant vista of mountain and sky. She nodded to herself, deciding to come back and photograph this before the light changed. Rising, she let her skirts fall and continued toward the livery, anxious to get started.

Morning was a photographer's golden time. And with the sun's arc slipping a little lower as the seasons changed, each day presented a different study of shadow and light. And today was perfect. Clear and still. No clouds to muddy contrast. No wind to blur images and shake off the tiny dewdrops sparkling on the tips of drooping leaves. The air was so crisp and clean, every curve and line and plane was sharply defined with that crystal clarity that came only in the fall after a wet night had settled the dust. She couldn't wait to capture the images already framed in her mind.

Perhaps Mr. Satterwhite had been right when he had accused her of hiding behind her camera. But right now she needed that.

She needed to narrow the world to a more manageable size and re-establish control. She needed to find in her lens a reality that made sense to her and brought order and balance to her reeling mind.

She needed to distance herself . . . from herself.

And from Ash.

And the chaos he brought.

Just thinking about him sent a shiver up her legs.

Mr. Driscoll graciously loaned her his pushcart and helped her load it with photography supplies from the wagon. Then calling the dogs from the manure pile, she went back down the street, pushing the cart before her. If she hurried, she would have ample time for several photographs before heading to church and Mr. Satter-white's service.

Clutching the note in his hand, Ash stood at his bedroom window and watched his wife push a canvas-draped wheelbarrow down the street toward the hotel. She looked brisk and efficient and seemed completely oblivious to the antics of Tricks and Agnes as they darted in and out of the trees in some dog game of chase. Early-morning sunlight glinted in her hair and he smiled, remembering the silky feel of it running through his fingers.

His wife at last.

But for how long?

Disturbed by that thought, he frowned down at the note, trying again to decipher the letters. There were only a few words. *Church 11. Dinner 2 at the Brodies'.* He was fairly certain of the numbers, and that the first word was church and not chicken, but he had no idea what the last word was. Disgusted with his own ineptitude, he tossed the note back onto his bureau and resumed dressing. The day wasna starting well.

He'd been surprised to find her gone when he awoke.

More than surprised. Panicked. What woman willingly left her bed at dawn?

He remembered that clench of fear that she had escaped him

again. That none of it was real. That the images in his mind of her sleek, flushed body, and the echo of her soft cries, and the sweet, salty taste of her on his tongue had all been conjured out of pain and his whiskey-soaked imagination.

Then he had seen her gown on the floor and smelled her scent on the pillow next to his, and he'd known it was real.

And he had finally been able to breathe again.

No battlefield, no whine of bullets or booming cannons, no advancing line of shrieking, sword-waving sepoys had ever put such fear into him. And he dinna like it.

After he finished dressing, he went back to the window. She had stopped behind the building next door and was pulling the canvas cover off the wagon to reveal her camera and several items of photography equipment. After carefully spreading the canvas on the ground, she set her boxy camera on one end of it, then sank to her knees and stretched out on the canvas behind it.

Bluidy hell. He leaned close to the window and scanned the street, fearing some horseman would trample her or a wagon would roll over her. But the track was deserted except for the dogs, who came charging toward her prone body, obviously thinking this was some new game. Ash laughed aloud at her desperate attempts to avoid licks and muddy feet while shielding her camera, until Tricks spotted a wee ground squirrel and took off into the woods again, Agnes yipping at his heels.

His delicate viscountess yelled something after them that made Ash grin, shoved away a lock of hair that had fallen loose, then rolled back into position behind her camera. Flipping the drape over her head, she reached around to remove the covering and focus the lens.

What was she photographing? A beetle? Horse dung? A butterfly?

He wanted to go down to her and demand the good-morning kiss she'd denied him. He wanted to reassure himself that last night was real and make her promise she would never leave him again.

Instead, he pulled a chair close to the window, settled back, and watched his wife work.

After setting up her tripod, she photographed trees, buildings, a mule dozing in its traces behind the mercantile, two children watching from the open back door. And as he sat in the shadows, watching her, a slow and troubling thought crept into Ash's mind. Something he dinna want to consider. Or even acknowledge.

Photography was more than work to Maddie. It breathed life into her step and brought a wondering, childlike delight to her face. It was passion. A passion as strong as the one she had shown him in the wee hours of the night. Satterwhite's words drifted through his mind.

You take away her photography, you take away her joy.

No.

Is that what you want?

"Bugger off."

But the words wouldn't go away, and with a curse, Ash rose from the chair and left the room.

Other than a few pleasantries when she delivered his schedule for the day—church at eleven o'clock, then Satterwhite's service, then dinner at the Brodies' at two o'clock—Ash scarcely shared a word with his wife as she bustled about taking her photographs. It wasn't that she avoided him but that she was busy with tasks that dinna involve him or require his help or presence.

Or so he told himself.

To combat the restlessness that always plagued him when he hadn't enough to do, he took Tricks and Lurch out for exercise.

It was beautiful country, Maddie's Colorado Territory. Bold and majestic and inspiring but lacking the subtle nuances of his Highlands, where cloud and mist and ancient voices drifted through the dells.

When they reached the flats beyond the mouth of the canyon,

he let the animals run. As always, the feel of a good horse beneath his knees—powerful muscles bunching and stretching in long reaching strides, the wind whistling past his ears, and the sun harsh in his face—set Ash's spirit soaring. For that moment, at least, he was unfettered by the past or duty or burdensome responsibility. It was just the horse beneath him and the roar of blood in his veins and the unknown future rushing toward them.

And the joy of it made him laugh out loud.

When he entered the lobby just after ten o'clock, he found Maddie sitting in one of the upholstered chairs, talking with the blond Hathaway woman. She had washed away the mud and put ribbons in her auburn hair and changed into a floaty yellowish dress that clung to her body in a way that made his palms sweat. A pretty picture, the ladies were, had one not looked at him as if she expected him to pounce, and the other one hoping he would so she could gut him.

Stopping before them, he bowed stiffly, hands clasped behind his back. "Morning, ladies."

Lucinda Hathaway looked at his muddy dog then up at him. Her smile was as warm as a Welsh winter. "We thought you'd run off." "Again" was implied, rather than spoken aloud.

"And miss a chance to be paraded before my wife's friends? Never."

"It's church, Mr. Ashby. Not an inspection."

"I'm delighted to hear it, so I am. And it's *Lord* Ashby," he corrected, his smile matching hers in sincerity. Had she been a man, the lass would have flourished in the military. She was certainly no coward.

Turning to his wife, he said, "And you look especially fetching, my lady. I feel a bit worn in comparison."

"The washroom is available," Miss Hathaway cut in before Maddie could speak. "I took the liberty of instructing Billy to put your laundered clothing in the wardrobe with the clean toweling. Please don't use the drying cloths on your dog." She made a shooing motion. "We'll wait."

Bollocks. "We? So you'll be joining us? What a delight."

"Only to services. Maddie and I will be taking my buggy. I'm sorry there won't be enough room for three," she added, not sounding sorry at all. "She said you would probably prefer to ride alongside anyway. And of course, you're welcome to use it later, since I won't be joining you for dinner at the Brodies'."

"No?" Ash hid his relief behind a look of feigned sympathy. "Cholera, perhaps? An overactive spleen? Bloat? I hear chamomilla works wonders."

This time it was his wife who broke in. "I hate to interrupt such a delightful Punch and Judy show," she said, laughing. "But if we delay much longer, we'll miss opening hymns."

"A blessing," Miss Hathaway murmured. "Biddy's last rendition of 'Come to Jesus' left me deaf for a week."

Twenty minutes later, Ash stepped out of the washroom to find his wife and Miss Hathaway chatting on the back stoop with Driscoll, who had brought Lurch and Miss Hathaway's conveyance from the livery.

It was a four-wheeled, open, one-horse buggy with a fold-down top, similar to the type doctors used. The long-legged pacer harnessed to it looked calm and capable. After helping the ladies board, Ash swung up on Lurch and they were off.

Five minutes later they arrived at the Come All You Sinners Church of Heartbreak Creek, situated at the edge of town where the canyon opened into a wide plain of grassy, rolling hills; Ash must have ridden past it earlier without noticing it tucked in beside the creek. It was so close to the hotel, he wondered why they hadn't simply walked.

The church was small, the flock smaller, which in no way diminished the arm-waving, pulpit-pounding enthusiasm of Pastor Rickman or his stridently vocal pianist wife, Biddy.

Ash couldn't have slept if he'd wanted to.

After a sermon decrying the temptations of the flesh, and a closing hymn sung with alarming gusto by two elderly ladies, the pastor herded his flock to the wee cemetery beside the church—for what, Ash had no idea, since Satterwhite was resting peacefully a day's ride away. But there they stood, staring mournfully down at a patch of ground that presumably would have been Satterwhite's final resting place had he made the trip home, while Biddy Rickman did more damage to "Amazing Grace" than a drunken piper with a bad cold. A few words about Satterwhite, a few tears from Maddie, a prayer tossed in for good measure, and they were on their way back to town with an hour to kill before they had to leave for the Brodies'.

Maddie spent it in her wagon, checking her supplies for the trip to Denver, while Ash perused months-old newspapers in the hotel lobby. A war had been fought and lost in Sedan, another Napoleon had been deposed, and a third French Republic had been declared. Wolseley had saved the day in Canada, infanticide had finally been banned in India, and women all over the country were demanding the right to vote.

Ash had been aware of none of it. Sad, that.

At half past one, he went back to the livery. As he had requested, Driscoll had folded down the canvas top on Miss Hathaway's buggy so they could take in the air. After loading in his carbine, Ash rousted Maddie from her wagon, handed her into the buggy, and took up the reins, imagining the laughter from his fellow cavalry officers had they seen him riding about in a carriage like a London matron.

The day was clear and bright, with a hint of fall in the breeze, but still warm in the sun. Glancing back at the mound of coats, hats, and blankets stuffed behind the seat, Ash asked his wife if she was expecting a blizzard.

"Laugh if you will," she retorted. "But it will be much colder tonight after the sun goes down. You'll be begging for a blanket."

He might be begging tonight. But not for a blanket.

At the edge of town, they crossed over a wooden bridge—the hollow thud of the horses' hoofbeats on the planks echoing like distant artillery fire—then turned left onto a track that paralleled Heartbreak Creek. Ash kept an eye out for bears gleaning the last of the berries in the brush, but all he saw were two rabbits and a fat marmot.

They spoke little. It was one of those highly charged female-type silences that eroded a man's confidence and had him scanning through recent events to determine what he might have done wrong. Ash tolerated it as long as he could, then looked over at his wife. "It was the uniform, right?"

In the slanted light, her eyes were as brown and clear as the medicine bottles that had lined the windowsill beside his hospital bed. Filled with promises and hope. Addictive.

"Uniform?"

"That caught your eye." When she still showed no understanding, he explained. "I can feel you drifting away, lass, and I'm seeking a way to draw you back. The ladies always seemed taken with the uniform. As once did you. Shall I send for it?"

"Drifting away? You can say that after what we—you and I—when we—after last night?" She clasped her gloved hands in her lap and looked away, her cheeks as red as strawberry ice in a paper cone.

"So it went well for you then, love? You dinna say, so I wasna sure. But with all the squealing and carrying on, I should have known."

Her head whipped toward him. "I did not squeal or carry on."

"No? Then it must have been me."

Caught off guard by the absurdity of that, she sputtered into a laugh, which made him laugh, which eased the tension a bit. He loved to hear her laugh. In fact, he loved all her little sounds.

"I must admit," she went on, pulling him from his pleasant musings of her naked body, "you did look most dashing in your uniform. Filled it out quite nicely, as I recall."

"Not as nicely as I would now, with all your tartish talk of bed sport."

"Tartish—? Don't be crass." But she checked before she hastily looked away. He was sure of it.

She sat stiffly for a bit, then wilted on a great sigh. "Ash, what are we going to do?"

He had some ideas but doubted their thoughts were pointed in the same direction. "About what, lass?"

"Us. This." Another deep exhale. "I don't want to go back to Scotland."

Ah. He'd figured that was the reason for the tense silence. Not sure how to respond, he waited as the wheels rattled across another wooden bridge where Elderberry Creek joined Heartbreak Creek, then turned toward her. She looked more sad than defiant, and it troubled him that the idea of living with him in Scotland would bring her such distress. "I'm aware you don't, love. You've made your feelings quite clear."

She went on as if he hadn't spoken. "And yet . . ." She raised her gloved hands in a helpless gesture, then let them drop back to her lap. "And yet I don't want to lose you again, either."

An encouraging sign. "You've made those feelings *less* clear." He sent her a hopeful smile. "Perhaps you'd like another go at it tonight?"

"Don't make jokes, Ash. This is serious."

"I see that. As was my offer." His smile faded. "I want my wife back, Maddie. Even if I have to chase her around England while she takes her photographs." He tried to put sincerity into his voice, but he could tell she wasn't fooled.

"A viscountess photographer." She gave an un-viscountess-like snort. "Society would never accept that, as well you know. And I'll not make a mockery of your position."

He couldn't give her words of reassurance. Not with generations of Kirkwells and a lifetime of familial duty rising up to hold his throat in a choking grip.

"So what are we going to do, Ash?"

"I'm thinking on it, lass."

"Perhaps if I had just a bit more time I could come to terms with it."

He looked over at her, saw a confusion on her face that mirrored his own. Taking her gloved hand in his, he brought it to his lips for a kiss. "We'll work something out, love." He punctuated that with a gentle squeeze, then returned her hand to her lap and faced the road again.

But that nagging question remained. What?

They clopped along through dappled shade cast by the tall cottonwoods and alders and firs that crowded the bank of Elderberry Creek running a few yards from the road. Ash kept the horse at an easy walk, enjoying this quiet time with his wife and in no rush to suffer the censorious looks and probing questions he was sure awaited him.

"I suppose I should tell you about the people we'll be dining with," she said, as if her thoughts had strayed in the same direction as his. "Prepare you, as it were."

That dinna sound good. "I've met the sheriff. Seems a good man."

"He is. I wish he would take the sheriff's position permanently so we could see more of him and Edwina and the children." At his questioning look, she explained, "He's a rancher by trade, but with his wife in a family way, and the regular sheriff, Buck Aldrich, away until spring, he's been talked into taking over the position temporarily. Again."

"They have other children?"

"He does. Three boys and a girl from a previous marriage. One that ended badly, not to put too fine a point on it. Edwina was the mail-order bride he married by proxy to come help with the children and ranch chores. What a fiasco that was. Edwina, a southern magnolia of the first water, and Declan." She laughed and shook her head. "I guess I should warn you. Edwina can play a piano blindfolded, flirt a dead man back to life, and find water with a willow switch, but she's an abysmal cook. Let's hope her sister has come to help out today."

"Sister?" Yet another woman waiting to skewer him?

His wife looked at him in surprise, her face partially shaded by the brim of her bonnet. "You didn't know Edwina and Pru are half sisters?"

"The dark-skinned woman is her sister?"

"Pru's mother was a slave on their plantation. They share the same father. He dearly loved both his daughters, which is why Pru is as well educated as Edwina, although she was apparently a far better student. The woman is brilliant."

"That must have complicated things at home."

"Vastly. From what Edwina says, her own mother was abusive, perhaps even insane. Both she and Pru have scars to attest to that. Pru's are worse, and she's quite sensitive about them. Because of that, and whatever happened when she was abducted by Lone Tree, she's a bit skittish."

"Lone Tree?" Ash was having difficulty sorting it all out. "Is he the Cheyenne Dog Soldier I've heard mentioned?"

"Heavens, no. That's Thomas Redstone. He's Declan's deputy. The two are like brothers." Leaning over, she added in a confidential tone, "And, although no one mentions it, he is madly in love with Pru. You'll see." She straightened with a sigh. "No, Lone Tree was a renegade Arapaho who had some sort of vendetta against Declan. He was quite vicious. Dead now, thankfully. Still, the ordeal he put Pru through still preys on her, and I think that's why she holds Thomas at arm's length. Poor man."

Ash knew firsthand how that felt. But no more. He'd happily and repeatedly reclaimed his bride last night. And he wasn't about to let her slip away from him a second time.

"There it is." Maddie pointed to a small whitewashed house that had been added on to, then added on to again, so that it looked less like a planned structure than a series of rooms tacked on when need arose.

As he lifted Maddie down from the buggy, the door crashed open and children stampeded down the porch steps and into the yard. Unfortunately that was at the exact moment that Tricks also arrived, his tongue lolling, a chewed-off length of rope dangling between his front legs.

The moment the children saw him, they erupted in shrieks.

"Hold!" Ash barked before the wolfhound mistook the frenzy as an attack on him.

Children froze. Tricks flopped onto his belly. At his side, Maddie sucked in a breath.

Ash dinna know much about children, but he knew how to take charge of unruly troops. And he also knew that the hysteria would continue until he'd allayed their fears about Tricks. Clasping his hands behind his back, he marched forward, his voice cracking like a whip. "Form ranks!"

One wee creature, dressed in boy's clothing and its face hidden beneath a hat so that Ash couldn't determine gender, leaned toward a thin boy with sharp brown eyes and a mop of light brown hair. "What's ranks?"

Ash stopped before the floppy-hatted urchin. He/she had the most remarkable gray eyes, the color of buffed pewter or newly cast lead bullets. He bent down until their faces were as close as he could get them without falling onto his knees. "Line up," he said softly.

"Why?"

Female, he guessed by the quavery-voiced defiance. Only a female would dare. "Because I order you to."

"Why?"

Never having been asked for a reason before, Ash wasn't sure how to answer. "Because you're frightening my dog."

Her gaze slid toward Tricks, who was stretched at Maddie's side, watching them with unblinking intensity. "He's very big."

Ash straightened. "Aye. He's an Irish Wolfhound."

"I what?"

"What's his name?" a new voice cut in.

Ash turned to the questioner, a blond boy with a hodgepodge of little teeth, big teeth, and missing teeth. "Tricks."

"Does he do tricks?"

"He does. I'll show—"

"Perhaps later, children," his wife cut in, moving to his side. "Right now, I would like to introduce you to my husband." She directed Ash to a gangly boy who looked like a younger, shorter, skinnier, chinless version of the sheriff. "R. D., here, is the oldest."

Ash offered his hand. The lad took it in a sure grip and studied him through dark, steady eyes. A fine soldier someday. Ash nodded approval.

"And this"—Maddie rested her gloved hand on the shoulder of the towheaded boy with the odd teeth—"is Joe Bill."

Joe Bill's grip was no less sure, but damper. Ash hoped it was sweat.

Moving to the last two in line, Maddie smiled down at the skinny boy with the sharp brown eyes. "This is Lucas—he's brilliant—and Brin, the beauty in the family. Children, this is Lord Ashby."

Clasping his hand once more behind his back, Ash gave a curt, military nod.

"Lord?" The girl's eyes widened. "You're named after God?"

"I'm not calling him lord." With that, the blond boy—Joe Bill—marched back up the weed-choked path to the porch where several adults, including the Indian and the sheriff, stood watching.

"Me, neither," the female, Brin, announced and followed her brother. "He talks funny."

The smart one, Lucas, gave a shy smile, then showing solidarity, traipsed after his older brother and younger sister. Which left the gangly adolescent, R. D., who studied Ash with the same probing intensity his father had exhibited when he had first met Ash several weeks ago. "I like your dog," he finally said. Then he, too, went up the steps and into the house.

"Recruits," Ash muttered, letting out the breath he hadn't realized he'd been holding. "They hadn't even been properly dismissed."

"Children," Maddie corrected under her breath. "Not to worry. They've defeated stouter men than you." Taking his arm, she steered him on toward the house, calling "Hallo" and waving as she went.

Ash wasn't easily impressed. He'd fought alongside Britain's finest and Scotland's fiercest. He'd battled Russians, Prussians, Sultans, and Sheiks. But when he saw the Cheyenne Dog Soldier planted at the top of the steps, arms crossed over his wide chest, he recognized a true warrior.

"Ash, I believe you've met Declan Brodie, our sheriff," Maddie said, pausing before the bottom step. Then she went on to introduce Edwina Brodie, Prudence Lincoln, and the Indian, Thomas Redstone.

"Welcome," Edwina said, her lively blue eyes alight with mischief. "We've never had lords and ladies to dinner before, and I declare I hardly know whether to bow or curtsy or faint dead away."

"You never faint," Prudence Lincoln said as Maddie started up the steps. "And in your condition, it wouldn't be prudent, anyway. Good afternoon, Lord Ashby," she added with a smile that almost made Ash miss the bottom step.

"Just Ash," he managed, aware of the sheriff's smirk and the Cheyenne's glower. "Delighted to meet you, ladies."

The dark-skinned woman spoke with the same drawling Southern accent as did the sheriff's wife, although it carried a softer, mellower tone. Neither woman made use of their *r*s. Perhaps they'd given them all to the Scots, Ash mused, as he stopped before their hosts. "Thank you for inviting us into your home."

"Oh, law's amercy," Edwina Brodie said in a breathless voice—probably a condition brought on by her substantial girth. "Did you hear that Declan? That's exactly the kind of manners I've been trying to teach the children. And do call me Edwina."

Brodie extended a hand to Ash. "Welcome back to Heartbreak Creek."

The Indian didn't extend a hand but studied Ash as thoroughly as Ash studied him.

The man was in full Indian garb—thigh-length leather war shirt decorated with beads and shells and bits of antler, leather legging, soft-soled fringed leather knee boots, and a red breechcloth hanging below the edge of his long tunic. The only thing missing was war paint. And the deputy badge.

Ash nodded. "Redstone."

The Cheyenne nodded silently back.

Ash sensed he'd met a man he wouldn't want for an enemy.

Turning back to Brodie, he said, "Could you spare something to tie up my dog? A chain would be best, I think."

Twelve

Dinner was a continuation of the chaos that had erupted earlier when the children had come charging out of the house. Edwina Brodie made gallant attempts to maintain order, but it was apparent that although the children loved her, they clearly dinna fear her. A true leader needed both if he—or she—was to maintain order, Ash had found.

Which the sheriff had in abundance, although he wielded his power with soft words and hard looks—and only after his wife had lost her gracious smile and turned to him with narrowed eyes.

"Children," he would say in his quiet voice. "Slops." And that ended it. For a while, anyway.

Watching the looks passing between the sheriff and his wife, and seeing the pride in their smiles when they looked at their children—who really weren't bad children as much as high-spirited and somewhat undisciplined—made Ash realize how different his own life might have been had he grown up in such an unstructured, boisterous, but affectionate household. If he ever had a family of his own to manage, would he be a benign ruler like Declan Brodie? Or a ham-fisted tyrant like his father?

"Quite different from Northbridge, is it not?" his wife murmured at his side as if she had read his thoughts. Unsettling how often that was happening of late. He dinna like to think he was so transparent.

"Aye." He smiled down at her. "And even though it gives me a headache, I like it."

Her smile faded. "Your head hurts?"

"No more than any sane person's would."

"You were a soldier?" the oldest boy—R. D.—asked, pulling Ash away from pleasant memories of his wife's soft breasts.

"Aye."

Brin leaned toward her brother, Lucas. "Why does he keep saying 'I'?" she whispered loud enough for the whole table to hear. For such a small mite, the wee bairn had a verra big voice.

"Not 'I.' Aye," the boy whispered back. "It means yes." Lucas's brown gaze swung to Ash. "Doesn't it?"

"Aye."

"See, he did it again."

"Did you kill a lot of people when you were a soldier?" the blond boy asked through a mouthful of half-chewed carrots.

A bit taken aback, Ash shrugged. "When necessary."

"Ed killed Lone Tree," the blond volunteered.

Edwina Brodie narrowed her eyes in warning.

"Slops," her husband said and took a bite of roast beef.

While Joe Bill's mother leaned over and whispered something in the boy's ear that took some of the color out of his cheeks, R. D. continued his interrogation of Ash. "Sword or rifle?"

"Both." Ash set down his fork and sat back, becoming uneasy. Not that he minded doing his duty as a soldier, but he dinna like discussing the gory aspects of it with a child.

"Were you ever wounded?"

"Aye." Without looking over, he knew the Indian was listening.

"How many times?"

Ash wiped his mouth with his napkin and placed it carefully beside his plate. "Four. Perhaps five."

Finally, the Cheyenne spoke. "What is the long gun you use?"

"When I was with the Rifles," Ash said, "we used the Pattern 1853 Enfield muzzle-loaders. Later, when I transferred to the Hussars, we were issued shorter barreled, breech-loading Snider-Enfield cavalry carbines. They don't have the range or accuracy of the long rifle but are easier to carry on horseback."

R. D. pointed to a rifle hung over the door. "That's a Sharps .50."

"Aye. I recognize it. A fine rifle, I hear."

"My, all this talk of guns is utterly fascinating, don't you think, ladies?" Edwina punctuated the pointed remark with a dramatic roll of her cornflower blue eyes toward Maddie and Pru.

They grinned back.

"Ever shoot one of them?" R. D. asked

"No, but I've heard they're verra accurate."

"Not that one," Brodie cut in with a look of disgust as he spooned a second helping of potatoes onto his plate. "Thing pulls left every time."

Ash thought for a moment to determine which direction was left so he could mark it in his mind if he ever had a chance to shoot the rifle.

"Bet it wouldn't pull left for me," the boy argued.

"No, it would probably break your shoulder, instead," his father retorted. "Get some meat on your bones, then you can try it." He must have seen Ash's look of interest. "You want, Ashby, you can try it after supper. But be warned. Thing kicks like a bluenose mule."

Ash doubted it would kick harder than his carbine with its shorter barrel, especially if he loaded it with one of his special long-range cartridges.

The talk drifted to more appropriate topics for dinner conversation. Prudence Lincoln mentioned two new students who had joined her little school. Ash could see she was as passionate about her teaching as Maddie was about her photography. She apparently even lived in the building that housed the schoolroom. Her dark eyes seemed to glow with excitement and her beautiful face became more animated and less wary. He wondered what had happened to make her so reserved even among friends—was it because of her mixed blood? Those pale burn scars he could see on her wrist? Or her ordeal when she'd been abducted by Indians?

He studied the Cheyenne, who—as usual—was looking at Miss Lincoln. The Indian had said little during the meal, and when he did speak, his voice was as flat and expressionless as his dark gaze. Ash wondered at the admiration these people obviously felt for the silent, hard-faced man.

Then wee Brin said something that made him laugh, and Ash immediately realized the reason for their affection. That broad smile brought a shocking transformation to his starkly sculpted face and spoke of deep feelings for this family he apparently had adopted as his own.

Ash understood that. He had harbored a similar affection for the men under his command. Almost paternal. Intensely protective. Even now, he mourned those he had lost.

Conversation shifted to talk of Denver and all that would be needed for the trip. Since Edwina Brodie would be traveling with them, Prudence Lincoln would stay at the Brodie house to watch the children, while Thomas Redstone would take over sheriff duties in town—and watch over Prudence Lincoln from his room in the carriage house behind the Brodie's house. He had a good start on that now, Ash noticed. The Cheyenne had scarcely taken his eyes off the pretty dark-skinned woman since they'd taken their seats.

An interesting group. Ash liked them and was even starting to enjoy himself when Brodie pulled a crumpled envelope from his back trouser pocket.

"Meant to give this to you earlier. Your first name is Angus, right? Angus Wallace?"

Ash nodded.

"Then this must be for you. Came in late today, in care of Heartbreak Creek sheriff." He studied the envelope, then held it toward Ash. "Judging by the cross-outs, it's been forwarded several times already."

With a sense of dread, Ash took the envelope, wondering how he was going to hide from these people his inability to read.

"I never got a letter," Joe Bill said morosely.

Brin sighed heavily. "Me, neither."

"Wouldn't matter, Brin. You can't read yet anyway."

Ash looked at the faces turned toward him. Most wore expectant expressions—letters were a rare happenstance, it seemed—but one person, Prudence Lincoln, seemed more puzzled than curious. His dread building, Ash opened the envelope and pulled out two sheets of paper covered with small handwriting. Letters swam across the page.

"What does it say?"

"Brin," Edwina scolded. "It's none of your business."

Ash studied the letters but could only make out a word here and there. Shame rising in his throat, he looked helplessly at the faces watching him. "I can't—"

"Of course you can't." His wife snatched the papers from his grip. "And you shouldn't, since it's not even addressed to you." She pointed to the name on the envelope. "A. Wallace." To the others, she explained that Alexandra Madeline Wallace was her full name, but she signed her photographs A. M. Wallace. "Perhaps it's from someone wanting to commission a portrait. Wouldn't that be lovely?"

While she scanned the letter, Ash sank back in his chair and wiped his damp palms on his thighs, aware that Prudence Lincoln was still studying him.

"It's from a man named Aaron Zucker in Pennsylvania." Maddie passed the letter to Pru, who looked it over then passed it on to Declan. "He's trying to find his brother, Ephraim Zucker. He writes that he's coming to Heartbreak Creek to question me about a photograph I took of his brother several months ago."

"Do you remember this Ephraim Zucker?" Edwina asked.

Maddie shook her head. "Apparently he planned to meet his brother in Omaha, Nebraska Territory, several weeks ago, but Ephraim never showed up."

Brodie handed the letter back to Maddie. "Says he'll arrive in Heartbreak Creek sometime next week."

"He'd best hurry, then." Folding the letter, Maddie slipped it into her skirt pocket. "Or he'll have to wait until we return from Denver."

When the meal ended, Declan took down the rifle over the door, and trailing children like goslings, took Ash and Thomas out back to set up a shooting area. Between the Brodie house and that of their nearest neighbor, Jeb Kendal, was a long open stretch that backed up to a brushy hill. As they walked out, Maddie heard Declan tell R. D. and Joe Bill to alert Jeb to what they were doing, then make sure no one was prowling the brush they'd be shooting into. Ash said he would get his British carbine from the buggy so they could try that, too.

As soon as the tromp of heavy footfalls descended the porch steps, Edwina pounced.

"So what's going on, Maddie? Tell us everything."

"About what?"

"You know what. Your husband. And whatever it is that put that rash on your neck. Looks like beard rash to me."

"Edwina!" Pru rose and began clearing the table. "You are the nosiest creature alive, I swear."

"I'm sure I don't know what you're talking about." Maddie hiked her shoulders and tried to shorten her neck, but knew it was to no avail. It was most inconsiderate of Ash not to shave before he snuck into her room last night and—

Edwina laughed and shook a finger at Maddie. "Then why are you grinning like a possum eating persimmons? Him, too. Why, that man was all but drooling into his plate whenever he looked at you."

"Was he? I didn't notice." A lie, of course. She had noticed everything about him, including his almost palpable dread when Declan had handed him the letter. An affliction, he'd called it. And also a horrible shame for a man as capable and intelligent as Ash to be unable to perform such a simple task as reading. Maybe there was something she could do to help him. Perhaps if she tactfully asked Pru . . .

As she rose to help Pru clear the table, Edwina started up, too. "No, you rest," Maddie said, motioning her back into her chair.

Edwina returned to her seat with a grateful sigh. "Don't try to change the subject, Maddie. It was obvious the minute you came up to the house. Didn't I say that, Pru? Something has changed. That's what I said."

"I believe your exact words were, 'Doesn't Maddie look fetching in that dress?' "

"Exactly. And it was obvious why you look so fetching, so don't bother to deny it."

"Deny what?"

"That you and Ash . . . you know . . ."

Maddie did know but was going to force Edwina to say it aloud. For all that she was an accomplished flirt, the southern belle was more modest than Queen Victoria ever thought of being. "Know what?"

"That you and Ash . . . consummated."

"Oh, Lord," Pru muttered.

Taking Maddie's silence for confirmation, Edwina pointed that finger again. "You did, didn't you? I knew it. Not that I blame you. He is your husband, after all. And almost as handsome as Declan."

Maddie thought Ash the handsomer of the two but let the comment pass unchallenged.

Pru set a stack of plates onto the plank counter, then turned to Maddie, a troubled frown on her beautiful face. "Does this mean you'll be going back to Scotland, after all?"

Edwina cut in before Maddie could respond. "Of course not. She'll stay right here. Why, look at how well her photography is going. She's practically almost famous! And she just *has* to be here for when the baby comes, and for the christening, and by then—"

"Edwina," her sister admonished.

Edwina's face crumpled. "But I don't want her to leave."

Hearing the wobble in Edwina's voice, Maddie rested a reassuring hand on her shoulder, trying to avoid a scene that would only lead to tears for all of them and do no one any good—especially Edwina, who was volatile enough even when not in a family way. "I don't want to leave you, either."

"So what will you do?" Pru asked.

Edwina sniffed into her table napkin. "She'll make him stay here, that's what."

Maddie picked up more dirty dishes and carried them to the counter. "As I said before, that's not possible. He's heir to an earldom, and earls carry great responsibility."

"But he's not an earl yet, is he?" Edwina argued. "So why can't he stay here until he inherits?"

Pausing at the sink, Maddie looked out at the men walking toward the open field. Ash looked so tall and proud, his long legs moving in a graceful, rolling gait, his heels coming down with authority and purpose. A big, able man, hobbled by duty and bound by honor. He would make a magnificent earl.

Turning away, she scraped plates into the slop bucket. "He has duties." But even as she said it, she thought of Glynnis, and all that Ash's sister did for Northbridge. She was the true manager of the lands. It was because of Glynnis's hard work that the earl and his two other sons had been able to spend weeks, even months, in Edinburgh and London. Did Donnan truly need Ash when he had Glynnis there to run Northbridge?

Maddie thought of London—damp, noisy, redolent of too many people crowding the narrow streets, and the pervasive odor of coal fires, refuse, and the river Thames hanging over the city like a dark cloud. "Did you know that in London, between the fog and rain and coal soot in the air, we often went weeks without ever seeing the sun? And Scotland was no better."

"In Louisiana we had our rainy seasons," Edwina put in. "August was always a veritable steam bath. Then those awful hurricanes. Remember that year, Pru, when all the cabins along the bayou washed away?"

Maddie glanced out the window at the clear, crisp sky. How could she take photographs in the rain? Would she have to wait weeks for the sun to show itself, or hide under an oiled canvas to frame her images? What about all the nuances of light and shadow that created depth and mystery?

Or would she even be able to pursue her photography at all?

"So," Edwina announced. "Now that we have Maddie and her Angus back together, we must get to work on you and Thomas, Pru."

"Oh, Lord."

Maddie watched Pru, thinking she seemed especially evasive today. "How have things gone with him while I was gone?"

Pru busied herself pumping water into the sink. "Same as always."

"Then why are you blushing?" her sister challenged.

Maddie studied Pru's smooth caramel-colored skin. "She's blushing? How can you tell?"

"I'd know she was blushing in the dark. So tell us, Pru. What are you hiding? Have you and Thomas . . . you know . . ."

"No!" Pru said emphatically. "We have not consummated."

"But you've done something . . ."

Throwing her hands up in defeat, Pru whirled from the sink. "All right. We kissed. There. Satisfied?"

Edwina grinned at Maddie. "I win. And I'll expect that beaded pink ribbon the next time I'm in town." At her sister's outraged gasp, she quickly explained. "It wasn't exactly a bet, Pru. Maddie wasn't sure if Indians even kissed. I was sure they did. And if anybody could get one from Thomas, it would be you. That's how much confidence I have in you. You should be thanking me."

"You are utterly impossible. And this conversation is over."

"I think she means it," Maddie said.

"She does." Rising awkwardly from her chair, Edwina grimaced down at her body, one hand splayed on her midsection as if holding it in place. "I feel like I'm toting around a full-grown Declan. And I still have three more months to go. Law's amercy." Once balanced, she motioned for Maddie and Pru to follow. "Forget the dishes and come to the back room. You *must* see the lovely cradle Declan made. He is so good with his hands." She sent them a look. "And you can trust me on that."

While Ash went back to the buggy for his carbine, Declan had R. D. set up four targets at the bottom of the brushy slope—two empty one-gallon cans from when they'd whitewashed the house the previous summer, an empty two-gallon vinegar bottle, and a leaky water bucket—then pace back to their shooting position beside the paddocks—which was approximately three hundred sixty yards.

When Ash returned with his rifle, Brodie was herding children to a safe distance and Thomas Redstone was leaning against a fence post toying with a sliding brass telescope. Two rifles—the Sharps and a Winchester repeater that looked to be the same model 1866 that Satterwhite had owned—were leaning against the bottom rail of the small corral off the stable.

Ash set the carbine beside the other guns, along with the box of cartridges he had loaded himself. Some he had modified for long distance shots by casting the bullets lighter by a third, which left more room in the cartridge for power. A trick he'd learned from an old rifleman and a man with the keenest eye he'd ever seen. But even though the lighter bullets traveled farther and flatter, the carbine was only accurate to a maximum of four hundred yards, which probably made it a little less effective in distance shots than the Sharps. Be interesting to see if he was right.

"Want to try the Sharps first?" Brodie asked.

"Aye."

He watched the sheriff pop the lever, slip the cartridge into place, then close it. Brodie handed him the rifle, then pointed across the open stretch. "Four targets at the base of the hill. We'll start with the bucket on the right. Remember, it kicks like a son of a bitch."

Ash had been kicked by both a son of a bitch and a mule. He suspected the Sharps couldn't be worse. Bending, he picked up a pinch of grass and let it drop to check the wind.

Target right. Wind left. While he set that in his mind, he raised the rifle and looked through the open ladder sight mounted behind the hammer. He found his target. Lowering the rifle, he adjusted the sight for range and drop. Satisfied, he motioned Redstone aside. Resting his elbow on the tall fence post, he peered through the sight with his near eye.

"Bucket right. Three hundred fifty yards." He took a deep breath, let out half of it, counted to two, and squeezed the trigger.

The barrel jumped, but the recoil wasn't as bad as his carbine with a modified cartridge. And because of its longer barrel, the Sharps wasn't nearly as loud. Before the sound left his ears, the bucket flew into the air, tumbled twice then rolled to a stop.

Ash straightened off the post and handed Brodie his rifle. "No pull. Left or right."

"You're sure?"

"Aye."

"He hit in front of it," Thomas Redstone said.

"No," Ash said calmly. "I dinna."

"See for yourself." The Cheyenne handed him the telescope.

Ash pressed the cup to his eye, adjusted the focus until he saw the hole in the wooden bucket, then lowered the telescope and turned to the others. "Square in the middle."

Both men and all four children burst into hoots of laughter.

Ash blinked in confusion.

"You got him!" Brin shouted, hopping up and down.

"He looks like a raccoon," Joe Bill crowed, pointing at Ash's face.

"A war pony with a painted eye," R. D. seconded.

Ash looked at the telescope, saw the remnants of black boot wax on the eyecup and knew the rest of it was now smeared in a circle around his eye. A trick recruits dearly loved to play on their sergeants.

"Sorry," Brodie said, not sounding sorry at all. "You know Indians. They love their pranks."

Ash laughed good-naturedly and wiped off the wax with his handkerchief. This wasn't the first time he'd been tricked. The military was famous for its pranks. At least this one didn't involve broken bones or scorched pants.

"Hell of a shot, by the way," the sheriff said to Ash as he reloaded the Sharps. "Think you can do better, Thomas?"

The Cheyenne studied Ash, laughter still showing in his dark eyes. "Better than a white man? Yes."

Ash smirked back. "But better than a Scot? No."

Ash was right. Neither Redstone nor Brodie could match him in marksmanship, even when they tried sitting behind the fence and resting the rifle on the bottom rail. With three of the four targets still standing, Ash picked up the Snider-Enfield. Now it was his turn.

He loaded it with one of his special cartridges, knowing that the added gunpowder would greatly increase the muzzle blast as well as the kick. After snapping the side breech closed, he held it out to the Cheyenne.

"Perhaps this will be easier for you to shoot," he chided. "With only a twenty-inch barrel, it's as light as a feather in your hands and has a kick as soft as a wee brownie's kiss."

"What is this brownie?" Thomas asked Brodie, taking the rifle. Brodie shrugged.

"Be sure to hold it soft," Ash advised. "This wee gun hasn't the power of the Sharps so you won't even need to brace it. Just lean close into it and aim through the sliding rear sight to the fixed sight on the barrel. Come." He motioned the sheriff closer. "You can watch over his shoulder."

Feet braced, his cheek against the stock, Thomas peered through the sight. Brodie leaned closer and squinted at the target in the distance. When Ash saw Thomas take a deep breath, he stepped back and put his fingers to his ears.

Thomas squeezed. The muzzle blast jerked the shortened barrel up and back, smacking the tall metal sight against the Cheyenne's forehead. He staggered back, almost stumbling into Brodie who had his hands clapped over his ears. Words in a language Ash dinna know exploded from the Indian's mouth.

"Looks like you missed," Ash called out. "Too bad." Clasping his hands behind his back, he turned to the sheriff, who was shaking his head like a dog with a bee in its ear. "We Scots," he said loudly enough to be heard over the ringing he guessed was still echoing through the sheriff's head, "like our pranks, too."

And that's when they jumped him.

Thirteen

" An entertaining afternoon," Ash said later as he helped Maddie into the buggy. Daylight was fading fast and he knew he would have to pick up the pace if they were to get back to Heartbreak Creek before dark. Tricks was probably halfway there already, having taken off as soon as Ash had removed the chain and returned it to the sheriff.

"Entertaining? You were fighting! And *laughing*! Rolling around on the ground like barnyard animals."

While Ash went around to the other side of the buggy, she yanked the coats and blankets from behind the bench and threw them onto the seat beside her. "My God, Ashby, you're a *viscount*!"

Shoving blankets and coats aside to make room, Ash took his seat. "That doesn't mean I canna have fun."

"Fun? You broke your finger!"

"Only knocked a wee bit out of joint, but I snapped it back in place. See?" He held up his hand to show the finger in question, which was now straight, although a bluish, purple color. He bent it as far as the swelling would allow. "All fixed."

She sniffed and looked away.

"A friendly tussle, lass. That's all."

"And yet your hand is injured, Declan's nose is still bleeding, and Thomas has that nasty bruise on his forehead."

"I dinna do that. The sight on the rifle left that mark."

"Which you caused. Brin told us all about it."

God love the lass.

After helping her into her coat and draping the blanket over her knees, he picked up the reins and released the brake. The air had turned brisk yet was far from being cold, but he told his delicate English rose that if she needed additional warming, he would be happy to provide it.

Or not, judging by her lack of response.

Reining the horse in a tight circle, he pointed the buggy back the way they'd come, then snapped the whip in the air above the gelding's rump.

"Declan's ears are still ringing," his wife scolded as she tied the strings on her bonnet. "You're demented. All of you."

The horse settled into a smooth pacer's gait. Ash relaxed against the cushioned seat, scanning the road ahead for wildlife moving up from the creek. "It was only a prank, love. And they gave me a black eye first."

"What black eye? I see no black eye."

Was that worry in her voice? "I wiped it away."

She stared at him.

"Black boot wax. And anyway, Redstone should be thanking me, so he should."

"For what?"

He grinned. "Did you not see the way Miss Lincoln rushed to his side when she saw the wee mark on his head?"

She pondered that, then gave a half smile. "He did seem rather incapacitated for such a minor injury."

"Aye. And enjoying every moment of her tender ministrations, poor lad."

"Grown men. Fighting. In front of the children." She let out a great huff of air. "You could have injured your side. Or brought on another headache."

"I'm fine, lass."

"And who is going to mend your torn shirt?"

Not you, I'm guessing. But he wisely keep that to himself and grinned at her instead.

"Oh, hush."

Because the night was clear, the temperature dropped with the sun, and by the time they rolled into Heartbreak Creek, even Ash was noticing the cold. Not wanting Maddie to take a chill, he stopped at the hotel before going on to the livery. "I'll wait while you get Agnes," he told her as he lifted her from the buggy and set her directly on the stoop so her dainty shoes wouldn't get mussed. "That way Tricks can tell her all about his big adventure as we walk back."

She went inside and a few minutes later returned with Agnes squirming in her arms. "Lucinda said there's a man waiting to speak to me," she said, handing the dog into the buggy. "Or rather to see A. Wallace. Perhaps that Zucker fellow. At any rate, I'll speak to him now." Her brown eyes flicked over him. She arched a brow. "Meanwhile, you might want to stop off at the washroom and clean yourself up. There's blood on your coat. Or maybe that's horse dung."

"Wait," he said as she started away. Evil things happened in this wild place. And a woman as beautiful as his wife would always be noticed by both the good and the bad. "Are you sure you don't want me with you?"

"I'll meet him in the lobby under the watchful eyes of Lucinda and Yancey. It will be entirely proper."

Ash was less worried about impropriety than safety. But he dinna want to crowd his wife, either. She was a capable woman. She dinna need a watchdog. "Send Yancey or Billy should you need me."

When Maddie entered the lobby after a quick stop in the washroom to tidy her hair, she found the blond gentleman Lucinda had pointed out earlier still slouching in one of the upholstered chairs, half hidden behind a tall fern.

She studied him as she approached. He seemed closer in age to Ash than to her own twenty-five years, and wore a poorly tailored suit and a shirt that had seen cleaner days, and impatiently bounced a dusty bowler hat on his crossed knee.

"You wished to see me?" she asked, moving to stand before him.

Startled, he looked up. When he saw her, he stood, hat in his hands. "A. Wallace?" he asked with a hesitant smile.

"Yes."

His smile broadened as his gaze slid over her. "You're a woman."

It was a lovely smile and might have rendered the man handsome, if not for the odd coldness in his mismatched eyes. Obviously he wasn't a longtime resident, because he had most of his teeth and none were darkened with rusty stains. "I am."

He scratched his head. No doubt his overuse of hair pomade made his scalp itch. That, or lice. Wanting exposure to neither, Maddie inched back a step.

"Kind of throws me, you being a woman, and all. Not that I'm complaining, mind you." He gave a brusque laugh and hooked a thumb in his vest pocket.

Maddie caught the scent of spirits in his breath. His hand showed several nicks and scars. She wondered if perhaps he was a miner.

"Never heard of a female photographer. And English, by the sound of it."

"I assure you I am all three, Mr. . . . ?"

"Oh, right." He dipped his head. "Aaron Zucker, ma'am."

Maddie nodded politely back.

"I'm looking for my brother, Ephraim."

From the corner of her eye, Maddie saw Ash come in with the dogs and pause by the front desk to speak to Lucinda. They both looked her way, then Ash went up the stairs, the dogs trailing after him. At the top, he paused again and looked down at her in a way that made her skin tingle. She was debating signaling him to come down when his gaze shifted to the man before her. All gentleness left his face. Did he feel it, too? Although Mr. Zucker had not said or done anything to alarm her, there was still something . . .

But then Ash turned and went on down the hall.

"Yes, Mr. Zucker," she said, turning her attention back to the tall man who was so blond his eyebrows appeared almost nonexistent. "I received your letter. You wrote you were to meet your brother in Omaha?"

She saw a momentary confusion cross his face before he quickly covered it with that broad smile that brought little warmth to either his blue eye or the brown one with the odd, pale flecks. "Yep. That's right. Omaha. But somehow I missed him, you see. And now I'm trying to track him down. I have this picture . . ."

He reached into the inside pocket of his coat, which was of a cheap, knobby wool and showed substantial wear along the lapels and elbows. The cuffs were stained along the forearms, as if Mr. Zucker had the habit of wiping his mouth on his sleeve when he ate.

He handed her a tintype that was smudged and frayed on the edges. "My brother sent me this a while back." He pointed to her signature on the bottom. "See, it's got your name on it. That's how I found you. I believe you took this somewhere up north, maybe around the Blue River area. Do you remember it?"

Maddie studied the image. A man standing outside a rustic cabin, his elbow resting on the handle of a tall pickax. She had taken dozens like it over the summer. Mr. Satterwhite might have known the man, or even the area where the photograph had been taken. He had carried a map of this whole territory in his head. But she saw nothing she recognized.

She returned the photograph with an apologetic smile. "I'm sorry, Mr. Zucker. But I took so many photographs over these last few months."

"You're sure? Look at it again." He thrust it toward her, the action brusque and a trifle menacing, as if he were jabbing with a knife.

There was something about the tone of his voice and that coldness in his eyes that put Maddie off. Instead of taking it, she clasped her hands at her waist and shook her head. "I wish I could help you, Mr. Zucker. But I cannot."

He must have seen her wariness. He put on that smile again, which didn't reassure her in the least. "I don't mean to appear forward, ma'am. I'm worried about my brother, is all. If you could just take another look at it. Maybe you'll see something in the area around the cabin or the creek. Anything would help. Please, ma'am."

Reluctantly, she took the photograph. There was something vaguely familiar about the surroundings. Maybe that stand of aspen or that odd-shaped peak rising behind the cabin. But she couldn't be sure. It looked like so many others.

Again, she handed the photograph back. "I'll think on it, Mr. Zucker. But I cannot promise anything. Perhaps when I return from Denver—"

"You're going to Denver?"

She almost stepped back, sorry she had mentioned it. "Yes, for the statehood convention."

"The Blue River area is on the way. If you take the left route over Hoosier Pass, you'll be right on it. Maybe you'll see something to jog your memory."

"I'm not sure which route we'll take." She glanced over to the front desk and caught Lucinda's eye. "But if you will leave me your direction, I will send word if I remember anything."

"Ma'am—"

"Good evening," Lucinda cut in, gliding up. "I'm sorry to interrupt." She gave Zucker an apologetic smile before saying to Maddie, "Your husband is looking for you. He headed upstairs a few minutes ago with the dogs." Maddie thought she might have put extra emphasis on "husband" and "dogs." Clever lady, Lucinda.

"Please leave your direction with Miss Hathaway here," Maddie told Zucker. "If I remember anything, I will send word." Then ignoring his attempt to delay her further, she bid them both good night and went up the stairs, thankful that the room was registered under the name of Ashby rather than Wallace.

There was something odd about Mr. Zucker . . .

When Maddie opened the door to the suite, she saw Ash seated in one of the chairs beside the sitting room window. He was leaning forward, elbows resting on his splayed knees as he studied dozens of photographs spread on the floor between his feet. The box in which they had been stored lay open by his chair.

"What are you doing?" she asked, slipping off her coat.

He picked up a photograph and studied it. "I watched you take this today."

She stepped closer to see which one he held. It was the ground-level view of the rutted road stretching away to the mountains. It had turned out rather nicely, she thought. "Do you like it?" she asked, going back to hang her coat on a hook beside the door.

"When I saw you lying on the ground behind your camera, I thought 'what is that daft woman up to now?' I dinna know what you were doing. Or what you saw. Now I understand."

"Understand what?"

" 'Tis magic you create, so it is. This picture pulls me in. It makes me want to be on that road. To follow it all the way to the mountains. The mystery. The freedom. The endless sky. You've captured it all right here. On this small square of paper."

His words brought tears to her eyes. How gratifying that a hardened, disciplined man like Ash, who had pattered his life around violent practicalities and unyielding realities, would appreciate the nuances of her work. "Thank you, Ash."

He looked up, his expression as serious as she had ever seen it. He looked quite . . . defeated. "You have a gift, lass. I dinna realize how great it was until now. I dinna understand."

She came forward and knelt on the other side of the photographs, facing him. Sitting back on her heels, she tipped her head to study him. "Understand what, Ash?" she asked again.

With a deep sigh, he slumped back, his eyes drifting closed. "I canna do it." He said it so softly, she knew the remark was directed at himself, rather than her. But before she could question him on it, he abruptly changed the subject. "How was your meeting?"

"What? Oh . . ." Troubled by his weary tone, she tried to inject energy into her voice as if to compensate for the lack of it in his. "It was Mr. Zucker. The man who sent the letter through Declan."

As she spoke, she sifted through the pictures, hoping to recognize the one Mr. Zucker had shown her. She always kept copies of her photographs. A vanity, perhaps. But she liked to look through them from time to time, to see if she had improved, or if one might have been better if taken from another perspective, or with a different angle of light.

"He showed me a photograph I had taken of his brother." Sliding one from beneath the pile, she studied it. "This one, in fact. He wanted to know if I remembered taking it. He was most insistent about it."

Ash's eyes opened. "How insistent?"

"Nothing untoward. Just deeply disappointed that I didn't recognize where I had taken it. But . . ."

"But, what?"

"There was something odd about him."

He sat up. Seeing the sudden concern on his face, she gave a dismissive wave. "I'm just being silly. Having Mr. Satterwhite gone has made me feel a bit . . . exposed, as it were. Rather at loose ends." She flashed a bright smile. "I keep forgetting I have you to watch over me now."

He didn't smile back. "Lass."

That's all. Just "lass." But the way he said it sent a shiver of unease all through her body. There was a note of finality in it that made her thoughts scatter in panic.

"What's wrong, Ash?"

"We must talk."

It was difficult to keep her voice from betraying her growing alarm. His tone sounded too much like his father's had the morning he'd come into the garden to tell her that her parents were dead.

Fearing what was to come, her whole body tightened, clenched inward as if to ward off a blow. "Talk about what?"

It was a long time before he answered. "I'm not a patient man. I thought I could change your mind. But it would be wrong."

"What are you talking about?" But she knew. She could feel it coming. And a voice screamed in her head. *No! Don't do this.*

Clasping her hands tightly at her knees, she tried to remain calm and refrain from shouting at him. Was he going to demand she go back to Scotland? Now that he had broken through all her barriers and exposed her weakness where he was concerned, would he use that to try to control her?

He leaned forward again, elbows on his knees. For a moment he stared down at the tintypes at his feet, then spread his big hands in a gesture of defeat. With a sigh, he lifted his head. "I canna do it, lass. I canna take you from this. It's wrong."

Did that mean he wasn't taking her back to Scotland? Or that he was returning without her?

She stared at him, her mind reeling. And even though he didn't move, she could feel him drawing away, and it sent a jolt of terror through her. "What are you saying? You're giving up? You're leaving?"

He didn't answer. Just looked at her, and the resignation in his eyes cut her heart to shreds. She couldn't breathe. Couldn't think. "Oh my God . . . you're leaving me . . . again . . ." And fearing what else she might say, she clapped both hands over her mouth.

"Lass." He reached toward her, but she jerked back. "I canna stay, love. And I won't ask you to give up your work. It would be wrong."

You arrogant, noble, bloody, misbegotten bounder. She took her hands away, saw that they were shaking but couldn't make them stop even when she clenched them into fists. If she thought her legs would hold her, she would have fled the room.

Dimly, through the buzzing in her head, she heard his voice, a low rumble that vibrated in the air around her. "I've watched you, lass. I've seen joy light up your face when you speak of your photography. And I've seen the results. You're an artist, so you are. And I'll not be taking that away from you."

"What are you saying?" *You bloody bastard.* "Good-bye?"

"It's for the best."

"Whose best?" She lurched to her feet. *Good-bye?* The word thundered through her head, drove the air from her lungs. She had thought he had simply been angling for a way to get her to go back to Scotland with him—not that he would leave without her. For a moment, she couldn't draw in a breath. "You—you're leaving?"

"I must."

"When?"

"I dinna ken. Soon."

"B-but . . ."

"I canna stay, Maddie. And you canna leave."

She stood before him, her legs trembling, her heart pressing against her lungs. Why now? It made no sense. Not after their night together. Not after finding each other again after all this time.

"B-but what about Denver?"

"Brodie will watch out for you."

"But I need you."

"No, lass, you dinna. You never have."

Wearily, he pushed himself out of the chair. He stood for a moment, his face in shadow, his big form blocking the frail light from the lamp behind him. "There's a saying in Scotland . . . dinna take a wife until you ken what to do with her." He gave a soft, joyless laugh. "I've never known what to do with you, lass. You were not what I expected, and more than I hoped for. You were a light burning just out of reach, and I was half afraid if I caught you, you would burn right through me. And for these last few days, you have."

She twisted her hands together. "Ash, don't do this. I don't want you to go."

Reaching out, he gently stroked his hand over her hair. "You've built a fine life for yourself here, Madeline. Found a new family . . . a better one than what you left behind." His hand fell away. "I wish you joy in it."

"But you can't just leave. What will you do?"

He shrugged. "I'll go back to Scotland and learn how to be an earl."

"You'll hate it." *And you'll turn into your father—choking on disappointment and taking it out on everyone around you.*

" 'Tis my duty."

Fury ignited, burned through her in a hot, bright rush. "And you would never forsake your duty, would you, Lord Ashby?" She wanted to strike him. Pound her fists against his chest. Scream at him that he was wrong, wrong, wrong!

"Lass . . ."

But she had some small measure of pride left. So she lifted her chin and somehow managed to keep her voice from breaking. "Go then." With a wave of her hand, she turned away. "Go tend your tasks, milord, and leave me to mine."

As soon as the door closed behind him, Maddie stumbled into her room and fell across her bed.

The upstairs maid had straightened it. The dented pillows and tangled sheets had been smoothed and tucked and covered with the counterpane as if last night had never happened. Even the scent of him was gone. She pounded the bed with her fists, too angry even to cry.

Tricks and Agnes, roused from naps in the sitting room, came in to see what she was doing. But she had no reassurances for them. She was almost senseless with fury. Pain writhed inside her, hot and bitter and sharp as glass.

Damn you.

Then suddenly, as if he was right beside her, Mr. Satterwhite whispered in her mind.

You're hiding . . . You need your husband . . . he's a good man.

No! She clapped her hands over her ears to shut him out, but still the words circled and echoed.

A life that'll amount to more than a collection of tintypes in some dusty book on a stranger's shelf.

But what about her work? She needed that, too.

Yet if she had to choose . . .

She flipped over on her back and stared up at the ceiling, ideas churning through her mind. There had to be a way to work this out. There had to be something she could do.

Ash hardly slept, plagued by regrets and an almost overwhelming need to go into Maddie's room, take her into his arms, and tell her it was all a mistake—he wouldn't leave—they would work something out.

But what?

When dawn was just a dim pink glow behind the peaks, he rose, dressed, and calling Tricks, quietly left the suite.

His breath frosted in the air as he walked to the livery. Driscoll had just doled out the morning feed, and rather than interrupt Lurch, Ash went into Maddie's wagon to wait for him to finish.

He sat on her wee bed, and the scents he would always associate with his wife settled around him like a perfumed mist. Flowers, soap, photography chemicals, Agnes. In the dim light, he studied the small space that held so much of her essence, picturing her before her tiny mirror, combing her hair, or warming her hands beside her wee stove. A life of status and luxury awaited her as a future countess, yet she was happier here in this crude wagon, surrounded by her photography plates and the tintypes pinned to the low ceiling above her bed.

He lay back and studied them, awed again by the artistry of her work. He could easily pick hers from the others, and not only because of her name across the bottom. There was a gentleness to it. A touch of magic in the lighting and the way she framed the images.

Satterwhite had been right: she did see the beauty in everything around her, and somehow was able to capture that feeling in photographic images.

A picture of him with Lurch and Tricks caught his eye. Then another of him sitting by the fire with Satterwhite, and one of Satterwhite leading the mules to water. But none of his wife, and that saddened him. He would have liked having an image of her to take out and look at in the long, lonely years ahead.

The sound of horses moving from the barn into the paddocks told him breakfast was over. Rising, he left the wagon and went to saddle Lurch. A good long run would clear his head. Then perhaps he could find another solution to this coil he was tangled in.

"Luce, I know it makes no sense, and it's exactly what I don't need . . . but I love him." Maddie's voice cracked on the last words, and tears welled up again. She had already cried so much her eyes felt like puffy slits and her nose was raw from blowing it. But she couldn't seem to stem the tears, no matter how hard she tried or how often she splashed her face with water.

Lucinda rose and crossed to where Maddie sat on the edge of the bed. When Miriam, the parlor maid, had come to freshen the suite she shared with Ash, Maddie had fled to the lovely rooms Lucinda had built for herself on the ground floor behind Yancey's office. It was done up in pale creams and beiges and greens, a perfect setting for Lucinda's blond, green-eyed beauty.

Sitting down beside her, Lucinda gave Maddie a one-armed hug. "I wish I could help."

"You can. Tell me how much you hate him. Or how rude he was to ignore me—no matter the reason. Or that I'm better off without him and it's good riddance to have him out of my life."

"But I don't hate him. Nor do I think you're better off without him."

Maddie pulled back to stare at her. "You don't?"

"I rather like him." At a knock on the door, Lucinda rose and went into the sitting room. Maddie heard Billy's voice, the clatter of crockery, then the sound of the door closing.

A moment later, Lucinda appeared in the bedroom doorway. "And judging by the way he looks at you," she said, picking up the conversation where it had left off, "I doubt he was ever indifferent, even if he didn't write or come for visits. Now come into the sitting room. I have lunch set up on the table by the window."

Although she had little appetite, Maddie rose and followed Lucinda. "But, Luce," she said, plopping into one of the upholstered chairs beside a tall window overlooking the road to the livery and the mountains rising on the other side of the creek. "I would have to go back to Scotland. I might never see you again."

"Admittedly, I don't like that idea. But you can't run around these mountains like a nomad forever. And giving up a title and a life of ease would be foolish. A woman needs security. Money will provide that."

Maddie sniffed, which made her cough. "You Americans," she chided, spreading a napkin across her lap. "You have such romantic ideas about titles. It's not all glamour and ball gowns, I assure you. Being in London society is like living in a fishbowl with a school of flesh-eating piranhas taking nips at you every time you pass by. And Scotland is rainy most of the time, and filled with sheep that stink and people who hate you because you're English. Not that I blame them. Dreadful practice, those Clearances."

"Well, it's certainly a lot better than living day to day in the poorest section of New York," Lucinda snapped, clearly out of patience. "Spending your days kipping food and dodging constables, and your nights fighting off rats and alcohol-soaked procurers."

Maddie's mouth almost fell open. Lucinda rarely spoke of her younger years. Maddie knew her parents had died very young and Luce had been raised by an elderly guardian. She had even mentioned her hatred for what she called "those industrialist types" who kept the working poor in grinding poverty while they grew rich, and the "runners" who preyed on the starving immigrants as they came off the boats. Still, there was a great deal about Lucinda that Maddie didn't know, like the full story of the man Lucinda had left at the altar and exactly how the New Yorker had come into possession of a valise full of money and railroad shares. But Maddie had never known how destitute Luce had been. How utterly without hope.

Battling new tears, she reached across the table and took Lucinda's hand. "Oh, dearest, I'm so sorry. How foolish you must think me . . . after all you've gone through, to turn up my nose at what Ash is offering."

Lucinda pulled her hand away. Maddie had forgotten that another legacy of Lucinda's childhood was that she didn't like to be touched.

"Not foolish. Shortsighted. We all have choices, Maddie. Didn't you once tell me you wanted a family and children? Can you see yourself having them with any man other than Ashby? I doubt it. All I'm saying is that you consider that before you let your viscount slip away. Now, pass the rolls."

Fourteen

Ash stayed out most of the day. Earlier, he had shot two grouse and had roasted them over a small fire. It felt good to be in the open again, tending such a simple task. It restored his balance, reduced things to an elemental level—find food, cook food, eat food. Out here it was just him, and his animal companions, and a vast windy silence all around. There was peace in that, comfort of a kind he had never found in cities and ballrooms and lofty castles. The soldier's life was an extension of that simplicity. Fight, protect your fellow soldiers, kill or die if you must.

But he was no longer a soldier, and not yet an earl. Instead, he was trapped somewhere between the two, yet belonging to neither.

Leaning back against the saddle he'd removed from Lurch after their long run, he laced his fingers behind his head and stared up into a sky that was slowly fading. Already the wispy clouds had gone from white to gold and pink and now trailed across the sky in tattered purple streamers tipped with red and orange. Such skies were a rarity in the islands he called home. But here, framed by tall, frosted peaks and towering deep green forests, they were as common as the game that roamed the hills, as plentifully as the sheep back home.

A magical place, these mountains. He saw that now in a way he hadn't before. Maddie had done that for him—taught him to see the beauty in the trees, rather than the enemy lurking within—to listen for the whisper in the wind, rather than the whine of musket balls. Maddie and her mountains had healed him. No wonder she dinna want to leave them.

Above him, in perfect silhouette, an eagle made lazy circles against the glowing sky. Envying its soaring freedom, Ash watched it drift down to the trees in a slow descent toward a huge nest atop a tall dead snag. Wings arched back, legs thrust out in front, it dropped down onto the nest, stretched once, then folded its great wings.

Safe for the night. Secure. Right where it belonged.

If a simple bird could find that, why couldn't he?

It was late and Maddie was beside herself with worry.

When she had left Lucinda's rooms after luncheon, and Yancey had told her he hadn't seen Ash all day, she had been so filled with panic that he might have already left she had dashed to the suite and checked his room.

His clothing was there, his shaving mug still atop the bureau beside the pitcher of cloudy water she had warned him not to drink. Satisfied he hadn't escaped her, and determined that he wouldn't until she'd had her say, she had returned to her own room to wait.

Supper came and went. The clink of dishes from the hotel kitchen below their suite grew fainter, then stopped altogether. She rose and lit her bedside lamp, then stretched out on the bed, Agnes tucked under her arm.

She must have dozed off, because the next thing she heard was Agnes scratching at the door into the suite. She rushed into the sitting room and flung open the door, expecting to see Tricks and Ash. But it was only Billy, sent by Lucinda to see if Maddie wanted him to take Agnes for her bedtime outing.

After they left, she checked Ash's bedroom again in case he had slipped by her while she slept, but nothing had been disturbed since her earlier inspection. Disheartened, she returned to the sitting room and sat in one of the chairs beside the window and stared out at the night. She still didn't know what she wanted to say to him. Or how she could convince him to stay with her here, instead of going back to Scotland.

Sighing, she tipped her head against the high back of the chair. If only there was some way to make him understand the utter joy she felt in translating a vision in her head into an image on a sheet of paper, and in a way that was uniquely hers. If only he could see how hard she had worked to build a new life here, an independent life. Didn't he realize there were only a handful of female photographers, and none who had their work published in a big London periodical? If only . . .

But then, it wasn't just about what *she* wanted, was it?

Then it came to her. The solution. The only way they could each gain what they wanted without losing each other in the process.

When Ash stepped through the door of the suite, it was dark except for the glow of the small lamp on the table by the window and a dim light shining through the crack under Maddie's door. He hesitated, wanting to assure himself she was all right, but recognized that for the weak excuse it was. Instead, he quietly crossed the sitting room, called Tricks into his bedroom, and shut the door.

He dinna light the lamp but moved in darkness to the window. Hands braced high on either side of the sash, he looked out at the starlit night. He would miss the stars. And the riotous sunsets. And Maddie.

Behind him, the door opened. He turned to see his wife silhouetted on the threshold. She was twisting her hands, as she did when she was nervous, and seeing that small show of vulnerability in such a strong, independent woman made something catch in his chest.

"All right," she said.

Someone who dinna know her well might have missed that tremble in her voice. "All right, what, lass?"

"I'll go back with you."

He tried to see her expression, but the light from the sitting room was behind her and her face was in shadow. He took a step forward and stopped. "Maddie, I canna—"

"Could you light the lamp, please?"

He hesitated, then did as she asked. When it was going, he turned back to her, and tried to hide his dismay at her ravaged appearance. It was apparent she had been crying and was fighting tears, still. "Lass—"

She raised a staying hand. "Please let me finish."

"Of course."

She stepped forward and stopped on the other side of the bed. An awkward but safe distance.

"I'll go back to Scotland with you, Ash," she said again. "I'll be your countess, and God willing, I'll bear your heirs. *When* it's necessary."

Before he could ask her to explain, she rushed on, as if fearing he meant to argue with her. "You said you have no lands or duties to attend as Viscount Ashby. And Donnan is a relatively young man. He could live twenty more years, and I pray God he will. So why go back now?"

"To help him."

"Do what? When I was there, he spent more time in Edinburgh and London than at home. As did the earl. Glynnis managed Northbridge and the Kirkwell lands. She's done it for years and loves it. Why not let her continue to do it for now?"

"Glynnis will marry our neighbor, Fain McKenzie soon. He's been after her for years."

She made a dismissive motion. "She's turned him down twice already."

"She has? Why? McKenzie is a good man."

"Perhaps so. But she doesn't love him as much as she loves Northbridge. As long as Donnan needs her, she'll gladly stay. And as long as she stays, your brother doesn't need you. Not as much as I do."

He sighed wearily. "For what, Maddie?"

"To be my protector. My friend. My husband." The tears started to flow, and her voice rose as her throat constricted. "Please, Ash. Make *me* your duty until Northbridge needs you. Give me this time, at least."

He realized his hands were shaking and clasped them behind his back rather than reach for her. "Donnan wasna well when I left."

"Then let us use the time we have." She came around the bed and stood before him, her cheeks sheened by lamplight and tears. Her eyes were dark pools of pain in her stricken face.

"And then what, love?"

"We'll go back. Together."

"But your photography—"

"I'll give it up."

He stepped back, shaking his head. "No, I canna—"

She clutched his arm to hold him to her. "It's not your choice, Ash. It's mine. Please. Give me this time now, then when duty calls you, I'll willingly go back and be the countess you need me to be."

He looked away, afraid she would see the wanting in his eyes. He would bargain with the devil himself to keep Maddie by his side. But he couldna let her give up her art. She would end up hating him for it.

He felt her hand cup his cheek and gently force his head around until their eyes met. "It's all right, Ash. This is what I want to do. My decision. Just give me a little more time, that's all I ask."

Tipping his head into her hand, he kissed her palm. Then he gave her a smile he hoped would hide his doubt. "As it happens, love, time is all I have right now." Then before she could see the despair in his eyes, he pulled her hard against his chest. He took a deep breath and let it out, knowing what he was about to do was wrong, but unable to keep himself from clutching at any reprieve he could find.

"All right. I'll stay here with you, lass. As long as I can." But he wasn't convinced it was the right decision. In the end, she still wouldn't be able to leave, and duty wouldn't allow him to stay.

She reached up and pulled his head down and kissed him hard. Then again, gentler, her tongue sweeping the seam of his lips.

That was all the invitation he needed. With shaking hands, he undressed her, then himself. He laid her across his bed and touched her with his hands and his mouth and his tongue until her breathing grew shallow and her body began to tremble. Then he settled into the warm cradle of her thighs. Resting his weight on his elbows, he kissed her, and whispered, *"Tha gradh agam ort,"* as he pushed inside.

Her passion rose to meet his in soft cries and gentle touches, and when her head arched back and her breath caught in her throat and her legs closed hard around his waist, he knew she had bound him to her forever, and he could never leave this woman, no matter what duty called.

KRIGBAUM MINE

HEARTBREAK CREEK CANYON

"I found the photographer," Clete said as he slammed through the door of the abandoned mine overseer's shack above Heartbreak Creek. "And guess what, Si?" He tossed his dusty black bowler onto the crate that served as a table. "It's a goddamn woman."

"A woman?"

"A woman. You know what women are, don't you, moron? The ones with tits who run when they see your idiot face." Clete laughed in that mean way that always made Si want to hide. "I ought to turn you loose on one, freak. You drooling and rooting around, trying to figure out what goes where, and her screaming like she had the devil up her ass. Be fun to watch."

"You didn't hurt her, did you, Clete?"

Si hated when his brother did bad things to women. When he heard them cry, it always made him cry, too, even though deep down he was glad. Because when Clete was sticking it into women, he wasn't sticking it into him, and he was always glad of that.

"Shut up, moron, and rustle us up some supper. I'm hungry."

While Si fired up the small cookstove, Clete sat at the table, taking sips from his bottle of Forty-Rod. Si watched him, his fear going up as the whiskey in the bottle went down. Clete was mean enough when he didn't drink. But when he did . . .

"Supper's ready, Clete," he said, carrying the pot to the table.

His brother looked into it, then spit a mouthful of whiskey into Si's face.

With a cry, Si staggered back, his eyes burning.

"Christ! Beans again?"

Si scrubbed at his face with his shirtsleeve. "That's all there is, Clete. I swear. That and a tin of peaches."

"You ain't having any peaches. Hand them over."

Si handed him the can of peaches, then watched his brother empty it in three bites, juice dripping down his whiskered chin. His own stomach rumbled like a growling dog. He hadn't had peaches in a long time.

Tossing the empty can aside, Clete pulled the pot closer. After eating his fill, he shoved the pot toward Si and picked up the bottle again.

Si ate quickly, fearing any minute his brother would jerk the pot away from him. But Clete seemed too busy studying the picture of the smiling man standing beside his cabin in front of the peak that looked like a face turned sideways.

"The bitch said she didn't remember where she took it," he said after a while. "I think she lied. I could see it in her face." Clete looked up, his spooky eyes boring into Si. "Same as I see it in yours whenever you try to lie to me. But I always know, don't I, moron?"

"Yes, Clete." Beneath the table, Si's legs started to shake. He clamped his knees together to make it stop. The bottle was almost empty now, and Si knew what that meant. "You're the smart one, Clete. Everybody says."

"Yeah, I am, moron. Which is why I have to look after you. And teach you. And show you how things are supposed to be." He tilted the bottle up for the last swallow, then tossed it over his shoulder. It hit with a thud against the wall, clattered down, and rolled across the floor. "Ain't that right, moron?"

Tears were burning now and pressing hard against the back of Si's eyes. He kept his head down, blinking fast to keep them back. "Yes, Clete."

"And what do I do when you lie to me?"

Si felt the beans ride up in his throat, and with a shudder, swallowed them down again. "You hurt me."

"That's right." Abruptly, Clete laughed. Shoving the chair back, he stood and stretched.

Si felt him looming over him, weaving a little, his breath hot and stinking of whiskey.

"But not tonight, Si. Tonight, I'm thinking maybe one of the sweet little Coolie girls from the laundry might smell a whole lot better than you." He took a step, almost tripped on the bottle, then kicked it aside and yanked open the door. "Pack the saddlebags, moron. We leave at first light."

Preparations for the trip to Denver began in earnest over the next few days. Because three women would be going, those preparations became as involved as redeploying a thousand troops three hundred miles across hostile territory. Ash tolerated it as long as he could, then assumed command.

Mustering them in the dining room during the midafternoon lull two days before their departure, he stood before his traveling companions, feet braced, hands clasped behind his back. When the ladies finally settled and ceased prattling on about hairdos, the color, style, and fit of each other's dresses, bonnets, shawls, et cetera, he announced, "You will be allowed one valise each."

Immediately, a chorus of feminine protests rose.

Declan Brodie sighed and shook his head.

Raising his voice, Ash continued over the protests, "Unless, of course, you ladies are willing to do without potable water, rations, weapons, tents, extra bedding, grain for the animals, photography crates, emergency items, tools, and extra wheels for Maddie's wagon and Miss Hathaway's buggy. I leave it entirely up to you."

Despite the mutinous looks directed his way, Ash maintained his smile, and after a bit of muttering, they reluctantly complied.

Mentally checking that one off his list, he moved on to travel arrangements. "In deference to her delicate condition, and should she feel the need to rest along the way, Mrs. Brodie will travel during the day in Madeline's wagon, either up front or in back. Her husband will drive."

Brodie was about to protest, no doubt preferring to ride horseback like Ash. But when Ash added that he and the sheriff would share driving detail on an alternating basis, he reluctantly nodded acceptance.

"Questions so far?" Ash asked.

The sheriff yawned. Mrs. Brodie smiled dreamily and stroked her protruding belly while Maddie looked out the window and Miss Hathaway leaned forward to examine something on the tablecloth. An attentive group.

Rocking on his heels, Ash proceeded. "Miss Hathaway has stated she is comfortable driving her own buggy. Madeline will ride with her, and Mrs. Brodie, too, should she choose. When not driving Maddie's wagon, the sheriff, or Tricks and I, will take the advance position to scout for problems ahead." He and Maddie had already decided to leave Agnes behind with Prudence Lincoln and the Brodie children. "That's it. So if there are no ques—"

"Where will we sleep?" Mrs. Brodie blinked up at him, her blue eyes round with worry. "We can't all fit into that itty-bitty wagon."

"No, you canna. But because you and Madeline have husbands to see to your comfort, you will stay with them in tents. Miss Hathaway will sleep in the wagon."

Edwina Brodie opened her mouth to argue when her husband leaned over and whispered something in her ear. Color inched up her neck. Her mouth formed an *O*, then widened into a speculative smile. Turning back to Ash, she nodded demurely.

Ash guessed the sheriff had used the same inducement on his wife that he had used earlier on Maddie—privacy, and all the benefits that came with it.

"Then it's settled. Muster behind the hotel at dawn, day after tomorrow. Dismissed—I mean, good day, ladies." As the females filed out, Ash motioned for the sheriff to stay behind.

"You don't know much about women, do you, Ashby," Brodie said, clapping a hand on Ash's shoulder in a friendly way.

"I know what's important," Ash defended, affronted by the accusation. His wife certainly wasn't complaining.

"It's like herding turtles," Brodie went on as if Ash hadn't spoken. "The harder you push, the slower they move. They've got one speed. Their own. Best accept that now, or you'll be chewing through your stirrup leathers before we get halfway to Denver."

Seeing the wisdom in the sheriff's words, Ash nodded.

Giving his shoulder a last pat, Brodie rested his hands low on his gun belt. "So what did you need to talk to me about?"

"Anything on that Zucker fellow?" Ash had told the sheriff about the tall blond man's meeting with Maddie. He'd also described him, asking Brodie to let him know if he saw the man about town.

Declan Brodie shook his head. "Nothing. I've alerted Thomas, too, since he'll be taking over as sheriff while I'm gone. Did you know Zucker wasn't traveling alone?"

Ash looked at him in surprise. "Maddie dinna mention that."

"Probably didn't know. Thomas did some checking, found sign that someone had been using the abandoned overseer's shack up at the mine. Two horses, both shod. Several discarded food cans and fresh ashes in the woodstove. By the size of the boot prints in and out of the shack, he guesses two men, probably blond, one with a scar on his forearm."

Ash stared at him. "You're jesting."

" 'Course I am." Brodie laughed. "One was probably more sandy-haired than blond. Thomas isn't so good with colors."

Ash realized he'd been the butt of another prank. "Bugger off," he said with a grin, liking this sheriff more every time he talked to him.

"Right. Anyway, seems they're gone now. One of the laundry girls took a beating, but those Chinese folks are pretty closemouthed and no one's talking. I'll keep checking. Seems too coincidental. If Zucker shows up again, Thomas will be sure to ask him about it." Brodie's smile carried menace. "He's really good at getting answers."

Two days later, when dusty blue and gold clouds hung in wispy disarray across a sky as pink as the inside of an abalone shell, Ash led his wee convoy out of Heartbreak Creek.

It felt good to be on the move again.

They traveled without incident through the morning, stopping near noon to rest the animals and "enjoy a nice luncheon alfresco" as Edwina Brodie put it. That lasted about ten minutes until black flies had the ladies running for Maddie's wagon.

After loading up again, they continued traveling through the afternoon, finally stopping when the sun was sinking toward the peaks. The temperature began to drop, which curbed the insects somewhat, and once Ash got a fire started, smoke drove the rest of them away.

While Declan tended the animals and set up the tents, Ash went to Maddie's wagon for the eight-foot angler's rod he had bought at the Heartbreak Creek Mercantile, along with a tin of wet flies and a simple reel wound with silk fishing line. Whistling under his breath, he headed downstream with Tricks to where the creek they had been following emptied into a sizeable lake. He had grown up with a fishing rod in his hand, although in Scotland he had fished more for salmon than trout. But he'd heard about the native cold-water trout in this area and was anxious to give them a try.

Within an hour, he had eight good-sized fish flopping on the bank. Pleased with his success, he strung them on a stick and headed back to camp.

It became immediately apparent none of these women could cook.

"My God," Miss Hathaway gasped when she saw that a couple of the fish were still twitching. "Are they alive?"

"Not for long," Ash said and picked up a rock.

Maddie fled for the wagon.

"I think I'm going to be ill," the sheriff's wife sputtered, reeling for the bushes, Miss Hathaway on her heels.

Ash looked questioningly at the sheriff, who shrugged. "She dressed a chicken once. Took her a week to get over it. She was doing better, though, until she started breeding and her stomach went south."

Yet, somehow, once the fish had been cleaned, dredged in cornmeal, and fried in bacon drippings, the lasses managed to find their appetites again. God love them.

Fifteen

Two evenings after the others left for Denver, Thomas stood on the porch of the Brodie house and watched a coyote weave in and out of the shadows along the track that ran in front of the house. A full blood moon perched on the tips of the mountains, and by its light, *okom* would eat well.

It was a good night for hunting.

He glanced back at the house. The sounds from the kitchen had grown quieter. The voices of the children had long since faded. Only the soft footsteps of his woman reached his ears.

He smiled into the darkness, hoping tonight would mean good hunting for him, as well.

A few minutes later, Prudence came onto the porch, the Englishwoman's little dog running past her and down the porch steps. Thomas glanced at the brush. *"Nenaasestse,"* he called to the little dog. *"Okom* is hunting."

"Okom?" Prudence asked, coming to stand beside him.

He pointed to the lean, bushytailed coyote watching from the bushes beside the creek. "The full moon lights his way." He smiled down at her. "Perhaps *okom* will not be the only hunter this night, *eho'nehevehohtse.*"

One who walks in wolf tracks. That was his name for her because she was smart like a wolf. There were other words he called her, but he did not tell her their meaning because she was not ready yet to hear them.

He frightened her. He knew this. He also knew it was not because of anything he had done to her, but because of what others had done. *Eho'nehevehohtse* was wounded in body and spirit. But she was strong, as well. He could see in her eyes and in the tremble of her body when he brushed his hand along her arm that she was coming to accept him.

That was good. His patience was not boundless.

The little dog made water, then came back up the steps and scratched at the door. Prudence let the animal inside, then returned to her place at his side. "It's a beautiful night."

"The children sleep?"

She let out a long sigh. "Yes, thank goodness. It's like being pecked to death by chickens. I don't know how Edwina can keep up with them."

By day, her skin was the rich color of tanned leather. But in the moonlight, her face glowed like dark, polished quartz. "You will kiss me now," he said.

She drew back with a nervous laugh. "I will?"

He waited, saying nothing.

After a moment, she rose onto the tips of her toes, and as gently as a butterfly seeking nectar from the flower, she brushed her lips against his.

He stood without moving, his arms locked at his sides to keep from pulling her body against his.

When she drew away, he forced a smile, even though his heart kicked against his chest. "Are you *katse'e*—a little girl?" he teased. "Or *nahe'e*—my woman?"

She gave that false laugh again. "Did you know that Maddie and Edwina made bets on whether or not Indians kissed?"

"That was not a kiss." Cupping his hands around her head to

keep her from pulling away, he leaned down and pressed his lips to hers. He felt her body go rigid, but he continued to hold her and run the tip of his tongue along her closed lips. She slowly relaxed. Her mouth parted beneath his. After a moment, he lifted his head and smiled at her. "That was a kiss."

She said nothing, but he saw the softness in her face and the way her gaze followed his mouth as he spoke. It encouraged him to be bolder. "Indians also do this." Taking one hand from her face, he put it on her breast.

She immediately pulled back as far as his other hand would allow.

"No, *heme'oono*," he said gently. "You cannot run from me forever. You must free your mind from the past. Do not let fear rule you."

He stroked her through the cloth of her dress, felt a tremble run through her, and heard her breath grow shallow. "Think of me," he whispered against her mouth. "No one else."

"I do." Her voice sounded thin and wispy as woodsmoke. "All the time. But I'm afraid."

"Not of me." Taking his other hand from her cheek, he began to loosen the long row of buttons down the front of her dress.

She shivered. "No. Not of you. But Thomas . . . I . . . please . . ."

"Please what, *heme'oono*? Look upon you?" He pushed the edges of her dress aside. A thin cloth still covered her, but he could see the fine web of scars rising above it and up across her shoulder. He trailed the tips of his fingers over the scars and tried to stem the fury rising inside.

Declan had told him what had happened. Edwina had dropped a pitcher of milk. A simple thing. But her mother began to beat her for it, and when Prudence tried to stop her, the enraged woman had dumped a pot of scalding water on her. Edwina had been six, Prudence, seven. Babies, still. Too young to know such evil.

Thomas spread his hand over the scars and wished he had the power to take them from her memory.

She was shaking now, her body poised for flight. He could feel the pulse of her fear beneath his hand, but she did not draw away from his touch. As he pulled the thin cloth down to bare her breasts, he felt something hot and wet drop onto the back of his hand and he knew she was crying.

"You are beautiful, Prudence Lincoln." He looked up and smiled.

Blinking against her tears, she gave that laugh again. But she did not try to hide herself from him and did not cringe from him when he bent and pressed his lips to her scars.

"Only a Cheyenne warrior would think so," she said.

He lifted his head and tried to read her expression in the slanting moonlight. "Why do you say that?"

She put her hand over his heart. Even though a shirt covered him, he knew she could feel the thick ridges of his own scars from the ordeal of the sun dance ceremony.

"Do my scars disgust you?" he asked.

"No. But it hurts me to think of what you must have endured."

He laughed softly. "Foolish *he'e.*" He kissed her breast, then followed the trail of scars up her shoulder to her neck, where he dipped his tongue into the hollow at the base of her throat. "Scars are badges of strength and courage. They tell the story of what we have endured. Only survivors wear them."

"Or the very clumsy."

He continued to stroke her and listened to her breathing change from fear to wanting. "*Nemehotatse,*" he whispered against her warm skin. *I love you.*

"This is highly improper," she gasped, her fingers twisting in the cloth over his arms. Beneath his lips, her heart beat like the wings of a trapped bird.

"What is the meaning of improper?"

"N-not right. Incorrect. Oh, my . . . that breeze is cool."

He smiled and warmed her with his hand. "Between you and me, *heme'oono,* this is most correct. You are my heart mate, Prudence Lincoln. As I am yours. You will never free your spirit until you accept that."

"By l-letting you d-do this?" It was a whisper, yet he heard the invitation beneath the sigh.

"And more. Tonight I will not sleep in the carriage house. Tonight I will sleep beside you." He started to loosen the sash of her dress, then paused when he heard a distant sound. He cocked his head.

A horse was moving up the track. A shod horse. Odd time to be out for an evening ride. Turning back to *eho'nehevehohtse*, he pulled her dress back over her breasts and kissed her lips. "You will go inside now and wait for me."

"Oh, will I?" She laughed a true laugh, and the sound of it made his heart sing. "I don't like being ordered about like a field hand. Even by you."

"Ho. Already your spirit grows stronger."

In the paddock behind the house, Thomas's horse whinnied. The horse on the road answered. "If you will not go inside, at least cover yourself. A rider comes."

"A rider? Oh, dear!" Prudence fumbled with her buttons. Thomas tried to help her, but she batted his hand away. "Why didn't you tell me?"

"I just did." He opened the door. "Go inside. I will see what he wants."

She continued to fuss with her dress, then her hair until all was right again.

Thomas moved his rifle from inside the door and leaned it against the porch rail.

"He could be going on to the Kendal place," Prudence said, taking her place once more at his side.

"Or he could be coming here. As sheriff, I order you to go into the house, Prudence Lincoln."

"What do you suppose he wants at this hour?"

Thomas sighed. "Then move to my other side, so you do not block my knife arm."

.   .   .

Ash's troops made better progress the second day, and long before dusk, they had left the road that continued toward Breckenridge and the Blue River area, and had turned right, onto the flatter, more southerly route into Denver.

"You want to stop here tonight?" Brodie asked, reining his big bay alongside Maddie's wagon. "Or go on a bit farther?"

Ash studied the small clearing for a defensible position. They needed to stay close to water for the animals, but he disliked these narrow canyons where visibility was blocked by tall firs and rocky bluffs. "Is there something more open ahead? Maybe a ridge or higher position that would give us a better view of approaching riders?"

"Higher position?" Brodie's brows furrowed over his deep set brown eyes. "How high? I don't much like high."

Ash shrugged. "As long as it's open. I could scout ahead and see what I can find."

"I'll do it. I'm already saddled. And I'll get something for supper, too. Something with fewer bones than those trout last night."

Ash hid his disappointment. He had been driving Maddie's wagon all day and would have welcomed a brisk gallop. "If you're not back in an hour, I'll set up camp here."

Brodie nodded and rode off.

Ash drove the wagon off the road, set the brake, and climbed down. After folding down the steps at the back door, he knocked on the side of the wagon and called to Edwina Brodie, who had been napping inside, telling her they would be stopping for a while if she wanted to get out and stretch her legs. Then he went to the buggy to tell Maddie and Miss Hathaway the reason for the delay.

Maddie gave him a grateful smile as he swung her to the ground. "It has been rather a long day. Would we have time for a spot of tea, do you think?"

Next they would be wanting scones and jam. But Ash nodded and soon had a wee fire going and the kettle heating. Once the ladies had tended their needs in the brush, he slung the strap of his carbine over his shoulder, and with Tricks zigzagging ahead of him, went to explore the creek. This time of year, bears often prowled the banks of rivers and streams, hunting fish, berries, bark, even insects to fill their bellies before their long winter hibernation. He saw horse tracks—shod—and signs of deer, elk, raccoons, and other varmints moving through, but naught that alarmed him.

Convinced there was no immediate danger, he went back to the wagons, accepted a tin mug of tea from his wife, and settled beside the fire to wait for Brodie's return.

As the rider approached, Pru watched Thomas move to the top of the porch stairs. He said nothing, did nothing. Yet lethal intent radiated off his strong, sturdy body like heat from a fire.

This was the Cheyenne warrior she had seen only one other time, when he and Declan had come to the Indian village to rescue her from Lone Tree. This was the savage side of the patient student who sat in the back of her little school, struggling to learn his letters, or the quiet guardian who walked silently beside her in the evenings when she headed to the hotel for supper or went to visit with Edwina at the Brodies'. This Thomas bore little resemblance to the gentle man who had held her in his arms in the sweat lodge he had built for her, waiting for Mother Earth to draw the evil memories from her mind.

She loved them both. Feared them both.

"Is this Sheriff Brodie's place?" the man in the road called.

Thomas nodded.

"I hate to be coming by so late, but I've been waiting in town all afternoon to speak to him. Is he here?"

Thomas shook his head.

Pru elbowed him in the ribs. "Be nice," she hissed. "It could be important. Find out what he wants."

Thomas gave her a warning look, then turned back to the man in the road. "I am his deputy. What do you want?"

"That's nice?" Pru muttered.

"I'm Aaron Zucker," the man called. "From Pennsylvania. I sent the sheriff a letter recently about my brother who's gone missing. Do you know if he received it?"

Pru looked at Thomas in surprise. "Wasn't that the name of the man who met with Maddie at the hotel?" she whispered.

Thomas nodded. She could tell by his closed expression he had reached the same conclusions she had. Even in the shadowed moonlight, the man in the road looked nothing like the man Ash had described to Declan—tall, blond, black bowler hat. This man was more round than tall and wore a porkpie hat.

Determined to get to the bottom of this, Pru stepped forward and down the steps. "Yes, your letter came, Mr. Zucker. Would you like to come inside and have a cup of tea while we discuss it?"

Thomas's hand clamped over her shoulder before she had gone two steps. "Go inside, Prudence," he said in a voice that carried the weight and warmth of steel. "I will bring Mr. Zucker in after he ties his horse."

Pru went into the house. She had just set the tea to brew when boots thudded on the porch. Only one set. Thomas wore soft-soled moccasins and never made a sound when he walked. The door opened, and Pru turned with a smile that spread when she saw the man in the doorway, standing with his hat in his hands and a white collar about his neck.

"Why, Mr. Zucker . . . I didn't realize you were a priest."

"A reverend, only, ma'am. And not even that to my wife. She calls me a pulpit-thumper with a hammer for a fist." He said it with a fond smile.

Liking him immediately, Pru introduced Thomas and herself, then motioned toward the table in the center of the kitchen. "Do please sit. The tea will be ready in a moment." As Reverend Zucker took his seat, she set the teapot and cups on the table beside the lamp, then took the chair across from him. "How may we help you, Reverend?"

Zucker smiled uncertainly up at Thomas, who stood with his

back to the closed door, feet planted, arms folded across his chest. He might be dressed in his town clothes, but there was no mistaking he was an Indian, and not a particularly friendly one, at that.

"I wrote to the sheriff," the reverend began, "asking him to pass on a letter to the photographer who took this." As he spoke, he pulled a photograph from his coat pocket and set it on the table beside his porkpie hat. His face softened as he looked at the image of a man outside a crude cabin. "That's my brother, Ephraim. This was taken outside his diggings in the Blue River area. I don't know exactly where. I was hoping the photographer might remember where he took it." He looked up, his expression hopeful. "Is he in town, do you know?"

"I'm afraid not. And the photographer is a 'she,' not a 'he.' "

He leaned back. "A she? A female photographer?"

While the reverend tried to cover his obvious surprise that there could be such a thing as a woman photographer, Pru poured the tea. Thomas, still standing, picked up the photograph and held it to the lamplight to study it. After a moment, he returned it to the table, pushing it to the far side as if wanting to distance himself from the image.

Pru knew many Indians thought cameras stole their spirits and considered the image of themselves on the piece of paper as proof of that. But she had thought Thomas too worldly to accept such a notion. Yet there was much about the Cheyenne Dog Soldier she still didn't know, which was one of her major reservations about him. As a mulatto, she had enough difficulty trying to fit into a world dominated by whites. She didn't know if she had it in her to bend to the Cheyenne culture, as well.

"One man has already come through Heartbreak Creek looking for your brother," Thomas said in that solemn way he had. "He also carried the name Aaron Zucker and had this same image on a piece of paper."

The reverend's round face went slack. He set his teacup down with a clatter. "Another man? Claiming to be me? But who? What did he look like?"

"Yellow hair. Tall. Eyes from two fathers."

"He means mismatched," Pru cut in, with a look of apology to Thomas. "One eye was blue and the other a grayish brown."

The reverend shook his head. "I know of no one like that. Oh, dear Lord." He pressed the heel of his hand over his brow as if to block a thought too horrible to face. "It's the claim. He's probably after my brother's claim." Taking his hand away, he looked up at Thomas, his eyes moist with unshed tears. "Ephraim wrote that he'd found gold. Not just placer nuggets in the river, but a real vein. He was most secretive about where. In his last letter, he wrote that the claims office in Breckenridge had mailed all the paperwork to the territorial office in Denver. He planned to check that everything was registered when he passed through there on his way to meet me in Omaha."

"Why Omaha?" Pru asked.

"To buy mining equipment." With trembling hands, he pulled a folded paper from his pocket. Opening it, he shoved it across the table. "Here's his letter, and the name of the bank where I was to meet him. But he never came, and no one at the bank had ever heard of him."

Thomas studied the obviously worried middle-aged man for a long time, betraying nothing of his thoughts. Finally, he spoke. "How do we know which of you is Aaron Zucker?"

The reverend blinked, as if he'd never been confronted with such a dilemma, which he probably hadn't. "I have this letter—"

"Letters can be stolen," Thomas cut in.

"I may have an idea." Rising, Pru went into the parlor, found a sheet of paper and a stub of pencil, then returned to the kitchen. She set them before the befuddled reverend. "Write as much as you remember of the last paragraph in your letter to A. M. Wallace. Then sign your name."

She had seen that letter and had noted the careful script and the way the reverend had penned his signature. She also had a keen memory of the text. If the wording and script matched the letter Declan Brodie had given Maddie, there was a good chance the reverend was Aaron Zucker.

Reverend Zucker did as instructed, then passed the paper back to Pru.

After looking it over, she nodded to Thomas. "It's the same."

"Then I will warn Declan." He turned toward the door.

"Wait." Pru touched his arm. "Warn him of what?"

"That the blond man is a trickster. They could be riding into an ambush."

The reverend lurched to his feet. "I'll go with you."

"They left two moons ago. It will be a hard ride."

"He's my brother."

The two men stared at each other. Finally, Thomas nodded. "Bring food and warm coverings. I will meet you at the hotel."

"You're leaving tonight?"

Thomas nodded. "The moon is full. The horses and I will find our way. You have only to follow."

After the reverend left, Thomas turned to Pru. "You will kiss me before I go."

Smiling to hide her worry, Pru walked toward him. "Yes, I will."

This time when she kissed him, she allowed herself the luxury of sliding her hands up his chest and across his thick shoulders. He felt warm and solid, and from the faint tremor in his arms when he pulled her hard against his body, she knew he was as captured by the kiss as was she.

When he finally pulled his mouth from hers, his breathing was ragged. "You will take yourself and the children to the hotel in the morning. You will be safe there. I will go now to ask Mayor Gebbers to find another deputy until I return."

She nodded, her gaze pinned to his lips, the taste of him still on her tongue. She wondered if he would kiss her again.

As she watched, those lips widened into a grin. "Do not look at me that way, *heme'oono*. Or I will not be able to leave you."

She saw the laughter in his black eyes. And the love. She knew what he wanted from her. But whenever she thought about what that entailed, the coil of fear lodged in her chest tightened a little more.

"And when I return, Prudence Lincoln," he went on, once again the solemn, austere warrior, "you will accept me as your heart mate. You will join with me and become my woman. If you cannot do this, we will part our ways. Do you understand?"

Pru felt an edge of panic cut into her heart. She wasn't ready. It was too soon.

His expression softened. "I see your fear, *eho'nehevehohtse*. It hides behind your eyes when you look at me, and in your hands when you allow yourself to touch me. But I am not your enemy, *heme'oono*. You will think on that while I am gone." Reaching out, he gently brushed his fingertips across her jaw. "*Nemehotatse*, Prudence Lincoln."

"What does that mean? I don't understand what you're saying?"

"Yes, *eho'nehevehohtse*. You know."

When Declan hadn't returned by the allotted hour, Ash set up camp.

He spaced out the wagons and tents along the edge of the trees so the animals had most of the small clearing to graze, then gathered enough firewood to see them through the night. He was debating trying his hand at fishing again when Declan rode up with a small doe tied behind his saddle.

And the deer wasn't the only thing he had brought back.

Behind him rode a man Ash dinna recognize—young, light-haired, his face bruised, a half-healed cut through one brow. The vacant look in his swollen eyes and the slackness of his jaw made Ash wonder if he might be simple.

But the other man—on foot and leading a limping horse—Ash did recognize. Tall, wearing a black bowler, the hair poking out beneath it so blond it almost appeared white, and mismatched eyes that had the color and warmth of dirty snow.

Aaron Zucker.

Sixteen

"You'll never get those wagons through Kenosha Pass," Zucker told Ash as he tied his limping horse to an alder and began to unsaddle.

Declan, trailed by the dog, had ridden on into the trees, where he had untied the deer from behind his saddle and was now hanging it from a branch so he could skin it before cutting it up. The ladies looked pointedly the other way.

The fellow Zucker had brought with him—who he had introduced as his youngest brother, Silas—stood on the other side of Zucker, watching them with the quick, darting glances of a kicked dog. Ash smiled to reassure him, but the lad—it was hard to tell his age—looked quickly down at the ground, his thin shoulders hunched as if to deflect a blow.

"Damn landslide," Zucker went on. "Already cost me two days."

Ash frowned when he saw the blond man toss the saddle to the ground. It was as poor a saddle as the beast that wore it, but Ash hated to see any equipment—or animals—treated with such neglect.

"Be a month before they clear it. You, Si. You going to unsaddle or stand there drooling all day?"

Ash hunkered beside the horse's injured leg. "What happened to your mount?" he asked, running his hand down the left front cannon bone.

No blood. No heat. Yet the leg was swollen double between the pastern and hoof.

"Hell if I know. Just started limping. Si, bring your saddle here by mine. And untie those saddlebags first."

Ash's fingers found what he had suspected. An old horse trader's trick; tie a tail hair tight around the pastern, circulation slows, and before long you have a limping horse with a swollen leg. He just couldn't understand why a man would do such a thing to his own mount. Snapping the hair with his thumbnail, he pulled it free, then stood and held it up so that the knot showed. "Now how do you suppose this happened?"

A craven look came over Zucker's face, then he whirled, his fist shooting out to slam into the side of his brother's head. "Damnit, Si!"

The boy cried out, the saddle flying.

The horse shied, his big body slamming into Ash.

"Ho, now!" Ash shoved back, trying to keep his boots clear of the stomping hooves. When the frightened animal calmed, Ash whipped toward Zucker. "What the bluidy hell was that?"

On the other side of the nervous horse, Silas cowered beneath his brother's kicks. "I swear I didn't do it, Cl—"

"Shut up! I mean it, Si! Not another word!" Zucker turned back to Ash, his mismatched eyes crackling with a fury he was barely able to contain. "Sorry. Quite a prankster, that one." He put on a look of concern. "Horse didn't kick you, did it?"

Ignoring him, Ash went to the boy and extended a hand.

The lad cringed.

"It's all right. Dinna worry. Take my hand, lad."

Reluctantly, the young man did.

Ash pulled him to his feet, dusted him off, and pulled a twig from his tangled hair. The lad smelled like a hog wallow; Ash doubted he'd had a bath in weeks. Resting a hand on a thin shoulder, he turned the boy toward the women gathered around the campfire. "See that lady with the dark red hair?"

Ash saw Maddie watching, her hands twisting nervously at her waist. He smiled and waved. "She's verra nice, so she is. Go on over to her and she'll tend you, maybe give you something to eat."

Si looked up at him, his pale blue eyes wet with tears. "She will?"

"Aye. She will. I swear it." He gave the shoulder a gentle nudge. "Off you go then, lad."

As the boy walked away, Ash turned back to Zucker. He tried to keep his tone calm and reasonable, but 'twas hard. "Dinna do that again."

Fury crackled in Zucker's eyes again. "You got no call to interfere—"

Ash hit him across the face.

Zucker staggered back, fingers pressed to his bleeding mouth. "Wh-what the hell?"

"See how it feels?" Ash closed the distance between them. "You're a coward to strike a simpleminded lad. Dinna do it again."

"I can hit him any time I—"

Ash hit him again, then grabbed him by the throat. "No. You canna."

Zucker clawed at his arm and tried to pull himself free, but Ash tightened his grip. "You willna hit the lad again. Do you understand?" From the corner of his eye, he saw Zucker reach down to his gun belt.

He smiled. "Oh, please do," he whispered into Zucker's ear as he pressed the thumbnail of his free hand at the corner of the blue gray eye with the odd brown flecks. "So I can pop out this eye for the ravens."

Zucker froze. He made a gagging noise.

Ash loosened his grip just enough to allow the man to breathe easier. "You willna hurt the lad again. Swear it." He punctuated the order by pushing his thumb a little deeper into the eye socket.

"Jesus. I-I won't. I swear."

Ash took his hand away from Zucker's throat. "As a show of

faith, you'll be giving me this." He slipped Zucker's pistol from the holster on his hip. "And that rifle in the scabbard on your saddle. I'll return both to you when you leave. Assuming you're still alive." He smiled.

Zucker dinna smile back. Instead, his gaze flicked past Ash's shoulder, and a different kind of fear showed in his mismatched eyes.

Ash dinna have to turn to see what had caused it. "That would be Tricks, I'm guessing. Fiercely protective. Deadly, so he is, especially if provoked. But you'll not be doing that, will you?"

"Christ."

"Good. Then you should get along fine. If not . . . well, we won't think about that. Come, Tricks. Let's see how that deer is coming along. I ken how you love fresh, warm meat." Resting an arm across Zucker's shoulders, Ash steered him away from the campsite and into the trees. "And meanwhile, Mr. Zucker, you'll be telling me why you were so rude to my wife last week. You upset her, so you did. And that upsets me."

Maddie watched her husband escort Mr. Zucker away from camp and breathed a sigh of relief. Glancing over Silas Zucker's head as he sat beside the fire, she gave Edwina and Lucinda a nod of satisfaction.

They had all seen the scoundrel strike his slow-witted brother. But before they could rush to the boy's defense, Ash had stepped in. His big body had blocked Zucker from their view, but whatever he had said to the weasel seemed to have had the desired effect.

"You're the lady who makes the pictures?" a tentative voice asked.

Looking down into the gentle gaze of Silas Zucker, Maddie wondered at the unforgivable cruelty of his brother. The boy's face showed evidence of other beatings, some long since healed into thin white scars, others so recent the bruises still showed.

"I am."

"She takes wonderful pictures," Edwina added cheerily. "Doesn't she, Lucinda?"

"She certainly does. Perhaps after we get you cleaned up, Silas, you might want to see some. Would you like that?"

He smiled and nodded.

A sweet smile, except for the broken teeth and the neglect of those that remained. This poor boy—even though he might be more than half-grown, he still seemed a boy to Maddie—sorely needed tending. A bath, a trim, a brush for those poor teeth. He'd been dreadfully neglected.

Lucinda rose. "Is that box of photographs in your wagon, Maddie?"

"Yes. Under the bed." Then an idea came to her and Maddie motioned for Lucinda to wait. "Would you like me to take a picture of you, too?" she asked Silas.

He blinked up at her, wariness in his eyes. "Will it hurt?"

"Not at all."

"My brother might not like it."

"Then we won't tell him."

"Well . . . okay, then. If you're sure it won't hurt." His hopeful, trusting smile almost broke her heart.

Lucinda brought the box of photographs for Silas while Maddie collected her camera equipment. As the boy carefully studied the images, his expression of wonder almost brought tears to Maddie's eyes.

She worked quickly, setting up her camera in the waning light, hoping to get at least one photograph of Silas before it became too dark to expose the negative plate. As she made last-minute adjustments to the lens, Tricks came up. But instead of the near hysteria that most strangers exhibited when seeing the ferocious-looking beast for the first time, Silas just smiled and reached out to touch the wolfhound's bushy eyebrows. Tricks rewarded him with a wet kiss, which made the boy laugh in delight.

Inspired, Maddie repositioned her camera back a few feet so she could center both the boy and the dog in the focusing screen. Satisfied with the framing, she instructed Silas to put his arm around Tricks and sit very still. Even Tricks cooperated.

After sliding in the sensitized plate, she pulled the drape over her head, removed the lens cover, and counted aloud to eleven, hoping that would be enough time to imprint the image on the plate in the fading light.

"All done," she said, replacing the lens cap. "That didn't hurt at all, did it?"

"What's your dog's name?"

"Tricks." Leaving him in the care of Luce and Edwina, she wrapped the entire camera in the dark drape and went into the unlit wagon to transfer the negative on the plate onto a piece of albumenized paper.

When she came back out with the photograph in her hand a few minutes later, Ash was walking up with an armload of firewood. Declan and Zucker were still working on the deer carcass. As Ash dumped the wood next to the fire ring, Maddie knelt beside Silas.

"Here's a picture of you and your friend, Tricks." She held it out. When he hesitated, as if expecting a trap, she put it into his hand. "Take it. It's yours."

"Mine? Forever?"

"Forever."

He studied it, careful not to smear it with his dirty hands. "It's me," he said in a wondering voice. "And Tricks."

The look of joy that crossed his poor battered face as he studied his own image made Maddie realize in a way she never had before how powerful a simple photograph could be.

Tears filled her eyes. Never had she been more proud of her talent, or more grateful for the gift of it, than she felt at that moment. To cover a sudden swell of emotion, she abruptly rose, almost stumbling into Ash, who was standing behind her.

She turned to apologize, then saw the way he was looking at her. In his face was a mixture of so many emotions she could scarcely separate one from the other. Pride. Love. Desire. Yet beneath it all was that undeniable trace of regret that she had glimpsed so often over the last days.

Her throat tightened. Unable to speak, she reached up and pressed her palm against his cheek, wanting to assure him that everything was fine, that she had no second thoughts, and when the time came, whether that was in a month or a dozen years, she would still choose him over her photography.

And she prayed with her whole heart that that was true.

Dinner was a tense affair. The venison steaks were tasty, as were the roasted potatoes and canned beans flavored with onion and bacon, but seeing the furtive glances Silas sent his brother—as if he expected to have his food snatched away at any moment or a fist to come flying at his face—rather dampened Ash's appetite.

As soon as the meal ended, Zucker rose. Thanking them tersely for the meal, he motioned Silas to come with him and walked to the far side of the clearing. There, they set up camp, which consisted of starting a small fire in a ring of stones, clearing the area around it of rocks and twigs, then spreading their bedrolls directly on the ground.

Taking Tricks with them, the ladies went to the creek, leaving Ash and Declan sitting at the fire. After they'd washed and tended their needs, the ladies gave their good nights and retired to their separate sleeping quarters.

Silence settled across the clearing. The moon rose and the animals, including the two horses belonging to the Zuckers, moved slowly in dappled shadows cast by moonlight shining through tall firs and hemlocks and alders, munching grass already withered by the first frost.

Tricks sat between Ash and Brodie, head up, ears pricked. Even a nightjar calling from the brush dinna draw his attention away from the small campfire across the clearing. Ash leaned forward to drop a limb on the fire, then sat back and waited for the smoke to clear.

"He lamed his own horse," he said to Brodie in a voice that wouldn't carry. He went on to explain about the tail hair tied around the animal's pastern, and the swelling it had caused. "It's only temporary," he added. "The beast will be sound by morning, but the question is why?"

"As an excuse to join up with us? Maybe hitch a ride in one of the wagons?"

"Perhaps." *But why?*

Ash tried to recall all that Maddie had told him after her meeting with Zucker in the lobby of the hotel. Zucker thought she'd taken that photograph of his missing brother somewhere in the mountains around Breckenridge. He had wanted her to take the more northerly, left-handed fork into Denver, which went through the Blue River area, thinking she might see something along the way to jog her memory. Which wouldn't happen if she took the right fork through Kenosha Pass—the road they were on now. But if he convinced them this road was blocked, they would have to turn back and take the other route—the one he had wanted Maddie to take in the first place.

"He wants to make certain we go through Blue River," he told Brodie. He went on to explain his reasoning. "That's what this is about. He thinks Maddie will recognize where she took that photograph, and that will lead him to his brother."

"So it's Maddie he's after."

Ash felt the cold, deadly resolve that had carried him into many a battle move through his chest. His hands itched to feel the saber in his grip. "He treads dangerous ground if he even comes near my wife."

"He must really want to find his brother," Declan mused. "I wonder why?"

"Or find something his brother has." Ash lowered his voice even more. "You saw the photograph—the pickax and sluice. Miner's tools. Perhaps his brother hit ore, and Zucker is trying to find it."

Brodie looked over at the smoking fire across the way. "Could be." He looked up into the sky. "There's a full moon tonight."

"Aye. If he moves, we'll see him. If not, Tricks will." He ruffled the wolfhound's rough coat. "The lad will know what to do, so he will."

"Jesus." Brodie looked down at the dog between them. "He's never killed anyone has he?"

Ash smiled. "Not yet. But I'm sure he would enjoy the practice."

"Jesus."

That night, Ash slept as lightly as he ever had on a field of battle. Twice he left Maddie's side to sit outside, well out of the fire's light so he wouldn't make an easy target.

He loved the night. It stripped away everything—sound and motion and substance—until all that was left was a vast, looming stillness that hung in the air like a hushed breath. It awakened his mind and sharpened his senses. It made him intensely aware that he was the intruder into this dark world, but if he curbed his impatience and cleared his mind, it would slowly reveal itself in furtive rustlings, a bird's startled cry, the silent fall of a star across the dome of the sky.

It was a whole other world, the night. Elemental and primitive and beautiful in its simplicity. His years as a forward rider with the Rifles had taught him how to use the darkness to his advantage— how to move silently through it, blending into the shadows until he reached his quarry, then strike before his enemy even knew he was there. The night was like one of Maddie's negative plates. Skewed, flat, and colorless. Beneath the stars and the pockmarked moon, even blood ran black.

And tonight, as Ash sat studying the two men snoring beside their dying campfire, he contemplated shedding some. Because of Maddie. And his fear for her. And his fear for himself if he had to live a life without her.

But the pull to her side was stronger than his need to kill a man he wasn't yet sure was his enemy. So after a while, he rose and went back to his wife.

.   .   .

Maddie awoke to the low drone of male voices. Ash was gone, all his blankets piled on top of her. She snuggled into them, smelled his scent in the rough fabric, and woodsmoke, and that lingering mustiness of coarse wool.

She smiled, remembering how he had wrapped his arms around her in the night and she had yelped and tried to roll away, startled by the coldness of his skin. But he had chuckled and pulled her back against his chest, and soon his hands had warmed on her awakening body and he was moving into her from behind and she was stifling her cries against the blanket so the others wouldn't hear.

That rogue. Tonight would be her turn.

Smiling at the prospect, she tossed the blankets aside, sat up, and lifted the flap of the tent.

Ash and Declan stood over the campfire, holding steaming mugs in their hands. Behind them, a thin coating of frost shimmered on the bowed roof of her wagon, and although a thin curl of smoke rose from the stovepipe, she saw no sign of Lucinda. She looked around but didn't see Edwina, either, or any sign of the Zucker brothers.

After digging through the blankets for the chemise Ash had removed from her in the night, she slipped it over her head, then pulled a skirt, a blouse, and a pair of long woolen stockings from her valise. She quickly dressed, finger-combed the worst of the tangles from her hair, tied it back with a ribbon, then stepped through the flap.

It was a glorious day. A perfect day for photography. She drew in a great breath of cold air and stretched the kinks from her back, then realized she had drawn the attention of the two men beside the fire.

Declan quickly looked away.

Ash didn't, his gaze sweeping over her in a possessive, hungry way that made something deep inside her pulse with memory.

She walked toward him, thinking some day she would photograph him as she saw him now, his hair silvered by sunlight, his eyes hot with desire, his tall form radiating male power.

But without the clothing, of course.

"What are you grinning about, lass?" he asked as she approached.

Ignoring that, she waved toward the cold fire on the other side of the clearing. "The Zuckers are gone?"

"Early this morning." He grinned. "I'm surprised you slept through it. Rough night?"

"Ah . . . restless, perhaps."

"But pleasantly so, I'm guessing by that wee smile."

"I'll go wake Ed," Declan muttered and abruptly walked away.

"You cad," Maddie scolded as soon as he was out of earshot. "Now he'll know what we were doing."

Ash laughed and pulled her close for a kiss. "I doubt he cares, love, since he was probably doing the same thing with his wife."

Maddie blinked at him in surprise. "But Edwina is increasing."

"Aye. And how do you suppose she got that way?"

"Good morning," Lucinda called, making Maddie jump back from Ash's embrace. "Is that coffee I smell?"

"Before he left, he apologized for being so forward with Maddie," Ash said later, when they were all gathered around the fire, finishing a quick breakfast of bacon and pan biscuits and stewed apples.

"I'm more concerned about Silas," Maddie muttered.

"Aye." Ash tossed the dregs of his cup into the fire, loosening a hissing gout of steam. "I almost wished Zucker had stayed so I could make sure he dinna hit the lad again."

"I'd feel better knowing where he is, too," Declan seconded. "I don't like the idea of him lurking up ahead somewhere."

"Assuming," Lucinda put in, "that we believe what he said about the landslide and change our route accordingly and head up toward Blue River."

Ash turned his head and looked at her. The woman had a sharp mind. He appreciated that she had so quickly grasped their dilemma. "If we do, we could be playing right into his hands."

"And into an ambush," Declan added.

Edwina Brodie looked from one to the other. Ash could see she was showing the strain of travel already. Brodie had told him she had a delicate stomach. She looked it this morning. Her face was drawn, her eyes shadowed by dark circles. He found himself imagining how Maddie would look with his babe growing inside her. Then remembering the one she had lost, he wondered if they would be given a second chance.

"But if we stay on our original route," Edwina Brodie argued, "and there really is a landslide, we would have to backtrack several days."

"And probably miss the statehood vote," her husband said.

"And I might miss my meeting with the owners of the Denver Pacific," Lucinda added.

"But the alternative could be worse," Ash stated, "if we ride into an ambush."

In the end, despite the possibility the road might be blocked and the delay might cost Declan his statehood vote and Lucinda her meeting with the railroads, they decided to continue on their original route. As the sheriff said, "Better late than dead."

Within an hour, they were packed, harnessed, and traveling again.

They crossed Red Hill Pass just after noon, and because the grade was relatively gentle and didn't overly strain the mules and Miss Hathaway's pacer, Ash allowed only a brief stop to water the animals and pass out cold rations of jerky and canned fruit before he had them moving again.

The ladies groused a bit, but he dangled before them the promise of a warm bath and soft bed if they made Jefferson by nightfall, which perked them up considerably.

It still felt like a snail's pace to Ash, and he was grateful he was able to spend the long day on horseback rather than bouncing along in a wagon like a bluidy sheep farmer. Even so, they made good time and were rolling down toward the Jefferson Creek bridge when Tricks warned him of riders advancing on their flank.

Wheeling Lurch, Ash rode back past the buggy. Waving Miss Hathaway to continue on, he pulled in beside the wagon to warn Brodie.

"Can you see who it is?" the sheriff asked.

"No. Keep going. I'll catch up." Reining Lurch off the track, he wound through the trees until he came to an elevated position with a good view of the road. He stopped and checked his weapons, levering one of his homemade scattershot cartridges into the carbine and making sure the chamber of his pistol was fully loaded. Then he called Tricks to his side and waited.

Two riders. Moving briskly, but not at a pursuit gallop. He watched them approach, then smiled when he saw who it was. Sending Lurch out of the trees, he galloped down to intercept Thomas Redstone.

"What are you doing here, heathen?" he asked as Thomas reined in. Ash glanced past him at the other man bouncing up behind him. A cleric. And one who dinna sit his horse particularly well.

"This man wanted to talk to your wife."

"About what?"

Thomas tipped his head toward the round-faced man reining in beside him. "His brother. Ephraim Zucker."

Seventeen

"Goddamnit!"

Si jumped to his feet as Clete came stomping down the path from his perch in a pile of boulders above the road. Quickly, he stuffed the photograph of him and the dog into his pocket. "What's wrong, Clete?"

"They took the other road, that's what! Bastards! How we going to get the woman now?"

"What woman, Clete?"

"What woman do you think, moron? The photographer." In a furious motion, he swiped his hat at Si's head. "Damnit, we need to find that claim!"

Silas stood for a minute, not sure what to do. When Clete was mad, he knew better than to talk to him. But they'd been sitting here forever, and he was hungry and thirsty and the wind was turning cold. Finally, the waiting got to him and he broke the long silence.

"So what are we going to do now, Clete?"

"Shut up, you idiot! How can I think with you yammering at me all the time?"

"Okay, Clete."

" 'Okay, Clete,' " his brother mimicked. "Christ! If I had a partner with half a brain, Zucker would have already told us where the claim is and we'd be sitting rich. Now we got nothing!"

"I'm sorry, Clete."

"Yeah, I know you are. You're the sorriest damn thing ever walked this earth. I ought to kill you now and do the world a favor."

Si watched an ant crawl across the toe of his boot. He wondered what it felt like to be so small. So small the wind could blow you far away and Clete would never even know you were gone. He smiled, imagining it.

Clete paced back and forth, kicking at rocks in his path. "We'll have to go to Denver. See if Zucker registered the claim. If he did, we'll have to forge a bill of sale, and reregister the claim under my name. If he didn't, we can file on it ourselves. Once we find the claim."

He paced and thought, then abruptly stopped. "Bud Purvis. Heard he was dealing faro at one of the hog ranches up there. He'll help us. Remember ole' Bud, Si?"

Si did. Bud kept a tarantula in a box. He would sometimes let it crawl around in his beard. But mostly, he liked to tease Si with it. Si hated crawly things. "Why do we need him? He's mean."

"That's *why* we need him, moron. And also because these foreigners we been following don't know Bud from Adam's house cat. Who else can I send into the registry office to ask about the claim? You, moron?"

"No, Clete."

"That's right." Clete paced some more.

Si sat down again. He didn't know what Clete was talking about. He was hungry and cold and tired and wished he was back with the picture lady and Tricks and the big man who talked funny. They had lots of food.

"After he checks on the claim, Bud can help me grab the woman out from under that crazy Scotsman's nose." Absently Clete rubbed the bruise on his neck. "Hell, maybe we'll take the Scotsman, too. Let him watch us take turns on his wife, then skin him and leave him staked on an ant hill. I owe him that, at least."

Abruptly Clete laughed and cuffed Si upside the head, almost knocking him off the rock he was sitting on.

"Maybe I'll give you a turn on the woman, too, since you seemed so taken with her. Or better yet, sell you to the perverts at one of the vice palaces. You'd like that, wouldn't you, Si? Yeah, I can hear you blubbering now."

Jefferson was a one-street village perched like a wart on a flat plain that was bordered by rolling hills sparsely covered with stunted, wind-bent pines. It looked like a town that wasn't sure of its purpose—ranching, farming, timber, or mining. So it made halfhearted attempts to cater to each and ended up meeting the needs of none. Like Heartbreak Creek, it was a ghost town in the making.

But it did have a hotel that served meals and a barn at one end of town that boarded animals. Tricks was posted there to stand guard over the buggy and wagon, while Thomas, who preferred to sleep outside, made camp in the trees nearby. It took Ash several attempts to make the dog understand he was to stay, but the wolfhound finally accepted the separation from his master and settled in for the night.

An hour later, the travelers met in the dining room. Because there were now seven in their party—probably the biggest group the dining room had ever served—the hotel kept the kitchen open late to accommodate them. A tureen of stew with vegetables, fresh rolls, and a warm berry cobbler sat on the table awaiting them when they arrived.

"There's no landslide at Kenosha Pass," Declan said as he took his seat beside his wife. "Hasn't been one in years."

"So I guess we avoided an ambush." Lucinda settled into the chair on the other side of Edwina. "But I still don't know what that other Zucker wants."

"Or who he is," Maddie added.

They had the room to themselves and so dinna have to worry

about eavesdroppers when the reverend repeated all he'd told Thomas and Prudence Lincoln at the sheriff's house on Elderberry Creek.

"I knew he was evil the minute I saw him last night," Edwina pronounced as she ladled stew into bowls and passed them around. "You can always tell. It's in the eyes. And his were different colors, at that. That man was as ugly as homemade sin."

No one argued the point. So the discussion moved on to speculation about what might be the purpose of such a ruse.

Declan Brodie remained silent throughout, and Ash guessed the sheriff had reached the same conclusions he had. "The only way he would know enough to pose as you, Reverend Zucker," Ash said during a lull in the speculations, "is if your brother told him about you."

Maddie shook her head. "I don't think he knew more about the reverend than his name. He wasn't dressed for the part, and when I mentioned the letter you sent me, sir, and that you were meeting Ephraim in Omaha, he seemed surprised."

"Perhaps he intercepted a missive from you to your brother," Edwina suggested. "If so, that would give him your name and that you were from Pennsylvania."

"But that wouldn't explain how he came into possession of the third copy of the photograph," Maddie argued. "Unless your brother gave it to him."

"Not willingly." Lucinda looked around at the doubting faces. "Think about it. If Ephraim told him about the reverend and gave him the photograph, why didn't he also reveal the whereabouts of the mine?"

"Maybe he did," Edwina said.

"Then why is he still harassing Maddie about its location?"

No one had an answer to that.

"So the only things we know for certain at this point," Brodie said between bites of biscuit, "is that Ephraim Zucker is missing, and the man impersonating the reverend doesn't know the location of the mine."

"Perhaps the claim was never registered," Edwina suggested. "And the imposter is trying to find it so he can file before Ephraim can."

The reverend shook his head. "No, he registered it. In his last letter, he said the paperwork was already on its way to Denver."

"Then your brother should have a copy of it," Brodie pointed out. "That way, if this imposter tries to jump the claim, your brother can prove he staked it first."

The reverend sighed. "I don't know where the papers are. I don't even know where my brother is."

Or if he's still alive, Ash thought, exchanging a look with the sheriff.

"Then how can we help the reverend and make sure this imposter quits harassing Maddie?" Edwina looked at Maddie, her blue eyes bright with worry. "It's all so unfair."

Ash reached over and put his hand over his wife's. It felt cold and small under his. "He'll not get near my lass," he said flatly. "Tricks and I will make sure of it."

Maddie rewarded him with a grateful smile. "I don't doubt it."

Brodie pushed his empty plate aside. "And meanwhile, we can check with the mining office in Denver. See if a claim has been registered to Ephraim Zucker. Then go from there."

Maddie smiled apologetically at the reverend. "I'm so sorry I can't remember where I took that photograph, Reverend. I took so many over the last two years."

"I understand, Mrs. Wallace. It was rather a long shot, I'm afraid."

"I will find this claim," a deep voice cut in. Everyone turned to stare at Thomas. Those were the first words he had spoken throughout the meal.

"How?" Brodie asked.

The Cheyenne took another bite of stew, chewed for a moment, then said, "I know where it is."

The reverend almost hopped to his feet. "You've been to my brother's cabin?"

"When I was there, there was no cabin. But the peak behind it is known among the People. Faces the Dawn, it is called."

The reverend's round face split into a hopeful smile. He grabbed Thomas's arm. "Can you take me there? Please?"

Thomas stopped chewing. He frowned down at the hand gripping his arm.

The reverend hastily took it away.

Thomas resumed chewing. "Yes, I can take you there. But first, I must take these people to Denver. They have been gone only two moons and already they are in trouble." He sighed and shook his head. "White people."

Denver was a bustling place. Situated at the confluence of the South Platte River and Cherry Creek, it sprawled across a high plateau, surrounded by distant snowcapped mountains. It was mostly a mining community, which was reflected in the vast number of establishments that catered to lonely prospectors who had more gold dust than sense.

After various name changes, the town had finally settled on Denver when it had become the territorial capitol three years past. And this year, with the completion in June of the Denver Pacific line from Cheyenne and the last spike of the Kansas Pacific being driven at Strasburg, it was a town ready to bloom.

Except for those pesky statehood issues.

"It's been going on for over a decade," Lucinda complained to Maddie and Edwina later as she deftly turned the buggy in behind Declan and Ash as they headed back out of the business district. The reverend followed in Maddie's wagon, and Thomas brought up the rear. "It's been a mess."

They had planned on staying at one of the downtown hotels, but when their husbands saw the desperadoes and drunken miners staggering in and out of the saloons, and the painted women hanging out of the windows calling to passersby, they decided it wasn't a safe place for their wives. Now they were all headed back to the less commercial area they had ridden through earlier.

"First, the residents voted against statehood," Lucinda continued, "because they didn't want to have to pay to operate a state government, then—what are you doing?"

Edwina, seated between Lucinda and Maddie, had leaned forward as far as her stomach would allow. "Look at that hussy!" She glared at a scantily clad woman on the balcony of a glitter palace. "She's waving at my husband. The nerve!"

"He's not waving back, is he?" Lucinda pointed out.

"He looked."

"So did you."

"Isn't this marvelous?" Maddie dipped her head to peer beneath the buggy's roof struts at a grizzled old man kissing a mule smack on the lips. "I could take photographs here for a month."

With a snort, Edwina squeezed back into her place on the crowded buggy seat, her arms crossed over her bulging midriff. "Lucky for him he didn't wave back, that's all I can say."

"Why would he, when he has you?" Maddie peered through the open doors of a saloon, then jerked back. "Oh my. Did you know they have paintings of naked women in there?"

"That's disgusting. Declan better not be thinking of going into one of those places."

"Then five years ago," Lucinda continued, "the residents finally approved statehood and petitioned Congress. But because of an alleged voting scandal or some such, President Johnson vetoed it. Twice. Can you credit that? Sometimes I think Booth should have shot him instead of Lincoln. But now that Grant is president, and if we can get Teller and Evans and Chaffee to quit squabbling long enough to agree on who is to be the second senator, we might pass the vote this time around."

"Are we almost there?" Edwina muttered. "I really could use the necessary."

"Again?"

"I can't help it, Luce. If you haven't noticed I have a giant Declan-sized baby bouncing around on my inner parts. It's a wonder I can function at all."

"Oh, you're functioning just fine," Lucinda said drily. "In fact, you've functioned three times in the last two hours."

"You're counting? I cannot believe you would count the—"

"They've stopped." Maddie pointed ahead to where Declan and Ash had reined in before a slightly worn but respectable-looking two-storied house bearing a sign in the yard that read, MRS. KEMBLE'S BOARDING HOUSE FOR PERSONS OF QUALITY.

"That doesn't look so bad," Edwina said. "Do you think they have an indoor facility?"

After the men conferred for a moment, Declan swung down, wrapped his horse's reins around a hitching post by the street, and walked up the stone path.

"I do wish he would hurry," Edwina muttered, tapping her foot on the floor of the buggy in the exact tempo of the painful throb bouncing between Maddie's temples. "Sometimes he can be as slow as molasses."

A few minutes later, Declan came back out, pointed Ash and Tricks around the side of the house, then walked toward the buggy.

"They have rooms for everyone but Thomas, who wouldn't stay inside, anyway, and a stable for the horses. Follow Ash around back. We'll unload there."

Though by no means elegant, Mrs. Kemble's boardinghouse was clean and the rooms were spacious and adequately furnished. Edwina was delighted to find a water closet at the end of the upstairs hall by their bedrooms, and Maddie was just as pleased to find a roomy washroom with a deep tub on the ground floor. It had been a long four days.

Once they had unloaded the wagon and buggy, Declan left Edwina napping in their room and rode back into town with Reverend Zucker to find out where the delegates would be meeting and where the claims office was located. While Maddie and Lucinda made use of the washroom, Ash and Thomas took care of the weary horses and Maddie's mules, rubbing them down with burlap, checking their hooves for stones and cracks, and applying salve to any cuts or rubbed spots left by the rigging.

Ash was trying to comb the tangles out of Lurch's tail when Thomas, working on his own mount beside Lurch in the narrow aisleway of the stable, finally broke the long silence.

"Your horse does not hear."

Working a twig free, Ash tossed it aside and started on another knot. "He was injured in an explosion."

"Yet you did not put him down."

"No."

"Why?"

Ash straightened, one hand resting on Lurch's croup. "He's a good horse."

"He is old."

"He does well enough."

"He is still old."

Ash knew that. He had inherited Lurch from a fellow cavalryman who had died of malaria in India. Rather than leave the horse behind, Ash had brought him back to England. That was over a decade ago, and they'd been together ever since. In fact, they'd been together longer than many of the men Ash had served with. They trusted each other. Depended on each other. And after suffering his own debilitating injury, Ash wouldn't do to this fine horse what had been done to him. Lurch wouldn't want to live a useless life. "He's a good horse," Ash said again and went back to combing.

"You brought him with you from that place you call home?" Thomas asked after a moment.

"Scotland. Aye." He gave Lurch's arse an affectionate pat. "He's been to India, Ireland, England, and halfway across this vast country. A well-traveled lad, so he is."

"I do not know those other places. Are they far?"

"Aye. Across oceans and seas and mountains as tall as these."

Resting an arm across his spotted pony's back, Thomas stared past Ash at the distant peaks framed by the open stable doors.

"Prudence Lincoln has told me of the big lakes the whites call oceans. But I have never seen one."

Ash chuckled. "I had my head in a bucket for most of the crossing, so I dinna see much of it, either." Seeing Thomas's questioning look, he made a face and rubbed his stomach.

"Ho." Thomas nodded in understanding. "Like Declan Brodie after I gave him *mataho*—peyote."

Ash had heard of the vision-inducing cactus buttons but had never tried any. He was glad he hadn't if it could bring down a man Brodie's size. He grinned, picturing it as he stroked the curry comb down Lurch's flank. "How did you and the sheriff become friends?"

"He saved my life." Thomas said no more for a while, then added, "And I saved his."

"A poor trade."

Thomas scowled at him over his horse's back. "Because I am not white?"

"Because he's a terrible shot and useless in a tussle. You're better."

Thomas's lips twitched. "He can fight when he must. But that is not his way. You like to fight."

"I dinna mind." Ash hung the curry comb on a nail protruding from an upright post. "A friendly wrestle now and then eases tension and clears the mind. We often had regimental matches."

"You will fight me."

Ash laughed. "Dinna be daft."

"You are afraid?"

"Of course not. But I'm taller and outweigh you by at least two stone."

Thomas grinned—a transformation that was so startling Ash could only stare. "Then I will use only one hand."

Ash laughed at the arrogance of the man. "You would have made a fine Scottish soldier, so you would."

"I am already a fine Cheyenne Dog Soldier. Why would I settle for less?"

That was it. Grinning, Ash motioned toward the open doors. "After you, heathen. And never say I dinna warn you."

Unbuttoning his shirt as they left the stable, Ash recounted the standard rules—no biting, eye gouging, hair pulling, kidney punches, kicks to the groin, spitting—then he faltered when Thomas removed his leather war tunic to expose massive scars across his chest.

"Good God, man. Were you caught in a bear trap?"

Thomas lifted over his head a leather strip from which hung a small pouch, then tucked his chin to study the two twisted ridges of scar tissue that covered him from collarbone to ribs. "It is from the sun dance ceremony."

Ash had heard of it, but until seeing Thomas's scars, hadn't truly believed that a sane man would willingly pierce himself with sticks then hang from them until the flesh ripped away. "Why would you do such a thing?" he asked, removing his own shirt and tossing it over a post.

"It is a sacred rite. I will not speak of it." Thomas's gaze drifted to the scarring on Ash's side. "You have rites as well?"

"Aye. It's called casualties of war." Seeing Thomas dinna understand, he added, "A powder keg exploded."

"You did not get those scars in battle?"

"No." Sensing that admission had somehow diminished him in the Cheyenne's eyes, Ash turned and presented his back. "But this one I did." He motioned toward a puckered dent where a bullet had entered his right side just below his rib cage. "And this." Turning back, he pointed to two long saber scars, one across his shoulder by his neck and another along his upper arm. "There's another bullet scar on my thigh, but I'll not be showing you that." Planting hands on his hips, he dared Thomas to belittle any of those well-earned marks.

"You carry many battle scars," the Cheyenne acknowledged in his expressionless way. "You must be a poor fighter."

Ash was about to take offense when he saw the laughter in the dark eyes. "We'll see about that." And in a single quick motion, he threw an arm around the Indian's neck and flipped him over his hip and onto the ground.

The Cheyenne rolled, swept a moccasined foot behind Ash's ankle, and yanked. Ash hit hard, scrambled into a half crouch, and drove his shoulder into the Indian's belly. Then they were both down, twisting, grabbing for handholds, throwing elbows, and maneuvering for headlocks and scissor holds. Ash had just gotten the Cheyenne down for the fourth time when a deep voice interrupted.

"This a friendly fight? Or should I get my manacles?"

Ash turned to see Brodie and the reverend watching from their horses. He spit dirt from his mouth and grinned just as Thomas's heel caught him behind the knee and sent him staggering into the fence. Wood cracked. The rail gave and Ash fell with a thud.

From the house came the slam of a door. Three women marched across the yard.

"Aw, hell," Brodie muttered. "Now look what you've done."

Ash rolled over to find Thomas extending a hand. He hesitated, half expecting a trick, but the panting Cheyenne grinned through the sweat-streaked dust caking his face. "You fight good. For a Scotsman."

Ash took the hand and pulled himself up. "As do you. For a runt."

"Cover yourselves," the sheriff ordered. "I don't want my wife to see those scars. Her stomach's unsettled enough as it is."

"Pay no attention to him, heathen," Ash said to Thomas as he pulled on his shirt. "He's probably afraid she'll see what real men look like."

"Men?" Thomas made a show of looking around. "Another Cheyenne has come?"

Ash laughed. "I hope so. Now we can have a fair fight."

"You people had better repair that fence," a shrill voice called.

Ash turned with a contrite expression as the woman who ran the boardinghouse stomped up, Edwina and Maddie in tow.

Edwina looked shocked. Maddie, furious.

"Aye, Mrs. Kemble, we will. And it's sorry I am for allowing this treacherous savage to throw me into it. As penance, I'll make sure he mucks out your stalls after he replaces the broken rail."

Behind him, Thomas snorted. Or maybe he was coughing up dust.

Mrs. Kemble's bright eyes darted from Ash to Thomas and back to Ash. She reminded him of a busy little hen deciding which worm to peck first. "I've a mind to throw all of you out."

"I'll see it doesn't happen again, Mrs. Kemble," Brodie promised.

"I'm sure they meant no harm," the reverend added.

This time, it was Maddie who snorted.

"Well . . . all right, then. But no more fighting. This is a respectable establishment." She glared at each of them a moment longer, then whirled and stomped back to the house.

"What on earth were you fighting about?" Edwina Brodie demanded.

When Thomas dinna respond, Ash stepped in. "Thomas, here, said the sheriff was a poor shot and a worse fighter. I was just defending your husband's honor, so I was."

Edwina glared at Thomas.

Thomas glared at Ash.

Muttering under her breath, Maddie took Edwina's arm and steered her back to the house.

"There was no claim registered to Ephraim Zucker," Brodie said a few minutes later, leaning against the wall while Thomas and Ash mucked out the last stall.

"I know he registered it," the reverend insisted from his perch on an overturned water bucket just inside the stable doors. "The imposter must have stolen Ephraim's copy when he took the photograph."

"Or maybe it just hasn't been processed yet." Brodie didn't sound hopeful. "Didn't they say it's not unusual for these things to take several months?"

"I suppose." It was obvious the reverend was starting to lose hope. His shoulders drooped and his kind eyes had dulled a bit more with each new disappointment.

Ash stuck the tines of the manure fork into the dirt floor and rested a forearm on the handle. "Perhaps your brother's copy of the paperwork is at the cabin."

"Perhaps," the reverend said without conviction.

After hanging his fork on the wall hooks, Thomas grabbed the handles of the overflowing wheelbarrow and steered it down the center aisle to the manure pile outside. He dumped it, left the barrow tilted up against the exterior wall and walked back, brushing bits of dirt and hay off his leather tunic. "I will take you to the cabin tomorrow."

"Will you?" The reverend immediately perked up. "What time?"

"Early."

"I'll be ready." After thanking Thomas several times, the reverend excused himself to wash before supper and inquire if Mrs. Kemble might sell him victuals for the trip. There was a new bounce in his step as he rushed to the house.

"I doubt his brother will be there," the sheriff said.

Ash carried a tin of grain to Lurch's stall and poured it atop his pile of hay. "I doubt his brother is even alive."

"How far is this place, Thomas?"

"Half a day. Maybe more for a white man."

"We may have a problem."

Both Ash and Thomas stared at Brodie.

"I think the other Zuckers are in town. They were at a distance, but I recognized the blond hair and bowler hat."

Bollocks. Ash doled out the last tin of grain to Buttercup, then closed the feed room door and slid the bar home. "Did they see you?"

"I don't know. Maybe. Si's brother—if they are brothers— knows I'm a delegate. Because of my size, I wouldn't be that hard to pick out amongst the others."

Ash stood in the middle of the aisleway and stared out at the fading sky, wishing he had acted on his impulse two nights ago and killed the bluidy bastard. If anything happened to Maddie because of that . . . he couldn't even finish the thought. "As long as he dinna follow you back here, we should be fine."

"Well, that's the thing."

"Oh, hell."

"I'm pretty sure it wasn't either of the Zuckers, but I got the distinct impression someone followed the reverend from the claims office."

"How? Si and his brother hadn't met the reverend, so how would they know to follow him?"

"The poor fellow made quite a stink when they couldn't find Ephraim's paperwork. Anyone within hearing would have heard the name. There were a lot of people standing in line."

"Bluidy hell."

Brodie turned to Thomas, who was leaning against a stall door. "Be watchful, Thomas. If they know who the reverend is, he could be their new target. They see you leave, they might figure you're going to Ephraim's cabin and follow you."

Thomas nodded. "The churchman is a poor rider and makes more noise than a buffalo, but I will do what I can."

Ash gave Thomas a meaningful look. One warrior to another. Men who, by training or by nature, were prepared to kill. "If there's trouble, Thomas, you'll know what to do, so you will."

The Cheyenne nodded.

Brodie raised a hand. "Hold up." He leveled warning glances at each of them. "No killing unless you're fired on first. You know that, Thomas. You're a duly sworn officer of the law."

Thomas looked down at his war shirt with its array of quills and beads and bones sewn in intricate patterns. "I see no badge."

"Damnit, Thomas! I don't want to have to come hunting you. Or keep a posse from hunting you."

Ash stepped in. "He's right, Thomas. Until we know what happened to the reverend's brother, we have to keep them alive."

Thomas smiled. "I will keep them alive."

"And there's the boy," Ash added. "He's simple. Dinna hurt him."

"I would not. It is against our way to do harm to those with troubled spirits. We will leave when the sun clears the mountains." Thomas pushed away from the wall, then hesitated and turned to

Ash. "While I am away, Scotsman, you will watch over the women when the sheriff and Miss Hathaway are at their meetings."

Ash nodded.

"And if anyone tries to harm them, *you* will know what to do."

"Aye. And if I fail, Tricks won't."

"Hell." Brodie sighed. "It's going to be a bloody week. I can already tell."

Eighteen

There were no empty seats at the dinner table that evening. In addition to the group from Heartbreak Creek, there was also a deaf widow with an ear trumpet she never used, her excruciatingly shy unmarried daughter, and a rail-thin Bible salesman, who spent most of the meal conversing with the reverend when he wasn't casting looks at Edwina.

Unkind looks.

Maddie couldn't decide if it was because Edwina's natural vivacity was an affront to his sour disposition or because of her obvious pregnancy. Even in a frontier area like this, where the practicalities of survival often outweighed the strictures of propriety, there were still those who felt a woman in Edwina's condition should remain out of the public eye.

Rubbish.

Just another example of the foolish thinking that awaited her if—when, that is—she went back into the bosom of society. Which she would gladly do, of course, rather than lose Ash.

She glanced at her husband, seated on her left, and felt a resurgence of the worry she had felt when she'd found him rolling in the dirt with Thomas.

Overgrown children. That's all they were.

She had been waiting in their room, primed to scold him soundly for risking injury to his side or perhaps bringing on another of his incapacitating headaches, when he had walked in, still damp from his wash, wrapped his arms around her, and whispered, "Thank you, lass," into her hair.

"For what?" she had asked, pulling back, her pique momentarily forgotten.

"For not telling them about . . ." He motioned vaguely to his head. "My troubles. They depend on me, so they do. And I'd not be wanting them to think I'm not up to the task."

At the time, she had wondered fleetingly if he had been trying to convince Thomas and Declan of that, or himself?

Ash's military career had meant as much to him as her photography did to her. He had been a decorated officer—a natural leader, respected by his peers and admired by his men. To have lost all of that so abruptly—and in such a violent and brutal way—must have been a terrible blow. A skilled soldier one minute, a near cripple, the next. That had to have shaken his confidence. And perhaps tussling in the dirt like a schoolboy was his way of proving to the world—and himself—he was still the man he always was.

Silly creature. In her eyes, he would always be larger than life.

Feeling a sudden desire to reassure him, she lifted her glass with her right hand, and—shocked by what she was doing even as she did it—rested her left on his leg.

His head whipped toward her, those startling green eyes round with surprise.

She took a sip, set her glass down, and smiled. "Would you please pass the bread, Ash?"

The way he looked at her made her feel bold and daring and a bit out of breath. Would a countess do this, she wondered, lightly tracing a figure eight on his muscled thigh.

Those muscles flexed beneath her hand when he leaned forward to rest his forearms on the edge of the table, shielding his lower body from view of the others. "Hungry, are you, lass?" he asked, his lips quirking at the corners.

"I find that I am. The long travel day, perhaps."

"That, and camp rations," Lucinda seconded. "I hate hard-tack."

Beneath the table, Maddie's hand wandered and explored.

"I so agree." Edwina helped herself to more vegetables. "I wasn't that hungry earlier, but I declare, Mrs. Kemble, this meal is good enough to bring tears of joy to a glass eye."

Mrs. Kemble preened and fluffed the limp gray curls poking out beneath her little lace widow's cap. "I was afraid the roast wouldn't be as tender as I'd hoped. It's so hard to come by good meat nowadays."

"How right you are." Maddie smiled as she found the heat of him.

He sucked in air. The hand beside his plate clenched into a fist.

"I'm partial to chicken," the deaf widow's daughter offered, then blushed furiously when Declan sent her a smile.

"You're sick, you say?" her mother shouted.

"I've often found," Maddie mused, lightly stroking, "that the key to a nice piece of meat is entirely in the preparation. Don't you agree, Ash?" She punctuated that with a little squeeze.

He jerked and cleared his throat. "But over preparation can lead to disastrous results," he warned in a strained voice.

At the other end of the table, Edwina nodded. "You're certainly right about that. I burn meat all the time."

"I don't mind," Declan said with a sideways glance at Ash.

"Is it overcooked?" Grabbing the serving fork, Mrs. Kemble jabbed at what was left of the roast. "Did I leave it in too long?"

"Not at all," Maddie assured her. "It's perfect. Firm, yet tender. An unusual thing in such a sizeable cut." Another squeeze.

"You'll pay, lass," Ash hissed through clenched teeth.

"I hope so," she murmured back. A final little pat, then she pulled her hand away and reached for the bowl of fruit. "Did you grow these plump blackberries yourself, Mrs. Kemble? I can't wait to give them a try."

Maddie was still abed, exhausted from Ash's tender punishments—that man was extremely exacting in his retribution, bless his heart—when she heard Thomas and Reverend Zucker ride past the window the following morning. If the pink glow of sunlight peeking through the crochet edge of the bedroom curtain was any indication, it promised to be a beautiful day. Perfect for photography.

Anxious to get started, she rose and quickly dressed, wondering if she had time for breakfast before accompanying Lucinda and Declan into town for their various meetings.

Ash had been adamant that she not go. "We know Si's brother is in Denver. Brodie saw him. You willna be safe."

"In plain sight? Among all those passersby? Don't be silly."

"I should go with you."

"And leave Edwina here alone?"

Eventually, she had distracted him by kissing her way down his restless body—she could be thorough, too. Now, realizing how late it was and fearing he might use her tardiness as an excuse to send the others on without her, she hurriedly left the room.

But when she crossed to the stable a few minutes later, she found Declan and Lucinda waiting while Ash dutifully harnessed the mules to her wagon. Beside him stood a gangly boy who looked a little older than R. D., Declan's oldest son. Ash introduced him as Chub Pennystone, a nephew of Mrs. Kemble.

"He's to stay with you at all times. If there's a problem, he'll find Brodie. Questions?"

Seeing the determination in her husband's stance and expression, Maddie didn't argue. In truth, she was glad of the help. There never seemed to be enough hands where photography was concerned. "I'm grateful for the assistance, Chub." She gave the boy a bright smile that sent a flush up his thin neck, over his freckled cheeks, and beneath the brown hair that hung into his hazel eyes. "I hope you can drive a wagon."

Chub—obviously not named such because of any excess weight—hitched trousers that were dangerously close to falling off his narrow hips despite the frayed braces over his narrow shoulders. "Yes, ma'am. I drive my pa's hay wagon all the time."

"Then we shall get along famously."

They left soon after, Declan riding ahead, Lucinda and Maddie in the driver's box with Chub, and both women carrying their double shot palm pistols in their skirt pockets.

"Are you ready for your meeting today with the gentlemen from the Denver Pacific?" Maddie asked Lucinda, who sat between her and Chub.

Lucinda nodded and patted the thick, ribbon-tied folder in her lap. "All that's missing is the paperwork on the water test."

"I thought you already took care of that."

"I did. But the results weren't as good as I'd hoped so I'm having it tested again."

The water in Heartbreak Creek was its major drawback, as was evidenced by the stained teeth of most of the longtime residents. Such a high mineral content was equally damaging to metal pipes, gauges, and valves on steam-driven locomotives, and for that reason, the railroad had avoided Heartbreak Canyon when they had laid tracks through this section of the territory several years earlier. But their alternate route presented its own problems, including a steep grade up Henson's Loop and a trestle over the gorge at Damnation Creek, which washed out each spring.

But now, with the mine shut down and the water cannon no longer in operation, Lucinda was convinced the mineral content of the water in Heartbreak Creek would be substantially reduced, which might induce the railroad to reroute through Heartbreak Creek rather than go through the costly and time-consuming task of rebuilding the trestle every year.

"And if the new results are still not favorable?" Maddie asked.

"I'll dig a new well."

"Won't that be a terrible expense?"

Lucinda looked over at her, her jade green eyes fierce in their resolve. "I'm committed to this, Maddie. I want to see Heartbreak Creek flourish again so we can be proud to call it home."

It suddenly occurred to Maddie that of all the ladies, Lucinda was the most displaced. Edwina and Pru had lost their plantation home in Louisiana, but they still had each other, and now both had men who adored them. Maddie still had Ash, although they had yet to establish a home—either in Scotland or here.

But Luce had nothing except the ladies, a few railroad shares that must be rapidly dwindling, and her hopes for Heartbreak Creek. She needed the town as much as the town needed her.

Reaching over, Maddie patted her friend's hand. "And I shall assist in any way I can. Hopefully my photographs will help."

She had taken a dozen of them—from the refurbished Heartbreak Creek Hotel to the livery, the Chinese laundry and washhouse, the bank, and even that rude Cal Bagley's mercantile—hoping to show the town as a thriving community.

A lie, of course. With the mine closed and few other employment opportunities available, the little settlement was dying a slow death. Maddie wasn't convinced that even if the railroad rerouted through the canyon, the town would ever flourish. But for Lucinda's sake, she fervently hoped the meetings today would bear fruit.

Before they had gone three miles, Thomas knew they were not alone. Two riders. A mile back. Only white men would make so much noise. "We have followers." He held up two fingers. "*Eneseo'o.*"

The reverend twisted in the saddle as if he expected to see them hanging off the tail of his pony. "You're sure?"

Thomas did not bother to answer such a foolish question. He pointed to the trail ahead. "You go. I will see who they are and what they want."

Instead of obeying, the churchman reined in, forcing Thomas to do the same. "They could be anyone, Mr. Redstone. We mustn't threaten them unless we know for certain they mean us harm."

"I do not threaten." First Prudence Lincoln and now this sad-faced man. Were all white people so disobedient?

"It would be unchristian of us to hurt them without cause."

"I am not Christian. I am Cheyenne." He pointed down the road again, amazed that they were arguing about this. "Go."

"I cannot, Mr. Redstone. Until you promise me you will not harm them unless they try to hurt you first."

Thomas studied the round face, with its hopeful smile and the trusting brown eyes of a man who saw no evil in those around him. A spotted fawn. A rabbit. Thomas wondered how he had lived this long.

"Remember what the sheriff said," the reverend prodded.

Thomas sighed. How could the Cheyenne be losing their lands to a people so foolish? "We will wait in the trees until they pass by. If they are the men the Scotsman described, we will know they are enemies." Without waiting for the older man to consent, he reined his pony off the road.

They waited in the shade of a tall spruce. Thomas marked time by tree shadows moving across the ground. The reverend used a round timepiece he kept in his pocket. He checked it many times. Finally he clicked it closed and said, "It's been over an hour. They must have turned off somewhere."

Or they waited for Thomas and the reverend to move again. "We will go now. The sun is low." And Thomas did not want to be caught in the open with this man who would not fight.

They had covered only a short distance when the followers were once more on their trail. But they made no effort to close the distance between them, so Thomas said nothing to the reverend and continued on.

The attack, if there was one, would come when they reached the cabin. The riders who followed would have no use for them then, and that was when the bullets would fly.

The sun sank lower. The reverend grew weary, but Thomas

kept the ponies at a fast trot. If they could reach the cabin, they would have protection.

It was almost dusk when he saw the dwelling through the trees. "*Hatahaohe*—there it is," he called just before a bullet slammed into his back and knocked him to the ground.

Time passed quickly for Maddie. By midafternoon, she had a full box of negative plates she was anxious to develop in the dark tent she had asked Ash to set up behind the boardinghouse. It had been a marvelous, historic day. How her father would have loved being in the thick of it. The only thing that marred her excitement came in late morning, when Chub told her he had seen a funny-looking fellow staring at her.

She had scanned the faces of the people milling about but had seen no one she recognized. "Describe 'funny looking.'"

The boy thought about it as he scratched at a bug bite on his arm. "Not tall or short. Regular-like. But skinny. I think he had light hair, but it was hard to tell, he was so dirty. Maybe he had a limp, but I'm not sure."

Since that described a goodly number of the men wandering the boardwalks in town, Maddie wasn't unduly alarmed; it wasn't as if she hadn't been gawked at before. But she did keep an eye out and advised Chub to do the same.

The rest of the afternoon passed without incident, except for an elderly fellow who kept peeking under her drape to see what she was doing, thereby overexposing several plates. No sign of the watcher. She and Chub were loading her equipment back into the wagon when Declan and Lucinda came up, their meetings finished for the day.

Lucinda was brimming with news. "I've got another meeting with the gentlemen from the Denver Pacific tomorrow morning, and I'm lunching with Edgar Kitchner of the Kansas Pacific at the Grand Hotel. Isn't that marvelous?"

"It is." Although Maddie wondered if the gentlemen were as interested in railroad matters as they might be in Lucinda. She looked especially vivacious today, her face alight with energy and passion.

"Perhaps I can play one against the other. What do you think?"

Maddie laughed. "I think if anyone could manage that, it would be you." Lucinda certainly had a head for business, as well as enough charm to easily bring a man to her way of thinking.

"And how was your day?" Maddie asked the sheriff, who was helping Chub load the crates.

"Boring. I don't know why the mayor insisted I come. Quibbling, name calling, and trading threats, that's all they do all day."

"It's politics," Lucinda reminded him.

"It's posturing."

"Exactly."

Declan turned to Maddie. "No problems here?"

Before Maddie could answer, Chub sidled up. "He's back. Over there."

Declan frowned and set down the crate he'd just picked up. He looked around. "Who's back?"

"Mr. Wallace said I was to watch for anybody watching Mrs. Wallace. There was a man earlier, but he went away. Now he's back." He tipped his head toward the colonnaded building across the street. "Slinking around behind that fat post over there."

They all turned to look but saw no one slinking around the columns outside the Cattleman's Bank.

"Looks like he's gone." Chub sounded vastly disappointed. As exciting as the day had been for Maddie, it had obviously been less so for him.

"What did he look like?" Declan asked.

Chub gave the same description he'd given Maddie earlier. Light-haired, skinny, dirty, maybe limping.

"That could be Silas," Maddie said, wondering why the boy would be watching her . . . unless his brother had put him to the task. A shiver ran up her arms. Did that mean his brother was watching her, too?

"Well, he's not there, now," Lucinda said, looking around.

Declan picked up the crate again. "It's time we headed back, anyway. Let's load these and go."

Ash had just finished brushing Lurch when he heard the wagon roll up outside the stable. Relieved, he went out to meet them, Tricks at his heels.

It had been bluidy boring, keeping watch over a woman who napped most of the day. To stay busy, he had repaired all the fencing, straightened the tack and feed room, rehung two broken shutters for the landlady, and had even resorted to giving Tricks a bath, just for the exercise.

"About time," he said, helping the ladies from the driver's box. "Mrs. Kemble's been threatening to start supper without you." After setting his wife onto her feet, he gave her arse a wee pat to hurry her toward the house. "Off you go." Ignoring the look of exasperation she sent him, he added, "Tell her we'll be in as soon as we unharness and tend the animals."

Chub stayed long enough to carry the crates into the dark tent, then headed to his own home down the road.

"Any problems here?" Brodie asked, coming out of the tack room after hanging up the harness rigging.

"None. You?"

"Maybe."

Ash stopped brushing Maisy and looked at him. "Explain."

The sheriff related what Chub had said about someone watching Maddie. "She thinks it sounds like Silas."

"Bluidy hell."

"Chub could be wrong."

And he could be right. *Bollocks.*

After turning the mules into the back paddock, Ash tossed the halters over a post and followed the sheriff down the aisleway toward the front doors.

"Silas seemed to like Maddie," Brodie said. "I doubt he'd do anything to hurt her."

But Ash heard the echo of his own worry in the sheriff's voice. "That poor lad would do anything his brother told him to do. He's terrified of him, and rightly so."

While Brodie secured the stable doors, Ash looked around. Already evening shadows were closing in. The wind had picked up. The rush of it through the tall pines surrounding the house would easily mask sound, and the brush along the back of the house could provide ample cover for a man. Or two. He would have to be extra watchful through the night.

Falling into step with the sheriff, he reached down to pat the wolfhound's head. "I'll see if Mrs. Kemble will allow Tricks to roam the house tonight."

Thomas lay on his back where he had fallen, the pain in his back so hot and consuming it stole away his breath. The whole front side of his torso was numb.

"Oh dear, oh dear." The reverend knelt at his side and started pressing against his ribs where the bullet had exited. Thomas arched, a cry rising in his throat.

"Can you move, Mr. Redstone?"

Thomas struggled to roll over and escape the searing pain in his back. He flopped facedown, his cheek falling against dirt that was warm and wet with his blood. Dimly he became aware—more as a vibration than a sound—of approaching horses.

"*Taaseste . . . taanaasestse . . .*"

The reverend's face appeared in his dimming vision. "What? What are you saying? How can I help you?"

"Go . . . now . . ."

"No, I won't leave you."

Thomas struggled to find the words, to evade the blackness that pressed against his eyes. "Tell them . . . I am dead . . . say . . . you have papers . . ."

"What papers? The claim papers?"

"Yes . . ." The drumming hoofbeats drew closer. Thomas fought to keep his eyes open. "Stay alive . . . I will come."

"God be with you, Thomas Redstone."

Darkness closed around him. Beyond it, voices rose in shouts—the reverend asking why they had killed his friend—horses milling close by. Thomas slowed his breathing and hoped the men who shot him did not know that dead men did not bleed.

After a while, the noise went away and only the pain remained.

He opened his eyes.

Dusk had fallen. The forest was silent and still. He smelled blood and felt the warm stickiness of it soaking the dirt.

He must move. He must not be here if they came back.

With a groan, he staggered to his feet, then stood shivering with cold even though tongues of fire licked at his back and his side.

There was no sign of the reverend or his pony.

Seeing blood seep from a hole in his shirt, he pressed a hand over it and gasped at the searing pain. When it faded enough that he could breathe again, he lifted his face to the darkening sky.

"Help me . . . *nehvestahmestse, ma'heone.*"

The wind swirled softly around him, then swept up the steep bank above him. Heeding the voices of his spirit guides, Thomas turned and climbed slowly away from the trail and up into the trees.

Nineteen

The intruder came after supper, when the diners, including Mrs. Kemble, had retired to the front parlor to hear Edwina Brodie play the piano blindfolded. It was a dare laughingly issued by Miss Hathaway and heartily accepted by Edwina after her own husband pronounced the idea "bunkum."

A private joke, Ash decided, amused by the heated glances passing between the sheriff and his wife. He looked at Maddie, seated beside him, wondering if she had noticed. She was smiling as she watched them, but it was such a sad, wistful smile, he felt a tug deep inside his chest.

His Maddie. His wife. But would she ever be completely his own? For all her passion and tender words, he sensed there was a small part of herself she wouldn't share with him. And he dinna know why.

Laughter across the room drew his attention, and he looked over to see Miss Hathaway tying a length of cloth over Edwina Brodie's eyes.

That was when Tricks, roused from his nap beside Ash's chair, lifted his head and stared intently at the window.

Ash followed his gaze. He knew the window overlooked the

backyard and stable, but all he saw was lamplight reflected in the glass panes.

He studied the dog.

Tricks showed no agitation, only curiosity.

A wandering cat, perhaps. Or a rider passing by on the road.

Resting his hand on the wolfhound's head, he murmured softly to him in Gaelic. When Tricks took no notice and his dark gaze remained fixed on the window, Ash caught Brodie's eye and gave a slight nod.

Without stirring from his slouched position, Ash leaned over and whispered into Maddie's ear, "Have I mentioned today, lass, how much I love you?"

"W-What?"

"I love you."

She reared back to blink at him. *"Now, Ash?"* As if startled by the loudness of her blurted response, she glanced around to see if anyone else had heard, then lowered her voice. "You finally get around to saying it and you do it *here?* In front of all these people?"

"I've told you many times, lass, so I have."

"You most certainly have not. I would have remembered."

Reaching over, he gently cupped her cheek. His hand looked big and clumsy and battered against the pale perfection of her skin. "Sweet Maddie," he said softly. *"A ghra mo chroi."*

"What?"

"Tha gaol mor agam ort."

"I don't speak Gaelic. What does that mean?"

He kissed her lightly. "I'll tell you later, love. Or, better yet, I'll show you." He kissed her again, then straightened in the chair. "But right now, Tricks needs to go out." Gratified by her look of consternation, he rose and left the room. As he and Tricks moved down the hall toward the kitchen, he heard the sheriff ask if anyone wanted more coffee.

A moment later, as Ash was tying a lead rope around the wolfhound's neck, Brodie came through the kitchen doorway. "What's wrong?" the sheriff asked.

"I'm not sure. But the lad senses something is amiss." Pulling his pistol from his coat on a hook beside the door, Ash checked the load, snapped the chamber closed, and pushed the gun into the waistband of his trousers. "If I'm not back in ten minutes," he instructed as he donned his coat, "come seek me." After closing the door behind him, he paused on the porch long enough for his eyes to adjust, then stepped into the yard.

Ash had excellent vision at night, but even without it, the near full moon rising over the mountains in the east cast enough light through the trees to light his way.

Tricks led him toward the barn, tugging against the rope in a determined way, but showing no intent to give chase. He stopped before the double doors, sniffed at the ground, then at the slide bar.

Ash saw that the doors were ajar—not the way he and Brodie had left them earlier. Gripping his pistol in one hand and Tricks's rope in the other, he shouldered the door open and peered inside.

Silence. The smell of sweet feed and alfalfa and horses. Moonlight illuminating the inside walkway with a pale glow.

Nothing moved. He listened but heard only the sounds of horses resting quietly in their stalls. A long, dark head peered over one of the half doors—Brodie's big gelding—but he showed no alarm.

Ash let go of the rope.

Tricks moved quickly past the stalls, nose to the ground. Stopping outside the tack and feed room, he cocked his head and listened, then lifted a paw and pushed against the door.

It swung open and he went inside.

A voice, then a laugh Ash recognized. Shoving the pistol back into his waistband, he stepped forward and looked into the room.

Pale strips of moonlight shining through the slats of the exterior wall fell across a figure huddled in a corner, laughing as Tricks licked his dirty face. Ash let out a breath. "Hello, Silas," he said.

The lad almost jumped out a foot off the ground. By the time he recovered from his fright and Ash had gotten the lantern lit, Brodie had arrived, which scared the lad all over again. They had just gotten him calmed down a second time when the ladies burst in, this time startling Ash so badly he almost drew his pistol.

"Aha!" Edwina Brodie crowed from the doorway, hands on hips. "Didn't I tell you something was going on, ladies? Didn't I?"

Miss Hathaway and Maddie appeared at Edwina's shoulder, gawking like deer caught in a sudden flare of light.

"Christamighty, Ed!" Holstering his own pistol, Brodie dragged a hand across his face. "Don't you know not to come sneaking around in the middle of the night?"

"Don't you?" she countered. "And just what are you two doing out here—oh my goodness! Is that Silas?"

"Mercy, he's been hurt!"

"Oh, you poor dear!"

Like a stampede of unschooled horses, the three women rushed into the small room, all talking at once and stirring up dust and such a ruckus Ash had to resort to drill commands to reestablish order.

"There's no need to shout, dearest. You're frightening Silas."

"What happened?" Miss Hathaway demanded, gently wiping dirt from the boy's bruised face.

"That's what we're trying to find out," Ash snapped, which earned him another chiding look from his wife.

"Is this it?" Brodie made a show of looking around. "Is anyone else coming? Because I don't want to have to go through this again."

His wife patted his arm. "Everyone else has retired. Now stop fussing and tell us what's going on."

"Ask him."

They all turned and looked expectantly at Silas.

It took a while, but once the lad was convinced he wasn't in trouble and no one was going to hurt him, he finally blurted out the sorry tale. Ash followed as best he could, mentally filling in the omitted details.

He wasn't really Silas Zucker, the lad tearfully admitted, but Silas Cochran, and his brother was Cletus Cochran, but he was pretending to be another man—*Reverend Zucker*—because he wanted the smiling man's—*Ephraim Zucker's*—gold. But the picture lady—*Maddie*—didn't know where the smiling man's cabin was, and Clete was mad because of what Silas did—*which he wouldn't talk about*—so his brother got Bud Purvis to help him, who was even meaner than Clete and had a tarantula, and they made Si promise to keep watch over the picture lady until they got back.

"Got back from where?" Ash asked.

"I don't know."

Luckily, Brodie intervened before Ash started shaking the lad. "Could they have gone to the cabin?"

"I don't know. I think they were following the fat man and the Indian, but I'm not sure. I'm hungry. Do you have any food?"

"Sure." Brodie sent Miss Hathaway to get something from the kitchen, then asked Maddie if it would be all right if Si slept in her wagon.

Maddie looked at the filthy lad, then backed up a step. "Perhaps if you bathed him first."

"Maybe tomorrow. For now, let's just make a bed for him out here. Ash, get your bedroll."

Ash had seen the lad scratching, too, and was as wary as his wife. "I'd rather you get yours."

In the end, Maddie suggested he use Mr. Satterwhite's bedroll, which was still in the storage box attached to the underside of the wagon. After she and Edwina went to get it, Ash turned to Brodie. "I'm leaving for the cabin."

"Now?"

"There's a near full moon."

"You don't even know where it is."

"Out toward Blue River. We crossed that road coming in. And Thomas described the bluff by the cabin well enough. Besides, I'll have Tricks. Do you have something of Thomas's I can let him smell?"

Brodie rummaged through a pouch hanging on a hook, then pulled out one of Thomas's town shirts.

Ash stuffed it into his saddlebag. "You'll watch Maddie while I'm gone. There's only you now."

Brodie looked surprised. "You're expecting trouble here?"

Ash glanced at Silas, who was happily trading fleas with Tricks, and wondered how much of what the lad had said could be relied upon. "If his brother follows Thomas and the reverend to the cabin and realizes the claim papers aren't there, where else would he look but here?"

"They'd have to go through Thomas first."

"Aye. That's what I'm afraid of."

Ash was in the center aisle, saddling Lurch when Maddie came back. Sending Edwina on into the feed room with the bedroll, she came toward him. He paused to watch her. She seemed to glow in the slanting moonlight—a wee highland fairy come to life, and so beautiful it brought a catch to his breath.

"You're going after Thomas," she said, stopping beside him.

He finished buckling the bridle, then turned to face her, one hand resting on Lurch's neck. "Aye. He could be riding into an ambush." If he hadn't already done so.

"So could you." Reaching up, she took his face in her soft hands and looked hard into his eyes. "You come back to me, Angus Wallace," she said fiercely. "I'll not be parted from you again."

He drew her tight against his body. If he could, he would have pulled her all the way into his chest to keep her near his heart forever. *"Tha gaol agam ort,"* he whispered into her hair. *I love you.*

She drew back, and rising on tiptoe, pressed her lips to his. It was less a show of passion than possession, and he answered it with all the love he held for this fey creature who was his wife. When the kiss ended and she stepped back, her eyes were wet and her smile wobbly. "Guard yourself well, dearest. *Moi aussi, je t'aime.*"

"I dinna speak French. What does that mean?"

"I'll show you when you get back."

For the first two hours, Ash and Tricks made good time because the road was well defined and no clouds obscured the moon. But when the track branched off toward Breckenridge, it began to climb sharply and trees often blocked the moonlight. Ash pulled Lurch back to a walk and tried to curb his impatience. Twice they surprised elk in the road and once chased off a bear that was digging at a rotten stump. Tricks knew better than to give chase, and they moved steadily on. Other than night birds and the distant howl of wolves, the night was quiet except for the rhythmic clomp of Lurch's shod hooves on the hard-packed dirt.

The higher they went, the colder it grew. Ash pulled the collar of his fleece-lined jacket higher, pinning the warmth of his woolen scarf over his ears. Even though he wore gloves, he frequently changed hands on the reins so he could slip the other beneath his jacket and under his arm to warm it up again. His breath dampened the scarf that lay over his mouth and nose, and after a while, the wool was crusted with ice.

Later, when the sky had begun to lighten into that gunmetal blue that preceded dawn, they came to another junction in the road. Ash reined in and studied the crude sign nailed to a tree.

Two letters looked nearly the same—like eights, or *b*s or *p*s. Blue River? He pulled Thomas's shirt from his saddlebag and held it down for Tricks to sniff.

The hound showed no interest and plopped on the ground, panting.

Realizing he had been pushing the animals too hard, Ash returned the shirt to the saddlebag and dismounted. He stood for a moment, listening, and heard the faint trickle of water off in the brush. Leading Lurch toward it, he found a seep of water running down into a puddle in a wee clearing.

He broke the ice with his boot heel, refilled his canteen, then let the animals drink. After loosening Lurch's girth and removing his snaffle so the horse could graze the sparse grass in the clearing, he settled against a downed log to wait for more light, hoping by then he might be able to spot the peak Thomas had mentioned. If not, he would have to go into Breckenridge and ask.

He must have dozed off. When next he opened his eyes, sunlight gilded the treetops and Tricks was chewing on something— something with hair, and by the smell, none too fresh.

Ash tightened Lurch's cinch, slipped his bridle on, then mounted and headed back to the road.

Faces the Dawn. That was the Indian name for the peak he sought. And an hour later, as they rounded a bend where the trail opened onto a long sloped valley, there it was, the profile of a face looking into the morning sun. Ash studied it for a moment, trying to orient the view he saw now with the perspective he remembered from Maddie's photograph.

He was on the correct side but several miles short.

Continuing at a slower pace, he scanned for recently used trails branching off on the downhill side, hoping he could find one that would lead to the aspen valley in the photograph. He did. After following it for less than a mile, he smelled woodsmoke.

He dismounted and tied the rope on Tricks, not wanting the dog to run off until he could do a thorough reconnaissance of the area. Then leading the horse, he continued down the trail. About a hundred yards farther, he saw a cabin through the trees. He was pulling his field glasses from his *sabretache* when Tricks started to whine and sniff at the ground several yards away. Then with a yip, he yanked the rope from Ash's grip and tore off into the trees. Ash looked to see what had drawn the hound's attention.

Blood. Boot prints. Several horses, one of which was unshod.

Scanning the brush, he saw more blood leading off the trail and into the trees in the direction Tricks had run. Swinging up onto Lurch, he followed.

From ahead came a yip, then a yelping bark that was abruptly cut off. Fearing Tricks had been hurt, Ash yanked out his pistol, dropped from the saddle to the ground, and sent Lurch trotting on ahead. Running at a crouch, he circled through the trees so he could approach from the high side. Through the trees, he saw Tricks standing over the prone figure of a man who had one hand clasped around his muzzle.

Just as Lurch trotted up from the other direction, Ash stepped out into the open. "Let go of my dog, ye bluidy bastard."

A burst of words in a language Ash dinna know—but in a voice he recognized.

"Thomas?"

He ran forward and saw that Tricks was trying to lick the figure he had trapped on the ground at the edge of a drop-off, not bite him.

"Get him off," Thomas choked out.

Grinning with relief, Ash dropped the pistol into his jacket pocket and pulled the exuberant hound away. But his amusement died when he saw that the front of Thomas's war tunic was stained with blood. Most of it had dried, but on his side, halfway down his rib cage, there was a tear in the leather and a seep of bright red blood.

"Bluidy hell, Thomas!"

The Cheyenne looked up at him, his eyes sunken, his mouth drawn into something barely resembling his usual smile. "What took you so long, Scotsman?"

"We'll be fine," Lucinda insisted to Declan. "It's not as if I'll be wandering the streets. I'll be in meetings all day. And Maddie draws so much attention with her photography doings, she's never alone. Besides, she'll have Chub."

They were in the aisle of the stable. Lucinda and Maddie had just brought breakfast to Silas, who was busily gobbling it down in the feed room, but instead of finding Declan hitching the buggy and Maddie's wagon, he was sitting on a nail keg, oiling his rifle.

The sheriff propped the gun against the wall and screwed the cap back on the tin of gun oil. He looked up, his face set in stubborn lines. "And what about Edwina? I can't take you two to town and leave her here alone. And I sure can't bring her to the assembly with me."

Maddie agreed. Edwina wasn't one to sit quietly by without wanting to be in the thick of it, especially if words were flying. "This is Friday, is it not? Won't the final vote be today?"

"Late this afternoon."

"Then stay with your wife this morning. Lucinda and I will go on with Chub, then he can bring me back at noon to watch over Edwina while you take the buggy into town to cast your vote. By then Lucinda should be through with her meetings and she can ride back with you."

"That'll leave you and Ed here unprotected."

"In a crowded boardinghouse?" Even though the Bible sales-man had moved on, the deaf widow and her daughter were still in residence, although they seldom left their room and would be scant protection even if they did. But Mrs. Kemble could certainly han-dle herself. Hadn't she had all three men jumping to do her bidding after that "wee tussle" two days ago?

"We both have our pistols," Maddie reminded him. "And we know how to shoot. We'll be fine for the three or so hours it will take for you to go vote and come back."

After a bit more arguing, Declan finally gave in. Chub came, helped him harness the mules, then climbed into the driver's box be-side Maddie and Lucinda, promising he would bring Maddie back in time for Declan to go cast his vote in the assembly that afternoon.

"Meanwhile, Sheriff"—shooting a glance at the open feed room door, Lucinda lowered her voice—"see if you can get that poor boy cleaned up. I'm sure Mrs. Kemble has some strong soap and a scrub brush."

Declan stepped back, hands raised. "That's not my problem."

"It is if he gives us all lice. That's how typhus gets started. I should know. I'm from New York, remember."

"This isn't New York and there's no typhus around here."

"Not yet."

"Hell."

If the size of the stain on his shirt and the pallor of his usually ruddy skin were any indication, Thomas had lost a lot of blood. Drawing on hard experience with battlefield wounds, Ash did a quick ex-amination.

The bullet had gone through. He saw no obstruction in either the entrance or the exit wound to indicate a piece of Thomas's shirt was still lodged inside. The blood seeping down his side wasna bubbling or frothy, so hopefully a lung hadn't been nicked, and Thomas's gut wasna distended as it would have been if he was bleeding inside. The Cheyenne wasn't showing fever yet, but Ash had seen enough battlefield wounds to know it was probably coming.

All in all, Thomas was lucky.

He dinna look it.

Once Ash had patched the Indian up as best he could with bandages made from Thomas's town shirt, held in place by strips torn from the woolen scarf, he covered Thomas with his jacket and helped him sit up against a boulder. "Drink as much as you can," he ordered, handing Thomas his canteen. "And here's jerky, if you're up to it."

While Thomas chewed the dried meat and took sips from the canteen, Ash told him what Si had said about his brother, Clete, and his cohort, Bud Purvis, leaving the lad to watch Maddie while they followed the reverend, hoping he would lead them to the cabin.

"I knew they followed." Thomas worked to bite off another piece of meat. Ash could see that even chewing was an effort for him. "But the churchman did not want to fight, so we went on. They shot me just as the cabin came in sight."

Thereby eliminating the one they dinna need and the fighter who posed the biggest threat. Made sense to Ash. "But they let you live?"

"The churchman told them I was dead. He told them the claim papers were down there." Wincing, Thomas twisted to point over his shoulder to the cabin in the middle of the clearing below. "That was more important to them than a wounded Indian."

"See what's happening down there. I'll get my rifle." Ash pulled his field glasses from his *sabretache* and handed them to Thomas, then went into the trees where he'd tied Lurch and Tricks. He pulled the carbine from the case hanging off his cavalry saddle, dug out a box of bullets from his saddlebag, then went back and stretched out on the ground beside the Cheyenne, who was on his stomach, peering through the glasses at the cabin.

"What do you see?" Ash asked.

Thomas handed him the field glasses. "Nothing. They do not work."

"That's because 'tis white man magic and ye're but a bluidy heathen." Bracing his elbows in the dirt, Ash adjusted the focus until the cabin came clearly into view.

He saw no people. No horses. If not for the smoke rising from the stone chimney, it looked the same as Maddie's photograph— aspen grove, meadow, small creek with a sluice, outhouse in back. But from this angle, with the side of the cabin facing him, he could see higher up on the hillside, where a pile of tailings spilled down below a hole dug into the earth. The mine, he assumed. He handed the glasses over to Thomas. "Where's the reverend?"

"Inside. But I have not seen him for a while."

"The horses?"

"Staked on the other side of the cabin in that ravine. Mine, as well."

A man came out the back door of the cabin. Short. Dark beard. Not the reverend and not Cletus Cochran. Bud Purvis? He stood for a minute, scratching and staring up at the mine, then went on to the outhouse.

"That is one of the men who followed us," Thomas said, squinting through the glasses at the distant figure.

Ash picked up the carbine and quickly loaded it. He adjusted the sliding ramp sight at the back of the barrel for two hundred and fifty yards, give or take ten.

No wind. Downhill. An easy shot.

He lifted the rifle to his shoulder. Once again propping his elbows on the ground, he lined up the rear sight with the fixed sight at the end of the barrel until it was square on the outhouse door. Then he waited.

From the corner of his eye, he saw Thomas set down the field glasses and stick his fingers in his ears.

The door opened and the man came out. After pausing to do up his trousers, he walked toward the house.

Ash tracked him through the sights until the cabin door closed behind him, then he lowered the rifle and let out a string of Gaelic curses.

"You did not shoot," Thomas said, taking his fingers from his ears.

"If I had, and the reverend is still alive, the other fellow might have killed him or used him as a shield to make his escape."

"So we sit here?"

"Aye. The reverend has got to relieve himself sometime, and I doubt he'll be alone. If he's in the clear and I can get a shot at the man with him, I'll take it, so I will. Bluidy, buggerin', humpin' sons of bitches."

He dinna have to wait long. This time when the door opened, two men came out. Ash studied them through the field glasses.

The one in front was more round than tall. No beard. The reverend. His hands were tied in front and there was blood on his shirt, but otherwise he seemed all right. The other was the same man who had come out earlier. Bud Purvis.

"Watch the cabin." Ash handed the glasses to Thomas and picked up the loaded rifle. "I've got ye now, ye bastard," he muttered as he lined up the sights.

The reverend tripped and went down on one knee. Purvis kicked him in the arse until the older man scrambled back onto his feet and staggered on to the outhouse. The reverend went inside.

Ash took a breath, let out half. He slipped his finger around the trigger.

Purvis stood at the open door for a moment, then let it close. He turned in Ash's direction the instant before Ash squeezed the trigger.

Noise exploded. A belch of acrid smoke burned in Ash's eyes.

The bullet entered Purvis's left eye and exited the back of his head in a red mist.

Flipping onto his back, Ash worked frantically to clear the side breech so he could reload. "Did the other one come out of the cabin?" he shouted over the ringing in his ears. "Did you see him?" Turning the rifle over, he tried to shake out the spent casing, but it dinna fall. *Christ.* "What is he doing? Talk to me, man!"

"The door opened, but I could not see if he came out."

"Maybe he went out a window." Ash dug the hot casing loose with his fingernail, then thumbed another cartridge into the side-hinged breechblock and snapped it closed. Swinging the rifle to his shoulder, he rolled back into firing position.

"There!" Thomas pointed past the cabin. "On the other side. He runs to the gully."

Ash tracked until he found movement in the sights. White blond hair. Cletus Cochran. Aiming just ahead of the running figure, he fired.

Cochran dropped from sight.

Ears ringing, Ash squinted through the haze of spent powder as he dug out the spent casing so he could reload. "Did I get him?"

"I cannot see him."

"Bollocks!"

The outhouse door opened. The reverend came out and bent over the figure sprawled on the ground. Two hundred yards past him, running a ragged course in and out the brush, a man on a saddleless bay horse galloped out of the gully and into the cover of the trees. Three other horses ran loose behind him—Thomas's spotted pony, the reverend's chestnut, and a third horse Ash dinna know. But they gave up soon enough, and after milling for a moment, dropped their heads to graze at the edge of the trees.

Ash lurched to his feet. "Bluidy hell! I missed the bastard!"

The urge to give chase almost overwhelmed him. But he couldn't leave Thomas and the reverend unprotected. Nor could he dally here, either. Cochran might head back to Denver. And Maddie.

Thomas lowered the glasses. Teeth clenched, he rolled onto his uninjured side. "You got one," he said in a strained voice. "Right in the eye. A fine shot. For a white man."

"Bugger that. I was aiming for the bastard's chest."

Thomas tried to laugh, but it came out a cough instead.

Ash studied him, wondering what to do. It was clear the Cheyenne was in no condition to ride. In fact, if Ash dinna get him covered, warm, and off the ground, Thomas would soon be fighting for his life.

"I'm going down to check on the reverend and see if there's a wagon. Have you any weapons, heathen?"

Thomas's eyes drifted closed. "Knife. They took the rifle."

"Here's my pistol." When Thomas dinna open his eyes, Ash set it on the ground beside his hand. "I'll leave Tricks with you. I'll have to tie him, but he'll still be able to let you know if anyone comes."

When Thomas still dinna respond, Ash hunkered beside him and rested a hand on his shoulder. "Thomas?"

The Cheyenne's eyes opened. "Why are you still here, white man?"

Ash forced a smile. "Can I bring you back anything, heathen?"

A faint smile creased Thomas's lips. His eyes closed. "Peyote."

"Praise God," the reverend said when Ash rode up. "I wasn't sure who was shooting. Did you find Mr. Redstone? Is he all right?"

"He's alive."

Ash dismounted and walked over to study Bud Purvis's body. A wee hole beside the eye socket, a fist-sized crater where the back of his head had been. Neat and to the point. Seeing an enclosure on the other side of the cabin, he led Lurch toward it. "Are you hurt?" he asked, eyeing the bruises on the reverend's face and the bloodstains on his shirt.

"It's nothing. I'm more concerned about Mr. Redstone. Will you take me to him? I was a chaplain in the war, but I often served as a medic, as well. Perhaps I can help."

"I'd rather bring him here. Is there a wagon?"

"On the other side of the paddock."

Lurch whinnied. A distant answer, and Ash looked up to see the three loose mounts galloping back, Thomas's pony in the lead. No sign of Cochran, but he might be lurking up in those trees, lining the reverend up in his sights even now. *Bluidy hell.* He needed Tricks to track him down. But first, he must tend Thomas.

He tied Lurch inside the paddock, leaving the gate open to lure the other horses in. "Get inside the cabin," he told the reverend as he checked the rigging on the small buckboard. "And stay out of sight until we're certain the other man is gone."

"What about Mr. Redstone?"

"I'll get him. Go. Before Cochran takes a shot at you."

"No fear of that. He's long gone, I'm afraid. And it's all my fault."

Ash turned to study him. "What are you saying?"

A look of deep distress came over the portly man's face. "Mr. Redstone told me to stall, to tell them I had the claim papers. They looked for them here. When they didn't find them, they started hitting me. Eventually, I told them they were in town."

Fear slammed into Ash's chest. "In town? You mean at the boardinghouse?"

"I-I'm sorry. I didn't know what else to do. I didn't think they believed me, but where else would that blond fellow go?"

Sweet Mary. The reverend had sent him straight to Maddie.

The next half hour was a blur for Ash. After harnessing a weary Lurch to the wagon, he went back up the hill and brought Thomas and Tricks back. The reverend was waiting with what medical items he could find in the cabin—wound salve, bandages, and gauze. He was also boiling beans and some dried meat to make a broth. After tending Thomas's wounds, they moved him to a cot beside the hearth. Even though Thomas had regained some color, it was obvious he was still too weak to ride.

"Thomas, I must go back." Ash hunkered beside the cot so their eyes were on the same level. "We think Cochran is headed to the boardinghouse. I canna take you with me."

Thomas nodded, his dark eyes shadowed with pain but also filled with that calm acceptance every wounded warrior must face when told he will be left behind.

"The reverend will bring you in the wagon if you're up to it. Or I'll come back for you. I'll not leave you here, heathen."

"Find him, Scotsman. Kill him."

"I will." Ash rose and looked down at the man he was just beginning to know but already thought of as a brother in arms. "I'll not fail you, my friend."

Thomas nodded. "My spirit rides with you, *hovahe*."

Ten minutes later, Ash rode out on Thomas's pony, Tricks at his side, and a familiar throb building behind his eyes.

Twenty

The morning was scarcely half done and Maddie was already wishing she was back at the boardinghouse. It was more than just worry over Ash and Thomas and the reverend that had her so out of sorts. Photography simply didn't seem that important when people she loved might be in danger.

Still, she went through the motions rather than give in to the fear that hovered at the edge of her mind. She was a soldier's wife. And that's what was expected of soldiers' wives—they waited patiently and worried secretly and put on a brave face despite the terror churning inside.

She had started the day by the government offices before slowly working her way through the commercial and business areas. But now, at the edge of the saloon district, where she had anticipated finding a wealth of material and people to photograph, she had run out of albumenized paper.

A bad day all around.

She and Chub were loading her supplies back into the wagon when she saw Lucinda coming down the boardwalk. Judging by the dragging steps, it seemed Lucinda's morning hadn't gone that well, either.

"What are you doing here?" she asked as Luce stopped by the steps at the back of the wagon. "I thought you were staying to ride back with Declan later."

"My meeting was canceled."

She was a shadow of the cheerful woman who had ridden into town with them that morning. Maddie wondered if she'd been crying, then discounted the notion. Lucinda never cried. Yet it was apparent something was troubling her. "Luce, what's wrong?"

"I'm not sure. Probably nothing." She made a dismissive gesture, then picked up a box of *carte de visite* cards and handed it up to Chub, who stood at the top of the wagon steps. "Anything else to be loaded?" she asked, looking around.

"I believe that's it." After cautioning Chub to make sure the door was locked and the steps secured, Maddie took Lucinda's arm and walked her toward the front driver's box. "Talk to me. Tell me why you're upset."

"Things didn't go as well as I'd hoped, that's all."

Maddie said no more as they climbed up into the driver's box. Lucinda was intensely private and didn't welcome prying. A few minutes later, Chub joined them, and they were on their way to the boardinghouse.

Maddie scanned the faces of the men on the boardwalk as they passed by, then realized what she was doing. She frowned, wondering when it had become habit to be so watchful and wary. Yet, without Ash by her side, she did feel exposed and vaguely uneasy . . . as if something was missing.

Her independence, perhaps.

They rode in silence for a while, then Lucinda blurted out, "It's the oddest thing, Maddie. Yesterday, they all seemed so enthusiastic about my plans. But today, they could scarcely spare me a glance."

"The men from the railroads?"

"It's as if overnight, I've become a pariah. Edgar Kitchner didn't even cancel our luncheon meeting himself, but sent his underling to inform me he would be unavailable."

"Perhaps he had a conflict," Maddie suggested, tracing the square face of the signet ring through the fabric of her glove. Would it be so bad, returning to her old life with Ash?

"That's what I thought. But when I pressed, the assistant said Mr. Kitchner would be unavailable . . . *permanently*. What do you make of that?"

Hearing the distress in Lucinda's voice, Maddie put Ash from her mind and gave her friend her full attention. "Obviously he's a fool. Just as well you won't be doing business with him. He'll come to regret missing this wonderful opportunity, mark my words."

Lucinda absently plucked at the ribbon tie on the folder she clasped in her lap. "I might have agreed, had he been the only one to cancel."

"The men from the Denver Pacific have dropped out, as well?"

Lucinda nodded.

"They gave no reason for their change of heart?"

"Oh, the usual excuses. Overextending. Labor shortages. Right of way issues. All polite ways of saying they're no longer interested. I just can't figure why. I don't know what's going on, but something's not right about all this."

She looked as despondent as Maddie had ever seen her. Luce wasn't one to dwell on her difficulties. She was far too practical and levelheaded for that. "Are there no other railroads that might be looking for a branch line across the southern Rockies?"

"Mr. Kitchner's minion mentioned one. A newly formed group called the Wichita Pacific. But I know nothing about them."

"Perhaps you should find out," Maddie suggested. "You've come too far to give up now."

"Perhaps." Luce gave a halfhearted shrug. "But sometimes, Maddie, I wonder if I'm wasting my time—and money—trying to bring Heartbreak Creek back to life."

Maddie had often wondered the same thing.

Declan came out to meet them when they rolled up to the stable. "What are you doing back so soon?" he asked Lucinda, lifting her down from the driver's box. "I thought you were coming back with me after the vote."

"I had no reason to stay." She explained about the canceled meetings. "I think this whole trip has been a waste of my time."

"Any word from Ash or Thomas?" Maddie asked.

"Nothing yet," Declan said, helping Chub unharness the mules. "But it's early yet."

Maddie hid her disappointment. "Where are Silas and Ed?"

"Worn out. Bathing Silas took it out of both of them."

Maddie shared a look of surprise with Lucinda. Silas might be a child mentally, but physically, he was a grown man. "She bathed Silas?"

"Not likely." Declan swung open the paddock gate so Chub could lead Maisy and Buttercup through, then shut it and sent the boy on home for the day. "As usual, I did the actual work. She just shouted orders through the door. That's what she does best. One of the things, anyway."

Maddie caught those last murmured words as he walked back into the barn with the harness leathers thrown over his shoulder. She assumed by his grin he wasn't referring to her cooking. "Well, at least he's clean."

"Mostly. Don't suppose either of you ladies has a spare brush for his teeth? He said the scrub brush tasted funny."

Lucinda shuddered. Maddie wasn't sure if it was because Declan had actually tried to fit a scrub brush into the boy's mouth or because the thought of Silas using one of her brushes was beyond disgusting.

The back door slammed. Mrs. Kemble marched purposefully toward them.

"Trouble," Declan muttered.

"I need to talk to you people." She stopped before them, hands planted on her aproned hips. "First you bring a red Indian to my house, then there's fisticuffs in the yard and that giant dog roaming everywhere, and now a simpleminded man is living in my barn. I don't know what kind of establishment you think I'm running here, but I've about had it with your shenanigans."

"What shenanigans, ma'am?" Declan asked in his calm way.

"Comings and goings at all hours of the night, that's what. People disappearing, then others showing up, and now strangers hounding me with their questions. I don't need this aggravation. I run a respectable place."

Maddie thought of Cletus Cochran and felt a prickle of unease. "What strangers?"

"I'm sure I don't know. Some fellow asking about Miss Hathaway here. He didn't leave his name. I told him you would be gone to meetings in town all day and sent him on his way. But now here you are. And your wife, Sheriff, says the other two—the reverend and that brawling Scotsman—will be back this evening. Do you people have any idea how difficult it is to plan meals when I never even know who all's going to be here? Now I'll have to go back to the market and get two more chickens. I've a mind to send every one of you people packing."

"What was he asking?" Lucinda asked.

"I'm sure it's none of my business. Something about a railroad, I think. And that town you're from. Heartbreak Creek. Is that simpleminded fellow expecting to eat, too?"

"If you don't mind, ma'am. I sure would appreciate it." Declan gave her the smile Maddie had seen him use to charm Edwina. It seemed to have little effect on the landlady.

"You people," she muttered, stomping back to the house. "No telling who or what you'll bring around next."

As soon as she was out of earshot, Maddie turned to Lucinda. "Do you suppose it could be someone from the Wichita Pacific?"

"I don't know."

But Maddie had seen that spark of interest in Lucinda's eyes. "If he's interested enough to come asking about you, perhaps you should make inquiries of your own."

"You're right." Suddenly her vibrant self again, Lucinda

grinned at Declan. "Harness the buggy. I've decided to go back to town with you this afternoon. I've come too far to give up so easily."

Ash had been on enough forced marches to know he couldn't push his mount at a constant fast gait. Trot forty minutes, walk ten, dismount and lead him at a jog ten. Luckily, the animal was strong and better rested than Lurch would have been. He just hoped Tricks could keep up the pace.

The ache in his temple was steady now. Every step the pony took jarred up his spine and exploded inside his head. When the sun hit him full in the face, it was like a knife thrust behind his eyes. So far, the dizziness was mild, but he could feel it spreading up through his head like eddies in a swirling pool.

He figured Cochran had an hour and a half head start. With luck he might be able to cut that to less than one. Then he would do what he should have done back at the clearing four days ago, and kill the bluidy bastard.

"Is she still angry?" Edwina asked when Maddie slipped into her room with a bowl of blackberries and two rolls left over from lunch.

"She's mellowed somewhat, although it's probably a good thing we're leaving soon. I think our dear landlady is running out of patience." Maddie set the bowl on the small table beside Edwina's bed, then munching on one of the rolls, went to look out the window.

The afternoon was dwindling away, and still no sign of Ash or Thomas or the reverend. Declan and Lucinda had gone to town an hour ago, and Mrs. Kemble had left for the market. The widow and her daughter had gone to afternoon mass at the Catholic church several blocks away. With just the two of them in the house, it was so quiet Maddie could hear the tick of the regulator clock in the hallway and the distant thump of the ax as Silas split the cordwood piled beside the stable. It was a task she had put him to earlier, as a way to pay Mrs. Kemble for his supper.

Seeing no riders coming down the road in front of the boarding-house, she sighed and sank into the chair beside the bed.

"Stop worrying." Edwina popped a blackberry in her mouth. "Ash and Thomas are fully capable of taking care of themselves."

She looked the essence of femininity—stretched out on the coverlet, stockinged feet crossed, one arm tucked lazily behind her riotous light brown curls, her body ripe with life. Maddie framed it in her mind, wishing there was enough light for a photograph.

"You love him, don't you?" Edwina observed.

"I do. I think I always have."

Edwina ate two more berries, then sighed. "Which means you'll go back to Scotland with him."

"Eventually."

Maddie watched tears rise in her friend's expressive blue eyes.

"I am sick to death of losing people I love," Edwina said in a quavering voice. "I hate the thought of losing you, too. But I can see he makes you happy."

Fighting her own tears, Maddie looked toward the window. The breeze had picked up, as it did in late afternoon, and tiny swirls of dust danced in the long shafts of light shining through the trees. The noise of the ax had stopped and Maddie wondered if Mrs. Kemble or the widow and her daughter had returned. But she heard no voices downstairs, and no footsteps in the hall. Forcing a smile, she turned back to Edwina. "Perhaps you could come for a visit. The family lives in a castle, you know."

"A castle!" Edwina gave that contagious laugh that always brought a smile to anyone hearing it. "Imagine that. Will you host grand balls and wear a coronet and have servants at your beck and call?"

Maddie laughed with her, trying to picture Ash wearing evening clothes. Then wearing a kilt that showed his ticklish knees. Then stretched across her bed, wearing nothing. A braw lad indeed.

Edwina's laugh faded to a wistful smile. "We had parties. Just before the war started, we had one every night." Waving a hand in pantomime to a waltz, she added dreamily, "All the handsome young men in their smart gray uniforms, and the pretty girls in their frocks and gowns, dancing the night away as if tomorrow would never come." She let her hand drop back to her lap and sighed again. "How foolish we were."

A muffled step in the hall drew Maddie's attention. A timid knock on the door, then Silas's voice. "Ma'am? You in there?"

Maddie exchanged a look of curiosity with Edwina, then rose and went to the door. She opened it to find Silas hunched in the hall, blood dripping from a cut on his brow, one eye swollen shut. Before Maddie could ask what had happened, he lurched forward into the room, almost plowing into Maddie.

A man appeared at his shoulder—a man with mismatched eyes and a knife in his hand.

"Hello, picture lady. Remember me?"

By the time Ash reached the main road into Denver, the pony was showing the strain, Tricks was starting to lag, and pain was a thunderous roar in his head.

The ache in the left side of his head had expanded to a pounding throb that pulsed with every heartbeat. Lights flashed behind his eyes and his vision had narrowed to a haloed tunnel. It was an effort to stay in the saddle.

He pushed doggedly on. Only a few more miles. He would tie himself to the bluidy horse if he had to. He wouldn't fail her this time.

To focus away from the pain, he mentally listed all the reasons everything would be fine.

Declan was there. Maddie wasn't even at the boardinghouse but was still in town. Chub was with her. She had her wee pistol. People were all around. Cochran wouldn't make his move in the idle of a crowd in broad daylight.

Would he?

Time inched by to the drum of the pony's hoofbeats. People

stared as he rode by, gaping at Tricks who struggled valiantly to stay up.

Ash cupped a hand over his left eye, but that dinna help with the dizziness. Leaning forward, he gripped the pony's mane in both hands and struggled to stay balanced.

Only a few more miles . . .

As Maddie stared down at the knife pointed at her chest, a great stillness came over her. As if she were focusing the lens on her camera, she centered her mind on one single thought—her sole purpose at this moment, and the only thing that mattered.

Stay alive.

Only then could she keep Edwina alive.

Help would come.

She shot a warning glance at Edwina, silently entreating her to remain calm and not do anything to excite the situation. But Ed was frozen in shock, perched upright on the bed, both hands clutched over her distended belly as if to protect the baby within.

Roughly shoving Maddie aside with his free hand, Cletus Cochran stepped in and shut the door. She watched him, fighting to keep her fear from showing even as her mind tried to reason why he was even here. Hadn't he gone after Thomas and the reverend?

Or had Silas lied about that?

"Which room is Zucker's?" Cochran demanded.

Zucker's? Why would he want the reverend? What could the reverend have that Cochran—*the claim papers!* Suddenly it made sense. Cochran hadn't found the claim papers at the cabin, so he had come here.

But where were Thomas and the reverend? And Ash? What had he done to them?

Panic jangled along her nerves. It took all of her will to keep it in check. "I thought you said you were Zucker."

He backhanded her in the face.

Pain exploded. Blinded, she staggered back, blood filling her nose and mouth. Beyond the pain and the buzzing in her ears, she heard Edwina's shrill voice and Silas crying. Lifting a shaking hand to her face, she felt the hot gush of blood through her fingers.

He grabbed her hair and jerked her head back. More blood dripped down her throat, making her gag. Mismatched eyes swam before hers as the knife pricked her side. "Which. Room. Is Zuckers?"

"At the other end of the hall," Edwina cried before Maddie could clear her throat enough to speak. "On the left."

He let go of her hair. The eyes went away.

Maddie doubled over and coughed, spattering blood on her skirts. Had he broken her nose?

"You done there, Si?"

Through the tangle of her hair, Maddie watched Silas finish tying a long pink ribbon around Edwina's hands, then bend to wrap a blue one around her ankles.

He was crying. Bright drips of red fell from his brow onto the coverlet. "Y-yes, Clete. All done."

"Here." Cletus held out the knife.

Silas stared at it.

"Take it, moron!"

When Silas gingerly took it, Maddie almost screamed at him to use it. Stab him before he killed them all. But she knew Silas wouldn't—couldn't—go against his brother.

Cochran pulled the gun from his holster. "You watch that one while we're gone, Si. If she does anything, stick her in the throat. You hear me, moron?"

"Y-yes, Clete."

Grabbing Maddie's left arm, Cochran wrenched it behind her and up between her shoulder blades with such force she cried out and rose on her tiptoes. "Move!" he barked and shoved her toward the door.

"If that one screams or gets away," he called back over his shoulder, "I'll come for you, Si. And you know what I'll do. I'll hurt you bad. Remember that."

Silas's sobs echoed through Maddie's befuddled mind. Pain assaulted her—from her nose, her arm, the socket of her shoulder—but it helped bring her thoughts back in line and rid her body of the terrible numbness that threatened to drag her down.

Cletus pushed her out the door, closed it, then using the arm behind her back, steered her down the hall.

Maddie felt the palm pistol in her skirt pocket bounce against her leg with every step. She knew if they were to survive this, she had to get him away from the house. Away from Edwina. Out into the open where she could use it, where someone would see.

"If you're looking for the claim papers," she gasped, trying to arch away from his agonizing grip on her arm, "they're not in his room."

He stopped. "Where are they?"

She coughed and wiped her right sleeve at the blood still dripping from her nose. "In my wagon."

"You better not be lying." Another vicious twist almost sent Maddie to her knees before he jerked her upright again. Pulling her so close she could smell the stink of his breath, he whispered in her ear, "If you try anything, anything at all, I'll come back up here and gut her. I'll cut that kid out of her and leave them both to die. Understand?"

"I w-won't. I promise."

He shoved her ahead of him toward the stairs.

When they stepped out the back door, the sun hit them full in the face. Cochran stopped. Using her as a shield—one hand pinning her arm, the other holding the muzzle of the gun against her side—he looked around.

The stable faced them. Both the front and back doors were open, and Maddie could see all the way through to her wagon parked in back. Nothing moved in the aisleway. No buggy stood by her wagon. Only the mules dozed in the paddock.

Maddie slid a hand into her pocket. But before she could grab the pistol, he pushed her so hard she almost fell off the stoop.

"Walk!"

They were out in the open and still forty feet from the stable doors when a figure stepped from a stall into the aisleway. Tall, bareheaded, holding a rifle to his shoulder. His face was in shadow, his lanky form silhouetted in the open rear doors.

But Maddie would have known that long body and those sturdy legs and that military stance anywhere.

Cochran stopped, cursed softly under his breath.

"Let her go and ride away," Ash called.

"I'll shoot her." Cocking the pistol, Cochran jabbed the barrel hard into her ribs. "I swear I will."

Ash took a step, then stopped, rifle still at his shoulder. He seemed to falter but slid his other foot forward to steady his balance.

A small, inconsequential movement.

But Maddie saw.

She searched his shadowed face, but it was partially hidden by the stock of the rifle. Yet she knew.

"Fifty feet. Your pistol against my rifle. Think about it, Cochran."

"You shoot me, you kill her."

"Last chance, you bluidy bastard."

Maddie slid a shaking hand into her pocket. This time she found the small pepperbox pistol.

Then Cochran's arm shot past her right shoulder, his pistol pointed at Ash. He fired at the same time a loud boom came from the stable.

Noise deafened her. Cochran stumbled back, dragging Maddie with him. Dimly she heard him screaming as he lifted his gun hand to the right side of his head.

In the barn, Ash sagged against the stall.

Gasping with terror, Maddie struggled one-handed to thumb back the hammer on the pistol.

The man behind her lowered his hand from his head. It was covered in blood. "You son of a bitch! You shot off my ear!"

In the stable, Ash cursed and worked frantically to reload.

Maddie saw Cochran's gun come up again. She butted it away

with her shoulder, then twisted, jammed the pistol into his stomach, and squeezed the trigger.

A muffled pop. Cochran jerked. Wrenching her arm free, Maddie fell forward onto her knees just as something huge and snarling leaped past.

Growls, screams, Ash shouting.

Then suddenly he was there, dragging Tricks off by the scruff of his neck and thrusting a long blade into what was left of Cletus Cochran's throat.

"Oh God, oh God," Maddie wept, trying to crawl away from the carnage. Blood was everywhere—she could smell it, feel it on her hands, taste the coppery saltiness of it on the back of her tongue.

"Lass."

She screamed when hands lifted her from the ground. Then she saw it was Ash and threw herself against him.

"Are you hurt, Maddie? Let me see if you're hurt."

But she couldn't let him go, and finally he had to reach up and pull her arms from around his neck.

"Let me look at you, lass." Trapping her face in his sticky hands, he squinted down at her. "Sweet Mary. There's so much blood. Where are you hurt? Did he cut you?"

"Oh, Ash—the gun w-went off and I saw you f-fall, and—"

"He dinna hit me. I just lost my balance. Did he cut you?"

"N-no. A bloody nose, that's all. Is he . . . ?" She started to look over at Cochran, but he pulled her face back around.

"Aye. He's dead."

"T-tricks?"

"He's fine."

A door slammed. Edwina and Silas stood on the stoop, gaping in horror from Ash and Maddie to Cochran's body, then to the wolfhound coming to greet them, his muzzle and chest wet with blood.

The buggy rolled into the yard. Footsteps came from the opposite direction, then a shrill voice cried, "Goodness gracious sakes alive! What have you people done now?"

Twenty-one

B linded by pain and shaking with relief, Ash barely stayed on his feet as shouts exploded around him—Maddie arguing with Mrs. Kemble. Brodie and his wife and Miss Hathaway running up to join in. Silas crying and running to hide in the barn with Tricks.

He dinna care.

He'd made it in time. Maddie was safe. He hadna let her down.

Pressing a hand to his temple, he stumbled away from the chaos toward the stable, desperate to wash off the blood and find a quiet, dark place to lie down before he fell down or heaved up what jerky was left in his stomach.

Maddie appeared beside him as he bent over the trough, scrubbing his hands in the murky water. After rinsing her own face and hands as best she could, she took his arm and gently led him into the house and up the stairs to their room.

He stood numbly as she stripped off his clothes and helped him into bed. With a groan, he stretched out, praying the spinning would stop.

"Stay," he said, reaching blindly out, afraid to open his eyes.

A moment later, he felt her slide in beside him. Pulling her close, he whispered into her hair. "Dinna leave me."

"I won't." She gently stroked his chest. "Sleep."

He put his hand over hers to anchor her to him, then let his mind go.

Sound faded. The throbbing eased. A few bright flashes of light, then weariness pulled him down into a place as black and thick as a peat bog.

When next he opened his eyes, sunlight lit the room. For a moment he thought he was back in the hospital in Ireland, awakening from another laudanum dream—his mouth dry, his limbs weak, his thoughts so disoriented for a moment he dinna know where he was.

Then it all came rushing back—the endless ride, the pain, the fear of what might have happened if he hadna reached her in time—and a sudden, choking panic squeezed his chest.

A hand stroked his brow, startling him. He turned his head to see Maddie, fully dressed, stretched atop the covers, facing him. Poor lass. Purple bruises shadowed her swollen eyes. A blanket of sticking plaster covered the bridge of her nose. Yet she had never been more precious to him. Emotion constricted his throat. He felt the burn of it behind his eyes and looked away before he betrayed himself.

What would he have done had he lost her?

"You're finally awake."

"Aye," he said, hoarsely. "It's morning then?"

"Afternoon."

He had slept that long? In control once again, he gave her a smile. "Have you been watching over me, lass, all this time?"

She gave him a smile he'd never seen from her before. Sweet and warm and full of knowledge. And love. He was sure of it. Yet she dinna say the words, and he wondered why. He also wondered why she was fully dressed while he was naked beneath the covers.

She brushed the hair from his brow. "How do you feel?"

Ready. Eager as a thirteen-year-old. But he could tell by the worry on her face that his wife had other things on her mind. Just as well. He was feeling a bit shaky yet. "Better. Hungry. Did Thomas come?"

Her expression deepened into a frown. "The reverend brought him a couple of hours ago. The doctor is with him now. Even as hurt as he is, Mrs. Kemble is fearful of having an Indian in the house—apparently an uncle of hers was killed by Cheyenne on the Overland Trail several years ago—so Declan put him in my wagon. I think he prefers that, anyway."

"I should be there." Ash started to sit up, but she put her hand on his chest and gently urged him back down.

"Later. Eat first." She rose and went to the bureau, returning with a plate piled high with leftovers. Only then did Ash see she wore a sling on her left arm.

"What's wrong with your arm?"

"Nothing. A wrenched shoulder. The doctor thought it would heal faster if I didn't use it for a few days."

"It's sorry I am, lass, that I wasna here to protect you."

Setting the plate on the bedside table, she sank onto the bed, her hip next to his, her free hand fisted in her lap. He saw her throat working, and the wee wobble in her chin, and knew she was struggling not to cry. "The reverend told us what happened, and what you did for him and Thomas. He said once you were sure they were safe, you didn't even rest or eat, but turned around and made the long ride back."

"I shouldn't have left you. If Cochran had—"

She put a fingertip to his lips, cutting him off. "You were here when I needed you, Ash. And at great cost to yourself, I fear." She lost the battle, and a tear began a slow descent down her pale cheek. "I need to say something to you, Ash."

He braced himself, not knowing what was coming or how he could defend himself against it. Doubt crystallized into a single, hard knot in the center of his chest.

"I have been so unfair to you for so long, dearest." Lifting trembling fingers, she brushed the tear away. Another started down. "Every time something went wrong in my life, I looked for someone to save me. And when you couldn't come, I blamed you for letting me down."

"I should have tried harder."

"No. *I* should have tried harder. I realize that now." Leaning down, she pressed a salty kiss to his lips, then straightened. "Life is full of heartache. People die, babes are lost. It isn't always as neat as we would like it to be. You couldn't have saved me from that, and I was wrong to expect it of you. I misjudged you. And myself, perhaps," she added with a weak smile. "I'm stronger than I think."

Relief made his throat tight. "Aye, lass. You are. I've known it from the first, so I have."

"Then know this, too, Angus Wallace." Her voice was starting to break now, and the words were hard to follow. "You have never let me down. I don't think you're capable of it. And even blinded by headaches and plagued by old wounds, you're still all the man I'll ever need."

He hid the joy those words gave him behind a shaky smile. "I should hope so."

"You nincompoop."

This time when she leaned down, he wrapped his arms around her so she couldn't pull back until he'd finished kissing her. When he finally let her sit up, she was still crying. And smiling. It made no sense.

"*Je t'aime*, Angus Wallace. I love you. I always have."

Finally. "You were supposed to show me," he reminded her.

"Was I?" Chuckling, she lifted her skirt to blot her wet cheeks. "Perhaps later."

"And let all this nakedness go to waste? You wouldn't even have to undress, love. Just lift those petticoats—"

"Hush!" Chuckles gave way to laughter, even as a maidenly blush inched up her tear-streaked cheeks. "As appealing as it would be to toss up my skirts for you like a back alley tart, I must insist you bathe first. You smell entirely too much of horse, and there's still blood under your nails." As she said that last part, she looked quickly away. "Besides, you need to eat to keep up your strength."

"My strength has been up since I awoke and saw you beside me.

Would you like to see?" Seeing she was about to scold, he laughed. God, he loved this woman.

"All right, lass. I'll do as you ask, and hope you'll be joining me later in the washroom to make sure I'm thoroughly scrubbed. Now pass the plate. If I canna nibble on you, I'll try that chicken. And you can tell me all that has happened whilst I lay abed, dreaming of you."

He hadn't been hungry until he took the first bite, then suddenly he felt ravenous. While he devoured cold chicken, potatoes, carrots, beets, and rolls, she related the events of the last day.

Brodie had managed to keep the landlady from throwing them out immediately, but she expected them to be gone soon. The undertaker had removed Cochran's body. The local marshal had come, and after talking to Declan, and Maddie, and Edwina, had decided Cochran's death was self-defense. "Declan thinks it was more a case of him not knowing who to charge for the actual killing—you, me, or Tricks."

Seeing the worry in her eyes, Ash mentally kicked himself. "It was my blade that finished him off," he reassured her. "Your wee gun would only have slowed him down for a while." Until infection set in, as it always did in gut shots. But Ash dinna mention that. The lass had been through enough without piling misplaced guilt on her shoulders. "He said naught about Tricks?" There were many who thought once a dog attacked a human, he could never be trusted again.

"He was concerned, but we assured him we would keep him secured until we leave."

"Secured? Where?"

"He's keeping Lurch and Si company in the stable. I'm more worried about Silas. Even though he feared and hated his brother, he seems quite lost without him. What will become of him, do you think?"

"I'll talk to Declan about it," Ash said between bites. "It's clear the lad canna live on his own. He's far too trusting and would be easy prey for unscrupulous types."

From there the talk moved on to when they could leave for

Heartbreak Creek. "Edwina and Declan are anxious to get back to their children. Lucinda is quite excited, too." Maddie told him about Miss Hathaway's canceled meetings, then finding renewed interest from a new railroad. "Apparently they're sending a representative to Heartbreak Creek in the next month or so. Lucinda is determined to do everything she can to put the town in a good light."

"Perhaps I can help. I'm verra handy with a hammer, so I am."

"I know."

"Saucy wench." Leaning over, he gave her a kiss as he set his empty plate on the bedside table, then ran his hand up her thigh.

She gently pushed it away. "Later."

He sat back with a sigh. "Since you willna join me for a wee bit of sport, lass, I might as well dress and go check on Thomas and Tricks."

"Bathe first. You wouldn't want to frighten them." She rose and picked up the plate. "I've left your shaving things in the washroom. See that you use them. I don't want Edwina commenting on my rash again."

Thirty minutes later, Ash arrived at the open door of Maddie's wagon, scrubbed and shaved, his hair still damp from his bath. The doctor had left and Brodie was moving boxes around to make more room.

"How's the heathen?" he asked from the doorway.

Startled, Brodie straightened, thumping the crown of his hat against the ceiling and unloosing a shower of photographs. Muttering under his breath, he bent to pick them up.

"Hungry," Thomas answered from the bed.

Ash saw the footboard had been removed and the runt's feet only stuck out a half foot beyond the mattress. The Cheyenne still wore his moccasins and breechclout, but he'd removed his war shirt and leggings. He lay on his uninjured side, thick wrappings swathing his ribs. He looked better than when Ash had last seen him, but that wasn't saying much. On the wee table beside the bed, he saw a familiar brown bottle, and noting the Cheyenne's drowsiness, guessed he had been given laudanum.

Wincing, Thomas rolled onto his back. "Declan Brodie says you killed Cletus Cochran."

"Aye."

"But you needed your woman and dog to do it."

Ash made a crude gesture to the smirking Indian, then turned to Brodie. "What did the doctor say?"

"That you and the reverend probably saved his life."

"Did he?" Now it was Ash's turn to smirk. "And how does it feel, heathen, to owe your life to a Scotsman?"

"My shame is great."

"If you ladies are through tossing insults," Brodie said, sitting on one of Maddie's photography crates. "We need to figure out when to leave and what to do with Silas."

"White people," Thomas mumbled. "You make such trouble for yourselves." Closing his eyes, he sank into a deep, drugged sleep.

Lowering his voice, Brodie gave Ash the doctor's report. Thomas had lost a lot of blood and would be weak for a while. The wounds looked clean, but there was always risk of infection. "Mrs. Kemble wants us to leave tomorrow, but he won't be able to ride, and I doubt we can keep him in the wagon the whole way back to Heartbreak Creek."

"What about the reverend?"

The sheriff sighed and shook his head. "He's still fixed on finding his brother. I don't have much hope of that happening. Says he'll go back to the cabin. He's convinced his brother registered the claim, and plans to keep looking for Ephraim's copy of the paperwork."

"When is he leaving?"

"I'm not sure. He's in the feed room, talking to Silas right now. The boy's pretty upset and confused about his brother's death."

"Let's go talk to him. Maybe we can figure out what to do with the lad."

Tricks almost knocked him down with his enthusiastic welcome.

"Your wife made us bathe him to get all the blood off," Brodie murmured, eyeing the wiggling, waggling dog. "Took me and Chub and Silas to get him in the trough. When we finished, he rolled in the manure pile, so we had to do it again."

"He's not too fond of his baths," Ash said, ruffling the dog's ears. "The Irish in him, I think."

Ash nodded hello to the reverend, who sat on an overturned bucket, then at Silas, who was hunched in the corner, watching the newcomers warily. Recognizing the defensive position, Ash hunkered in front of the lad and smiled in reassurance. "Good day to you, Silas. I thank you for taking care of my dog. He's verra dear to me, so he is."

"I like Tricks. He likes me, too."

"I can see that." Ash turned his head to pet the wolfhound.

Silas gasped.

Startled, Ash looked back to find the lad staring at him with an odd expression on his battered face.

"Did God send you?" Silas asked.

"God?" Ash glanced at Brodie and the reverend. They seemed as confused by the question as he was. "Why would you think God sent me?"

Instead of answering, the boy dug in the lining of his coat. "I got one, too. Ma gave it to me. She said if I told the truth and didn't hurt anybody, God would watch over me." Papers and photographs and letters spilled out before he finally found what he sought. "She said anytime I was in trouble or afraid, all I had to do was hold it and everything would be okay. See?" He held out his hand. In his dirty palm was a pendant bearing the same five cross design that was on the back of Ash's neck.

"Did God send you to make Clete stop hurting me?"

Taken aback, Ash wasn't sure how to answer.

The reverend stepped in. "I think perhaps He did. I think the Lord sent this warrior to do His work."

"No. He dinna." The idea was repugnant to Ash. He had never been one to cling to that pious justification for the brutal tasks he had been required to perform as a soldier. He had seen enough carnage and violence and bloodshed on the battlefield to know God had naught to do with it.

But Silas clutched at Ash like he was his salvation. "I'm sorry," he choked out, tears rolling down his dirty face. "But he started yelling and it scared me. Then he ran at me and hit me and the knife slipped and then he stopped moving. I didn't mean to hurt him, I swear."

With a soft sound—something between a sigh and a moan—the reverend dropped his head into his hand.

Ash already guessed the answer but made himself ask. "Who did you hurt, lad?"

Silas wiped a sleeve over his runny nose. "The smiling man."

"Do you know his name?"

"I don't remember. But he lives in a little cabin with trees all around and a mountain that looks like a face turned sideways. I had a picture of him, but Clete took it."

With a shaking hand, the reverend pulled a photograph from his pocket and held it out. "A picture like this?"

"You found it!" Smiling broadly, his tears forgotten, Silas took the photograph and held it up to Ash and Brodie, pointing at the figure beside the cabin. "See? The smiling man and the cabin and the mountain that looks like a face turned sideways." His grin faded. "I wanted to go there. Whenever Clete hurt me, I pretended I was safe with the smiling man by his cabin. But I never was."

After a long silence, the reverend cleared his throat and said, "Would you like to go there with me, Silas?"

Si looked up, his bruised face so desperate with hope Ash had to look away.

"Are you sure about this, Reverend?" Brodie warned softly. "By his own admission, the boy—"

"Didn't know what he was doing," Zucker cut in before the sheriff could finish the sentence. "He's a gentle soul that has been sorely used. It's time he had a home, I think. And I can surely use the help fixing up the cabin for when my wife comes. What can be the harm, Sheriff, if we give this poor boy a second chance?"

Brodie dinna respond, and when Ash looked over to see why, he found the sheriff staring at the papers and pictures that had spilled into Silas's lap.

"Where did you get the pictures and those papers, Silas?"

The fear came back in the lad's face. "I'm sorry. I didn't mean to take them. But Clete was going to throw them away, and I didn't think the smiling man would need them anymore."

"Can I see?"

"You won't hurt the pictures, will you?"

"No. I won't hurt them. But if you're worried about it, I'll just look at the papers. All right?" Brodie held out his hand.

Reluctantly, Silas handed them over.

Brodie sifted through them. A letter from the reverend to his brother—which he passed over to the reverend—and some folded papers. He opened them to find a printed form with a seal stamped on the front. "Son of a bitch," he said wonderingly. "They were right here in Silas's jacket the whole time." Laughing, he held them up for Ash and the reverend to see. "The missing claim papers. It's all here. Take a look."

The reverend studied them carefully, his expresssion bouncing between wonder and joy and sadness. Everything was properly registered—description, location, assay report. Ephraim Zucker had definitely struck gold.

"I guess it's settled then," he said, tucking the papers into his jacket pocket. "I'll go back to the claims office first thing tomorrow and have the deed registered in my name as Ephraim's next of kin. Then I'll pick up some supplies, and Silas and I will head to the cabin. It's time to put all this pain and ugliness behind us. Right, Si?"

"Okay. Can Tricks come with us?"

The reverend must have seen Ash's instantaneous rejection of the idea, because he smiled and shook his head. "I think Mr. Wallace needs Tricks to stay with him. But perhaps we can find a pup along the way."

"Okay."

Ash nodded his gratitude to Zucker. Odd, how things had turned out. The reverend was sitting rich, Silas had a good home, and Cletus Cochran was roasting in hell where he belonged. Maybe the long arm of Providence had had a hand in all this after all.

Before leaving the stable, Ash got a blank bank draft from his saddlebag, filled it out as best he could, then went to the kitchen, where Miss Hathaway and Edwina Brodie were sitting at the table peeling potatoes, and Mrs. Kemble was bent before the oven door, basting a ham with a honey and applesauce glaze that made Ash's stomach rumble. Nodding to the two at the table, he turned to the landlady. "If I might have a word with you, ma'am?"

She straightened, her expression none too friendly. "So you're finally awake. Never knew a body could sleep so long. But at least when you're asleep, you're not causing trouble."

"My apologies." He put on his best smile. It dinna even faze the hardhearted shrew. "I thought we should settle up before we leave tomorrow." He held out the bank draft and hoped he had written it correctly.

Wiping her hands on her apron, she eyed it suspiciously. "What's that?"

"Payment for our rooms and the fine meals you've provided and for stabling the animals. I trust it will be sufficient."

She took the draft and studied it, a frown drawing her gray brows together. "More than sufficient. In fact, double sufficient. Why's that?"

"For the aggravation our shenanigans have caused you."

"Humph." She squinted at the signature. "I can hardly read this chicken scratching. Looks like it says Fifth Viscount of Ashby. Who's that?"

"Me."

She glared up at him. "I thought you were Angus Wallace."

"I am."

"Is this more of your shenanigans?"

"It is not," Maddie's voice cut in as she entered the room. "My husband is indeed Viscount Ashby, a Scottish lord and member of the British peerage. But rather than attract mawkish attention, he prefers to go by his given name when visiting America."

Ash stared at his wife in amazed amusement as she glided by, every inch the grand dame. The two black eyes and sticking plastered nose rather tarnished the effect, but she nonetheless cut a striking figure.

"Lord Ashby was also a decorated colonel in the Prince of Wales's Own Tenth Hussars," she went on, proudly. "Which is, of course, the most famed cavalry unit in the entire British Army."

The *entire* army, Ash mused, sharing a glance with the ladies at the potato bowl and wondering how the other regiments would feel about that.

Mrs. Kemble sniffed. "I never heard of someone having two names."

His viscountess leaned over to whisper in her ear, "His family lives in a castle."

That got the old biddy's blood pumping. "Do they? A real castle? Like real lords and ladies?"

"Exactly like real lords and ladies." With a triumphant smile, his lady wife sailed on by, her work complete. "May I help you set the table, Mrs. Kemble? I daresay you've never before had a real viscountess do your bidding."

Edwina Brodie rolled her eyes. Miss Hathaway coughed into the peelings.

"A viscountess," Mrs. Kemble breathed. "Wait until I tell Ruby." Then rushing into the dining room after Maddie, she called, "Would that be better than a baron?"

The reverend and Silas departed early the next morning amid invitations for them to bring Mrs. Zucker to Heartbreak Creek for a visit. "So you can meet the children and help us christen the baby," Edwina urged.

"And I should have the last of the rooms in the hotel refurbished soon," Lucinda added. "If you'll let me know when you're coming, I'll set aside one of the suites."

"And Tricks would be so happy to see you, Silas," Maddie put in, dabbing at her eyes.

Ash smiled dutifully and rocked on his heels, wondering how much longer these bluidy good-byes would drag on. By his calculations, they were already an hour late if they planned to billet in Jefferson that night.

While the women prattled on, he mentally went through the list of preparations: The landlady and Chub had been paid. The doctor had checked Thomas, pronounced him fit for travel—as long as he dinna ride horseback or sit too long—then collected his fee and left. Maddie's equipment and the ladies' valises had been stowed, along with extra water and food. Weapons had been secured. He had personally inspected the vehicles, and the animals were harnessed and waiting. All that remained was to load three wee women into the buggy.

A monumental task, apparently. He looked over to Brodie for help in moving things along, but the sheriff just shrugged like there was nothing he could do. He would have made a poor drill sergeant.

Finally the reverend released the brake. As soon as the buckboard rolled out into the street, Ash politely herded the women toward the house, advising them to attend their needs and muster by the wagons in ten minutes.

Thirty minutes later, they came out the back door, followed by the landlady, the deaf widow, and her simpering daughter. Fearing another series of protracted good-byes, Ash marched toward them.

"Thank you for your hospitality, Mrs. Kemble. It has been a delight to meet you all, but now we must bid you good-bye. Ladies?" He made a shooing motion.

They looked at him.

"Mount up."

They continued to look at him.

"Now!"

Fifteen minutes later, they were on their way back home to Heartbreak Creek.

Home?

When had he begun to think of Heartbreak Creek as home?

Twenty-two

It was Tuesday afternoon, and Pru and the children were walking back from school and speculating on whether or not it would snow that night, when Brin shrieked, "Pa!" and took off down the boardwalk so fast her floppy hat flew off her head. Before it touched ground, the other three charged after her, shouting and waving.

Pru stopped to retrieve the hat, then watched in amusement as Declan staggered under the assault of his three youngest children trying to climb all over him. Only R. D. remained aloof—being too big and old for such childish displays—until Edwina came out of the hotel and launched an attack of her own on him.

Not seeing Thomas and thinking he might be around back, Pru slipped into the alley that ran beside the mercantile to the back-street.

She had thought of little else but him in the days he had been gone. "Heart mate" he had called her. A fanciful word. But there was an element of truth in it. She did feel connected to Thomas on a level beyond the physical or even the intellectual. It was a spiritual bonding that transcended everything that had gone before. In his eyes, she was not just the scarred daughter of a slave, or Edwina's half-black half sister, or Lone Tree's captive, or the negress teaching in the little schoolhouse by the creek.

She was his heart mate.

The idea of that—of him, of seeing him again after their short separation—made her laugh out loud.

Quickening her steps as she reached the backstreet, she turned toward the hotel. Maddie's wagon was parked by the stoop. Lucinda's buggy stood beside it, with Thomas's painted horse tied to the rear.

Filled with equal parts of anticipation and nervousness, Pru walked briskly down the track, searching for his sturdy form among the figures milling at the back of the wagon.

Tricks raced by, Agnes nipping at his heels. Pru smiled, watching them. If it was possible for dogs to laugh, they would be doing it.

Ahead, voices rose as Maddie supervised her husband in the lowering of the stair at the back of the wagon. Lucinda hurried out of the hotel, followed by a white-haired man carrying a black satchel—Doc Boyce? Mr. Wallace spoke to him for a moment, then the doctor hurried up the steps and into the wagon.

Why? Who needed a doctor?

Pru walked faster, dread growing as she noted everyone was accounted for except Thomas.

"Pru!" Declan called from behind her.

She stopped and waited for him to catch up. What she saw in his face as he drew near sent dread blossoming into full-blown fear. "What's wrong? Is it Thomas? Has something happened?"

"He's been shot. But he's alive."

Shot. Alive. Hurt. "How bad?"

"He was doing okay, but this morning when he woke up, his fever—"

She whirled and started walking again.

He fell into step beside her.

"Where are you taking him?" she asked, a part of her amazed at how calm her voice sounded despite the terror clawing at her throat.

"He can't stay at the sheriff's office or in his room in your carriage house all alone with nobody to see to him."

"Ed can—"

"In her condition? And what if he tries to get up, or needs to be sponged, or . . . something."

"He won't stay in the hotel. You know that."

"Then bring him to the school. We can clean out the storage room."

"I don't know if that would be wise, Pru. People might talk."

"Then let them!" She rounded on him, patience gone. "There's always talk—about me, Thomas, anyone who's different. I don't care. I'm used to it." Realizing she still held Brin's hat, she thrust it toward him and resumed walking. "Bring him to the school. I'll tend him."

"But—"

"Bring him, Sheriff! Or I'll find a way to do it myself."

He said no more until they reached the wagon. The Wallaces and Lucinda still hovered at the back steps, looking lost in the way people did when faced with a crisis they could do nothing about. "Is the doctor still inside?" Pru asked.

"Aye," Mr. Wallace said.

"Please don't unharness the mules just yet," she instructed him. "We'll be moving Thomas to the school when Doc Boyce is finished. I could use your help clearing the storeroom and getting him inside."

"Of course."

"Have you everything you'll need?" Lucinda asked.

Pru shot her a look of gratitude—not just for the offer, but for not questioning her decision. "Perhaps some bedding. A cot, if you have one."

"I'll have Yancey check the storeroom." Motioning Maddie to follow, she started back inside, issuing instructions as she went. "Ask Cook to pack a basket. Miriam can collect bedding. We'll take everything over in the buggy so it will be there when he arrives."

Pru looked up at the closed door, gathering courage to face what she might find when she went in there. She knew it would be a shock, seeing Thomas laid low. He had always seemed so indomitable, so unstoppable. Even wounded, he had ridden days to find her after Lone Tree had taken her to the Indian encampment. It seemed impossible that now that she'd allowed him into her heart, he might be torn from it forever.

She couldn't bear it. Wouldn't allow it.

Bracing herself, she put a foot on the first step.

A hand touched her shoulder. "Miss Lincoln."

She turned, impatient to reach Thomas, then saw the worry in Angus Wallace's startling green eyes. "Yes?"

"Anything you need, ma'am. Anything at all. He's a good man, so he is. He deserves everything we can do to save him."

"Yes. He does," she said and continued up the steps.

It was late. Wind howled at the door like a starving beast, and already snow had formed crescents on the bottoms of the windowpanes.

Shivering, Pru settled deeper into the chair beside the bed and pulled her shawl closer. Even though the little woodstove in the classroom down the hall was blazing as high as it could go, the chill reached into her very bones. She doubted she would ever grow accustomed to it. Having lived most of her life at near sea level in the sultry bayou country of Louisiana, she still struggled with the thin, cold air of the Colorado Rockies.

She watched the slow rise and fall of Thomas's chest and felt her own lungs take on the tempo, expanding and contracting in unison with his, as if to encourage him to take the next breath. The rhythm soothed her.

Over the last week, her life had been pared down to simple, rote responses to the most basic needs of the man lying in the bed—warmth when he shivered, cool cloths when he burned, water if she could force it down him. Keeping him alive.

She refused to fail him. To do so would wrest all hope from her life.

Thomas made a restless movement, then lay still again.

She checked the small watch she wore pinned in her skirt pocket, wondering if it was time to give him more medicine. His fever had started up again earlier this evening after Declan and Mr. Wallace had stopped by with another basket of food from the hotel kitchen. He had become agitated despite the laudanum the doctor insisted she give him for pain and restlessness. But after dosing him with two droppers of aconite solution, he seemed to have settled somewhat.

The wound had improved but was still oozing. Doc Boyce had shown her how to flush it with carbolized water but said it couldn't be allowed to close, since it had to heal from the inside out. He had instructed her on how to fix a drawing poultice made from flaxseed and ground mustard, which she was to keep applying as long as it was still drawing out infection. For almost a week now, she had flushed the wound every time she had applied the poultice, and it seemed to Pru the oozing was less and the redness was beginning to fade.

But that could be wishful thinking.

She rolled her head, trying to ease the stiffness in her neck and shoulders. As she did, her gaze fell on the small leather pouch sitting on the bedside table. Declan had given it to her when they'd first brought Thomas to the schoolhouse.

"Keep it safe," he had said, handing it to her. "It's sacred to Thomas, and he'll want it when he wakes up."

It weighed next to nothing and felt empty except for a single hard, round thing. It had no beading or painted symbols like on his war shirt, and the stitching was crude. "What's in it?" she had asked Declan.

"He'll tell you if he wants you to know. Put it where he can see it."

She had done as he'd asked, thinking this was just one more thing about Thomas she didn't know. There was so much she might never truly come to terms with . . . his language, the myths and spirits that guided him, his reverence for all living things even though he would willingly take a life, as she had seen when he had come to take her from Lone Tree. And she was certain she would never understand the sacred sun dance ceremony that required self-mutilation to prove manhood.

But she did know the heart of the man who bore those terrible scars, and she loved him.

"*Eho'nehevehohtse . . .*"

Pru jerked upright in the chair, realizing she had fallen asleep. Her gaze flew to Thomas, who had rolled onto his uninjured side. His eyes were open and fixed on her.

She stared back, trying to find her Thomas in that dark, unwavering gaze, rather than the stranger who had drifted in and out of fevered sleep over the last days.

He smiled weakly. "Prudence."

"You're awake." Rising quickly, she went to rest a hand on his forehead. Cool. No fever. A giddy relief made her hand tremble. Tucking it behind her skirts, she let out the breath she hadn't even been aware of holding and smiled down at him. "You're better."

"Better than what?" He grimaced and licked dry lips with a coated tongue. "Did you give me *mataho*?"

She shook her head, not sure what that was. "Laudanum."

"I do not like it. You will not give it to me again."

She smiled at the haughty command even as tears clouded her eyes. He was going to be all right. He was going to live. "Are you hungry?"

"Water, first. Then buffalo steak."

"Water, first. Then broth." She was unable to stop the tears from overflowing.

He frowned, his dark eyes shadowed with weariness even though he'd slept a day and a half. "Why do you cry, *heme'oono*?"

She blotted her face with her apron, but still the tears came. "Because I'm happy. Because you're going to live. Because I couldn't have borne it if you weren't."

He patted the bed beside him. "Come, Prudence. Lie beside me and I will dry your tears."

She had to laugh. Did the man actually think to come at her in his condition? "Let me get the water and broth. If you're still awake after that, maybe I'll let you read to me from the primer."

She returned several minutes later with a pitcher of fresh water and a bowl of broth. He was sitting on the edge of the bed, one hand clasped to his injured side, the other clutching the leather pouch. As she set the tray on the table, he looked up with a stricken, almost panicked expression—if such an emotion as panic was possible for Thomas.

"I thought it was gone. I thought I lost it."

She sat in the chair beside the bed, and leaning forward, braced her crossed arms on her knees. "Declan saved it for you. He told me to put it where you could see it, but I must have accidentally pushed it behind some of the medicine bottles. I'm sorry for worrying you. I know it's sacred to you."

"Not sacred. Necessary."

She waited, but he said no more, and his closed expression forbade her to pry.

After he drank two cups of water and half the broth, he sank back onto the pillows, the pouch still clutched in his hand.

"Would you like for me to put it around your neck?" she asked.

But he was already asleep, the hand holding the pouch resting on his scarred chest.

She pulled the covers over him, then quietly left the room.

He slept most of the next two days. When she went in on the third morning after the fever broke, she found him standing at the window, fully dressed, squinting out at the snow-covered street. The glare of sunshine off the unbroken white was almost painful to the eyes. "You shouldn't be up," she scolded, setting the breakfast tray on the chair so she could clear space on the small bedside table.

He didn't respond but turned to watch in silence as she carefully set the pouch aside, then moved the tray from the chair to the table. This time she'd brought oatmeal with honey and cinnamon, stewed apples, and two coddled eggs.

"Still no meat?" He eyed the tray with a look of disappointment.

"Perhaps tomorrow."

He started to say something, then changed his mind and came to sit on the bed. He ate in silence and with such single-minded determination she wondered if he was that hungry or simply intent on rebuilding his strength as quickly as possible.

She poured a cup of water for him, then sat back and studied him as he ate. His improvement was remarkable. No fever, the tremble in his hands was gone, his appetite was back. Yet she sensed a distance growing between them and didn't know what had caused it.

When he finished the last bite of oatmeal and had returned the empty bowl to the tray, she asked if she could check the wounds. He nodded and lifted the leather tunic to expose his bandaged ribs.

She removed the wrappings and was relieved to find no new evidence of infection. She flushed both wounds. His continued silence created an awkwardness that hadn't been there before. She hated it. Feared it.

"The children do not come for lessons today?"

"It's Saturday. They won't be here tomorrow, either." She didn't mention that she had closed the school the previous week, as well, because she had been too involved with Thomas to teach the lessons.

"Where is my horse?"

"In the pen around back. Mr. Wallace brought hay and grain."

"He is Mr. Wallace now? That Scotsman has too many names."

Smiling at the description, she smeared carbolic ointment on two bandages, then motioned for him to hold them to the wounds while she applied sticking tape.

"He says I owe him for saving my life. When I am well, I will wrestle him and let him win. That should make him happy." He tipped his head to study her face. "I owe you even more, I think."

"There is no debt between us, Thomas."

"I am glad." He said no more until she finished wrapping the gauze around his chest, then he dropped the shirt back over his torso and stood. "Thank you, Prudence. Now I will walk."

"Walk where?"

He pointed down the hall to the far wall of the classroom. "Fifty times. You will listen to me count and tell me if I miss numbers."

He began stronger than he finished, but he completed the fifty laps, drank copious amounts of water, then slogged through a foot of melting snow to the outhouse rather than use a chamber pot. He ate lunch with the same grim-faced efficiency, washed in a bucket of warm water she brought him, then slept for two hours.

And still that space between them remained.

Pru was beside herself. What had she said or done to cause this breach between them? She could feel him drifting away but had no idea how to stop it. By the time she brought him supper, she was bouncing between anger and fear that she was losing him.

He was at the window again. She set the tray onto the table with a bang, then faced him, hands on hips.

He studied her for a moment, then walked over to take his seat on the bed. He took a bite of chicken, swallowed, and said, "You are angry."

"No," she lied. "I'm confused."

"Why?"

"Why? Because you won't talk to me."

"Talk to you about what?"

Throwing her hands up in disbelief, she whirled and left the room.

When she came back later for the tray, she found him doing laps again. She picked up the tray and was turning to leave when he appeared beside her so suddenly she almost ran into him—how did the man move so silently?

Taking the tray from her hands, he set it back on the table, then pulled her into his arms. "Do not be angry, *eho'nehevehohtse.*"

"I'm not angry. I'm confused."

"Between us nothing has changed. All is well."

Well? After his silent treatment? Yet she allowed herself to lean into him, drawing strength from the steady beat of his heart beneath her cheek. He was her anchor, her slender thread back to a life of joy and love and hope. But she doubted she would ever understand him.

Moving his hands to her shoulders, he dipped his head and kissed her, then stepped back. "Sit, Prudence," he said, motioning to the chair. "I will tell you what is in the pouch so you will understand and put away your anger."

"I'm not angry." But she sat and waited for him to speak.

He sat on the edge of the bed across from her, their knees almost touching. "Not long ago," he began, "I was a Dog Soldier." As he spoke, he stared past her at some distant point in his mind, his thumb idly stroking the worn leather of the pouch.

"We were foolish. We thought if we were brave enough and fought hard enough, we could defeat the bluecoats. Many died. Still the whites came. When I saw we could not win this war, I talked of finding a better way to take back our lands. But my Cheyenne brothers were too angry to listen."

She saw the heartache in his eyes, heard it in his voice. Instinctively she reached out to brush her fingertips against his cheek, wanting him to come back to her and away from that sad place.

He seemed not to notice and looked down at the pouch, blinking hard. "I was not afraid to die, Prudence. But I did not want my family to struggle on without me, either. So I took them into the mountains where we could live in peace."

He opened the pouch and pulled out a short length of straight black hair tied with a leather strip. "This belonged to my wife," he said and set it on the table at his side. "And this was my son's." Another lock, baby fine and glossy as a crow's wing.

Pru pressed her hand over her mouth.

"And this"—turning the pouch upside down, he shook out a small, misshapen piece of metal—"was the bullet that killed them." He set it carefully on the table beside the locks of hair. "One bullet.

Through my wife's back and into my infant son as he slept in her arms."

When he looked at her, Pru saw the sadness had been replaced by a coldness that took all expression from his face.

"One bullet, *eho'nehevehohtse.* Sent by a trapper who did not even know them but only sought to rid the world of two Indians with a single shot."

Swallowing hard, Pru clasped her hands in her lap and looked toward the window. Beyond it, darkness turned the snow a ghostly gray. *It will freeze tonight,* she thought. In the morning, they would awaken to a crust of sugary ice crystals that would melt away by afternoon to expose the mud and withered foliage beneath.

It explained so much. That unshakable strength in him. That amused tolerance with which he viewed life, and his protectiveness toward his new family in Heartbreak Creek. There were no surprises left for Thomas. He had seen it all and endured the worst. He had watched his dreams destroyed by a single, random, senseless act of evil and had seen beneath the glittering façade to the harshest reality a human could suffer.

And yet here he was. Still caring. Still trying. Still believing in second chances.

"I will find him, Prudence. I must."

She looked back to see him slipping the locks of hair and the spent bullet into the pouch. He pulled the drawstring closed and set it on the table. "I owe it to my wife and son so that their spirits can rest."

"Is this why you disappear into the mountains for days at a time? To find the man who killed them? Trying to find the trapper who did this?"

"Yes."

"And if you don't find him?"

"I will find him."

She saw the determination in the set of his chin, and felt something twist in her chest. He would die rather than fail in this task. He allowed himself no other outcome.

"I ask that you understand, *heme'oono*. I must do this thing before I can begin again with you."

She swiped her tears away and nodded. "I understand." She didn't like it, but she would accept it. It was all part and parcel of this complex man she had grown to love.

Rising from the chair, she began unbuttoning her dress. "But not tonight. Tonight you'll give me a memory to hold in my heart until you come back to me. That's what I ask of you."

A slow smile took the bleakness from his face. "I am still weak."

She laughed and hoped he didn't hear the catch in her throat or see the tremble in her hands as she let her dress slide to the floor. But if he did, he would know why and understand. She loved that about him most of all.

"You've never been weak, Thomas. But if you're worried about your wound, I'll be content to lie beside you and watch you sleep."

The smile spread. "Will you?"

"For now." She pulled the shift over her head and stood naked before him, scars and all. It was a terrifying, liberating moment, but when she saw something kindle in his eyes that had nothing to do with pity and everything to do with desire, she smiled. "Or perhaps we can think of another way."

"There is always another way. If not, we will make one." He held out his arms.

It was only a single step. But it was the hardest she had ever taken.

"Do not be afraid," he whispered, gathering her close. "*Nemehotatse, eho'nehevehohtse.*"

"I love you too, Thomas."

Maddie awoke with a jerk, her body rigid with terror. Gasping, she stared frantically into the darkness, her heart slamming against her ribs. But the attack never came. After a moment, the snarls and screams faded into a droning snore.

Turning her head, she saw her husband sprawled beside her, head back, mouth open, his big hands resting on his chest. She lifted a trembling hand and touched his shoulder. "Ash."

"Sent arms," he mumbled and rolled onto his side away from her. After a moment, his breathing settled into the slow exhalations of deep sleep, barely audible over the pounding of her heart.

She stared up at the ceiling while inside her head the images continued to flash, one after another, like projections from a magic lantern on a distant wall—Cochran, Tricks, Ash, blood.

"Time," Ash had said that first night she had awakened from night terrors. "Give it time, love. And remember I'm right beside you."

But the fear remained. In fact, it seemed to have grown stronger as the days passed. It colored everything—each decision, every thought. It followed her onto the boardwalk, tricking her into hearing footsteps behind her or voices whispering her name. It hovered just beyond her vision, a shadow there then gone, ready to slip into her mind the moment she closed her eyes.

She didn't know how to make it go away.

And it wasn't just fear for herself that kept her twisting at night.

She pressed her palm against her belly. Even now a babe might be growing inside. A son and future earl, his life predetermined by position and rank rather than his own desires and the happenstance of luck, choice, and hard-won experience.

But safe.

In Scotland, he would have a life of wealth and privilege, surrounded by servants, tutors, people charged to watch over him and keep him from harm. Far away from this violent, lawless place.

How could she deny her child that?

This was no longer just about her and her photographs. It was about building a future that was safe. It was about Ash and the children they might have, and putting her own ambitions aside and doing what was best for them. She had asked Ash to make her his duty. Now she must do the same for him.

Understanding in a way she never had the restraints of duty that bound Ash so tightly, she rolled over and put her arm around his waist.

He shifted, murmured something, and let out a great sigh.

She smiled. Blotting her tears against his strong, sturdy back, she nestled against his warmth and closed her eyes.

She would talk to him tomorrow.

Perhaps it was time to go back.

Twenty-three

Church again. Ash had withstood cavalry charges, cannon bombardments, and three months in an Irish hospital. He could probably withstand another round of Pastor and Biddy Rickman's evangelical enthusiasm. But he dinna want to.

At least this time, he had convinced his wife to walk the entire half mile to the Come All You Sinners Church of Heartbreak Creek, rather than go in Miss Hathaway's buggy. He enjoyed any time alone with her he could get. Living in a hotel suite put limitations on privacy.

"You were gone when I awoke," Maddie said, leaning slightly into his shoulder as they strolled along, her arm linked through his.

"Aye. It was a braw morning, so it was, and you were sleeping so soundly I decided to take the dogs out for a walk."

She pretended to look around. "Did you lose them along the way? I haven't seen them all morning."

"Driscoll is letting them rid the manure pile of mice."

As they left the canyon, he looked out over the rolling flats, feeling again that lift in spirits that always came over him whenever he was surrounded by so much sky and unbroken land. Perhaps they might build a home out here, in view of the mountains but not crowded against them. Room to stretch. He needed that. Here, he could breathe.

In the distance, several large animals came out of the trees to graze. Elk, he guessed by the size. Magnificent animals, so they were. The highlands had naught to equal their majesty.

"It's beautiful country, your mountains. There is nothing quite so lovely as a Colorado dawn."

She slanted him a teasing glance. "Even lovelier than your Highlands?"

He thought for a moment, comparing the two. "In a different way, perhaps. In Scotland the morn comes as a slow awakening. Mist rising out of the dells, draping the hills in a soft, gray shroud, the air growing thick with the scent of gorse and heather. But here . . ." He made an expansive motion with his arm and laughed. "Here the day bursts on you like a challenge. A hush stillness, a faint glow behind the ridges, then suddenly streaks of sunlight are racing down the slopes at full charge. I can see why you love it here. It's a seductive place."

"Seductive?"

"Aye. Perhaps because it's still new and untainted by politics and failure and the wanton destruction that has left its mark on the islands of home. It pulls you in. Opens up possibilities you never knew were there."

"You sound as if you don't want to go back to Scotland."

Did he? Perhaps, a bit. "Here, men are judged by accomplishment, not bloodlines. For the first time in seventeen years, I'm not under orders or having my future dictated by my birthright. I like the freedom of that, so I do."

She pressed her cheek against his arm. "My father would have adored you."

"Wise man."

She chuckled, then slowed, her attention drawn to the figure walking ahead of them down the track. "Is that Pru? But why would she leave Thomas? Pru!" she called, waving her free arm.

Miss Lincoln stopped and waited for them to catch up.

As they drew alongside, Miss Lincoln fell into step beside them. "Where's Thomas?" Maddie asked.

"Gone."

"Where?"

"Into the mountains. He said he had some unfinished business."

"Was he well enough?"

A smile tugged at Miss Lincoln's full lips. "He's a fast healer."

Maddie shook her head. "I can't believe he would just up and leave in his condition. He said nothing?"

"He left me this." Reaching into her pocket, Miss Lincoln pulled out a piece of rose-colored quartz carved in the shape of a heart.

"Oh, how lovely." Pulling her arm from Ash's, Maddie stopped to study it, marveling over the beauty and color of the smooth, opaque stone. "That's so sweet. I never realized Thomas was such a romantic."

Ash was a bit surprised himself.

At a call, they looked over to see Edwina and Declan Brodie waving as they went past in their buckboard, the back filled with restless children. The girl, Brin, wore a bonnet in place of her floppy hat, a dress, and a scowl. The boys wore clean shirts and slicked-down hair. Ash wondered how long Mrs. Brodie had labored to bring about the improvements.

Behind them, in her buggy, came Miss Hathaway. As she rolled by, she slowed to call out. "Don't forget. Dinner at the hotel after the service." Then she snapped the reins and sent the pacer moving smartly along.

Another boisterous gathering. Not that Ash minded spending time with Maddie's Heartbreak Creek family, but he would also enjoy an intimate dinner with just his wife every now and then. He was about to suggest they get their own place so they could do that, then remembered his wife couldn't cook.

The Brodies and Miss Hathaway were waiting outside the church when they arrived. Greetings evolved into questions about

Thomas then "ohs" and "ahs" over the stone he had given Miss Lincoln.

Ash refrained from snorting. It was a bluidy rock. What was so special about that? Although he had to admit all he had given his wife was a used signet ring. He must rectify that. He couldn't allow the heathen to win the day with a bluidy rock.

The Rickmans were in fine form that morning and managed to keep Ash awake for the entire service. It helped that he sat directly in front of Brin, who spent the hour bouncing the toe of her wee boot off the back of his pew.

They arrived back at the hotel just as Miriam was setting up their table. The hotel kitchen was gaining a fine reputation for its excellent fare, and more tables were full than empty. They were just finishing an excellent repast of roast beef, potatoes, several bowls of vegetables, fresh rolls, and blackberry cobbler when Yancey came in and told Miss Hathaway that visitors were waiting in the lobby.

A look of excitement came over her face. She pushed back her chair and rose. "Perhaps it's the gentleman from the Wichita Pacific. Although he isn't due for several more weeks."

"He's not a he," Yancey said. "And she's not asking for you." He pointed a gnarly finger at Ash. "It's him she came to see. She brought two fellows with her." He leaned forward and dropped his voice. "And one of them is wearing a dress."

Ash turned to look back through the open door at the three people waiting in the lobby. The air went out of him.

"Isn't that Glynnis?" Maddie asked.

What was his sister doing here? Tossing down his napkin, he rose and walked quickly into the lobby.

"Glynnis!" Grinning, he wrapped his arms around his sister. Then seeing the kilted man behind her, he laughed aloud. "Fain McKenzie?" Releasing Glynnis, he held out a hand to his Scottish neighbor. "What are you doing here?"

"Looking fer you. Ye've left a twisted trail, so ye have. Luckily yer Boston banker kept us apprised o' yer progress." After they shook hands, the big Scotsman wrapped an arm around Glynnis's shoulder. "And I couldna let yer wee sister come sae far withoot her husband, now could I?"

"Husband?" Ash looked from one to the other. "Have you finally settled for this glaikit numptie, then, sister?"

"So I have."

Fain smiled down at Glynnis. "These few months. We would have liked ye tae be there, but even if yer banker could have pinpointed yer exact location, ye wouldna have made it back in time. 'Tis a verra big country, America is."

"So you traveled all this way to tell me?"

"Aye." The laughter faded from Glynnis's eyes. "And to bring you this." She motioned the third visitor forward. In his hands he held a linen-wrapped parcel.

This man wasn't dressed in a kilt but wore a suit of clothes in a somber shade over a starched white shirt with a high collar. His bright red hair and fierce blue eyes Ash recognized from his youth. "Is that you, Colin MacPherson?" The last Ash had seen of MacPherson had been at University, where Colin had been studying to be a solicitor in his father's law firm—the same firm that had served the Earls of Kirkwell for several generations.

"It is, my lord." He gave a slight bow. "You're looking well, sir," he added as he handed the parcel to Glynnis.

"As are you, my friend." Ash was a bit surprised at the formal tone. He and Colin and Harry Ridgeway had shared many a pint during their university days. Besides his family and Harry and now Maddie, Colin was the only outsider who knew of Ash's affliction.

Distracted by footsteps behind him, Ash turned to see Maddie and the others coming out of the dining room. But before he could motion them forward for introductions, Glynnis touched his arm.

"This is yours now." She held out the parcel.

The way she said it caught Ash's attention. A feeling of foreboding gripped him as he looked from his sister's somber face to Fain's and MacPherson's. None was smiling now.

He took the parcel, and with suddenly clumsy fingers, unfolded the linen.

Inside was a thick woolen tartan in the Kirkwell plaid and his father's sporran. Lying atop it was the signet ring that bore the crest of the Earl of Kirkwell, and the brooch showing the family coat of arms, which his father, then later, Donnan, had pinned at their shoulders when they wore their great kilts. The final item was Donnan's *sgian dubh*, the small ceremonial knife he slipped into the folded top of his knee hose when he donned his *philabeg*, or small kilt.

A terrible, hollow feeling spread through Ash's chest. He looked up, saw the sadness in his sister's face, and shook his head. "Not Donnan, too."

"Aye." Tears filled her eyes. "Over two months ago."

The ground seemed to waffle beneath Ash's feet. Images flashed through his mind. Donnan, Neil, his parents. So many lost. "I should have been there," he said, still trying to digest that Donnan was gone, and now he was the last brother left.

"Dinna do that to yourself, Angus. It happened in his sleep. He dinna suffer." In a stronger voice, she said, "Colin, here, has come to handle all the legalities of the transfer. They're a maze to me. I ken you shy away from paperwork, but you can trust Colin to help you sort through it all. Fain has helped me handle things until we could find you, and now that we have, we can complete the transfer, then all go back home together."

His sister's voice barely penetrated the numbness in his mind. He blinked at her, trying to make sense of the words. *Go back?*

A feeling of suffocation gripped his throat.

No. 'Tis too soon.

He turned, seeking Maddie, and saw her watching from the doorway, a tormented look on her ashen face. He wanted to reassure her, tell her this was a mistake and they would figure something out. But the words couldn't get past the clog in his throat.

Glynnis put her hand over his. "I know you grieve for Donnan, Angus, but you must—"

"No." He wanted to thrust the plaid back at his sister. Deny that any of this had happened. "I dinna want this." *'Tis too soon.*

I'm not ready. His body started to shake. He couldn't breathe, couldn't think.

" 'Tis your duty, Angus. There's no one else."

"Bugger duty!"

"Lord Kirkwell." MacPherson gave a nervous cough. "If we could go someplace private where we could discuss—"

"No! There's naught to—"

"My office," Miss Hathaway cut in, stepping past Ash toward her suite of rooms behind the front desk. "This way, if you will. May I get you refreshments?"

At a sound, Ash looked over to see Maddie racing up the staircase, Edwina Brodie and Prudence Lincoln staring after her. "Lass! Maddie!"

She stopped and turned, her face white, her hands clutching the rail. He saw the glisten of tears on her stricken face, and everything inside of him rebelled at what he was doing to her.

"Dinna run from me now," he begged, not caring who heard. "Please, lass. We'll work something out."

"I k-know." Then she whirled and continued up the stairs and out of his sight.

Maddie burst through the door of the suite, Edwina and Pru moments behind her.

Oh God, oh God . . .

"Maddie! What's happening? What's going on?"

"He's dead."

"Who's dead?"

"Donnan. His brother." Stopping in the middle of the sitting room, she clapped shaking hands to her head and tried to stop the spinning. "Ash is now the earl. He'll have to go back."

"Back? To Scotland?"

"Yes." *Oh God. It's too soon.*

"Will you go, too?"

"Yes—No—I don't know." She took a deep breath. Then another. And another. She took her hands away. The shaking slowed. Moving on unsteady legs, she went to one of the chairs by the window and sank down before her knees gave out. "Yes. I have to go back, too."

Pru knelt beside her. "Is that what you want?"

"I gave my word."

"I knew it," Edwina wailed, plopping into the chair across from Maddie's. "We'll never see you again."

The door opened. Lucinda came in, carrying a bottle of brandy and an armful of glasses. She set them on the table, pulled the stopper from the bottle, and with a trembling hand, poured a small measure of amber liquid into each glass. With a fixed smile, she passed them around, then lifted hers high. "To our new countess." She tossed hers back in a single swallow, carefully set the glass on the table, then burst into tears.

Within seconds, all of them were crying.

"It's probably for the best," Maddie said, once she had regained control.

Edwina dabbed at her puffy eyes. "For whom?"

"Our children, if we have any. His family. Ash."

"What about you?" Lucinda asked. "Is this what you want?"

"And what about your photography?" Pru cut in.

Blinking back more tears, Maddie looked out the window beside her. The lowering sun outlined the snowy peaks in gold and pink. Already aspen leaves coated the ground and soon the snow would come to stay through the long winter. She envisioned a whole new world of light and shadow emerging from the frozen ground— stark, bare alder branches—tall firs rising like white-capped sentinels, their limbs drooping beneath a burden of snow—icicle daggers hanging from the eaves—tracks cutting across an unbroken drift of powdery snow. She would miss trying to capture all that with her camera.

But if she stayed, she would miss Ash more. So much more.

Turning from the window, she smiled weakly at her beloved friends. "Mr. Satterwhite accused me of hiding behind my camera.

I think perhaps he was right. Being here with all of you—seeing Edwina with her new family, and Pru with Thomas and her school, and watching Lucinda give this crusty little town new hope—has made me realize there can be so much more for me than a collection of photographs in some dusty book on a stranger's shelf. I want it all. And with Ash I can have it."

Tears were starting again, and she didn't want it to end that way. Forcing a smile, she poured another swallow into each glass. "Here's to us," she said, raising hers high. "Still and always the ladies of Heartbreak Creek . . . no matter where we are."

Behind her, the door opened, and Maddie turned to see Ash in the doorway. His face was as pale and drawn as if he were in the throes of one of his headaches. "If you don't mind, ladies, I need to talk to my wife."

While they murmured their good-byes and filed out, he went to the table and poured a brandy. He was on his second drink when he heard the door close and the rustle of her skirts as Maddie come up behind him. His nerves were so frayed he couldn't hold back a shiver when she rested her hand on the small of his back. "Ash, I'm so sorry about Donnan."

"Aye." He stared down into his glass, afraid to turn and look into her face. "And I'm sorry, too, lass, to let you down once again."

"Let me down? How?"

"The earldom." He downed the last swallow, then carefully set the glass back on the table. "I tried to give it to Glynnis, but she wouldna take it."

Moving around to his side, she stared up into his face. "The earldom? To Glynnis?"

"In Scotland it's possible for a daughter to inherit. But only if there's no male heir. I told her we could pretend she dinna find me and have me declared dead. But she wouldna do that. I'm sorry."

"Oh, Ash." He expected tears and regrets, but instead, she put her arms around him and hugged him close. "You nincompoop."

Rising on tiptoe, she pressed a kiss against his neck, then settled back and rested her head over his heart.

He looked down at her glossy auburn curls and felt an unfamiliar sting in his eyes. His love for this woman was like a living thing lodged in his chest, and with every breath it seemed to grow. "Nincompoop?"

"Only a nincompoop would apologize to his wife for making her a countess."

"In name only."

"What?" She drew back to look questioningly up at him again.

"Glynnis wouldn't accept the title, but she is happy to take over Northbridge to hold for our son, should we have one."

"What?"

He brushed a curl off her cheek. "Have you gone deaf, lass? You canna hear what I'm saying?"

"We're not going back?"

"Perhaps every few years for a visit. But not to live. Unless that's what you want."

Her brows drew together. "But what do you want, Ash?"

"You, lass. Any way I can get you."

She dinna seem impressed by his gallant turn of phrase. Hope dwindled. "What's wrong, Maddie? I thought you'd be pleased."

"That you've given up your birthright? I told you I'd go back with you. There's no need to give up Northbridge and the duties that await you there."

"I dinna give it up. I only left it in my sister's care. I never wanted it, lass. But Glynnis does, and she'll do right by it, so she will."

"So you're no longer Ashby, but now Kirkwell. Or both, until we have an heir. That should confuse these Americans thoroughly."

"Then let's just use Angus, love, unless you'd rather tout the title. I dinna feel much like an earl."

"You *look* every inch of one." She studied him through narrowed eyes, her mouth slightly askew as it often was when she was puzzling something through. He could almost hear her sorting it all out in her fine mind.

"So you *want* to stay here?" she finally asked. "In Heartbreak Creek?"

"Aye."

"You're certain?"

"Well . . ." He shrugged at her befuddled expression. "Not precisely *in* Heartbreak Creek. But perhaps out on the grassy flats where the view stretches all the way to the sky. Not too close to the church, of course. I wouldn't want the pastor dropping by too often. Someplace with enough room to breed a few horses—a man must do something useful with his life even if he's an earl, so he should. And I could seek buyers when we travel about to make your photographs. Would that be all right with you, lass?"

She dinna answer because she was crying again. And laughing. And trying to pull his shirt over his head. It made no sense.

But he wasna complaining.

Maddie awoke to the sound of a shrieking cat caught in a trap. She lurched upright and looked frantically around until she realized it was not an injured animal, but the screech and wail of bagpipes coming from behind the hotel. Throwing aside the covers, she rose, wrapped herself in a blanket, and crossed to the window her husband insisted be left open at night.

Ash stood beside the back stoop, talking to Fain and Glynnis and the solicitor, while Fain helped him adjust the pipes under his arm. He was dressed in full highland garb as befitted an earl of the realm, and he looked utterly magnificent.

"Lass," he called, catching sight of her in the window. "We're piping Donnan to the cemetery. Will you come?"

It's barely even dawn, for heaven's sake. "Of course." Ducking back into the room, she quickly dressed. As she struggled to brush the tangles from her hair, Glynnis came in. Maddie rushed over and put her arms around her, as she hadn't had a chance to do the previous afternoon.

"Oh, Glynnis, I'm so sorry about Donnan."

"He's at peace now," the older woman said, brushing away a tear. "And all is as it should be. Here, I brought you this." She held out a folded tartan. "As the Countess of Kirkwell, it's yours now."

"How lovely." Smiling uncertainly, Maddie accepted the plaid. "What do I do with it?"

Glynnis grinned and shook her head. "You wear it, ye daft Englishwoman. And proudly. Here, I'll show you."

Draping the long length of soft wool under one arm, she pulled it back up to cross over the opposite shoulder then pinned it in place with the Kirkwell brooch. After fluffing the folds so that it hung evenly three-quarters of the way down Maddie's shirts, she stood back to admire her work. "Och, lass. You look quite grand, so you do."

Maddie felt grand, too.

By the time they came out the back door of the hotel, Lucinda, Pru, all the Brodies, Mr. Driscoll, both dogs, Doc and Janet Boyce, Mayor Gebbers and his wife, and even that rude Cal Bagley were standing in the street, while still more townspeople were arriving.

Seeing Maddie's surprise, Glynnis whispered that Lucinda had passed the word that the Earl and Countess of Kirkwell were paying tribute to the earl's deceased brother, then hosting a dinner at the hotel.

"Are we?"

"Aye." Glynnis grinned. "You're verra generous, so you are."

Another bleat, then a long rattling sigh as Angus adjusted the bass drone and tuning slide on the pipes.

Maddie refrained from covering her ears. "I cannot believe you brought Angus's bagpipes all the way from Scotland."

"Those are Fain's. He willna be without them. The man is more Scottish than Robert the Bruce ever was. But dinna fret, lass, we'll be sending Angus's pipes with his other belongings after we return to Northbridge."

"Or we can get them when next we visit," Maddie offered hopefully. "Angus said we'd be coming over every few years." And perhaps by then, the dampness would have rotted the sheepskin bag.

"I doubt he'll be wanting to wait that long. He loves his pipes."

Maddie sighed. Then she would learn to love his bagpipes, too.

The procession lined up behind Ash, with Maddie first, followed by Glynnis, then Fain and the solicitor. The Heartbreak Creek ladies, Declan, and his children came next, then various other people fell in behind them.

Ash puffed into the blowpipe, the bag under his arm expanded, the drones coughed to life, and the pipe chanter emitted the first high note. And suddenly, the strains of "Amazing Grace" blasted the air.

Maddie winced. Birds fled. Somewhere a dog howled.

Then just as the sun burst above the frosted peaks, crowning the treetops with bright golden light, the procession marched forward toward the little church at the end of the canyon.

Ash was right, Maddie thought, watching the play of light on her husband's tousled silver hair and the sway of the kilt above his braw legs—there was nothing quite like a Colorado dawn, especially when accompanied by the haunting strains of the pipes of Scotland.

Deep in her heart, she felt Mr. Satterwhite's smile.

Here's a preview of
Kaki Warner's next Runaway Brides novel . . .

BRIDE OF THE HIGH COUNTRY

Coming soon from Berkley Sensation!

NEW YORK CITY, 1855

The first fire wagon raced past Father O'Rourke as he turned onto Mulberry Bend in the wretched Irish district of Five Points. Within minutes, two more rattled by, the horses blowing steam into the chill evening air, the men manning the sirens and bells pumping furiously.

Quickening his pace, the priest continued toward the reddish glow up ahead, partially obscured by swirls of dark, oily smoke.

The street became more crowded as ragged people came out of the dilapidated tenements, their faces drawn with worry. Father O'Rourke recognized the hopeless, helpless fear in their eyes. He had felt it himself and had seen it too often in the faces of his fellow countrymen as they had filed off the disease-ridden ships by the tens of thousands, only to find the conditions awaiting them in these tenements were as bad as those they had left behind in famine-stricken Ireland.

As he drew closer to the burning structure, Father O'Rourke realized it was Mrs. Beale's, the building he sought and a well-known brothel that catered to the basest tastes of a dissolute clientele. For the last month, ever since he had heard of the auction of prostitutes, some of whom were still children, he had been on a one-man crusade to have it shut down. Having failed in that, he had come tonight in hopes of appealing to the buyers. Apparently, that wouldn't be necessary now.

Angling through gawking onlookers, he worked his way toward a fireman shouting orders through a long brass speaking trumpet. Raising his voice over the roar of the fire and the clang of fire bells, he shouted, "Can I help? Is anyone hurt? Did everyone get out?"

"Don't know yet," the man shouted back. "All we know for sure is it started on one of the upper floors."

In a sudden blast of heat and exploding windows, the roof caved in. Pandemonium broke out as shrieking people fled the shower of shattered glass and flaming timbers, taking Father O'Rourke along with them. He was several doors down before he could escape the shoving throng by ducking into a side alley where a girl stood staring intently at the flaming building.

She was a wee, fragile thing and couldn't have been more than ten or twelve years old. Smudged and dirty, her blond hair falling loose down her thin back, her skimpy dress so sheer her thin legs and naked buttocks showed clearly through the pale muslin. She was shivering so hard he could hear the chatter of her teeth from several feet away.

But even more bizarre was her face. A child's face, but marked with kohl and rouge and lip paint until she looked like a player on a stage—or a depraved man's plaything.

"Child." When the girl didn't respond, O'Rourke reached out and touched her thin shoulder.

With a cry of terror, the girl whirled away. She would have escaped if O'Rourke hadn't been expecting it. Scooping her up, he pinned her flailing body against his chest. She was all bones and flying hair, and she smelled of overly sweet perfume and smoke and kerosene.

"'Tis all right, lass," he murmured over and over into her ear.

"You're safe with me. Sure, and I'm a priest, and I've come to help you, so I have."

It was several moments before the girl stopped fighting him, more out of exhaustion and defeat than trust. "Can I put you down now, lass? You'll not run away from me?"

The girl didn't answer. But she didn't tense up for another fight, so O'Rourke gently set her back down on her bare feet. Taking off his coat, he draped it over her then, keeping his hands on her shoulders, knelt and looked into her painted face.

No tears. No fear. Nothing. As empty as a battered china doll with a blank, glassy stare.

"I'm Father O'Rourke. Who might you be?"

She didn't answer and continued to stare fixedly past him. He didn't need to turn to see what had captured her attention. The flames were reflected in her sad green eyes, and the distant roar of the flames continued.

"Were you at Mrs. Beale's?"

No response.

"What is your name, child?"

No response.

"Are you hurt, lassie?"

She didn't answer, but he saw her hands flatten against her thin gown. Red hands with blisters showing on the small fingers. The smell of kerosene wafted up to him again, and a terrible thought arose—one he didn't want to pursue. All that was important right now was getting her away from this place. Finding a safe haven for her. Someplace where she could be a child again.

"Can I wipe that paint off your face?"

No response.

He took out his handkerchief and, moistening one corner with spit, began wiping her face. Mostly it smeared, but at least now she just looked dirty rather than whorish. He put the kerchief away.

She still hadn't moved or spoken.

"Do you have parents nearby?"

Silence.

"You're an orphan?" There were thousands of them. The conditions here in Five Points were so deplorable most adults didn't last six years. For children it was even worse. Without God's intervention, this one wouldn't have lasted another month.

"Cathleen." It was the merest whisper, barely heard over the shouts of firefighters down the street. Spoken less to him, he suspected, than to herself.

"Your name is Cathleen? Cathleen Donovan?" He had heard of the girl—the wee blond star of tonight's auction. Her body, her sanity, probably even her soul up for sale to the highest bidder. He closed his eyes against sudden nausea and gave silent thanks to God for sparing this poor lost child.

He wasn't sure what to do with her. The shelter where he ministered to the starving and sick would be the first place Mrs. Beale's henchman, Smythe, would look—assuming he had escaped the fire. The orphanages were little more than workhouses. Then he remembered a man who owed him a debt from years ago, when Father O'Rourke had pulled him from the gutter where footpads had left him to die. The man—a judge—was dead now, but perhaps his widow would find a place in her home for this lost child. He had no other option.

He rose, and letting go of her shoulders, held out his hand. "Come, Cathleen. Let's leave this place."

The girl finally looked away from the burning building and up at him. Her smudged eyes carried more pain than any child's should. "Am I going to hell, then, Father?"

O'Rourke forced a smile. "No, child. You're leaving it."

One

It had been written and talked about for weeks.

"A fairy-tale romance," the gossip columns called it. *"Doyle Kerrigan, dashing railroad mogul brought to bended knee by Margaret Hamilton, ward of Ida Throckmorton, widow of the late Judge Harold Throckmorton."*

Margaret supposed there was a certain make-believe quality to their whirlwind courtship—the penniless nobody plucked from obscurity and thrust into the world of opulence. Who would have guessed that an Irish orphan from Five Points would someday be mistress of a home as grand as Doyle's new town house in the most fashionable area of New York?

Hopefully no one. The only way to protect herself was to ensure that no one ever found out about her Irish immigrant roots. Especially her fiancé. It was a betrayal on every level—not just of Doyle Kerrigan, but of her homeland, her parents, and especially little Cathleen Donovan. But she would do it. She would do anything to stay alive. She had already proven that.

Shutting her mind to that troubling thought, Margaret studied her reflection in the cheval mirror in her third-floor bedroom at Mrs. Throckmorton's Sixty-ninth Street brownstone.

The lilac silk gown Doyle had chosen brought out the green of her eyes. The diamond and amethyst necklace he had given her shimmered against her skin. More gems glittered in the pins securing her blond upsweep. Everything was the finest. Proof of Doyle's success. At the engagement ball tonight in his lavish new home, when he introduced his unknown but well-connected fiancé to New York's finest, he would be proclaiming to the world that he had reached the highest level of society that money could buy. And she would finally be safe.

A triumph for the Irish in both of them.

Then why did she feel such a sense of loss?

Irritated that she had let her happy mood slip away, and having almost forty minutes to spare before Doyle came to pick her up, Margaret moved restlessly about the room, finally coming to a stop at the tall window overlooking the street.

The day was fading. Smoke from thousands of coal stoves hung in sluggish layers in the still air, adding bands of deeper gray to the overcast sky. The distant oasis of the still-unfinished Central Park project seemed less green, as if painted with a muddied brush, and even the sheep dotting Sheep Meadow looked dingy. She scarcely remembered what stars looked like.

"So you're going through with it," a querulous voice said from the doorway.

Bracing herself for another argument, Margaret turned with a smile. "Yes, ma'am, I am. And you shouldn't be climbing those stairs on your own. I was just about to come down to you."

With the hand not gripping the ivory handle of her cane, Mrs. Throckmorton impatiently waved aside the notion that she would need help. "He's a ruffian and a thug. Do you know the kind of people who will be there tonight?"

Margaret waited, knowing the question didn't require an answer.

"Jay Gould, that's who. And Jim Fisk, and even that Tweed fellow from Tammany Hall. Crooks, all. The judge would never have countenanced an association with such disreputable types. My word, they're Democrats!"

Margaret knew that despite her criticisms, her guardian had only her best interests at heart. But she would never understand Margaret's driving need for the security this marriage would provide. How could she? Having been insulated by wealth all of her life, Mrs. Throckmorton had little knowledge of the squalor that prevailed in the Irish tenements of the sixth ward. She could never have imagined the kind of depravity that went on behind the closed doors of the house on Mulberry Bend. Yet when Father O'Rourke had appeared on her doorstep with a frightened twelve-year-old Irish orphan, Ida Throckmorton had honored her late husband's debt and taken her in.

But the benign tyrant of this staid brownstone on Sixty-ninth Street had her rules, so she did—the foremost being no Irish tolerated.

From that moment on, Cathleen Donovan had ceased to exist. Margaret Hamilton had taken her place—a distant relative of some twice-removed cousin of the late judge. She had been fed, clothed, and patiently tutored in academics and deportment and elocution until all her rough edges had been buffed away and she was able to pass for one of her guardian's own class.

It hadn't been that difficult. Most of Margaret's Irishness had been beaten out of her by Smythe during the two years she had spent at Mrs. Beale's. And with her blond hair and rosy cheeks she looked more English than Irish.

But sometimes, in that dark hush just before dawn, when the silence was so heavy it pressed like a weight on Margaret's chest, the ghost of Cathleen Donovan would come calling, bringing with her a confusing mix of good memories and choking terrors that would send Margaret bolting upright in her bed, gasping and clawing at her throat as if Smythe's hand was still there.

Those were bad nights. Hopefully they would plague her less frequently after her marriage.

The thump of the cane heralded Mrs. Throckmorton's progress across the room. "I wanted you to be taken care of when I'm gone. But not like this. Not in marriage to this upstart Irishman. Perhaps I can break the trust or arrange for—"

"You mustn't," Margaret cut in. "The judge wanted his estate to benefit his charities, and so it shall. Please don't fret. Doyle and I will do well together."

"Unless he finds out you're not the blue blood he thinks you are."

"He won't. You did your work too well."

Margaret almost laughed at the irony of it. In transforming an Irish orphan into a proper society miss, Ida Throckmorton had also created exactly the sort of wife Doyle Kerrigan wanted—an impoverished but genteel woman on the fringe of the upper class who was willing to marry an immigrant Irishman in exchange for a life of wealth and privilege. Fate was full of tricks, it seemed.

"I can see you won't listen to reason and are determined to marry the man." Leaning onto her cane with one hand, Mrs. Throckmorton reached into her skirt pocket with the other. "So you might as well have these." She thrust out her hand. Resting in her palm were two diamond pendant eardrops. "Call it my wedding gift, if you must."

Margaret blinked in astonishment. "My goodness, Mrs. Throckmorton. I-I don't know what to say."

"Then you may hug me instead."

Margaret did, noting how frail the small, thin frame felt against her own. "You're too kind to me, ma'am."

"I agree." Pulling back, Mrs. Throckmorton waved her away. "Now stop fussing about and help me to the chair so I can get off this foot. It took me forever to climb those stairs."

As the elderly woman settled onto the cushions of the armchair by the coal stove, her gouty foot propped on a damask footstool, Margaret went back to the mirror to put on the diamond earrings. She turned to show them off. "They're beautiful. Thank you so much."

"At least when you come to your senses and decamp, you'll have something of value to see you through. Turn. Shoulders back."

Margaret twirled a slow circle, then awaited the verdict.

"Humph. That neckline is too low. It was highly improper of him to pick out your gown, but at least he was right about the color. You look lovely. Too lovely for the likes of that parvenu." With a sniff, she turned her head away. A dab at the long, aristocratic nose with the hanky, then a deep, labored sigh. "I suppose because he's Irish, you feel some sort of absurd connection."

Margaret was taken aback. They never spoke of her Irish roots. After fifteen years of silence, all that remained—other than her night terrors—was the memory of endless hunger, living in a dark, windowless room with three other families, and an abiding hatred for the Irish runner who had hastened her father's death. If that was her connection to Doyle, it wasn't a good one.

"He's uncommonly ambitious," Mrs. Throckmorton mused, coming at her from a different direction.

"If so, it has served him well."

"I hear he has a temper."

"Does he? I've never seen it."

"Ask the workers building his railroads. And what kind of man would exploit his own people?"

"He's not exploiting. He's providing jobs to the Irish when no one else will."

"Stubborn girl." Mrs. Throckmorton's expression soured even more. "I thought you were too intelligent to be so blinded by love."

Love? Hardly that. Although Margaret might want to love her fiancé, she had little expectation of it. Which was certainly not his fault. Blond, hazel-eyed, generous—at least with her, less so in business—and so full of life he seemed to draw all the air from a room, Doyle Kerrigan was a man who easily inspired female admiration. But Margaret wasn't sure she was capable of love, or that it would even be wise to open herself to that possibility. If she had learned anything during those first devastating years in this great land of opportunity, it was that love was an illusion, and God didn't care, and the only thing lower than the immigrant Irish were the despicable runners who preyed on them.

Another deep sigh caught Margaret's attention and she looked over to see Mrs. Throckmorton dabbing at her eyes. She refrained from snorting. Bribery, condemnation, and now guilt? What ploy would the crafty old woman try next? Full-blown hysteria? Margaret couldn't even imagine such a thing.

"I know why you're doing this." Watery blue eyes looked up at Margaret out of a face that suddenly looked old and defeated. "It's because of what that vile woman did to you, isn't it? You don't think you deserve true happiness, so you're punishing yourself by marrying this man."

Shame rose in a hot flush, even as a dark coldness closed around Margaret's heart. How did Mrs. Throckmorton even know about Mrs. Beale? And why now? After avoiding the subject for fifteen years, why did she bring it up on what was supposed to be one of the happiest days of Margaret's life? So angry she couldn't find words to express it, she glared at her guardian, hands fisted at her sides.

"If only I had known—"

"How could you?"

"Your papist priest should have told me."

"It doesn't matter, ma'am." Realizing she had grabbed handfuls of her silk skirts, Margaret forced her fingers to straighten. "It's all in the past."

"I'm so sorry."

Shocked to see real tears roll down those wrinkled cheeks, Margaret let her anger go. Crossing to the chair, she put her arm around the thin shoulders and leaned down to kiss the cool, papery cheek. "Nothing happened, ma'am," she lied. "No one touched me. Father O'Rourke found me before the auction."

"I never thought I'd be grateful to a Catholic priest."

Irish and Catholic were synonymous in the elderly woman's mind, and she had scant liking for either. It still vexed her that Margaret had chosen Father O'Rourke to officiate at her wedding rather than her own Lutheran minister.

A few more tears, then with a pat on Margaret's arm she gently pushed her away. "Do stop hovering. You know I can't abide it."

Grateful to escape, Margaret went back to the window. To rid herself of the emotions still churning inside, she took several deep breaths, watching the cold glass fog with every exhalation. Closing her eyes, she reached deep into her mind for happier memories— rolling emerald hills, misty dales, waves crashing in frothy disarray against treeless bluffs. Instead of the strident voices of the newsboys hawking the late edition three stories below, she heard the call of terns on a chill north wind, the warble of her father's tin whistle, her mother's soft laughter.

It frightened her how hard she had to work to recall those memories now and how much they had dimmed over the years. Even Cathleen appeared to her less and less frequently. When those memories faded altogether, would she be more or less whole than she was now?

Footfalls sounded in the hall.

She turned to see Pringle in the doorway. "Mr. Kerrigan's carriage has arrived, madam," he said solemnly, his bushy white brows raised in his usual expression of disdain whenever he mentioned her Irish fiancé's name.

"Thank you, Pringle," Mrs. Throckmorton said. "Please have a cup of warm milk and a piece of toast sent to my room. That will be all."

"Very well, madam."

As the sound of Pringle's footsteps receded, Margaret crossed to the mirror. Her mood lifted as excitement gripped her, making it hard to take a full breath against the stays around her ribs. This was it. Her night. "I wish you would change your mind and come with me," she said over her shoulder to the woman watching from the chair. "I wouldn't be so nervous if you were there beside me."

"Nonsense. You will be a stunning success. I have trained you too well for it to be otherwise."

A last look to be sure everything was in order, then Margaret turned to face the woman who had been almost like a grandmother to her for over half of her life. "Well? How do I look, ma'am?"

The pinched lips thinned in a reluctant smile. "Like a princess."